Water Witch: The Deceiver's Grave

Water Witch: The Deceiver's Grave

Nene Adams

P.D. Publishing, Inc.
Clayton, North Carolina

Copyright © 2007 by Nene Adams

ISBN-13: 978-1-933720-20-3
ISBN-10: 1-933720-20-4

9 8 7 6 5 4 3 2 1

Cover art and design by Nene Adams
Edited by Penelope Warren/Barb Coles

Published by:

P.D. Publishing, Inc.
P.O. Box 70
Clayton, NC 27528

http://www.pdpublishing.com

Author's Note & Acknowledgements

Thanks and much gratitude are due to the gang who keep me honest, and never fails to point out where I've gone right or wrong. As always, I dedicate this book to my much beloved partner, *mijn liefje* Corrie Kuipers, who is an artist in her own right and my biggest source of inspiration. In gratitude, I also dedicate *Water Witch: The Deceiver's Grave* to the many wonderful people world-wide who have taken an interest in me and my writing, and whose amazing generosity in troubled times has helped us stay afloat. Thank you all so very much! Thanks are also due to my editor, Kay Porter, who is no lubber at all.

Please check my website http://www.corrieweb.nl/library.htm for news of my latest projects and other works. I also have a blog at http://neneadams.web-log.nl where I post serialized stories as time permits.

Water Witch is set at some point during the late eighteenth century in an alternative universe. The tale incorporates fantasy elements and therefore, does not conform to the actual Golden Age of Piracy with stringent exactitude. This is a highly romanticized view of an often brutal and violent world where the real pirates experienced short lives and bad ends, as did the majority of their victims. While I have tried to avoid glaring anachronisms – with notable exceptions – many facts have been changed to suit the narrative of my story. *Water Witch: The Deceiver's Grave* is romantic and fantastical fiction, not historic fact, and should be taken as a pleasant adventure tale rather than a scholarly work. Any errors are my own.

As a final point, the herbal cures and medicines described in the *Water Witch* are meant to be a curiosity only, and should not be attempted.

The thunder roar of cannons, the blood of many a brave,
Raise up your cutlass, strike a blow, and feed the crimson wave!
We'll ask no quarter of our foe and he will do the same,
For the roaring boys will live or die in the Water Witch's name!

Death rides on her shoulder, the Devil at her side,
She'll fight the wide world over, for she is hell's own bride!

   ~ Bess O'Bedlam's Song

CHAPTER ONE
Dead Man's Baggage

The West Indies
On the island of Antigua, in the capital St. John's Town
During the Glorious Golden Age of Magic, Piracy and Sail

The attack, when it came, was swift as a lick of lightning from a clear summer's sky and equally unexpected.

Black Harry Rye reeled down a dark alleyway, trying without much success to avoid splashing through reeking pools of filth or stepping on dog or cat or bloated rat carcasses. He passed three men leading a bleating goat on a tether. The animal's glossy hide was marked with the sacrificial symbol of Belial. Harry brushed off a scrawny whore who clutched at his arm; the woman's glassy gaze spoke of the pox. Her curses followed him as he continued down the alley. His belly was full of good mutton and bad ale; the night was humid but tolerably so, though sweat still soaked his shirt and breeches, and stung the galls in his armpits to irritated fire. He found a flea in his beard and cracked it between his thumbnails, taking some satisfaction in the tiny death.

The next moment, he was pinned against a wall with a hard arm across his throat and eight inches of steel glittering not a breath away from his wide-open eyes.

"Well, well, well," his attacker said in a low growl, "if it ain't Black Harry himself, piss-proud and just as useless. Good e'en, Harry."

"What...what do you want?" Harry was unable to focus on the person holding the knife; his vision was filled with quicksilver trails of light glinting from razor sharp edges. He reached down to the hilt of his cutlass, then let out a hiss when the knife jabbed forward and pricked the side of his nose, perilously close to his eye. "Damnation!"

"Keep your ass at anchor, m'lad, or I'll carve out those peepers in a trice!"

Harry was suddenly aware of a warm trickle of blood on his whiskered cheek. A sour belch bubbled up from his stomach, threatening to cast up his dinner. He swallowed thickly past the lump in his throat that felt as big, heavy and complicated as a Monkey's Fist knot. "Easy now, yer lordship," he said. "I ain't the fighting sort."

"Not even when you sailed with Tom Carew on the *Deceiver*?"

Startled, Harry bit back an oath. The heat of another body pressed close to his own; an uneasy silence bloomed between them, but he could feel the unspoken threat from his attacker, the faint vibration of violence held on a fraying leash. He shuffled nervously, coughed, spat a glob of sputum on the ground and said, "I don't quite take yer meaning. Don't know no Carew. Never heard o' *Deceiver*. You've got the wrong fellow, yer lordship."

"I think you know. I think you're hiding something." The dagger withdrew and the person stepped away from him, a shadowy figure abruptly revealed in a pool of lambent silver light as clouds scudded away from the horned witch's moon.

"By the sweet bleedin' Christ!" Harry blurted in surprise. *A woman!*

She was lean and lanky, about equal to Black Harry's height; her hair was concealed beneath a blue kerchief and a tricorn hat. Her eyes were gray, cold and bright as polished steel. A gunpowder tattoo curved over one cheek like a smudge from a dirty thumb. Five gold rings dangled from her earlobe. She grinned as recognition dawned. A weight settled in Harry's chest, and ice invaded his bowels.

"Bess O'Bedlam!" Harry felt his testicles trying to crawl into his body cavity. Fresh sweat broke out over his body, and with it came the bitter stench of fear. "By the sweet bleedin' Christ!" he repeated, and spat on the ground again to ward off bad luck.

"None other." Bess shrugged open her coat to show a cutlass thrust through her wide leather belt, as well as the pair of flintlock pistols she wore in a red ribbon sling looped over her shoulders. A dagger rode in the top of each sea boot. "Have you naught to tell me of Carew's *Deceiver*?" she asked, fingering the butt of a flintlock with her free hand.

"Nobbut a sea tale, captain! I swear on me mother's grave!"

Bess snorted. "Aye, as if I'd believe an oath from a motherless dog like you! I know you sailed with Fancy Carew, m'lad. It's been nigh onto twenty-five years since the *Deceiver* was swallowed whole by the sea, all hands lost or so they say, but here I stand talking today to a dead man, and if he don't sing me a pretty song, he'll be dead in truth. No mistake, Harry, you're worm's meat unless you tell me what I want to know. Mayhap I'll leave you livin' and a bit richer for your trouble if you please me with your warblin'."

Harry shook his head. Terror made his mouth dry but he ground out, "I know naught, captain. I never served with Carew."

"Lying's a mortal sin."

"I know naught!" Harry rolled his eyes from side to side, but there was no escape. Two tough-looking men materialized in the alley and for a moment he thought his salvation might be at hand. If he called on them to aid an old tar against this harpy, he might have a chance... Then the men muttered low greetings to Bess, and Harry felt as though he had been struck a blow in the cods. All the air rushed out of his lungs and he gasped weakly, clutching the wall for support as his knees wobbled, threatening to spill him over.

"Speak to me, Harry." Bess shoved her knife back into its sheath. With blood-chilling nonchalance, as though she had all the time in the world, she removed a cheroot from the pocket of her crimson waistcoat; a gesture from her sent one of the men to the end of the alley, where the narrow passage between a whorehouse and a warehouse met the main thoroughfare. Cresset torches burned there, a flickering of dirty orange against the gloom. He returned with a bit of flaming kindling, which she used to light the cheroot.

Puffing smoke idly, Bess said, "I'll make this simple for you, Harry m'lad. You've two choices. Tell me about the *Deceiver* – no lies, no fiddle-faddle, no flummery – and I'll cut you into the game. Give you a full share of the treasure and an easy berth on my ship. Damnation, man, I'll even give you a thousand *livres* as good faith right now, free and clear. If you say no, I'm going to use this cheroot and take out your eye; if you keep your bone box shut, I'll do t'other one. Not much use to be got from a blind sailor, Harry. You'll be beggin' for your supper till they roll you into a pauper's grave."

Harry swallowed hard. He braced himself against the wall and debated taking to his heels. As though they could read his mind, the other two men took up flanking positions. Harry wilted. He was too fat to outrun them, too old to fight and win his freedom. Internal ice melted as a surge of burning liquid in his bowels made him clench his buttocks together; he strove to control himself, lest he bewray his breeches and complete his humiliation.

"What's it to be, eh?" Bess removed the cheroot from her mouth, knocked off the feathery white ash, and examined the glowing crimson tip. "You know, a man's peepers make a noise when you take somethin' hot to them. Sounds somewhat like steppin' on a ripe grape; soft and liquid as a love-struck woman's sigh." She watched him tremble. A humorless grin stretched across her face, deepening the creases that fanned out from the corners of her eyes.

"Oh, you'll tell me everything in time," Bess continued in an almost seductive purr. "Why not save yourself the trouble? Your crewmates are dead, naught but empty bones surging with the tide. No one's left who'll begrudge you sharing the secret. This is just betwixt me n' thee, Harry Rye. Carew's lying snug in Abraham's bosom. He don't care about the treasure, he don't care if you break faith with him. Such things ain't no concern to any but the livin'. Telling me won't do you no harm. Where's the *Deceiver*? Where does she lie? Where's the reef that gutted her belly and left her foundering?"

Harry was mesmerized. His tongue flicked out to soothe dry lips. "I swore 'n oath!" he said, panting. "Never tell or 'tis the black spot for certain."

"None need ever know," Bess said coaxingly.

His guts roiled and he thought he might vomit. A dull thudding ache in his chest, which Harry had noticed earlier that evening, now exploded into fiery agony. Pain rippled down his left arm. Demons were excavating between his ribs; each pickaxe blow seemed to strike directly upon his convulsing heart. He cried out, "Cap'n!" and fell to his knees. A bloody haze obscured his vision, the edges tinged with hungry shadows.

"*Merde!*" Bess dropped the cheroot and knelt down beside the stricken man. "Talk to me, Harry! I don't reckon you're a good Christian, but confession's good for the soul!"

Harry tried to speak but something was squeezing his lungs; he could not catch his breath. It felt as though his bones were cracking and splintering under the intolerable pressure. Excruciating torment also squeezed his heart until he thought it was going to burst. He retched, bringing up a gush of barely digested mutton and bile that poured from his mouth and nose, and splashed on the cobblestones. Harry panted, toppling over sideways.

"By God, you'll not die on me yet," Bess growled, grasping him by the coat collar. "Where's the *Deceiver*, Harry? Tell me, damn you!"

Harry's lips drew back from his teeth in a rictus. "F-F-F-Fiddler's...Green," he stammered.

Bess frowned. Fiddler's Green was a mythical paradise where sailors went after they died, to carouse forever with women and wine. Harry Rye was telling her in so many words to kiss his arse and dance to the Devil's tune.

"A curse upon you," she spat in bitter disappointment, rising to her feet. "You've cheated me for the moment, Harry Rye, but when I see you in hell, I'll ask the Old Horned One to give you a clap of brimstone to remember me by."

The man's body stiffened. His fingers curled, claw-like, as his heels beat a tattoo upon the ground. He scrabbled at his waistcoat. His face was engorged, almost purple with the force of his distress. A long exhalation rattled in his throat. His eyes had rolled up, showing a crescent slice of blood-veined whites behind the drooping lids. Harry was beyond threats or curses.

A crewman asked, "Shall I fetch a gallipot, Cap'n?"

"He's past the 'pothecary's help. I reckon not even a miracle will save his worthless life, and I wouldn't waste a healer's charms on his like." Bess squatted once more, her attention attracted by something shining between the dying man's fingers. It looked like a silver coin; on reflex, she took it, tucked the object into her coat pocket, and jerked her head at her two companions. "Let's go. There's naught for us here."

They left him alone in the alley. His fingers twitched and went still. Dark clouds boiled across the moon once more. Mercifully, Black Harry Rye was dead before the stray dogs, and hungry cats and rats found his corpse and made a midnight feast.

Bess O'Bedlam, known to many in the Caribbean as the Water Witch, stalked through the streets of St. John's Town in a towering fury. The long full skirts of her black satin frock coat flared out around her legs as she moved stiffly but purposefully in the direction of the harbor. The two crewmen followed her without comment. They knew better than to interrupt their captain when she was angry. Bess' temper was as legendary as her penchant for trouble.

Suddenly, she paused. Something had caught her attention – a little tavern that was hardly more than a collection of boards lashed together, crammed between two other buildings, and leaning tipsily to one side. There were no windows, just wide cracks between the boards and a doorway covered by a ragged blanket. It looked slatternly and foul, thoroughly unsavory, and ready to collapse at the slightest shock.

A wooden signboard hung by a rope over the doorway. There was no writing on it – most sailors were illiterate, finding little use for letters – but someone had daubed the sign with dirty green paint and a crudely drawn violin. *Fiddler's Green*, Bess thought, eyeing the tavern with speculation. *Could it be a trap?* Absently, her short-trimmed nails drummed on the scabbard of her cutlass.

After a few moments of thought, she turned to her crewmen. "Get ye back to the *Mad Maudlin*," she ordered, "and tell Lovelock to wait for my return. If I ain't come by then, he's to get her away from Antigua and turn command over to Mister Dunn."

"Aye-aye, Cap'n," one of the men said. His companion looked as though he might protest, but a sharp glare from Bess made him reconsider. He shrugged and tugged his forelock. The sailors walked away without a backward glance.

Bess stood still for a while, ignoring the streams of people who passed by her. She was jostled once; well-honed reflexes caused her hand to shoot out, grabbing the cutpurse's thumb and snapping the bone with a practiced twist of her wrist. The would-be thief cursed hoarsely and disappeared into the crowd. No one else approached her too closely; she had shown that she was predator, not prey, and therefore to be avoided.

While she examined the tavern, a sailor was forcibly ejected out of the building by unseen hands. The man seemed hopelessly drunk; he reeled, stumbled, then slipped into a puddle of sewage, falling with a noisome splash. The hapless sailor was immediately set upon by a pack of child thieves who stripped him of valuables in a trice, leaving him naked and unconscious, or possibly dead. Shortly afterwards, a harlot in a tattered Madras cotton dress went inside the place, followed by a juggler whose glass balls were filled with dull red witch-fire, the occult-born flames that burned without burning.

At last, sensing nothing overtly suspicious that might be a trap, but still on her guard, Bess settled her shoulders and entered the Fiddler's Green. The tavern was dark, smoky and filthy, and reeked of stale beer, unwashed bodies and blood – old blood as well as more recently spilled. Every surface was covered with an oily film; the blackened ceiling beams fairly dripped with soot. Sand crunched underfoot. The tables and benches were cheap and badly constructed of scrap ship boards, seemingly ready to fall apart at a sneeze. A few spluttering candles in cracked dishes did little to dispel the gloom. It was the sort of place where a drowned rat or two in the ale barrels was thought to add a certain piquancy.

The customers matched the ambiance; they were rough-faced and ragged, true scoundrels who respected nothing but strength and brute cunning. The men reminded Bess of a pack of hungry dogs – fearless and vicious unless confronted by someone who proved to be stronger and meaner. Then they crawled on their bellies, pretended to submit and waited for the opportunity to tear out the stronger one's throat. There was a hum of tension in the air, prickling her skin like the tingle of nearby lightning. A sharp pain lanced through her thumbs. She knew what the warning portended; Bess was no stranger to savagery.

She eased the side of her frock coat back over her cutlass hilt, freeing the blade for action. Bess had visited this sort of establishment before. It was common sense to keep your weapon loose in its sheath, and your money next to your skin. She glanced around the dingy room, taking particular note of a number of card and dice games. If the gamblers had their knives stuck into the table tops – a sign of imminent bloodshed – it would be prudent to leave. She could always return later with a few of her own bully boys. Bess would back *Mad Maudlin's* crew against this scurvy lot anytime, but it looked like blades were sheathed, meaning the games were relatively honest.

A dreadlocked man in breeches and a dirty shirt – a cargo handler, judging from the boathook hanging on his belt – spied her in the doorway and made a coarse jest. The room erupted into sniggers. At first glance, Bess was definitely not the tavern's average customer. She was conscious of intense scrutiny by dozens of eyes as the patrons judged her appearance.

The oversized cuffs, lapels and collar of her black satin frock coat were decorated with swirls of flat gold braid. Fine lace spilled over her wrists, and cascaded down the bosom of her white linen shirt. Her hip-length waistcoat of cerise silk was embroidered with acanthus leaves in olive green, which matched her knee-length breeches; a thick, tooled leather belt supported the scabbard of her cutlass. A Burmese ruby ring glittered on her index finger, looking like a drop of petrified blood set in gold. From the top of her tricorn hat to the tips of her sea boots, Bess O'Bedlam cut a magnificent, even foppish, figure.

Because her breasts were small, her body lean and tall, she was usually mistaken for a young man, an impression she preferred not to correct unless it became necessary. Not everyone recognized the infamous pirate captain on sight, despite the Water Witch's formidable reputation in her own corner of the world. Black Harry Rye's instant identification was the exception, since common seafarer's gossip held Bess O'Bedlam to be ten feet high at least, with horns on her forehead, a set of clashing fangs between her legs and fireballs shooting from her arse. The reality might be ludicrously commonplace in comparison, but the real woman was more dangerous than any tale-teller's fantasy.

"Hey, bum boy!" a drunken wit called out, "Did you lose your way? Or are you looking for a real man to pry open that dainty bung-hole of yours and fill it full o' cream?" There was a great deal of laughter at this sally, but some of the other patrons kept quiet, watching to see how Bess would respond.

Bess bared her teeth in a snarl. "That's a damnable boast for a man who's lost his pizzle to the pox. Did you get the French disease from a quayside doxy, or was it your mother gave you the rot, you damned goose-witted whore's son?"

Infuriated, the man let out a bellow and leaped to his feet, nearly upsetting the table. His mates, spotting the flintlocks beneath Bess' coat, tried to make him sit down. He pulled away, too drunk for sense, and came at Bess swinging a broken chair leg.

Bess ducked the awkwardly aimed blow, drew back her leg, and kicked the man full in the face. He fell to the floor with a bone-rattling thump, spitting teeth and blood. She squatted and drew one of her flintlocks in a swift, fluid motion. Before he had time to defend himself, she had the barrel of the pistol pressed against his forehead. Bess cocked the doghead with her thumb. The twin clicks sounded ominous in the otherwise silent room.

"Easy, lad," she said as he blinked at her. His mouth was already swelling from the blow she had dealt him; blood smeared his lips and chin. "We've no real quarrel and 'tis too fine a night for killin' out of hand." She rose, keeping the flintlock aimed steadily at the man's face. "I'm feeling fairly peaceable, so you and your mates can pay up and get out, and I'll not stop you. Otherwise, I'll put a lead ball in your brainpan. S'trewth, by thunder, and you can make of it what you will."

He mumbled something unflattering and blasphemous, his expression sullen. Bess' smile grew wider. "Do you think your mates'll help you?" She shot a glance at the other patrons. Most had gone back to their drinking and gambling. The man's friends were watching the tableau but did not seem anxious to get involved. One by one, they threw a few small coins on the table and slunk out of the tavern.

Bess gestured with the pistol. "On your feet and find the door, quick, afore I change my mind!" she snapped.

He scrambled to his feet and fled, blood dribbling down the front of his shirt.

The landlord, a big-bellied, dusky-skinned man whose apron was covered in dubious stains, put away the spiked club he had retrieved from behind the bar at the first sign of trouble. Bess returned her flintlock to its sling beneath her coat and sauntered over to him. After bidding the landlord a polite good evening, she dipped into her pocket and slapped a Spanish doubloon down on the scarred counter. His hand flickered and the doubloon disappeared. Bess nodded, impressed by his speed.

"What will ye, m'lord?" the landlord asked. His voice was a rasping croak – no doubt the result of whatever had caused the thick scar on his throat—and his gaze was steady, cold and calculating. "Ain't got no wine, nor hock nor other fancy stuff. Only beer n' ale, rum n' arrack." He suddenly leered; the expression did not suit his weather-seamed face. "Less'n you wants a trip to Gropecunt Lane. I've got tail, m'lord, the likes of which you won't find outside the heathen Orient! Just sit yerself in the corner and I'll send over one o' me best doxies. Ol' Lizzy knows what the gentlemen likes. Hoy, Liz!"

"None o' that," Bess answered, shrugging away the caress of a blowsy, near toothless woman who had come at the landlord's call. She paid no heed to the harlot's hissed insult; instead, she gave Lizzy a flat stare that sent her scurrying away. Leaning an elbow on the bar, Bess beckoned the landlord closer. He hesitated, then complied.

"Black Harry Rye," she half-whispered, certain that no one could hear them over the buzz of conversation. "He sent me here."

The landlord looked startled. He glanced from left to right, and put his hands flat down on the counter. "Is that so, m'lord?" he asked warily.

"Aye, 'tis so," Bess replied, allowing some of her exasperation to show. "Well? Have you aught to say about that, or shall we stand here all evening, dumb as fish?"

"Perchance." The landlord considered her for a moment and finally shrugged. "Black Harry was here all right. He had some baggage with 'im."

Bess' interest was piqued. "Baggage?" she asked casually, although her heart beat a little faster. This could be it. The end of her long quest seemed within reach, and excitement sang through her veins.

"Aye." The landlord pushed a leather jack of ale towards her. When Bess did not touch it, he lifted it to his own lips and took a long swallow.

Bess had to restrain herself from punching the man, or at least giving him a good shake. If he knew how badly she needed the information, he might turn coy. Her instincts told her that trying to torture it out of him would be a prolonged and possibly fruitless endeavor. He was no Harry Rye, a tired old man who could be bullied to the breaking point. This fat fellow in his food-stained apron would hold out long after she was weary. The more she pushed him, the more stubborn he would become; besides, he probably had supporters among the snarling crowd of cutthroats that patronized his tavern.

Accordingly, she waited, keeping her face expressionless by force of will, until he relented and continued, "This is how 'tis, m'lord, and the Devil take me if I lie. Black Harry's credit ain't no good, not in St. John's Town. Not in the whole o' the godforsaken West Indies. He pays cash or kind, slap bang or nothing."

The landlord took another drink; a thin stream of ale spilled down his shirt. He wiped the wet spot carelessly with his palm. "So, Harry comes in tonight. He's got a fistful o' gold, m'lord. Gold." The man repeated the word reverently. "It weren't too long afore a sharper seen Harry's flash and gulled him into cards. Ye knows, m'lord, that poor Harry is befuddled most o' the time so that he can't tell his arse from his elbow. He lost the gold to the sharper – who was fast away soon as he had it, and no man the wiser – and Harry still owed me for the night's carouse. He went home to fetch more coin, so I'm keepin' his baggage till he pays the bill. 'Tis my right to settle a debt in such-like fashion."

"Harry won't be coming back tonight," Bess said. "He sent me to pay his bill. How much does the old sea-dog owe?"

"Well, that's mighty kind of yer lordship." The landlord's forehead crinkled; his look of cunning calculation increased. "I reckon he owed me...fifty shillings all told."

Bess rolled her eyes in disbelief. "Do I look like an addle pate fresh off the boat from Cádiz? I could buy this louse haven for half as much, free n' clear."

"Ah, but Harry's a good soul. Likes his mates jolly, he does. Bought the whole house a few rounds o' my best ale. Played the beast with two backs in Gropecunt Lane – twice. Then there's the damages, o' course. Damages is most costly."

"Damages?" Bess made a show of looking around. "A fire would do the place a world of good. Anythin' less is an improvement."

"I s'pose I could take thirty-five. No less," the landlord said, crossing beefy arms over his chest. "Bein' as how yer a great lordship who ain't but doing a kindness for a friend."

"Ten is all I'll offer, master grumbleguts. Not a ha'penny more." Bess took out her purse, counted the correct number of coins, and laid them on the counter. The landlord hesitated, and she added, "Take it. You've had a good doubloon from me thus far, more'n enough to pay for a whole night's carouse."

Still, the man seemed unwilling to accept the lesser fee. Greed had gotten the better of him. She could read that clearly on his face. She also noticed one of his hands creeping under the counter. "Pick up that cash and give me the baggage, or I'll gut you like a herring where you stand," she said, searing him with a cold glare. Her hand slapped against the hilt of her cutlass, and her muscles coiled, preparing to draw and strike.

The landlord froze in place. Slowly, he brought his hand back into sight, scooped up the coins, and gave her an unfriendly look. "Ye tells Black Harry, when you sees him, that he ain't welcome in my place no more," he said. "And if I sees yer poxy face again, m'lord cock o' the company, I'll push yer teeth out yer arse with one good punch."

"The baggage?" Bess lifted a brow, not at all affected by his threat.

The landlord came around the counter and stumped towards the back of the tavern. Reaching a door cobbled together from planks and stuck in a warped frame, he produced a key from his apron pocket and unlocked it. He shoved the door open with a foot and said, "Take yer damned baggage n' get ye gone."

He used his big belly to shove Bess aside as he returned to his place behind the counter.

Carefully, Bess entered the room, if it could be called that. It was a sort of cobbled-together lean-to tacked onto the back of the Fiddler's Green. Mildewed tarpaulins, propped up with more planks, served as walls and roof. The floor was simply the cobblestones of the alley behind the tavern. A sweet, stomach-churning stench permeated the atmosphere. She closed the door. It was oppressively dark, but Bess located a candle stub in a bracket on the doorframe, along with flint and steel. It took her only a moment to strike a light.

What she saw made her gasp in astonishment.

Black Harry Rye's "baggage" was a woman.

CHAPTER TWO
The Butcher's Bill

Marguerite De Vries was both furious and terrified.

She had been bound and gagged, and left to stew inside a dark stinking hole for hours, with only insects and rats for company. Her head ached – a dull throbbing pain that kept rhythm with the beat of her heart. The feeling in her arms and legs had progressed from excruciating muscle cramps to needle-sharp prickles and numb patches that somehow hurt far worse. It was the humiliating – and frightening, she admitted to herself – culmination of an evening that had gone from very, very good to very, very bad in little more than an ill-considered moment.

Marguerite was a thief. More specifically, she was a counterfeit crank, who employed a disguise to lure her prey into striking range. She often posed as a prostitute, soliciting for customers in the rowdier and most disreputable parts of town, where no one was likely to summon the town wardens over anything less than a full-scale riot. Hers was usually a successful scheme, since she took care to choose only the drunkest victims, persuading them to take her to their lodging-houses or into a convenient alley to transact their "business". Once out of the range of potential witnesses, Marguerite used the leaded sap she carried under her petticoats to knock her victims unconscious, steal their purses and any other valuables they owned, and be gone before they awoke, poorer but perhaps wiser, if sore of head.

It's a risky profession, she thought, remembering the times she had come close to getting killed. Sailors took being fleeced very seriously, as the loss of precious pay meant that unless their mates took pity on them, they could not afford any of the port's pleasures that they had lusted after while at sea for months on end. Marguerite had a nasty scar on her abdomen where a Royal Navy officer – who had proved to have a head as unyielding as a cannonball – cut her with a folding knife before she broke his nose with a swipe of the sap and fled, a hand clapped over the wound to hold in her guts until she could find a chirurgeon who asked no questions to mend it.

Enough of the past, she told herself sternly. It was the present to which she ought to turn her attention; specifically, this present mess that she had gotten herself into, and how she was going to get out of it again.

Marguerite's evening had gotten off to a spectacular start. She had picked up a Spanish captain, whose arrogance was scarcely tempered by strong drink, and went with him to a squalid room over a tavern. Marguerite let him paw at her titties as a distraction, then gave him an expertly judged crack on the back of his skull with her sap. Just a moment later, she stepped over his unconscious body and was on her way home, his heavy purse jingling in the hidden pocket of her skirts. In case of a pursuit, she zigzagged her way through a number of alleys and by-ways until she reached her own quarters.

The purse turned out to contain an impressive number of gold and silver coins, enough to keep her in relative ease for a few months. There had been no reason for Marguerite to return to the streets that night. She could have stayed in her rented room with a jug of wine and a roasted chicken, or gone shopping for clothes in the second-hand stalls at Petticoat Market. There was a sweet baby monkey that she had had her eye on, too; its fur was dyed green, and she had some notion of training it to climb into people's open windows and steal whatever valuables it could carry. However, she had taken her luck with the Spaniard to be a sign of further riches, and gone out to seek another victim.

That old bearded sailor – what a stupid mistake to make!

He had looked fat and sloppy, but there had been muscle under his bulk, and he had not been quite as drunk as he appeared. Marguerite's instincts would normally have warned her against the man, but flushed and heady with her earlier success, she had not heeded the warning bells in her head. She lured the sailor into an alleyway as usual, plying him with sweet words, but when she moved to strike him, he disarmed her and knocked her out instead – a solid fist to the side of her skull whose echo still throbbed in her temples.

When Marguerite woke up, she was in an unfamiliar place, with ropes tied tightly around her wrists and ankles, and a foul tasting gag in her mouth. As near as she could tell, the Spaniard's bulging purse was gone. Cheated by a cheat, *godskannonne*! Had pure rage been able to sizzle through her bonds, Marguerite would have been free already.

As it was, she could only wait and hold herself in readiness. It was hard, so hard, to push back the fear that threatened to overwhelm her. There were many fates in store for a woman in St. John's Town who let down her guard, many special sufferings only relieved by the blessing of a merciful death. Instead of dwelling on the horrors that might be visited upon her – and her imagination was fertile enough to supply several blood-chilling examples – Marguerite concentrated on what she would do to the bearded old bastard when he came back for her. Geld him, certainly. Slowly and with great attention to detail, using a nicked, blunt, rusty blade. White-hot pokers also sprang to mind. She did not know how many hours she lay there, trying futilely to stretch her muscles against the ropes that pinioned her so that she would not grow too stiff. Mildew-mottled tarpaulin was all that separated her from the street, but calling out for help was impossible and besides, she was not stupid enough to draw attention to her vulnerable state. The best thing to do was wait. She was cleverer than any sot of a sailor; she would somehow get away.

Marguerite was startled out of her thoughts when the door opened. She squirmed, using her heels to push herself backwards until she bumped into a barrel and could go no further. There was a scritch of flint striking steel, a spark and a guttering candle flame that chased away some of the shadows.

Marguerite squinted against the light, but she never took her gaze away from the person standing in the doorway. To her surprise, it was not the fat old man who had taken her.

Some high flying dandy, she thought immediately, taking in his fine clothing. *Hardly more than a boy. No hair on his cheeks, and I doubt there's much thatch below. Some Lord High Admiral's get, or most like, a plantation brat with more cash than sense. Carries himself like a regular banty rooster. I'll wager he diddles the slaves behind Daddy's back.*

She felt a touch of relief at this assessment. Such youths were susceptible to manipulation. She could turn him to her will, possibly use him to help her escape. *Aye, laddie buck, I'll give you a peek at my dainties and a sniff of my petticoats, and you'll follow my heels like a puppy.* Marguerite was not above using any weapon – including her own body – to survive. She drew the line at fornication if it could be avoided. She was choosy about her bed partners, much preferring the company of women to men.

Then she saw the gunpowder tattoo smudged high on one cheek, the five gold rings dangling from an earlobe, the cutlass and flintlock pistols in their ribbon sling, which were visible as the person moved further into the room and his coat flared out slightly. Marguerite's heart sank as she realized that this was not an inexperienced youth but a pirate, probably a captain judging from his bearing and his rich suit of clothes. In that split-second, she re-learned an unwelcome lesson – that no matter how dire the situation seems to be, it can always descend that little bit further into the purest of hells.

Eyes the color of polished steel stared down at her, holding as much warmth as conjured ice. Marguerite shrank back, shaking her head. She had heard tales of what pirates did to female prisoners, taken in a raid; rape was the least of the torments she could expect. Although she thought of herself as a bold woman, Marguerite was not really surprised to realize she was whimpering behind the gag. She had always steered clear of pirates, preferring less feral and unpredictable prey.

This particular pirate's expression was difficult to fathom. Amusement, perhaps. A certain amount of exasperation. Disappointment mingled with curiosity. Not a hint of naked lust showed in those depths, but Marguerite was unsure if she should feel relieved or even more apprehensive. She was not ugly; in fact, there were many who had complimented her looks. Marguerite was almost insulted by the indifference he displayed towards her physical charms. The pirate knelt down, studying her face, and that intense scrutiny made her feel like a specimen in a butterfly hunter's killing-jar. Marguerite's temper flared. No longer afraid, she tossed back her hair and gave him a scorn-filled glare.

"I like a wench with spirit," he said, chuckling. His voice was a little higher than she expected, but not out of line with his apparent youth. "You're a pretty thing, all right, if somewhat wet. Related to the fishes, are we?"

Marguerite realized that her gag was spittle-soaked and drool was escaping from the corners of her mouth. His patronizing attitude made her even angrier. She raked him with her most scathing look, and received only a pat on the cheek for her trouble. Marguerite immediately decided that she detested this cock-sure pirate.

You mincing beau nasty, she thought, fuming. *You simpering dog! Were I free, I'd crack you open like a melon and suck the marrow from your bones.*

The pirate grabbed her wrists and hauled Marguerite to her feet. He clucked his tongue and held her close when she stumbled, his arm hard around her waist. She was pressed against his chest, her face near his throat. He smelled of sandalwood and salt and tobacco. Despite the rage that still smoldered within her, Marguerite became aware of the heat that poured off his body. She lifted her head. His gaze captured her own. A smirk turned up the corners of his generous mouth – a sensual mouth that seemed to be made for kissing, she realized, slightly dizzied by the knowledge and her own surge of lust. His hands were very strong, forcing her to yield towards him. Marguerite felt the play of muscles in his compact body, the small, firm breasts beneath the embroidered cerise waistcoat...

Breasts?

Marguerite reared back, staring at the pirate in horror. Not a man at all, but a woman!

"Bess O'Bedlam," said the woman, touching the brim of her hat.

There were few females daring and bold enough to lead a rover's band, and Bess O'Bedlam was the most notorious. Marguerite had listened to tales about the legendary captain who commanded one of the toughest and most vicious cut-throat crews on the Spanish Main. She had too much sense to believe half of what she was told, but if only a portion of the myth was true, she was in serious trouble indeed.

Bess grinned. "And who did you expect, dear heart? The Holy Ghost and the Twelve Disciples of Christ to come and settle your hash?" Bess kept Marguerite on her feet and took a clasp-knife from her pocket, flicking it open with a practiced motion.

Terrified, Marguerite tried to turn away, nearly fell, and was jerked back into place by a hand on her arm.

"Hold still, girl. I ain't goin' to eat you whole," the pirate growled impatiently. "Leastways, not without salt and a savory sauce, b'God."

Bess bent and adroitly sliced through the ropes on Marguerite's ankles with the knife. Marguerite moaned through her gag and tears slid down her cheeks as the pain of restored circulation made her feel as if her legs were on fire. The worst of the agony and stiffness passed after a few minutes, however, and she was able to take a few tentative steps.

"Good, good. You'll have to walk, as you're a healthy seemin' lass and I doubt I could carry you to the harbor," Bess said in a matter-of-fact way that made Marguerite's blood run cold. "Come along, dear heart. There'll be time for talk and so forth on my ship."

Still gagged, Marguerite shook her head in mute protest. She was not going anywhere with a pirate.

Bess frowned at her. "I'll not ask so nice again," she warned. "Come you must and come you will, though I drag you through the streets by your hair. You'll like that even less, I warrant."

Marguerite's heart banged painfully against her ribs, but she kept her head. She looked in every direction, seeking some avenue of escape, some weapon to use against this cool monster with a woman's body and the soul of a murderer. Her resolve faltered when Bess drew her cutlass. Marguerite flinched and let out a mewling sound.

"Quiet, girl!" Bess' voice held such a tone of command that Marguerite instinctively obeyed, her throat closing around the muffled whimpers that were about to burst free.

The pirate crept to the door, which was hanging open a crack. She put her eye to the narrow opening. After a moment, she grunted and drew back. "The landlord and some of his bully boys," Bess said. "Seems that damned ale draper is spoilin' for a row. He's cleared the place out otherwise, so it's through him and we're clear. Stay close, dear heart. I'll have us out in a trice."

She sheathed her cutlass, reached inside her coat, and produced a blunderbuss that had been hanging from a second shoulder sling. It was short, but the wide bore flared at the end, giving it the look of a funnel. The scatter gun was a nasty weapon and highly unpredictable, with a habit of exploding in the shooter's face if overloaded with gunpowder. As a short-range clearer of decks, however, the blunderbuss had no peer.

Marguerite made an emphatic gesture to show her bound wrists, hoping this lunatic pirate would at least untie her so she could defend herself. To her renewed fury, Bess merely bestowed a patronizing smile.

"I think not," she said. "Any weapon you pick up is liable to get stuck in my back. Are you ready, girl?" Bess winked and took hold of Marguerite's arm with her free hand. "'Tis time to pay the butcher's bill."

And with that, Bess braced the wooden stock against her shoulder, kicked the door open and stormed into the tavern, dragging a reluctant Marguerite at her side.

CHAPTER THREE
Trapped!

The landlord had armed himself with an ancient wheel-lock pistol and a spiked club. The four men with him were armed with blades. They appeared to be old hands at violence, ready and willing to kill. Every man was braced for a fight. Nevertheless, none of them seemed prepared for the sheer thundering hell that blasted out of the doorway, affording them no warning and no quarter whatsoever.

A blunderbuss was a very effective weapon at short-range, often used to repel boarders at sea or rid the decks of mutineers. When Bess fired, a volley of heavy grape-shot scattered wildly from the trumpet-flared end of the gun, wreaking complete havoc on anything and anyone in its path. One man who took the brunt of the hot lead-storm was literally shredded, an explosion of blood and ragged tissue that painted walls and ceiling with streaks and splatters of dripping crimson. The rest were sore wounded, taking myriad injuries that left them groaning on the scarlet-washed floor.

When the thick cloud of smoke cleared a little, Bess stepped forward, allowing the spent blunderbuss to slide back under her coat. She shrugged to settle the weapon more comfortably in its sling, ignoring the dull ache in her shoulder where recoil from the gun had bruised her flesh down to the bone. Bess looked down at the landlord, who lay on his back on the floor, eyes closed. His filthy apron was now spotted with blood, a stain that quickly spread over the bulk of his torso. A ball of shot had taken away a chunk of his cheek, exposing his decaying teeth to the gum-line. He might live, she judged, then she saw bubbles in the crimson on his lips. Very rarely did a man survive such damage to the lungs.

The air was acrid with gunpowder; she could taste the rusted iron tang of blood droplets in her mouth. Bess checked the other men quickly. All but one had suffered mortal injuries. The survivor stared up at her in a daze; she thought the shot had broken his thigh bone. Bess dismissed the man as unimportant – he was not likely to leap up soon and there was no firearm within reaching distance. She took a firmer hold on her prisoner.

Whoever this girl was, whatever she had meant to Black Harry Rye, Bess O'Bedlam meant to find out the truth.

She left the Fiddler's Green with the young woman in tow and headed towards the harbor at a trot. At this late hour of the night, the streets were virtually deserted. Even the whorehouses were quiet, though red-tinted lamps still burned in the windows, indicating they were open for whatever licentious business could be desired by their patrons. The busiest place seemed to be a fortune-teller's shop; the sign blazed with multi-colored witch-fire, flames that leaped and glowed but did not burn, and needed no fuel save magic itself. Several sailors in British Naval uniform reeled out of the shop door clutching good luck talismans, their brows smeared with soot and chicken blood. One of the men carried a bedraggled cat on his shoulder, confined by a tether around its throat. The cat had pinfeathers stuck to its whiskers, and a satisfied smirk on its feline face.

Bess paid very little attention to the few folk she passed in the street, except for a quick assessment of potential threats. She was grateful that the girl was coming along meekly, since she had no wish to drag a struggling female through St. John's Town, even if most of the people she might encounter would cheer her on rather than attempt a rescue. Certainly, none of the night watch in the quarter called Wool-packers Quay who had charge of the *baracoons*, the dingy pens and warehouses where slaves were kept prior to the daily auctions, would lift a finger to help anyone but themselves.

They crossed the corner of the main square, where the stocks, pillories, ducking stool, cage, gallows and whipping posts stood, the implements of the King's justice as ordered by the town wardens and the Crown-appointed Governor. Some poor sod was still there, his ears nailed to the pillory, moaning and sobbing softly to himself. The rotting remains of a condemned criminal filled a small iron cage hanging from the top of a pole. The chain creaked in the wind. Bess wondered how long it had taken the fellow to die, and if he had been raving at the end. That would be her fate if she was caught, to be beaten with the dread *látigo para desollar*, the Spanish flaying whip with its innumerable leather tails and knots and sharpened metal stars that would strip the meat from her bones, then to be locked into a snug-fitting cage that would allow no movement at all, and finally hoisted aloft to dangle till she was dead. She would perish of her wounds, of the baking sun and horrific thirst, further tormented by birds that came to take their share of her flesh while she was still living.

Bess shivered and spat to avert ill luck.

Her flagship, the *Mad Maudlin*, lay at anchor in the sheltered harbor in the midst of dozens of other ships, mostly merchant traders from a dozen nations and a few military vessels. By day, the harbor was a chaotic bustle of brigantines and barques, Spanish galleons and Dutch galliots, jolly-boats and gigs, sloops and frigates, as the lucrative sugar and slave trades made St. John's Town one of the busiest ports in the West Indian Isles. At night, the harbor was silent save for the slap of waves against wooden hulls, the sleepy mutter of the middle watches with an occasional female giggle floating across the calm sea, answered by a deeper, murmuring male voice. There was little for honest men to fear here. Fort James reared on the north side of the harbor, protecting the waters with thirty-six long-range guns, any one of which was capable of sinking or otherwise eliminating an imprudent attacker.

Bess felt the skin between her shoulder blades crawling when she finally reached the docks. There was no one about; the watchmen were too far gone with drink to be much trouble at this hour of the night, but it would not be wise to linger. Honest men were abed, while those who plied more questionable trades were just beginning their nightly prowl. Bess found an unattended rowboat, got her captive aboard without too much trouble, and sculled out into the harbor to find her ship.

Mad Maudlin was akin to a three-masted Dutch cromster, which was, in its turn, similar to a galleon, possessing a high stern transom filled with a double row of mullioned rose glass windows, and a hull that bulged out around the keel like a tulip bulb. The ship was smaller than its Spanish cousin and more maneuverable as well. She carried a relatively small complement of seventy souls, and had room for about a hundred if they did not mind cramped quarters. Although the ship looked ungainly, *Mad Maudlin* was fast and heavily armed; sixteen twelve-pound guns stood on her gun deck, and a full dozen swivel guns were lashed to the top deck. Her timbers were sound, and she did not suffer from the iron sickness that plagued many West Indian vessels. With her sails aloft and a freshening wind to drive her onwards, the ship could do better than ten knots in the open sea.

Because of her piratical history, *Mad Maudlin* was flying Dutch colors instead of Bess O'Bedlam's crimson flag that depicted a skeleton and a heart pierced by a sword, coupled with an hourglass to signify that Death Ends Life In Time. The escutcheon had also been covered with a new one bearing the name *Vrouwe Cornelia*. This deception was necessary; Bess and her cutthroats had prices on their heads in English pounds, French *livres*, Dutch *florins*, Portuguese *moidore* and Spanish pieces-of-eight. Coming to St. John's Town, even in disguise, had been a huge risk.

At that moment, Bess could not say if this latest twist in her long quest for the *Deceiver*'s treasure had been worth the possibility of discovery by the authorities. She had killed five men; Black Harry Rye was also dead, though she had no direct hand in his demise. At the end of her search in Antigua, she had only a pretty girl and more of a puzzle to show for her efforts. *Deceiver*'s resting place remained lost, but Bess was confident that the wrecked ship would be found, no matter what had to be done to accomplish her goal.

Bess worked the oars in their tholes, her shoulders rolling in an even rhythm, her sea boots braced for purchase against the thwart. The girl was in the bow, head hanging and hair obscuring her face. Bess felt a touch of concern but had no inclination to coddle her prisoner at the moment. Whoever she was, the girl was high-spirited and feisty, not a delicate flower that might wilt at a touch. Life in the poor and rowdier sections of St. John's Town was not easy for anyone, but women especially were targets for abuse.

She passed under the hulking shadow of a British Royal Navy man-o'-war, and freed a hand to flick an insulting gesture at the unknowing captain. Like all pirates, she loathed the arrogant British who believed that naval superiority over other nations gave them the God-given right to do as they pleased. At last, Bess reached the *Mad Maudlin* and let out a low whistle. Someone on deck flung out a rope ladder and a line. She secured the rowboat and swarmed up the ladder, sure-footed and limber. It was but a moment before she pulled herself over the rail. By the faint illumination of a lamp held cupped in his scarred hands, Bess recognized her quartermaster, Solomon Lovelock.

"Mr. Lovelock," Bess said, "bring our guest aboard, put her in my cabin and cut loose that tub. We'll be leaving Antigua as soon as practical. I've no wish to remain under Fort James' eye any longer than we must. Set course for Hotspur Cay at sunrise."

"Aye-aye, Cap'n," Lovelock murmured. He was a big man, with a solid paunch that strained the seams of his patchwork leather vest. His meaty arms were covered with tattoos, and his head was shaved, but he sported a flamboyantly thick red mustache whose ends were carefully curled and waxed to points.

"Wake the gunnery master and have the guns loaded with case shot. Quietly, Mr. Lovelock." Bess' gray eyes gleamed. "If any mother-be-damned Britisher or other sea-hog gets in our way, she'll be fair surprised."

Lovelock smiled. "That she will," he replied. The big man moved away, motioning to a few crewmembers to join him.

Having given her orders, Bess sought the captain's cabin, tucked beneath the poop deck at the stern of the ship. As she ducked through the door, she reached for flint and steel to light the lantern hanging in its gimbals nearby. A mellow golden glow spread through the room, deepening the shadows in the corners. She breathed a sigh of relief and tossed her coat onto a brass hook, placing her tricorn hat over it. Unbuckling her wide leather belt, she laid it and the cutlass on top of her sea chest. The flintlocks and blunderbuss, with their accompanying ribbon slings, she hung on a second hook within easy reach. A needle-pointed dagger in a spring-sheath remained strapped to her forearm; she felt completely vulnerable without a weapon of some sort, even when she was ensconced in the safety of her flagship.

Lastly, Bess sat on the bed to remove her mud-spattered boots and woolen stockings, leaving her barefoot in breeches, waistcoat and shirt. It felt good to be free of the heavy clothing, the woolens and silks of old England that had been transported to the West Indies along with the natives of that cold, misty, rain-soaked country. Bess had enough vanity to enjoy dressing in the finest fashions when she could, but there was also something to be said for simplicity.

The captain's cabin was well-appointed with furniture, from the bunk box piled with feather mattresses and blankets, to a mother-of-pearl and gilt inlaid table bolted to the floor in front of the two rows of leaded, rose glass windows that ran the width of the stern. A dainty French writing desk held place along a wall. Bess moved to a cabinet beside the burled chestnut *escritoire*, shoved aside a bundle of rolled charts, and found a cup and a bottle. She poured herself a measure of rum before sitting behind the table.

The liquid burned its way down her throat and settled to a warm glow in her belly. Bess pulled off her headscarf and let the blue kerchief fall to the floor. She wore her chestnut brown hair sliced off shoulder length and pulled back into a sailor's queue at the nape of her neck. Damp strands clung to her throat. She scrubbed fingernails through her scalp, easing an itch caused by dried sweat and salt air.

There was a blue-and-white Delft dish of salmagundi sitting on top of the navigation chart that covered the table. The scent of pickled pork, herring, eggs and onions, highly spiced and oily rich, suddenly reminded Bess that it had been a long time since breakfast. Her stomach growled. Despite her weariness, she felt equally faint with hunger. Bess grabbed an ivory-handled spoon and began to eat, careful not to soil her precious charts. The salmagundi tasted good despite the fact that it had cooled off and congealed.

The same person who had left her the meal had also provided a pewter pitcher of water. She used it to dilute her cup of rum. Bess was as fond of spirits as any of her men, but she was rarely drunk at anchor, and never at sea. She controlled herself ruthlessly and expected her crew to do the same. Every hand drank a measured ration of watered rum and lime juice daily, for Bess had observed that doing so helped ward off the dreaded scurvy that caused teeth to loosen in the head, and made gums bleed and joints stiffen. The practice of rum-and-lime had proved a more effective preventative than sauerkraut or extract of malt. She had made a point of ordering the captains of her other four vessels to follow *Mad Maudlin*'s example, and any sailor who defied this order would soon find himself beached.

As she ate, the *Mad Maudlin*'s second-in-command, Henry Dunn, came into the cabin, herding the captive girl in front of him. Dunn was short and thick-set, with shoulders like a bull and thighs like tree trunks. He went shirtless, the better to show off the thick mats of black hair that covered his body; hard muscle bulged beneath his sun-bronzed skin. By contrast to the hirsute nature of his torso and arms, Dunn kept his face clean-shaven – not an easy task aboard ship, when a swell might make the cut-throat razor slip at an inopportune moment. His legs were so bowed that he waddled rather than walked.

"A gift for the crew?" he asked, shoving the girl down onto the bunk box.

"Not likely," Bess answered, wiping her mouth on her sleeve. "Black Harry's dead, Mister Dunn. I'd say the Good Lord struck him down for his sins, but I doubt e'en the Devil would cherish his company in hell."

"And the *Deceiver*?" Despite his brutish appearance, Dunn spoke like an educated man. He was, in fact, a former British Royal Navy officer who had deserted his ship after killing the second mate in a brawl over a gaming debt. On a pirate vessel, the unspoken rule was that no man had a past; Bess knew about Dunn's because he had told her years ago, figuring she might consider him a spy otherwise, if the truth came out.

Bess tilted the cup and finished her watered rum. "I've had no luck yet, damn his eyes. The last thing Harry said afore he died led me to the lass. Now you know what I know, and the whole of it wouldn't make a carriage for a louse to ride to Coventry."

Dunn turned and regarded the young woman. She made a muffled sound, blue eyes snapping with ire over the kerchief that held her gag in place. Dunn frowned. "The wench looks like trouble," he commented mildly. This was as much protest as he was willing to make, and Bess knew it.

"Perchance." Bess was equally laconic. Dunn supported her decisions and rarely contradicted her orders; he was one of her most loyal and trusted officers. She stood, filling her cup with plain water from the pitcher. "I reckon you've duties to attend, Mister Dunn. We'll be getting underway soonish."

"Aye, Captain," Dunn replied. "Is it Hotspur Cay, then?"

Bess nodded. "We'll rendezvous with the *Mistress Moon* and the *Medusa*," she said, naming two of the other vessels in her pirate fleet. The remaining ships – *Swiftsure* and the *Red Queen's Revenge* – were cruising for merchant vessels off the coast of Massachusetts, along the trade routes that passed between the New World and England. They were scheduled to join the rest at Bess' island haven as soon as practical.

"I'll see to it, Captain." Dunn waddled out of the cabin, closing the door behind him. When he had gone, Bess gave the prisoner her full attention.

"You'll want a drink," she said, coming around the table with the cup of water in her hand. "I'll wager you're dry as a beggar's bone."

Bess worked the handkerchief knot with her free hand, aware that the girl was giving her a death's head glare. *If looks could kill*, she thought, amused by the show of petty defiance, *I'd have pennies on my peepers, only a shroud for company, and me to the Diet of Worms in a handcart.*

For her part, Marguerite was very angry and very afraid, but she knew better than to reveal any hint of weakness to a pirate. Her survival depended upon forcing her captors to respect her on a level equal to their own. Cowardly or soft behavior would likely spell her doom. Marguerite repressed her fears and fanned the flames of outrage to a healthy glow. Pirates respected strength, therefore she would be strong. She had to live long enough to effect an escape. That was her goal, and she focused on it with every fiber of her being.

As soon as the handkerchief was untied, Marguerite managed to spit out the gag, and a cup was immediately pressed to her lips. The first taste of water – though stale and warm with a tinny tang – was like ambrosia. She had not had anything to drink since earlier that day, and her body was starved for liquid. Marguerite sucked greedily at the water and made a choked sound of protest when it was taken away.

"Not too much at a time," Bess cautioned, "or you'll cast up your accounts. We've plenty of sweet water, dear heart. There ain't no need to guzzle."

This slight kindness made Marguerite suspicious. Her fears were confirmed when Bess put the cup on the table, out of her reach. *I'll never beg for it, you black-hearted bitch*, she thought. *I'd rather do without till my flesh crumbles to dust.*

Bess used her clasp knife to saw through the bonds on Marguerite's wrists. Her hands, so long deprived of normal circulation, felt like useless clods of meat dangling from the ends of her arms, and her wrists were bruised and scraped raw. Marguerite gritted her teeth as the numbness gave way to hellfire. For several long minutes, she forced her fingers to flex until some of the feeling returned.

Marguerite was given the cup again, and she sipped at it, watching Bess over the rim. The pirate handed her a Delft dish containing a portion of some disgusting mixture that reeked of cold grease and spices. The smell made Marguerite's stomach turn.

"You'd best dine while there's a chance," Bess said, leaning her hip on the table. "There'll be a time when we're down to maggoty hardtack and scraped slime from the bottom of a water tun, and you'll be wishin' you had a nice salmagundi to fill your belly."

Marguerite realized that she was appearing too delicate. She steeled herself to eat, no matter if her belly protested. Lacking an eating utensil, she used her thumb and index finger to pick out pieces of meat from the mess in the dish. It was as searingly hot as its smell suggested. She bit into something small and hard; the resulting burst of spice made the color mount in her cheeks and tears spring to her eyes.

Bess smacked her helpfully on the back until the worst of the coughing fit ceased. Marguerite managed to wheeze, "Keep your paws to yourself, sea dog!"

Bess leaned back, hands spread wide in mocking surrender. "Why, dear heart, I'd no notion your tongue was so sharp! Small wonder Black Harry disarmed you with a gag."

Marguerite laid the dish aside and licked her fingers clean. "'Tis all I had for an eating knife," she replied tartly. "Do you treat all your guests in such a churlish fashion?" She finished off the water and held out her cup for more.

Bess shrugged and refilled the cup from the pitcher. "Those who fail to please me," she said, "will fare the worse for it."

Marguerite also shrugged, although inwardly she quailed at the dark meaning behind Bess' offhand remark. "Well, you'll get little pleasure from me," she said. "What do you want? Why did you bring me here?"

Bess was impressed by the girl's spirit. She was a handsome piece, even with her blonde hair matted with dirt, and a bruise blossoming like a grape stain beside her jaw. Eyes as blue as a stormy sea stared back at her. The girl was plump – her freckled breasts swelled over the bodice of her gown and threatened to spill over – but Bess liked her women with some meat on their bones. In other circumstances, she might have acted on the attraction, but this was no time to let lust rule her head. There was business to be done.

Bess bent forward and took hold of the girl's chin. "What's your name?"

"Marguerite De Vries. Let me go, you *vuile tyfus hoer*! You're hurting me!"

"Who is Black Harry Rye to you?"

Marguerite tore herself free of the pirate's grasp. "Damn your eyes!" she spat, drawing back her hand and dealing Bess a ringing slap across the face. "I know naught of any Harry Rye. Is he the fat bearded bastard who left me in that stinking hole?"

Bess rubbed her burning cheek. Marguerite was a healthy young woman with a strong arm. The blow had made her ears ring. "That one smiting I'll give you for nothing, Mistress Margo," she murmured. Her gaze was like gray ice. "Next time, you'll get the wrong end of my belt 'crost your arse."

Marguerite was aghast. She wanted to crawl away and hide, but dared not show her apprehension. Instead, she lifted her chin, allowed irritation to make a sharp groove between her brows, and said, "Then stay well away from me. I'm no doxy, *Captain*." This last word was pronounced with all the sarcasm at her command.

Tension thrummed between them. Marguerite could feel it, crackling along her skin, stretching her nerves to the snapping point. She held herself upright and proud, well aware that this might be the crux. She had no reason to believe that Bess was anything other than a common pirate, albeit an extraordinarily successful one. Marguerite expected a swift and brutal response to her impudence, and steeled herself accordingly.

"You speak Dutch," Bess said calmly, as though she was a participant in a pleasant conversation between old acquaintances instead of a pirate interrogating her prisoner. "Are you a cheese-scraper?"

Marguerite did not relax her guard in case this was a trick. "My mother was Dutch. My father was French. I was born on Antigua." That was all she intended to say.

"You're no plantation owner's daughter," Bess said as a statement of fact. "I can't see you servin' swill in a tavern. You've soft hands, but I doubt you're in the cloth cutting trade. Not a doxy, eh? A thief, then. What do you do, shake them dugs of yours in a lusty sailor's face and cut his purse when he ain't paying mind?"

It was a relatively accurate assessment of Marguerite's strategy, but she did not acknowledge the hit. "We're all sinners," she said, and gave Bess a pointed look. "Some have more to confess than others."

Bess smiled. "Aye, I'm a murderer and a thief. I've committed acts against God and man. I know I'm hell-bound, Mistress Margo. So be it. I make my own way in the world. I'll die knowing that I ain't beholdin' to no one. Everything I have, I took with my own hands, and paid for with my own blood."

Marguerite snorted, but she had no reply to give.

Bess changed the subject. "Do you ken the *Deceiver*, captained by Fancy Tom Carew?"

"Is he another of your poxy ilk?"

"Carew was a sea-rover some five-and-twenty years ago. Black Harry Rye served with him, and a prime condiddler he was, too. That man would steal anything in reach that weren't red hot or nailed fast."

Marguerite toyed with a lock of her hair. "What's that to me?"

"I've no idea, dear heart, saving that Black Harry named you with his last breath." Bess paused, then asked with studied casualness, "Did he give you aught? A love token, mayhap a key, a chart?"

"*Godskannonne*! That thrice-damned dog gave me nothing save a knock on the head! Did you kill him?"

"Nay. He paid the wages of his sin without me actin' as a heavenly debt collector." Bess was not convinced that the girl was not involved somehow. She briefly contemplated the merits of whipping cords and the *bastinado*, but she was loath to spoil Marguerite's prettiness. There were other ways of obtaining the information she sought.

Rather than continue the interrogation, Bess got to her feet and smoothed back her chestnut-brown hair with both hands. "We'll be underway at the tide," she said. "Make yourself at ease, Mistress Margo. I've matters to attend on deck."

"You're not... I won't go with you." Marguerite struggled to keep her voice from breaking.

"You've no choice." Bess went to the door. She paused, glancing at Marguerite over her shoulder. "Do naught to draw attention to yourself, dear heart. For most of the crew, a woman ain't but three holes on two legs. Less'n you want to be raped to death, keep your ass at anchor and your rattletrap shut. I'll send along the ship's boy with some grub in a bit."

"I won't go! I won't!" Marguerite was close to hysteria. Her worst nightmare was about to come true. Once the ship was at sea, there would be no escape, no hope. She would be at the complete and utter mercy of the most dreaded pirate in the Caribbean.

"You've no choice," Bess repeated bleakly. She went through the door and shut it behind her.

Marguerite distinctly heard the scraping sound of a key turning the lock. She was trapped!

Panic swelled in her throat. Despair almost choked her. She almost wished herself back in the Fiddler's Green tavern, facing an unknown fate. That had somehow been easier to accept than the certain knowledge that with Bess O'Bedlam as her captor, she would likely not survive; or if she did, then she would wish that she had not.

Marguerite lay down in the bunk box, so chilled she believed that she would never be warm again.

CHAPTER FOUR
The Speaking Bones

Bess leaned against the carved teak taffrail that ran round the edges of the poop deck and stared out at the harbor. Anticipating dawn, the sky had lightened to lavender-gray, shot through with streaks of rosy pink and yellow. A slender slice of blood-red sun was visible on the horizon, where the dark waves turned to a diamond-shot shimmer that stung the eyes. The stars were fading but she could still make out the constellation Orion as well as the Pleiades, called the Seven Sisters, in the south. The *Red Queen's Revenge* and the *Swiftsure* would keep the Sisters on their larboard beams during their run from the American colonies to Hotspur Cay. It was a course she knew very well; she could have sailed it in her sleep.

As her navigation tutor had taught her long ago, Bess checked the sky for the *Triangulum Australe*, the distinctive Southern Triangle that lay left of the now dimly glittering stars in the southern constellation Centaurus. She also automatically sought the subdued sapphire glimmer of Vega, the orange-tinged ruby of Arcturus, and the long graceful coil of Draco the Dragon in the north, as well as the faint splendour of Cassiopeia in the east, and golden-clothed Venus playing Star-of-Morning in the western sky. No matter if one was at anchor or at sea, it was always good to know the positions of the stars, and thus, one's own position in the wide, roaming world.

As above, so below.

Bess' focus shifted. All around them were other vessels, where crewmen were stirring on decks; on a nearby British Royal Navy sixth-rate frigate, rope slings had been lowered over the sides, and men were touching up the waspish yellow-and-black checkered paint pattern of the gun ports. From other ships came the crunching grind of holystones and sand, the splash of water followed by the slap of swabs flogging the decks dry. A dinghy full of raddled females with far too much paint on their faces was sloping away from an American schooner, the watermen working the oars together as the boat headed for the quay, its load of whores clutching their coins, their shawls, and their skull-shaped talismans against pregnancy. Bess followed the dinghy's progress. On the quay itself, a group of surly-looking men loitered, smoking pipes; she thought they were likely the whores' masters.

Bess idly wondered if the schooner had a chirurgeon on board, and if so, did he know the proper charms to ward off pox and gleet, for Antiguan girls were notoriously unclean. A cool breeze struck her face, making her squint; it was the *brisote* trade-wind from the northeast that was scented with salt and fish, human and animal waste, and the cast-off rubbish from dozens of ships at anchor – the filth that invariably collected in the morning tide that slopped along the edges of the docks.

She heard the American bosun and his mates piping and rousing the hands in terrible roars that were muffled by bulkheads but nevertheless carried: "Shake a leg, there! Up all hammocks! Out or down! Out or down! Here I come with a sharp knife and a clear conscience!"

Bess smiled. On *Mad Maudlin*, the crew had already been wakened and were hard at work hauling the chain-pumps to clear the bilge and the ship's well where foul water drained and collected at night. She glanced at the sky. Venus' dazzling brilliance was growing fainter as the sun overtook it. Bess sighed.

Her thoughts turned to Marguerite De Vries. It was possible that Black Harry's last words had meant nothing. He had been dying, after all. Mortally stricken men sometimes raved in their final moments. Or perhaps he had retained enough sense to send her on a wild goose chase, a dead man's final jest. Mistress Margo might be exactly as she claimed – an innocent bystander caught up in events not of her choosing.

On the other hand, Bess was not willing to give up her quest for the *Deceiver*. Three months ago, a chance meeting in Nassau had led her to the sole surviving crewman of the lost vessel – Black Harry Rye. Discreet inquiries at various ports suggested that Black Harry had a source of income that was not dependent upon circumstance. He had been seen paying his debts as well as passages to several islands, all with good Spanish gold doubloons. Bess reckoned that gold was part of the *Deceiver*'s cargo. She wanted it. Her mouth watered at the thought of that treasure, the richest prize ever plundered. Her soul swelled at the thought of the glory to come, the immortality of her name forever remembered as the one who had, against all odds, found the *Deceiver*'s grave.

Bess had to make a decision, and soon.

The sun crept further above the horizon. On the quarterdeck, Solomon Lovelock and Henry Dunn were overseeing preparations for the *Mad Maudlin*'s departure from St. John's harbor. The helmsman was already at his station by the great ship's wheel. The boatswain, a swarthy Bostonian named Toby Falconer, supervised the crewmen who were raising the bow anchors. The men bent their backs and pushed the wooden bars as they plodded in a circle around the drum-shaped capstan. The metallic rattle of spooling chain cable mingled with the slap of their bare feet on the deck.

"Weigh, ho!" Falconer shouted in his flat nasal twang. "Clean to the catheads, boys! Best and small, the bowers all! Weigh, ho!" He began to sing an old work chanty, the rhythmic rise and fall of the melody spurring the men's effort:

Ships do come and ships do go, and so do lassies' love and so,
But I, a roving jolly tar, do crave a wave that's deep and far,
For bum and 'baccy is the way a sailor such as I do pray,
And druther rum than landsman's beer, and go to sea with all that's dear,
Than plowing fields of wheat and rye, and ne'er an isle to catch my eye!
To sail through endless waters fine, why that's the only dream o' mine!

The starboard and larboard anchors rose from the water, dripping harbor mud. They were drawn up and secured home at the catheads, short projecting timbers that were carved into snarling lion's heads. Under the direction of Lovelock and Falconer, crewmen on the yards, nimble and apparently unafraid of the long dizzying drop below them, set the main topsail and the fore staysails. Canvas belled out with a crack as the sails caught the warm, salt-scented wind. Rigging creaked; the hull shuddered beneath Bess' feet, *Mad Maudlin* surrendering to the tide's inexorable pull.

Lovelock boomed more commands. "Make fast that clew line, you rot-gutted son of a Barbary ape!" the bald man called, shaking a fist the size of an oak knot at a careless man on the yard. "Keep us aloof of that man-o'-war," Lovelock said to the helmsman. "She's athwart-ships. Bear us up a point."

A Royal Navy man-o'-war, a 120-gun wooden behemoth, was also under sail, and ponderously turning directly into the *Mad Maudlin's* path. Livid, Dunn waddled forward, cupped his hands around his mouth and shouted, "Make way, you pig-wallowing bitch!"

The commander of the man-o'-war could not have heard him; the ship was not close enough yet. Dunn returned to the quarterdeck, his face flushed with rage. "Order Master Levalier to open the gunports, Solomon. If that Britisher don't shear off, then by the sweet bleeding Christ, I'll blast that God-be-damned whore's get out of the water."

Just then, a sultry wind gusted and *Mad Maudlin* put on speed, leaping forward like a dolphin. Lovelock called to Falconer, "Bring the mains'l flat in!"

Under the boatswain's direction, the linesmen hauled the aftmost corner of the mainsail towards the middle of the ship. *Mad Maudlin* slewed around on her beam, narrowly missing a Portuguese merchant vessel and an American schooner with raked-back masts and the lean lines of a greyhound. The helmsman adjusted his course and they shot past the man-o'-war, close enough to see the dismayed expression on the captain's face as that splendidly uniformed gentleman stood on his ship's quarterdeck, the sun glinting from the gold epaulettes and polished brass buttons on his dark blue coat.

There were no further incidents. *Mad Maudlin* sailed smoothly past the harbor mouth and into open water, making good headway. Bess was pleased by her crew's performance, especially the helmsman. He was new to the *Mad Maudlin*, but he had served with Captain Sullivan on the *Swiftsure*. Charles Halifax was a scrawny fellow with a pock-marked face, but his touch on the wheel was masterful.

Lovelock ordered more sails aloft in the light wind that came abaft the stern, and soon *Mad Maudlin* raced southeastward, the cutwater unscrolling fast from her bow, blue water hissing along her quarter. Only a few thin clouds marred the turquoise bowl of the sky, where the sun hung like a hot copper disk and turned the air hazy. Bess went from the poop deck to the quarterdeck and checked the weatherglass that hung in gimbals next to the door of her cabin. The liquid in the spout was low, indicating clear weather, but storms could be unpredictable in the tropics; a lightning-laced ship-killer could literally blow out of nowhere. Bess relied on the weatherglass, but more on her own instincts. She could smell a gale brewing hours in advance of the storm-front, though unlike the forecasts of a true weather witch, her predictions were based on experience rather than magical ability.

Crewmen clambered down the shrouds, using their toes for purchase on the ropes that ran down from the masts at larboard and starboard. One soul slid down a backstay, landing on the deck with a bone-jarring thump. His mates whooped in appreciation of his bravado, and the crewman turned a cartwheel for good measure. Falconer gave the man a slap on the shoulder and set him to splicing rope. The ship's cat, a white moggy with a comical black mask across her eyes, raced over the deck with a wounded rat clamped in her jaws; the squeaking rodent left a thin drizzle of blood behind. At once, some of the hands began to make wagers on how long it would take for Sheba to dispatch the rat in her leisurely but murderous way. Wagers began flying thick and fast forward of the foremast, then Falconer himself took charge of the book to avoid quarrels, and sent for a swab to mop the blood from the deck.

Bess went to the binnacle that stood next to the ship's wheel and checked the compass on its wooden stand. They were on course; the wind was fair, not the baffled and confused airs that were often to be found near the Tropic of Cancer. The sea was calm and, barring the unpredictable, the ship should arrive at Hotspur Cay within nine days or so.

"Keep your course thus," Bess said to Halifax, who acknowledged her order crisply.

Dunn approached her. The thick mats of hair on his body were covered with sparkling water beads. "I hope I meet that ill-mannered bitch of a man-o'-war someday, Captain."

Bess smiled at him. "Pride goeth before a fall," she quoted, knowing that the *Mad Maudlin* would likely not survive such a direct encounter, being out-gunned and out-manned. Dunn knew it, too. "Don't let it stick in your craw, Mister Dunn," she replied. "The job's well done. You gave that Britisher a poke in the eye she'll not soon forget. I reckon her captain will think twice afore running foul of us again."

Dunn's weather-beaten face creased as he grinned savagely. "Aye, Captain. That he will."

"I'm off to the galley," Bess said. "Pass the word round, Mister Dunn – our guest, Mistress Margo, ain't common property. She's mine alone. The men are to treat her like their very own virgin baby sister, and I'll keelhaul any dog that even thinks of touching her. Am I rightly understood?"

"Aye, Captain," Dunn replied. "There were doxies a-plenty in St. John's Town, and I doubt there's any man aboard who hasn't had a belly full of swiving. Nonetheless, I'll put a flea in the ears of those likely to offend."

Bess left the quarterdeck and sought the galley, located aft of the crew's quarters. The space was defined by an L-shaped oak table, above which hung nets filled with limes, yams, bananas, plantains, papayas, eggs, onions, gourds, dishes and cups and other items. Pots and pans swayed on hooks that had been hammered into the beams that curved overhead. Beneath a scuttle in the bulkhead was an iron firebox standing in a sandpit, positioned so that smoke could trickle out through the hole. Behind the table were cages of clucking chickens. An open barrel held live lobsters, destined to be made into pies. In one corner were several long cages of turtles. Every article that might shift upon the ship's movement was secured with lines.

A bubbling pot of gruel was on the firebox, stirred with a long-handled spoon by the cook, who glanced up as Bess entered. Hephzibah's skin was black as ship's pitch; she had high cheekbones, a broad flat nose and a proud set to her calico-turbaned head. As was her habit, she wore wide-legged petticoat-breeches and a man's shirt with the sleeves rolled to her elbows. Multiple gold and silver bracelets clashed on each wrist. Hephzibah's blind left eye was milky from corner to corner, but the right eye was sherry brown, sparkling with intelligence and spirit.

She smiled at the captain, exposing a gap between her front teeth. "Come to break your fast?" Hephzibah asked, gesturing towards the pot.

Bess shook her head. "Have the ship's boy take a bowl of the stuff to my cabin, along with whatever else you think might suit a wench's appetite."

"Have we a lady on board, then?" Hephzibah asked, raising a brow. She put the spoon down and went to the table.

"Ha!" Bess snorted, made a grab towards a slice of papaya, and snatched her hand back as Hephzibah threatened her fingers with a wicked looking chopping blade. "The wench ain't no lady. She's a thief, our Mistress Margo, and a hell-cat born."

The cook chuckled, reaching into one of the overhead nets to retrieve a battered tin bowl. She limped back to the firebox and ladled out a portion of oatmeal. Bess watched the woman's stiff movements, remembering the reason for the limp. Hephzibah had been wounded in a sea battle some years ago; a wooden splinter, blasted from the hull by a piece of shot, had cut through her ankle and chipped away part of her heel bone. She never complained, not even when Bess, acting as chirurgeon's mate down in the cockpit after the fight was over, had cauterized the wound with hot pitch to stop the bleeding. The resulting scar was ugly, but her foot was otherwise sound and would bear her weight. Hephzibah returned to the table and plunked the bowl down in front of Bess.

"Eat that right up," Hephzibah said in a no-nonsense tone, crossing her arms over her generous bosom. "You'll waste away to naught but skin and bones. A captain needs belly fodder to get through the day."

Bess grimaced. "I had salmagundi when I came aboard, not but an hour or so ago."

"Eat!"

Hephzibah's fierce glower made Bess pick up the bowl and swallow a mouthful of thin gruel. Burgoo was fairly tasteless stuff, and the flavorless dish made her long for spicier fare. Regardless of her feelings, however, Bess obeyed without another murmur. Hephzibah was the finest galley-master she had ever met, a veritable wizard who raised ship's cooking to a fine art. When the ex-slave was offended, though, her dishes were burnt or over-salted or otherwise unfit for consumption.

Bess knew her men well enough to realize that, while they would endure culinary hardship when they had no choice, they preferred to eat well when they could. Therefore, it was wise to keep Hephzibah happy; or the crew would have to subsist on ship's biscuit and plain salt beef, and such a situation made for grumblings and discontent. When the crew was in good spirits, the ship ran more efficiently. In recognition of the black woman's importance, there were standing orders on *Mad Maudlin* that within the confines of her galley – like the captain on the quarterdeck and the chirurgeon in the sick-bay – Hephzibah was the sole mistress and commander. Woe betide the sailor who offered offense; he would not only suffer the wrath of Hephzibah herself, but of his crewmates and the captain, as well.

When Bess finished the burgoo, Hephzibah rewarded her with a small portion of plum duff, a boiled suet pudding sweetened with dried currants. This was more to Bess' liking, and she polished the dessert off quickly, licking the spoon clean of every crumb. Hephzibah gave Bess a keen glance with her good eye.

"You didn't come down here just to magpie with me," the cook said, sliding the dirty dishes into a small barrel of water. She picked up her knife and began slicing open another papaya. "You look like there's something on your mind that's itching to get out."

Bess rubbed the gunpowder tattoo on her cheek and sighed. "I need you to speak to the bones for me, mistress."

Hephzibah froze, then slowly put the knife back down on the table. "Is your need so great?"

"Aye," Bess replied. "You know I'd not ask otherwise."

Until now, she had avoided requesting this service for two reasons. First, because she was aware of Hephzibah's reluctance to risk herself unnecessarily; and second, Bess preferred to rely on her own wits rather than consult the spirit world at every turn. There was always a price to be paid for such dabblings. The ex-slave was reliable and trustworthy, but the possibility that something could go horribly wrong was never far from Bess' thoughts.

Not all ships lost at sea were due to storms and other natural disasters. Sometimes, unnatural forces took vengeance on those who tampered with things best left alone. Everyone knew the cautionary tales about spook binders and creatures of darkness and fates worse than death. Bess would rather roll naked through fire than endanger *Mad Maudlin*. On the other hand, she needed to put her mind at ease regarding Marguerite De Vries and the role she played – or not, her conscience nagged – in the matter of the *Deceiver*.

"Is this to do with the woman in your cabin?" Hephzibah asked.

Bess nodded. "Mistress Margo might be part of the *Deceiver*, and she might not. If she ain't, then I'll put her off at the next port with a fat purse for her troubles. Speak to the bones, 'Zibah. The matter's a sore vexation to me. If there ain't no hope of findin' the *Deceiver*, I'll chart a new course, I swear. There's treasure a-plenty to be had elsewhere."

"But none as great as Fancy Carew's," Hephzibah said.

"Aye." All Bess could do was wait for Hephzibah's decision.

Above them on the deck, men's voices rang out in song as they hauled in the sheets.

> *O, the cook is in the galley, boys,*
> *A-makin' cakes with honey,*
> *And the captain's in the cabin, boys,*
> *A-eatin' tasty cunny!*
> *Let's heave away together, ho!*
> *Together heave away!*
> *We're bound to heave away, and ho!*
> *No honey, boys, this day!*

Bess watched Hephzibah; there was a deep crease between the woman's brows that indicated serious consideration. Finally, Hephzibah nodded. She cleared a space on the table and limped to a wooden chest tucked into a corner of the galley. The chest contained her private things, clothing and jewelry and other cherished articles. She came back holding a worn leather pouch. Cowrie shells and beads decorated the front of the *gris-gris* bag, which was closed with a drawstring. A tiny skull that looked appallingly human was fastened to one end of the string.

Hephzibah held the pouch tightly between her hands, then she opened it and cast the contents on the table. Bits of yellowed bone scattered across the scarred oak surface. Seemingly at random, the black woman chose a sharp curved piece and jabbed it into her thumb. A drop of blood welled up. She let it fall amidst the bones and closed her good eye. The cataract-clouded eye stared blankly ahead.

Bess held her breath. She had witnessed this a few times before. There was no doubt that Hephzibah had an uncanny power. Her talent did not lie in hexes or other spells, but she could, with some difficulty, summon certain spirits and compel them to grant her a glimpse of the past, present or future. Like all magic practitioners, she had paid a hefty price for her power, small as it was; Hephzibah's eye had not gone blind by accident. The spirits gave, but they also demanded payment and left their mark upon the magically gifted.

The black woman moaned, swaying a little. Her mouth dropped open; twin streams of saliva ran from the corners of her mouth. She mumbled something guttural, and the hairs on the back of Bess' neck prickled. The air smelled of lightning, crisp and stinging to the nose. A shadow crawled across the bulkhead, then another and another until the galley was crowded with shifting darkness. Suddenly, Hephzibah's milky white eye flared crimson, and a trickle of blood ran from her nostril. Her face took on a more skull-like quality, as though skin and flesh had shrunk down in an instant to cleave to her bones.

"Child of bone and blood, she be," Hephzibah said in a voice that was too deep, too hollow to be her own. "Child of kin-ties, bearing the way." Her fingers clawed at the table a moment, then stilled.

Bess dared not interrupt. The bones on the table began to vibrate and skitter about the surface. Hephzibah – or rather, the spirits controlling her – went on in a high girl's voice, "Seek the token, gift of the false-faced dead. Beware! A black curse on *Deceiver*'s grave."

Blood dripped on the front of Hephzibah's shirt. Her lips were covered in a liquid sheen of crimson. Again, her voice changed, becoming a smooth baritone. "She is the key."

"The key! The key!" other voices whispered. "She is the key!"

Bess shuddered.

The scuttle-cover banged open and a stiff breeze swept through the galley, gathering up the shadows and shepherding them outside. Hephzibah wailed, clutching the edge of the table with both hands. Her eyes were squeezed closed. After a few moments, Hephzibah shook herself, her breathing thick and slow. The woman's face was dripping with sweat, her complexion an unhealthy gray. "Too strong," she muttered. "Almost too strong for me."

"How do you feel?" Bess asked, suddenly regretting that she had put the woman through such an ordeal. "Will you take a tot of rum?"

Hephzibah ignored the question. "Did you find out what you wished to know?"

Bess frowned. "Perchance," she admitted. "'Twas all knotted up and tipsy-turvy."

"They speak as clearly as they're able," Hephzibah replied tartly. "Some things can't be told in plain words. You've got to puzzle it out for yourself. I've done *my* best."

"I know, 'Zibah." Bess' expression softened; she had a genuine fondness for the woman. "I'm grateful to you. Is there aught I can do in return?"

"Just leave me be for a while." Hephzibah swept the bones back into the pouch and pulled the drawstring tight. Her blind eye had returned to its normal milky color. Her complexion had also renewed itself, and she appeared to be sweating less. She picked up a cloth and mopped the blood from her face. "What of your young lady?"

"She's part of it somehow, and I'll crack that riddle yet. My thanks for the duff, mistress." Bess took one of Hephzibah's hands and pressed her lips to the knuckles. "I'm beholdin' to you, forever and aye."

Hephzibah flapped the bloodstained cloth at Bess' head. "Belay that sugar-talk, you dog! Away with you afore I take a merry rope's end to your useless hide!" A smile took the sting out of her command.

Pleased that Hephzibah seemed to have recovered from the worst effects of her efforts, Bess left the galley and returned to the poop deck. She found her place at the taffrail and propped her elbow on it, cupping her chin in her hand. Marguerite De Vries was the key to *Deceiver*'s treasure. Thus said the spirits, and Bess had never known them to be wrong. Tricksy, yes, and much given to enigmatic prophesy...but never wrong.

A token, she thought, rolling the spirit's puzzling words around in her mind. *A curse. A key.*

She did not know what it meant, but by thunder, Bess O'Bedlam meant to find out.

CHAPTER FIVE
Fancy's Folly

After spending some time feeling sorry for herself, her stomach knotted with dread, Marguerite finally shook off the worst of her upset. She was a survivor, pure and simple. As long as there was breath, there was life; as long as she lived, there was hope. Marguerite believed that with all the fervent faith of a Christian towards her God. She also knew that no one – not the authorities, not the Church – cared what happened to a common thief, a woman without relations, fortune or influential friends. She had only herself to rely on. That was the way of the world, cruel and harsh and pitiless. She had learned the lesson early; orphaned at the age of nine, Marguerite had made her way by sharp wits and sheer bravado.

Well, the time for tears is over, she thought ruefully, smoothing the full skirts of her bottle green gown. Water-spots had joined the stains on the bodice; she felt wet from cheeks to breasts from the force of her weeping. The sullen beat of a headache made her rub her temples to soothe the throb.

Now 'tis time to see what may be done. I'll not surrender – aye, not till the last drop of my blood is spilled, and even then I'll save my final breath to curse the dog who did for me.

She wrinkled her nose at the sour stench of her dress, and the acrid stink of her body. Most days, Marguerite sponged herself down with water, which she mixed with cheap *eau-de-cologne* when she could afford it. Prostitutes frequented public bath houses, and she had no wish to fight off lusty men just to be clean. A sponge-bath was usually sufficient, but there had been no time to indulge that day.

Marguerite spied a washstand against the bulkhead; there was a small scrap of mirror above it, and a railed shelf with brushes and silver-topped bottles. Remembering how Bess had smelled of sandalwood, she scooted out of the bunk box to investigate the contents of the washstand and shelf. The bottles held various oils and perfumes, including the smoky-sweet scent favored by the pirate. Marguerite sniffed until she found a fragrance that she liked – an orange flower water with a hint of spice.

She unlaced the bodice and peeled out of her dress, then held it at arms length to try and decide if the garment could be salvaged. The back of the dress in particular was soaked with a disgusting filth that reeked like an open sewer pit. Marguerite did not think it would ever be clean enough to wear again, but she thriftily laid the gown aside rather than discard it. This was her only gown and she doubted that Bess – who seemed to prefer men's costume – had anything else suitable.

Her stockings were a complete ruin; she balled them up and tossed them into a corner. The shoes needed cleaning and were missing a buckle, but were otherwise intact. The chemise and petticoats she wore beneath her dress were in slightly better condition, but not by much. Her chemise was ripped a little at the shoulder; the damage was easily mended if she could find a needle and thread. The linen undergarment was much patched and soft from many launderings; a thin line of scrolling grapevine embroidery around the neckline and hem was still in good condition. Marguerite smiled. Living as she did, it was difficult to obtain nice things, and she cherished the few luxuries that came her way.

Recalling her other gowns with regret – abandoned on Antigua, and forever out of reach – Marguerite sighed, untied her petticoat strings and stepped out of the plain cotton undergarment. Now clad solely in her chemise, she raised her arms, running her hands through her hair. She winced when her fingers caught on tangled blonde locks. *First things first*, she thought, reaching for the silver-backed brush on the shelf. Some vigorous brushing got rid of the worst of the dirt and mats. Lacking any pins, Marguerite found a bit of ribbon, gathered her hair at the nape of her neck and secured it with a neat black bow.

There was a sea sponge on the shelf. Marguerite poured water into the bowl from the pretty porcelain pitcher, and added a measure of orange flower scent. She began to wash her arms, throat and face, almost purring as the cool, refreshingly perfumed liquid trickled down her skin. After a few moments, she caught another glimpse of her face in the mirror.

Wide blue eyes stared back at her; a scattering of freckles stood out starkly against the paleness of her cheeks. Her smoothly rounded arms and shoulders glistened. Water had wetted the front of her chemise; the saturated fabric was translucent, clinging to her full breasts. Her rosy nipples were visible, straining against the front of the garment. Marguerite smiled and squeezed the sponge, letting more water drizzle between her breasts. The chemise was loose enough so that a thin stream of wetness ran down her belly, soaked her thighs, and pattered on the floor in fat droplets. Wickedly, Marguerite brushed a swollen nipple with her thumb, shivering as the sensation sent chills coursing through her blood. She wondered what Bess might think if she saw her prisoner in such a tempting light.

The idle thought alarmed her, chasing away the fleeting impulse and leaving her feeling like a naughty child with a guilty conscience. Marguerite finished her sponge-bath in a hurry, and cleaned up the floor with one of her petticoats. She got into the bunk box and sat down cross-legged, pulling a blanket to her chest. After a while, the ship began to move, gliding smoothly forwards, and Marguerite bit her lower lip.

She had never been aboard a ship or a boat in all her life, despite growing up on an island. Marguerite became violently nauseated standing on a quay, with nothing but an endless horizon of rippling water before her. *Mal de mer*, it was called – sea sickness – and the affliction was a source of much ribald jesting among professional sailing men.

Marguerite moaned as a long swell made the ship bob up and down. The motion was relatively gentle, but she was already experiencing dizziness, and her headache worsened. Her skin prickled, as though ants were crawling on her. There was a lurch; *Mad Maudlin* swung round in a way that made her feel sick, as though her stomach was trying to crawl up through her throat. She clutched the blanket and swallowed hard, willing the illness to pass. As the ship entered the open sea and put on more sail, the pitching and rolling motions became stronger, harder to ignore. Marguerite whimpered. Saliva filled her mouth. Pain squeezed the bones of her skull until she was nearly blind from the agony. Her skin felt clammy as a frog's. She bent over the edge of the bunk box and vomited uncontrollably.

Marguerite felt no better afterwards. She fell back into the bunk box, still retching, but at least her stomach was empty. She had not known such intense misery existed, and would have been glad to have met the end of her days without such knowledge. *This* was hell; not a place of fire and brimstone, but a watery Gehenna where blue devils sawed at her brain-pan and twirled her guts around their fishing gaffs. Marguerite wished heartily that she was dead.

After what seemed like an eternity of torment, there came the scraping of a key in the door lock. Marguerite did not have the strength to lift her head. At that moment, if the Devil himself had entered the cabin and offered to end her life in exchange for her immortal soul, she would have accepted the bargain, for the brimstone-scented flames of eternal torment could not possibly compare to her current suffering.

Bess came through the cabin door and paused. Marguerite was lying in the bunk box, wearing only a thin chemise that was rucked up around her thighs. Pink-tinged sunlight streamed through the windows and striped her flesh rose and gold. Bess was, however, unable to appreciate the otherwise tempting sight; at first glance, she thought that a crewman had attacked the woman against her orders. An immediate flash of rage made her jaw clench until her teeth protested, and her hands clench into tight fists. Bess was about to sweep out again to find the bastard whoreson when she noticed the mess on the floor and registered the sour odor of vomit. Marguerite's face was pale, gleaming with sweat, pinched around the nose and mouth. Bess' lips twitched as she fought back a smile.

"*Mal de mer*, dear heart?" she asked. When she received no reply other than a groan, Bess nodded and composed herself. Seasickness was really no laughing matter, despite the sea farer's gruff contempt for those who succumbed to it. She had known a sailor to die of *mal de mer*, although she suspected that he had been ill with fever already.

Bess leaned her head out of the doorway. "Jim Monk! Where the Devil are you, lad?" she shouted.

As if by magic, a young man appeared. His dark hair was twisted back into a tarred queue, and his shirt was far too big for his scrawny frame; it had been taken in at his waist with a broad leather belt. A wooden pipe was thrust into the belt, along with a small dagger. He gave Bess a cheeky grin. "Aye, Cap'n," Monk said, his eyes alight and curious. "Here I be." He tried to edge around Bess' body blocking the doorway, no doubt trying to get a glimpse of the mysterious lady in the cabin.

Shipboard rumor, already rampant, claimed that she was lovely beyond a man's wildest dreams, even more beautiful than the Sirens of Anthemoessa, off Sicily's turbulent shore – or so Bess had heard murmured around the scuttlebutt. Aware of the boy's interest – and of the crewmen who would surely corner him and demand every detail of what he might have seen – Bess settled herself more firmly in the doorway. "Send my compliments to Mistress Hephzibah, and ask for a cup of ginger tea and some ship's biscuit. Fetch 'em right smart to the main deck. When you're done with that, get in there and swab out my cabin. 'Tis worse than a pig's wallow!"

"Ain't no fault of mine," Monk answered, and dodged the swat aimed at his ear.

"Get along, you damned jackanapes, and save your breath to cool your porridge!" Bess made as if to kick him and Monk scampered away, still grinning.

That task accomplished, Bess turned her attention to Marguerite. It was clear to her that the girl was suffering. It was equally obvious that taking her on deck in such a state of dishabille would cause a riot. Not wishing to be forced to kill half her crew to save her reluctant guest from gang-rape, Bess opened the sea chest strapped down at the foot of the bunk box and rummaged through the contents. Eventually, she unearthed a clean shirt and a pair of canvas petticoat-breeches, the wide-legged garments that several of her crew, including Hephzibah, habitually wore. Bess went to the side of the bunk box and stared down at Marguerite. The blonde woman opened an eye and swore at her weakly.

"I see that upsettin' your tripes ain't dulled your tongue a whit, Mistress Margo," Bess replied. She reached for Marguerite, frowning when the woman rolled over to face the bulkhead. "On your feet, dear heart. Some sea air will do you good."

Marguerite protested and tried to resist, but Bess was adamant. Using a combination of merciless bullying and brute strength, she got the woman out of the bunk box and dressed in the shirt and breeches, merely pulling the clothes over her damp chemise. Once that chore was complete, Bess draped Marguerite's arm over her shoulder, helped her out of the cabin, practically towing her out on deck.

The main deck and the forecastle were bustling with crewmen. Some were working, others mending gear or chatting in small groups. It seemed that the ship's cat had dispatched her rat, and the betting circle had dissolved. Sheba herself was curled in the center of a coiled rope, carefully cleaning a forepaw. When Bess and Marguerite appeared, all conversation ceased. Every face turned towards the pair. A low buzz rippled across the deck. A hot-eyed man with a hungry expression took a step towards the women, then halted when Toby Falconer called him sharply to task. Apparently sensing trouble, the white-and-black cat fled. Bess ignored them all and took Marguerite to the rail.

Behind her on the quarterdeck, Henry Dunn scowled fiercely. "By

Christ's wounds! I see these surly sodomites don't have enough work to busy themselves, since they've time to stand idle and gape like bone-wits," he said to the air in general, though loud enough for his words to carry clean to the foredeck.

Solomon Lovelock sneered, teeth flashing white beneath his red mustache. "Aye, 'tis a while since the bilges were pumped and scrubbed to a polish."

Immediately, the crewmen took the hint and went back to their chores, although many of them continued to cast surreptitious glances.

Bess stood behind Marguerite, her arms around the woman, her hands braced on the rail. "Look at the horizon," she instructed. "Breathe. Sea air's a sovereign cure for the belly-gripes."

Willing to try anything to end her torment, Marguerite did as she was told. After a few minutes, she began to feel somewhat better. The tang of salt-laden air was delicious. Her headache eased. The crippling nausea abated. With this lessening of her illness came an awareness that Bess was pressed up against her. She could feel small, firm breasts against her back, the muscles of Bess' thighs shifting in rhythm with the ship's motion. The pirate captain was a little taller; her body was lean and hard. Marguerite inhaled deeply, then let out the breath in a sigh, more relaxed than she had been in a long time.

"Better, eh?" Bess released Marguerite reluctantly. The woman smelled of orange flowers; her hair was golden in the blazing Caribbean sunlight, tiny wisps gently curling and clinging to the nape of her neck. For a split second, Bess had the impulse to press her lips against that soft, pale, vulnerable spot. She controlled herself with an inner shake. *Belay that! Are you some moonstruck calf to fly into pieces on account of a pretty bit of woman-flesh? The wench is a means to an end, no more.*

When Jim Monk came on the main deck, carrying a piece of hardtack and a pewter mug of hot ginger tea, Bess was grateful for the interruption. Hephzibah obtained a supply of the fresh root from Jamaica, where the Spanish had transplanted it from the East Indies a hundred years ago. Apart from culinary use, ginger tea was soothing to an upset stomach. It was one of the few bits of wort-cunning that Bess had learned in her checkered career.

She took the cup from Monk and pressed it into Marguerite's hand. "Drink to the dregs," Bess said. The words came out a little more harshly than she had intended.

Irritated out of her moment of serenity, Marguerite jerked her hand back. Hot tea slopped over the rim of the cup; she hissed as it burned. "Clumsy oaf!" she spat, turning around to face Bess. "Have a care next time!"

"Just drink the damned tea," Bess ordered abruptly, willing herself not to look at the red mark on Marguerite's hand. An idea came to her, and she deliberately softened her tone. "My apologies, Mistress Margo. I meant no harm. Ginger's good for the *mal de mer.*"

You catch more flies with sugar than vinegar, Bess thought. *I reckon Mistress Margo might be sweetened a trifle if I play her up. Mayhap I'll act the mooncalf, too. A little wooing goes a long way with wenches. I need her – the spirits said as much – and when the deed's done, when I've got* Deceiver's *treasure, I'll be free to cast her adrift. Aye, 'tis a good scheme. I'll work my charm till she's cross-eyed with love and willin' to do aught for me.*

"Here," Bess continued, taking the piece of hardtack from Monk. She knocked it on the rail to drive out the weevils. "Nibble on this, dear heart, but dunk it first or you'll likely lose a tooth. Ship's biscuit ain't tasty but it's fillin'."

Marguerite almost snatched the hardtack and hurled it over the rail. Pride stiffened her spine. She bared her teeth at Bess in a not-smile. "Why, thank 'ee kindly for the advice, my lady all-a-gog," she said, her voice dripping poisoned honey. "I must've left my wits behind in St. John's Town."

Jim Monk was watching this by-play avidly, his mouth hanging open. Bess shot him a glare. "Have you no duties to attend?" she snapped.

Monk closed his mouth, swallowed hard, and took off as though the Devil himself was at his heels.

Bess gave Marguerite a more pleasant expression, including a smile that caused the creases at the corners of her eyes to deepen. "Shall I spin you a yarn, mistress?" she cooed. "There ain't nothin' like it to while away the time whilst a body's taking air n' exercise."

Marguerite sopped the hardtack in her tea and gnawed carefully. Even soaked, the stuff was tough and difficult to chew. She nodded, but kept a wary eye on the pirate captain.

"Well, then...five-and-twenty years agone, Fancy Tom Carew and the *Deceiver* was cruisin' the Straights when they spied a Spanish galleon run aground on the teeth of a ship-eating reef," Bess began, warming to her tale. She watched Marguerite to gauge the effect it was having.

"That galleon was the *Concepción*, making her way to Cádiz. Fair to bursting her seams she was, with gold and silver and emeralds and pearls and such, taken from godless heathens in the Americas. Carew was a lusty old hell-hound, and he weren't about to let that plunder go," Bess continued. "He and his mates was a fortnight scavenging the cargo. Carew worked his crew nigh unto death. In the end, *Deceiver* was ridin' damned low in the water but Carew had his treasure. A man couldn't spend it all in a lifetime. 'Twas the richest haul made in these waters – a king's ransom, fit for the pirate king, Carew."

Drawn into the narrative despite herself, Marguerite stood spell-bound, the hardtack and tea forgotten.

"Problem was," Bess said, "Carew was greedy. He didn't want to share the treasure but keep every coin for himself. So he made anchor at an isle – no man knows where it lies – and set his crew to foraging. I reckon he planned to maroon 'em all, and sail *Deceiver* home to Nassau by himself, only he forgot about the ship's boy who was still aboard. The boy gave the alarm. The crew hot-footed back and Carew had to do some fancy talkin' to stave off a mutiny. But that night in the middle watches, Fancy Tom tipped poison in the water tuns.

"Come mornin', Carew was a grinning devil. He put salt in the crewmen's burgoo. When the poor thirsty sea dogs drank the befouled water, they died to a man. All except one, so they say." Bess paused, a smile playing about her lips.

"What happened?" Marguerite asked breathlessly, blue eyes wide and filled with wonder. It was clear she was caught by the narrative.

Bess' smile widened. "Most say it was the seaman what done for Fancy Carew," she said. "Shot in the back, or mayhap a knife slit his gizzard. I don't reckon he lived, anyhow. Neither hide nor hair of Carew or the *Deceiver's* been seen ever since. Just think on that, Mistress Margo." Bess' gray eyes gleamed. "A king's ransom for the taking."

Marguerite frowned. "Do you think Black Harry killed Carew?"

Bess shrugged. "Perchance, mistress. The truth died with that black-faced liar."

Marguerite was about to say something more when Solomon Lovelock interrupted them. The quartermaster's red mustache bristled. He did not wait upon ceremony but said shortly, "Captain, there's trouble."

Instantly, Bess adopted a more business-like attitude. "Escort Mistress Margo to my cabin, Mister Lovelock, and secure it stoutly. I'll join you on the quarterdeck."

She hesitated, then took Marguerite's hand, removing the half-eaten piece of hardtack. Bess gallantly raised the woman's palm to her lips and kissed it, giving a slight flick of her tongue at the end of the caress that made Marguerite jump and shiver. Bess smothered a grin. Her plan was working. She made her best courtly bow and said, "*A bientôt*, Mistress Margo. My thanks for the pleasure of your company."

As Marguerite was led away by the burly quartermaster, she could not help glancing over her shoulder towards Bess. The wind ruffled short chestnut curls around the woman's lean face, and belled out the full sleeves of her linen shirt. The gunpowder tattoo seemed like a piece of shadow curving over her cheek. Marguerite was startled to realize that Bess O'Bedlam cut quite a romantic figure.

She wondered if she were losing her mind. Her palm tingled where Bess had kissed it. Marguerite clenched her hand into a fist and allowed herself to be returned to the captain's cabin, torn between confusion and a rising rage.

CHAPTER SIX
Nil Desperandum

Bess stalked the quarterdeck, waiting for Solomon Lovelock to return. Her first mate, Henry Dunn, was below decks with the gunnery master, Jacques Levalier. There seemed to be nothing untoward happening on the decks or in the yards. She paced to and fro impatiently, hands clasped behind her back. When Lovelock appeared, Bess went to him. "What's amiss?" she asked, her gaze keen.

"A brigantine off our starboard quarter, Cap'n," Lovelock replied. The sun struck a glare from his clean-shaven head. "She's flying British colors."

Bess' eyes narrowed and she frowned. "Fetch me the spyglass, Mister Lovelock."

He handed her a brass-bound spyglass. Bess walked to the rail and put the instrument to her eye, searching for the British vessel. It was not long before she found it.

"She's making sail in chase, the lively bitch," Bess observed. "Aye, there's Royal Navy ensigns aloft and a cut to her jib that I mislike. 'Tis the King's boot-lickers, spoilin' for a fight. Well, we'll see about that. She can't have more than ten guns. I reckon the captain's spied our butterbox colors and thinks we're a damned Lowlands merchant. He's got an itch for prize money, that one. Comin' on like hell was nippin' at his stern, and his gun ports wide open, the dog, hopin' we'll fire first so he can claim *Mad Maudlin* for a pirate. Hah!"

Lovelock made no comment, but he smiled at the sarcastic assessment.

Bess grunted and snapped the spyglass closed. "Prepare for battle, Mister Lovelock. Clear for action. Order the gun crew to make ready with chain-shot and case-shot. Have the helm hove to southward and eastward."

"Aye-aye, Cap'n," Lovelock said. He turned to the helmsman. "A point to starboard, Halifax."

"Brace the mains'l and clew up the fores'l," Bess ordered. "I've no wish to out-run her." She waited while the command was carried out under Falconer's direction.

In the lofty yards, crewmen furled the foresail. The mainsail was hauled close to the mast and secured so that its surface was flat and shivering under the wind. This had the effect of slowing the ship. In addition, Falconer ordered the remaining sheets set so that they were spilling wind; the sails, apparently full, were adjusted so as to prevent them from drawing with their full force, slowing *Mad Maudlin's* progress even further. There was a danger that the British captain might catch on to the trick – he would surely be observing the pirate's progress from his quarterdeck – but it was worth the effort if they took him unawares.

Henry Dunn arrived on the quarterdeck, somewhat out of breath.

"Kind of you to join the rest, Mister Dunn," Bess said. "We've a British brig to fight."

"I humbly beg your pardon," he replied. "M'sieur Levalier had some trouble on the gun deck."

"Couldn't fit his ramrod to your muzzle, eh?" Bess asked with a sardonic grin. It was well-known that Dunn and Levalier were lovers. She did not care, as long as their affair did not affect her ship's performance. "Don't he know that you're a breech-loader, Mister Dunn?"

Dunn had the decency to blush at this rough humor, although the heightened color was scarcely visible on his weather-beaten face. "We were neither of us on watch," he murmured.

"So be it." Bess summoned Dunn closer with a jerk of her head. "'Tis an engagement for sure, unless yon Britisher decides to beg off. Issue arms to the boarding party. Make ready the grappling hooks. When we're within half a pistol shot's range I want musketeers on the yardarms, too, for the brig will have armed Marines ready to pick us off. I ain't lookin' for a fight this day, but I'll not turn tail and run, b'God. Don't hoist our own colors till we've fired a broadside or three. That'll put some yellow in their livers."

"Aye, Cap'n," Dunn said. He squinted at the outline of the British ship. "She's about seven miles off. Do we fire first or wait till she hails us?"

Absently, Bess fingered a gold ring slotted through her earlobe – she wore one for each vessel in her pirate fleet, a total of five. "Hold our fire till I give the order," she said. "If she luffs off and hails us, have Willem de Woeste jabber some Dutch from the fo'c'sle to give them easement of their nerves. Then we'll favor the Britisher with a broadside salute and rake her with our swivel guns. After that, 'tis time for a grand killing."

"And if her captain surrenders?"

"I'm in no mood to take on prisoners," Bess said. "However, if the captain gives his parole, we'll take the pick of his provisions and any other dainties aboard, and leave the rest. We'll spike his guns for good measure. He can limp home to harbor, God rot his soul, and count himself fortunate."

Dunn nodded in acknowledgement. He and Lovelock issued crisp orders, and crewmen flew to obey. A swarm of sailors raced up into the yards, becoming black silhouettes against the white-hot glare of the Caribbean sun. Renewed energy crackled on *Mad Maudlin*'s decks. The hum of speed, the rhythmic vibration of the crystal-blue waves leaping beneath her hull, the creak of rigging and blocks, and the snap of sail conspired to make the ship a living thing, coursing gleefully away from the enemy to lure him into a trap. In the midst of making preparations, Bess spared a thought for Marguerite and asked Hephzibah to look in on her.

In the cabin, Marguerite had scrubbed at her palm until it was red and raw. The kiss Bess had placed on her hand – such a light, meaningless caress, hardly more than a butterfly's brush – felt as though it had been branded into her flesh. She hated her body's unconscious response to the pirate, and hated Bess for causing such a startling and unwelcome result with her flirtatious ways.

Am I a strumpet, Marguerite thought, enraged, *that with a bit of oily charm and a simple hand buss, I'm ready to haul up my petticoats and spread my thighs? Am I a child to be so mazed by a tale that I forget who and where I am?*

A murrain upon that pot-valiant peacock! That rot-gutted ape leader! When I clap eyes on Bess O'Bedlam again, I'll tear the hide off her in strips, from neck to marrowbones! She'll get no tenderness from me. I'll not yield an inch. If she thinks to bow and scrape and win favors from me, she's sore mistaken.

The more she considered the matter, the more Marguerite believed that Bess was trying to manipulate her. The kindness that the pirate had shown thus far had to be no more than a ruse. There was no proof of Bess' sincerity; indeed, the pirate captain, like all that scoundrel's breed, had a reputation for indiscriminate wenching.

She'd tup anything not fast enough to outrun her, Marguerite seethed. *Bess O'Bedlam has no heart. She can spin a pretty yarn but that's all it is – a false face to cover the beast beneath. Well, if she thinks I'm fool enough to fall arse-over-crown for her huskering, I'll soon prove her wrong.*

While she stewed, Marguerite stripped out of her borrowed clothes. The shirt and petticoat-breeches were comfortable, but not when bundled on over a knee-length chemise. She stripped the undergarment over her head and laid it on the table. Naked, she knelt to open the sea chest at the foot of the bunk box.

The garments within were typical, she thought, of a braggart pirate buck. No less than four fine *justaucorps* coats, each more resplendent with gold frogging and braid than the last, and one with genuine sapphire buttons. There were satin breeches to match; shirts of fine lawn, some boasting cascades of cobweb lace at wrists and throat; silk waistcoats; and kerchiefs, neck cloths and stockings. A few canvas petticoat-breeches and plainer shirts were present, clearly meant for everyday wear. At the very bottom of the chest, Marguerite found a woman's breech-clout and a stack of well-laundered rags. This evidence of Bess' monthly menses gave her pause.

How can she do it? Marguerite wondered. *How can she play the man while the moon mocks her with a woman's blood-tide?*

Something bulky, rolled and folded tightly into a corner of the sea chest caught her eye. She pounced upon the bundle and shook it out. As soon as she realized what the item was, all other thoughts disappeared from Marguerite's head. She stared at it with awe and more than a touch of envy.

The revealed gown was made of ivory satin, the full skirts split down the front to show the attached decorative petticoat beneath. The petticoat was a marvel of sky-blue Chinese silk embroidered with colorful winged serpents and clouds. A stiff, square-necked bodice was finished with a cockade of faded crimson ribbons and a discreet lace edging. The sleeves were tiers of ruffles tied with satin bows. The gown was crumpled, the ivory discolored in patches, but it was still beautiful enough to take Marguerite's breath away. She had never seen anything so lovely in her life.

Immediately, Marguerite began to speculate about what this dress might mean. Why did Bess hide it away in her sea chest? Was it a token of conquest or something more meaningful? Marguerite decided that it was probably the former. This was a court costume, or at least the sort of thing that a wealthy lady might own. That usually meant a member of the peerage. She had heard stories about noblewomen and their supposedly insatiable sexual appetites. According to rumor, the higher a woman's status, the less her morals became. Marguerite supposed that sometime in the past, Bess had taken a rich, possibly titled lover and kept the gown as a memento.

She sneered. *I knew it! The pirate thinks to make me but one in a long string of lovers. Ha! I'll show her that I'm not so easily gulled. I'll cast her sweet words back into her teeth with a good helping of sauce besides. Dear heart, indeed!*

There was a sharp rap on the cabin door. Marguerite hastily tumbled the gown back into the sea chest, adding the rest of the clothing on top of it in a haphazard way. The gown's existence was a secret, and she meant to keep her knowledge of it as a future weapon.

I'll play O'Bedlam's game and beat her at it, she swore to herself.

Donning the petticoat-breeches and shirt, Marguerite called out, "Come in, then, unless you've a mind to wear away your knuckles!"

The door opened and a black woman entered. Marguerite was astonished, wondering if the woman was a slave. Her bearing was proud enough to belie that initial assessment, but free blacks were a rarity in the West Indies, where sugar plantations were always hungry for slave laborers. The woman's left eye was sightless, milky with cataract; Marguerite noted the weakness, but she also took notice of the alert glitter in the other eye.

"Hephzibah's my name," the woman said. She was carrying a tray, and came limping into the cabin. "There'll be fighting soon. Best you stay here, girl. You'll be safe enough."

"Fighting?" Marguerite asked, feathery blonde brows drawing together in a frown.

"Aye." Hephzibah placed her tray on the mother-of-pearl inlaid table, nudging aside Marguerite's discarded chemise. She reached out and touched the garment. "Fine needlework. I see it's torn. I've a hussif with needle and thread; I'll fetch it to you later."

Marguerite edged closer. The tray contained a wooden platter with a slab of toasted cheese bread. The smell was delicious, and her mouth began to water. She was ravenously hungry. It seemed that either her time above deck or her subsequent spleen had cured the *mal de mer* for the nonce. There was also a dish of lobster pie and a portion of plum duff.

Hephzibah smiled at the greedy expression on Marguerite's face. "Eat while you're able," she said. The black woman picked up Bess' cutlass scabbard and the ribbon sling of flintlock pistols, collected more pistols from the cabinet, and turned to go.

With difficulty, Marguerite forced her attention away from the tempting dishes. "Wait, please!" she cried. "What do you mean about fighting?"

"There's a Royal Navy brig that the captain thinks needs a good thumping," Hephzibah explained, her hand on the door latch. She had not bothered to turn around. "You stay put, girl, hear me? I'll not lock you in, 'cause trouble ain't but a breath away at such times, and you may need to jump ship to save your life if it comes to that. But I reckon you'd best stay below where you ain't likely to catch lead shot. The captain finds you wanderin' about during hot action, she'll clap you in irons for sure."

Hephzibah departed, leaving Marguerite alone.

She sank down behind the table, picked up a two-pronged fork and ate, not really tasting the food. Marguerite's mind was a-whirl. There was a possibility – the slimmest of chances – that the British Navy brig might prove to be her salvation. She would have to be clever. It was a risk, but by her calculation there was very little to lose.

Appearance was everything in the world. One's clothing was the best indication of one's status in society. A soldier's uniform, a baker's smock, a clergyman's black coat, an Earl's glittering satin panoply, all indicated where each of them lay in the all-important tally of social rank. Noblemen commanded far more respect than farmers, and a respectable tradesman stood head-and-shoulders above a street beggar. Obtaining the best and most fashionable garments, usually from the second-hand trade, was one of the ways in which confidence tricksters fooled their victims. A man who appeared to be a gentleman of means was trusted automatically by his peers, whereas a penniless man who looked the part was spurned out of hand.

A poor woman – one without connections or fortune – would never be able to afford a gown like the ivory confection in the sea chest. Only a wealthy female could command such fabulous fashion. Marguerite knew that if she appealed to the British commander for rescue while wearing her filth-stained dress, or while absurdly clad in petticoat-breeches, he would not risk himself or his men to save a common female who was clearly of the lower classes. He would leave the supposed strumpet to her fate. However, if she appeared in the gown, he would believe that she was a lady, and therefore worthy to be rescued. Indeed, he would have an obligation to give her every aid as a gentleman in the King's employ. Once aboard the English ship, Marguerite could continue the deception. She thought that she had nerve enough to ape the manners of her betters. Any lapses in her behavior, as long as they were not too obvious, could be blamed on her fictitious upbringing as a provincial plantation owner's daughter who had not been raised in fashionable society.

The more Marguerite thought about it, the more she realized that her plan had merits. It was dangerous, of course. The failure of such a desperate endeavor could mean death. At the very least, she would remain trapped on the pirate vessel and be forced to deal with Bess. Nevertheless, Marguerite was determined to make the attempt.

She began to undress, and paused when an unexpected explosion made her nearly jump out of her skin. Marguerite could feel the vibrations of a gun's roar coming up through the floor under her feet. Another blast, and another, and she smelled the black-scorched, spoiled egg stink of gunpowder. Men's voices were raised in a lusty shout on the deck above her.

The attack had begun.

With feverish haste, Marguerite tore off her shirt and petticoat-breeches, and flung open the sea chest, reaching for the dress.

CHAPTER SEVEN
Thunder, Smoke and Blood

"Fire as you bear!" Bess shouted, her command echoed by men's voices until it reached the gun deck. The full-throated bellow of cannon fire pierced the air, and puffs of thick white smoke quickly dissipated on the wind. "Shift helm a-larboard!"

"Larboard, aye!" Halifax replied, his hands steady on the ship's wheel.

Boom! Boom! Boom! Smoking hot iron chain-shot screamed towards the British brigantine, the *H.M.S. Winchester*. The linked balls flew in a diagonal course across the deck of the ship, wrecking complete havoc where they struck wood and canvas and flesh. Equally deadly were the foot-long, razor-sharp splinters torn from the masts that ended more than one man's life despite the presence of netting and fearnought screens. *Boom!* A shot-storm chewed through *Winchester's* black-and white painted side. There was a loud explosion that had nothing to do with *Maudlin's* batteries, and a ball of fire erupted from a gunport on the British ship. Bess thought one of their guns had misfired; that happened sometimes during a hot engagement, when the cannon's bore was not properly swabbed out between charges, and the leftover gunpowder ignited with disastrous results. The scream of a wounded man, shrill and thin with agony, carried across the water like the piping of a curlew. On *Mad Maudlin*, the swivel guns let loose with high, resounding cracks. The sky was cloudless, the sun unrelenting; sharp-edged bars of light and shadow fell across the waist and decks of both ships, and turned blood an unreal shade of vermilion.

Winchester returned fire, but most of the shots fell short, splashing ineffectively into the water. One nine-pound ball carried across *Mad Maudlin's* main deck, clipping the larboard rail in passing, but otherwise did no damage; another clanged off a bow anchor and splashed, spent, into the ocean. The British ship's foresail and mainsail were in tatters. The spanker boom at the stern had been shot away. Nevertheless, the commander of the *Winchester* attempted to maneuver his stricken vessel. Luck was not on his side. The ship came sharp to the wind and lay dead in the water, her stern quarter exposed.

"Brail the main course!" Bess called. "Swivel guns to fire as you bear! Musketeers, fire! Lively now, lads! Mister Halifax, bring us alongside."

The lowermost sail of the main yard was hauled up. Graceful as a prowling cat, *Mad Maudlin* turned her bow towards the *Winchester*. Swivel guns and bow-chasers barked again, sending a hail of lead shot towards the becalmed British vessel. The pirate gunners, their faces blackened and greasy with soot streaks, raked *Winchester's* decks, sweeping men from the quarters. On the yardarms, sharpshooters lying prone along the spars took aim with their muskets and fired. A lucky shot carried off the Union flag on the main stay, and *Mad Maudlin*'s men cheered.

"Steady on your course," Bess told the helmsman, Halifax. She nodded to Dunn. "Make ready the grapplers and stand by the boarding party."

She checked the six flintlock pistols that she was carrying in a ribbon sling over her shoulders, to see that they were primed and powdered. Bess had borrowed a kerchief and tied it around her head to keep her unruly chestnut hair out of her eyes. Her shirt sleeves were rolled up, exposing sun-tanned, corded forearms. Ready for action, she unsheathed her cutlass, holding the blade naked in her hand. The well-sharpened steel glinted blue-white, a wink of diamond brightness that would soon be dulled by blood.

Solomon Lovelock was similarly armed with cutlass and flintlock, while Henry Dunn carried a boarding ax in one hand, a broad-bladed machete in the other. The gunnery master, Jacques Levalier, joined them on the quarterdeck. A vain man, he wore a white-powdered wig with a long braided queue that stuck out stiffly, and a heart-shaped beauty patch on his cheek, signifying a flirtatious nature. Levalier was taller than Dunn, and lean as a whippet compared to the first mate's muscular bulk. He favored his lover with a wink and a bit of muttered French that caused the color to mount upon Dunn's weather-beaten cheeks.

Bess grabbed the rail with her free hand as Halifax guided *Mad Maudlin* to the *Winchester*'s side. The pirate ship collided with the British vessel, the shock of impact shuddering through both. Crewmen standing ready on *Mad Maudlin*'s deck hurled grappling hooks across to the enemy vessel. Many of the steel hooks bit deep, and tangled in the ratlines and hammock-netting; the pirates hauled in their lines, using main strength to lash the two ships together while Toby Falconer screamed encouragement. The wooden hulls crackled and groaned where they met and rubbed together. *Mad Maudlin* surged up on a wave and shouldered *Winchester* hard, causing the slightly smaller ship to heel over a strake or two, then right itself with much screaming of strained oak planks. The clash caused a thin plume of white-foam water to spray high into the air, and fall as glittering droplets on upturned faces.

"Cease fire, damn your eyes, and God rot your soul in hell!" Bess shouted to an overly enthusiastic swivel gunner. She ordered the sails furled and the best and small bowers dropped; she had no intention of permitting the *Winchester* to escape until she was ready to let her go.

"Mister Falconer," she called down to the bos'n on the main deck, "strike those damned butterbox colors and run up our proper ensign."

Some of *Winchester*'s Marines had begun firing their muskets at the pirates, but dismayed moans were heard when Bess' skeleton and heart-pierced flag was hoisted up the mainstay. The bold crimson colors fluttered and snapped, bright as a patch of blood against the turquoise sky. Bess came down from the quarterdeck and into the press of her men who were milling about the waist, close to the rails, waving their weapons at the enemy. One of the men – a solidly paunchy native from Zeelandia Nova with a hip-length queue of jet black hair – screwed his tattooed face into a hideous grimace and shattered the air with a war cry, accompanied by intimidating gestures with a boarding axe.

"Follow me, boys, and lay on till they cry pardon!" Bess cried, leaping onto the rail and balancing there by an act of will. She easily jumped across to the *Winchester* and blocked a sword blow from a junior officer whose face was a mask of liquid scarlet that poured from a forehead wound. Steel rang on steel. Jumping back a step, Bess drew a flintlock with her free hand and fired point-blank. The officer collapsed, his head a shattered ruin. She blinked blood and bits of flesh from her eyes, suppressed a cough at the sulphuric reek of gunpowder discharge, discarded the spent pistol and drew another.

Black smoke billowed upward from a hatch, and thin flames licked at the edge of *Winchester*'s mainsail. Bess kicked aside a severed leg, then shot a British Marine who was about to stab Dunn in the back. She grabbed the collar of one of her crewmen and shouted in his ear, "Take some hands and put that fire out afore it finds the powder magazine!"

He nodded, an expression of sudden consternation on his swarthy face, and sprinted away, bawling for buckets.

Bess fought her way to the quarterdeck, using cutlass and flintlocks to clear a path. Pirates and Marines grappled; struggling knots of men broke apart and came together with roars and the clashing of arms. The scuppers ran red with blood. Beside her, Dunn chopped down an opponent with his boarding ax, then swept the machete in his other fist around to sever the man's head completely; the wide blade passed easily through the neck bones. The head bounced and rolled across the deck, finally coming to rest beside the mainmast. A huge jet of blood arced from the spasming trunk, flying through the air and splashing back down. Dunn dodged the worst of it, but his face caught some of the spray. The Marine fell dead, his neck still pumping blood.

Dunn shook his head to clear his eyes. Levalier hastened to protect Dunn; the Frenchman's white wig was askew and a shallow cut bled across his cheek. The two men stood back to back, and those foolhardy enough to engage them died. Nearby, Lovelock hacked down a British sailor. Eyes bloodshot and stinging from sweat and smoke, Bess continued to the quarterdeck.

A Marine came at her, swinging an iron marlinspike. His lips were drawn back in a crazed grin, and flecks of foam dotted his jaw. Bess had no more flintlocks – each pistol was good for one shot, for there was no time to reload in the midst of battle. She caught the marlinspike on the edge of her cutlass, and turned it aside, but not in time to avoid a cut across her eyebrow. Balling her free hand into a fist, Bess rolled her shoulder and punched the man with enough force to send him staggering backwards. He tripped over a coil of rope, leaped to his feet and brandished the marlinspike at her, rotten teeth bared in a snarl.

She made a cut at his head, shaving a strip of flesh off his ear, and reversed the cutlass to punch him with the hilt. The blow landed with a satisfying crunch. The Marine reeled, nose flat and dripping blood. Before he could recover, Bess whipped the cutlass across his vulnerable belly, reversing the blade after the first strike to deal a second . Loops of wet, pinkish-gray intestine bulged from the gaping wound. He let out a choked sob and dropped the marlinspike. Fight forgotten, his hands scrabbled to stuff his guts back inside his body.

Another Marine ran at her with a musket, holding it butt-first over his head. She blinked more blood away – the cut on her brow was not serious, but it was messy – and drove the heel of her boot into his unprotected knee. He went white. Bess drew back her leg again, this time kicking him hard in the crotch. The Marine turned red, then purple, and collapsed, wheezing, his mouth opening and closing in soundless agony. She felt a sudden whiplash across her leg, and the upper part of her thigh began burning. While she had been otherwise occupied, a British sailor had crept up and slashed her with a broad-bladed knife.

Bess cursed and swiped at him with her cutlass. He danced back, knife held professionally low. She brought her foot up and removed the dagger from her boot, flipped the weapon and caught it by the tip. A quick snap of her wrist, and the hilt of her dagger sprouted from his throat as if materialized there by magic. The sailor's knife clattered to the deck. He gurgled, scarlet spilling over his lips. Bess turned to catch the hobbling Marine coming towards her with his musket, his face set in a grimace.

Levalier calmly walked up and shot him through the skull with the small crossbow he carried. A quiver of deadly little darts was strapped to the Frenchman's outer thigh, over his breeches. Levalier made an elegant bow to Bess, who nodded in acknowledgement and paused to catch her breath.

"*Votre serviteur, capitaine*," Levalier said, spurning the body with the toe of his boot.

Bess nodded again and took her leave of the white-wigged gunnery master. With no further incidents, she finally arrived on the quarterdeck where *Winchester*'s commander waited, the right sleeve of his tailored uniform coat tattered and stained.

"Lt. Robert Coulter," he said coldly, his upper lip curling in disdain. He held an unsheathed sword in his left hand. "Acting commander of His Majesty's Ship *Winchester*. You would do well to give yourself up, pirate. Perhaps the Crown will grant you mercy, but I will not if you continue this attack."

Bess saluted him with her cutlass. "Captain Bess O'Bedlam," she replied. "Your ship's crippled and afire, Coulter. Your crew ain't likely to resist much longer, seein' as how they're mostly dead or wounded. Surrender and give me your parole, as officer and gentleman of His Majesty's Navy. I'll leave enough provisions to see you through to a friendly port, spare your injured, and take none of your crew prisoner."

Coulter's face was pale, shining with sweat. The sword in his hand trembled. Bess realized that he was very young, hardly more than a cub in her eyes. *What else to expect when treble-damned naval officers are promoted on account of cash and connections, and better men get no chance?* she thought. *I doubt the boy shaves regular yet. Gone adventuring to sea with daddy's blessing, and found himself a shark when he sought to take a minnow, the poor stupid wight.*

Bess grinned. "Where's your captain, Coulter?"

He licked his lips. His proud facade was cracking. "Sick-bay," Coulter finally admitted, although he did so sullenly. "He's fevered, you damned pirate. Yellow fever. You've condemned yourself, too. The sickness will spread to your ship and you'll all die."

"I doubt that," Bess said. She cocked a hand on her hip and gestured with the cutlass. "Were it the fever in truth, you'd have a yellow jack aloft to warn of quarantine. Your flummery don't fool me none. This was naught but a shake-down cruise, I reckon, meant to give a green crew the taste of the sea. Then your captain fell ill, and you decided to try for a prize. Ha! More guts than brains, that's a young pup's mistake. The game's over. Surrender, boy. Give me your solemn word and I'll let you live to fight another day, or by the sweet bleedin' Christ, I'll cut you down where you stand and turn *Winchester* into a funeral pyre."

Coulter hesitated. On the main deck, the fighting was beginning to abate. It was clear that *Winchester*'s crew were no longer resisting as fiercely. A bald pirate with a flaming red mustache was taking down the remaining British flags. More rough-looking men were putting out fires and dispatching the most grievously wounded sailors, delivering the necessary grace-stroke to ensure a relatively pain-free death.

"I hereby surrender His Majesty's Ship, *Winchester*, to you, madam, and give you my word as an officer and a gentleman to abide by such terms as you set," croaked a male voice near the ship's wheel. It was an older man dressed in a food-spotted shirt and breeches, but from his rigid bearing and air of command, Bess guessed he was the captain of the unfortunate vessel.

Her conjecture was proven true when a startled Coulter exclaimed, "Captain Reed, sir! Surrender to a pirate? Surely you jest!"

Reed was clearly suffering. His face was gray with strain and pinched white around the nostrils, his eyes bloodshot and bruised, but he held himself upright and approached the lieutenant. "Inform our men not to resist, but to lay down their arms at once. That is my order, Coulter. I'll not explain myself to you. I expect to be obeyed."

Visibly torn, Coulter shot a glance from Reed to Bess. At last, he drew himself upright and snapped off a salute, despite his obvious resentment. "Aye-aye, sir."

"Now, madam," Reed continued, speaking to Bess, "shall we discuss terms? I trust you are prepared to offer clemency."

Before Bess could reply, there was a commotion on the *Mad Maudlin*. A woman wearing an ivory dress with a sky-blue embroidered petticoat ran out onto the quarterdeck, shrieking, "For the love of God, save me, sir! Save a poor lady's life!"

Bess recognized the woman at once. It was Marguerite.

Behind her, a triumphant Coulter pressed the muzzle of his flintlock to the small of Bess' back. He looked at Captain Reed over the pirate woman's shoulder. "We cannot leave a lady in such obvious distress," he said. "Now tell your men to surrender," he continued to Bess, "or I'll blow you to hell."

An explosion of white-hot rage made Bess clench her jaw tightly, until it felt as though her teeth were being ground to splinters.

When the cannon fire dwindled at last, Marguerite was fussing over her appearance, waiting to judge the proper moment to come out on the open deck and make her appeal to the British captain. She had donned the ivory gown and was fairly pleased at the effect, although there were no stiffened under-petticoats to hold the full skirts out properly. The dress had been made for someone more petite than Marguerite; it was far too tight in the shoulders, bodice and waist; the seams were strained almost to the bursting point. She had managed to squeeze into it with difficulty, but at least she would look the part from a distance.

Her blonde hair was left loose, artfully tousled. She used lamp soot mixed with spittle to darken her eyelashes, but could find no rouge to color her pale cheeks. *'Tis just as well*, she thought. *A whey-faced lady is more to be pitied than one who's healthy-looking as a country milkmaid.* Rummaging in the delicate French desk, Marguerite found a porcelain patch-box, and stuck a black beauty mark in the shape of a star near the corner of her mouth.

She gazed at her reflection, satisfied. The tightly laced bodice pushed her breasts into quivering, blue-veined mounds, and even reduced her waist a bit. For good measure, she took a crescent moon patch and affixed it on one of the swelling curves exposed by the low, square-cut bodice.

Aye, that's more like it, she thought, smoothing her hands down the rustling skirts. *A dead man couldn't resist such a tempting bit of bait.*

Prepared at last, Marguerite took deep breaths to settle her nerves. The noise of fighting lessened. She decided that it was time. Without allowing herself to hesitate, Marguerite burst through the cabin door, flew up onto the quarterdeck, and screamed to the British captain for rescue. She knew that she made a dramatic sight, with her loosened hair streaming behind her like a golden banner and the wind billowing out the dress' ivory satin skirts.

She noticed the British ship's escutcheon, naming it the *H.M.S. Winchester*. Marguerite waved her arms in the air, wincing when a shoulder seam tore open. "For the love of God, save me, sir!" she shouted. "Save a poor lady's life!"

On the *Winchester*'s quarterdeck, Marguerite saw Bess standing with two men, both of whom were wearing blue uniforms and cocked hats. It appeared to her that the pirate captain had been captured. Marguerite was simultaneously dismayed and relieved. There was no time to consider this mixed reaction, however; someone grabbed her from behind and she let out a loud shriek, trying to pull away from the painful grip.

"Hold still, you damned hell-cat!" the man growled in her ear. His arm was like an iron bar across her stomach. A callused hand clamped over her mouth. Marguerite struggled and tried to bite him, but his palm was as tough as pig leather. Her bare feet scuffled on the deck as he dragged her towards the mainmast.

Something was happening on the *Winchester*. Marguerite was helpless to do anything save watch as Bess whirled about and struck the British officer with her fist. His flintlock discharged and the second man fell, a red stain blossoming on his shirt front. Bess lunged with her cutlass and ran the officer through, the scarlet-dripping tip of her sword emerging from his back. He, too, collapsed. She raised her boot to scrape his body off the blade.

Marguerite's captor used a bight of rope to lash her wrists together and left her bound to the mainmast. She shouted curses and imprecations at him, but he and the rest of *Mad Maudlin*'s men ignored her. Frustrated and furious, Marguerite spat at him when he passed, and received a cuff on the head that made a whirling constellation of stars explode in her black-tinged vision. After that, she huddled close to the mast and seethed quietly.

The longer she stood there, the more her initial rage abated, and fear took its place. What would Bess do to her? What punishment could she expect? A lump rose in Marguerite's throat. She felt as if she had swallowed a stone. Her knees grew weak and she clung to the mast, nails digging into the smooth wooden surface. After what seemed like an eternity, pirates began returning to *Mad Maudlin*, bearing casks and boxes and other goods.

Two men carried a long narwhale's tusk on their shoulders, a twist of ivory that resembled the fabled unicorn's horn. Several others had items of clothing, including a gentleman's pink satin coat with silver buttons. A sailor, grinning widely, sported a big, bright blue parrot on his shoulder; the empty cage was clutched in his hand. The wounded were brought below-deck by their mates, destined for the chirurgeon's sick-bay. The last to arrive was Bess O'Bedlam. Marguerite's heart sank down to her toes.

Bess paid no heed to the captive young woman, but calmly directed the storing of the spoils. When everything was accomplished to her satisfaction, she ordered her crewmen to cut the grapple lines, setting the *Winchester* adrift. The pirate ship's anchors were raised, her sails set, and the vessel took on speed under a fast wind abaft the stern. Another helmsman replaced Halifax at the wheel. Soon, the crippled *Winchester* was left in *Mad Maudlin*'s wake.

Dunn and Lovelock, both bearing only minor injuries, were tending to the running of the ship. Toby Falconer had taken a ball of shot in his hip, and was down in sick-bay awaiting treatment. Bess stood on the quarterdeck for a while, her hands clasped behind her back. The gunpowder tattoo on her cheek stood out starkly. She issued orders in a cold, clipped tone. Men tiptoed around her; not even the first mate seemed daring enough to approach the captain in such a dangerous mood.

At last, Bess came down from the quarterdeck and untied Marguerite, releasing her from the mainmast. She said nothing, but the muscles in her jaw writhed. A fierce light burned in the depths of her gray eyes. The intensity of that gaze dazzled Marguerite and left her breathless with terror.

During the fight, Bess had lost the kerchief covering her head. The left side of her face was scorched, the flesh livid and beginning to swell. Her hair was singed, too, and her left ear was covered in a film of gunpowder residue. There was a wound across her upper thigh, showing red through the slashed leg of her breeches. The material was wet with blood. A shallow cut had split her eyebrow open; more blood ran in lacy streams over her eye and dripped off her chin to stain the front of her shirt.

Marguerite opened her mouth to speak, but the words died unuttered in her throat when Bess gave her a quelling look. "Say naught," the pirate said, her voice ripe with the promise of violence, "or I cannot vouch for your life."

Marguerite pressed her lips together, suppressing a surprised yelp when Bess took hold of her wrist with such strength, the bones ached in protest. Bess dragged her unresisting to the cabin door, opened it, and shoved her inside. Marguerite fell against the bunk box, staring up at Bess with wide, terrified eyes. Her heart fluttered. She could not breathe.

Slowly, Bess removed the thick, black leather belt she wore and doubled up the silver-studded length in her fist. Her gaze was scorching.

Marguerite lay still, paralyzed in horror.

CHAPTER EIGHT
Consequences and Resolutions

"Take it off," Bess said tightly, a vein throbbing in her brow.

Marguerite caught her bottom lip between her teeth. "Wh-what?"

"Take off that dress, damnation to your soul!" Bess spat, swinging the belt at the bunk box. It hit the wooden side with a crack that sounded like thunder in the confines of the small cabin.

"No." Marguerite wished she had thought to provide herself with a weapon. Her plan had failed, and the consequences were going to be very unpleasant. She had faced death in the past, but Marguerite's instinct told her that this confrontation with Bess was going to be far, far worse than anything she had ever experienced. Pride beat back her fear. Whatever came, she would rather die than give the pirate any satisfaction.

Bess leaned down and grabbed a handful of Marguerite's hair. "Take off that dress...NOW!" The belt swung back, descended, and slapped against the bunk box once more, close enough for her to feel the breeze of its passage against her cheek.

Marguerite flinched. "Nay, *godskannonne!*" she repeated defiantly. "You'll have to tear your whore's precious gown from my back, for I'll not lift a finger to help you." She squeezed her eyes shut, waiting for the first blow to fall. When it did not come, Marguerite opened her eyes again. Bess was still leaning over her, but there was a queer expression on the woman's battered face.

"Are you calling my mother a whore?" Bess asked softly, letting go of Marguerite's hair.

Shocked, Marguerite blinked.

"Aye, that gown was my mother's," Bess said. She stood upright and swung her belt at the bunk box a third time. "Now take it off, you poxy bitch!"

Fingers made clumsy by haste and a deep, sickening shame, Marguerite unlaced the bodice, slipping the dress off her shoulders. Under Bess' searing glare, she managed to remove the gown without damaging it further. Once she stepped out of the pool of ivory satin, Marguerite skittered to a corner of the cabin, snatching a silver letter opener from the desk in passing. Clad only in her thin chemise, she pressed her back against the bulkhead, her makeshift weapon pointed at Bess. She knew that she stood no chance in a genuine fight against her captor, but Marguerite was determined to defend herself as long as she could.

Bess ignored the shivering woman. She picked up the dress, rolled it up, and placed it back into her sea chest. That accomplished, she went to the door, opened it and called for Jim Monk. The ship's boy appeared, looking somewhat subdued. He had not been involved in the fighting on the

Winchester, but Monk had been required to assist *Mad Maudlin*'s resident chirurgeon in the battle cockpit and the sick-bay – a grim and bloody task.

"Aye, captain," he said. There were black lines of dried blood beneath his fingernails.

"Fetch my bath and water to fill it," Bess said. "Then nip down to sick-bay and give my compliments to Mistress Glasspoole. I've a need for some of her sovereign grease and wound balm. Step lively, lad."

"Aye-aye, lively it is," Monk said, and fled to obey his orders.

Bess shut the door. Wedged in her corner, Marguerite continued to hold the letter opener at arm's length, but her muscles were beginning to tire. She controlled her trembling with an effort. "What are you going to do to me?" she asked.

"Naught for the nonce," Bess answered wearily, not looking at Marguerite. She sat down on the edge of the bunk box, dropped her belt on the mattress, and unbuttoned her embroidered crimson waistcoat, then let the garment slide off her body before she blew out her breath in a heavy sigh.

Marguerite did not trust the pirate's seeming complacence. She remained alert until Jim Monk returned with a copper hip bath, the scrolled rim engraved with mermaids and sharks. He placed the tub in the middle of the floor, left the cabin, and returned with buckets of sea water, dipped directly from the ocean. The boy had to make several trips before the hip bath was full. His immediate chore finished, Monk tugged his forelock and said, "I'll leave Mistress Glasspoole's medicines outside the door, Cap'n."

"S'good, lad. Off you go. Come back in an hour for the tub." Bess waited until he had closed the door behind him before she pulled her shirt over her head and slipped off her tattered breeches. She wore nothing underneath.

Marguerite could not help but stare at the woman's revealed body. Bess was lean, her muscles like whipcord over long, strong bones. Her face, throat, arms and legs below the knee were tanned to the color of fine bronze, but the rest of her skin was pale as cream. Her small, firm breasts were tipped with pale pink nipples. There was a long scar across her rib cage; another rippled from collarbone to shoulder. Puckered silver starfish – scars that were the legacy of lead shot – dotted one calf and a neatly rounded buttock. A network of thin scars criss-crossed her back, the marks of a long-ago whipping.

Bess stepped into the cold salt water with a grimace. "Come here, Margo."

Marguerite shook her head. She tore her fascinated gaze away from the tangled vee of dark curls at the juncture of Bess' thighs. "No. I won't," she said, brandishing the letter opener. "Stay away from me."

"We must come to a right understanding, you and I," Bess said, her tone so completely reasonable that Marguerite was instantly on her guard. "I've not yet raised a hand to you, but by the sweet bleedin' Christ, you'd tempt a saint to fisticuffs. Now come here, woman, and defy me no more, or I swear to God Almighty that I'll have Mister Dunn keep you chained to the mainmast till you learn some manners."

Warily, Marguerite came around the end of the table. She jumped when Bess barked, "Put down that pig sticker, Margo. I ain't goin' to hurt you."

As Bess sank into the hip bath, Marguerite laid the letter opener on the bunk box and moved to stand by the side of the copper vessel. It was not long enough for Bess to lie full-length, so she sat in the water with her knees up, leaning against the back, her arms outstretched along the rolled rim. Light from the mullioned rose-glass windows played on the water and tinted her skin pink. Marguerite avoided looking directly at the pirate.

"Shall I tell you what was accomplished this day by your foolishness?" Bess said, paying no attention to the sharp sting in her thigh as salt water leeched the dried blood away and opened the wound again. "I'd have let the *Winchester's* captain sail on unharmed, as he'd given his gentleman's parole and surrendered. Then you, mistress addle-pate, stole my mother's dress and put on a show for the benefit of a young jackass with more balls than brains. Aye, I killed him, but 'twas a near thing."

"I'm not responsible for your murdering ways," Marguerite said, tossing her hair back over her shoulders.

Bess did not acknowledge the interruption. "You put *Mad Maudlin* in jeopardy. You nearly had me shot through the breadbasket. But worse than that, Margo, you condemned them poor British bastards to a slow death."

"What do you mean?" Marguerite felt a touch of dismay and brushed it aside. She would not let herself be blamed for the pirate's actions.

"Are you so damnably ignorant as that?" Bess asked. She reached back, pulled the black ribbon from her hair, and shook out the short queue of chestnut locks. "Well, mistress, 'tis a fact that sailors sail, but navigation ain't no common deck-treader's trade. The captain and his officers keep the charts and quadrants and such-like things. There ain't no officers left unhurt on *Winchester* on account of your meddlin'. If them Britishers are lucky, they might strike land afore the water tuns are dry. Or mayhap they'll meet a friendly ship and cry mercy. More likely, they'll be dead and *Winchester* a ghost ship in less'n a fortnight. A man dyin' of thirst is an ugly sight. Chew on that and see how you like the flavor."

"I don't...I won't...*godskannonne!* If you hadn't attacked them in the first place..."

Bess raised a dripping hand. "Belay that! Aye, I don't care much for the King's men, but I ain't without mercy. I'd sooner slit a man's throat and kill him quick than make him suffer the agonies of the water-clemmed and damned. This fight was none o' my choosing. 'Twas the British pup in charge of that brig what showed fangs first. Would you druther I let him sink *Mad Maudlin* with you and all my crew aboard?"

"The officer was doing his duty," Marguerite insisted.

"His duty?" Bess guffawed, but there was nothing good humored in the sound. "Margo, we was flyin' Dutch colors. For all *Winchester* knew, *Mad Maudlin* was a Lowlands merchant. He didn't have no call to make sail and chase us down, still less with his gunports open. The commander hoped we'd fire first, and give him cause to take us as a pirate back to Portsmouth, and *Mad Maudlin* condemned as a prize. He'd have lined his pockets, sure enough, and all his crew would take their piece of the value of my ship. Take no false comfort, mistress. 'Twas not duty that goaded *Winchester* to a brawl, but greed."

"*Godskannonne*," Marguerite whispered. She had heard about unscrupulous British commanders who deliberately picked a fight with another nation's merchant vessel. If the English commander could claim that he had been fired upon first, that made his target legitimate prey. It was not a common practice but it had been known to occur.

"Make yourself useful. Fetch me soap and sponge," Bess grumbled, "afore I come out wrinkled as a damned raisin and none the fresher."

Her cheeks coloring, Marguerite did as she was bid.

Bess worked the rough-cut bar of soap to soften it, and began to wash herself clean of grime and blood. "Have you never done a man to death, Margo?" she asked, her voice gone cold and distant again. She scrubbed her gunpowder-blackened ear with care.

"No, I have not," Marguerite answered softly, her conscience greatly troubled. If what Bess said was true – and she supposed discreet questioning could check the statements for truth – then she was to blame for the deaths of *Winchester*'s captain and the remainder of his crew. Although Marguerite thought she could kill in self-defense, her resolve had never been tested. In truth, she did not think of herself as a killer; a thief, certainly, but never a cold-blooded murderer.

"Then you may hold yourself proud," Bess said, "for there's thirty men that'll lie restless in a sea-grave on your account." She ducked her head under the water, soaped her hair, and ducked again to rinse it. Finished with her bath, Bess rose and sluiced off her skin with her hands, then stepped out of the copper tub. A thin stream of blood mingled with water ran down her injured leg.

Marguerite turned her eyes away, the better to avoid the strange, conflicting feelings that arose in her at the sight of Bess' naked body. Finally, she said, "You've no right to keep me here against my will. I'm a prisoner; 'tis to be expected that I'll try an escape."

"If you try again," Bess grunted, "I'd consider it a kindness if you don't kill quite so many men next time. I doubt my own butcher's bill stands as high. 'Twould do my reputation no little harm to be surpassed in murder by a soft-handed wench like you."

A knock on the door interrupted whatever reply Marguerite was about to make. Bess found a clean shirt in her sea chest and pulled it over her head. The garment covered her to the knees. She called for the person to enter, and Henry Dunn waddled into the cabin. With the addition of the broad and hairy-chested first mate, the space felt incredibly cramped. He seemed to blot out the late afternoon sun streaming through the curved stern windows.

"Mistress Glasspoole's compliments," he said, dropping a pair of earthenware jars on the bunk box mattress. The burly man seemed completely unaffected by Bess' semi-undressed state. "We suffered twenty wounded, none too severe save for Toby Falconer's hip and Willem de Woeste's broken leg," Dunn continued, not acknowledging Marguerite's presence with so much as a flicker of his eyes. "Three casualties, which I'll write later in the log. Mister Hidalgo reports *Winchester* yielded a goodly supply of ammunition and powder – thirty barrels of large grain and ten barrels of fine grain for priming. In addition, we've acquired a side of fresh beef that's hardly green, three goats, four crates of chickens, two tuns of salt beef, a tun of soused hog, and spare sails, spars and cables. Some of the men took aboard clothing and such-like things, and one liberated a parrot." His teeth showed as a flash of white across his sunburned face when he grinned.

"Give the men an extra rum ration, and order Hephzibah to cook that side of beef for their supper, saving a steak or two for the officers," Bess said. "How fares Mister Falconer?"

Dunn's lips stretched in a slight smile. "In a foul humor, Captain. His hip bone was spared, but Mistress Glasspoole had to dig deep for the ball. She claims he'll recover in full if the wound heals clean."

Bess ran a hand through her wet chestnut-brown hair, wringing water from the dripping ends. "I've faith in Mistress Glasspoole, for she's more physician than 'most any other leech that calls himself by the name. Where's the *Winchester*'s strong-box?"

"Safe in my berth," Dunn replied. "I reckon it holds a hundred pounds or so of the realm's coin."

"We'll divide it up amongst the crew tomorrow. Is there aught else?"

Dunn paused. At last, he said, "Some of the men are wondering about Mistress Margo. Coming out on the deck during a battle wasn't wise."

"Oh?" Bess arched a brow. "Well, you tell those blasted dogs that she ain't their concern. You've my leave to give any flapping mouth a good buffet, Mister Dunn. She's my property. Thus I've spoken and by God, I mean to be obeyed without any sea lawyering."

"Aye-aye, Captain." Dunn turned and left the room.

Marguerite stood uncertainly while Bess sat down behind the desk. The pirate took a leather-bound book out of the drawer, and opened it. After a few minutes of page flipping, she found her place. Bess opened the silver top of the inkhorn, dipped in a quill, and began to write in the book.

"What are you doing?" Marguerite asked, after much hesitation.

Bess did not answer. Her quill scritched over the surface of the paper.

Stymied, Marguerite drifted to the bunk box. She felt quite subdued, even a little sick at the fate of the men on the *Winchester*, destined to meet a terrible end. Marguerite was not sure that all the blame could be laid entirely at her door, but she had to bear a portion of it. It had never occurred to her to wonder about the end result of her thief's trade, and how it affected her victims. She thought about all the men she had lured, all the money she had stolen. They might have had wives and children to support. Having gone hungry herself in lean times, Marguerite could sympathize with their imagined plight.

On the other hand, she had few alternatives. If she had not stolen, she would have died. That fact was unimpeachable. In her world the predators survived by preying on the weak. She had existed from day to day, paying little heed to yesterday or tomorrow. Now Marguerite sat for a while, contemplating what to do. At last, she resolved upon a new plan.

I'll show Bess O'Bedlam that I can be civil and civilized, Marguerite thought. *I'll lull her to complacency. I'll dote upon her like the sun shines out of her arse. I'll speak softly, gorge her with sweetness and moonshine and lover's sighs. Then when she trusts me, I can find an escape that will not end in another's death. 'Twill not be an easy road, but I'll keep my eye on the prize.*

When Bess snapped her book closed and stood, Marguerite was waiting. "Shall I dress your wounds?" she asked, gesturing towards the jars.

"If you must," Bess replied ungraciously. She sat down on the edge of the table, swinging her feet to and fro. "The blue's for burns; the white is wound balm."

Marguerite took the earthenware jars and set them on the table next to Bess. She opened the top of the plain one first, exposing a white salve flecked with green and orange. She sniffed at it, but could not identify the contents. Scooping up a finger full of the stuff, she smeared it delicately on Bess' thigh wound. The cut was not deep, but it was long, and Marguerite dipped into the jar frequently.

She tilted Bess' head more towards the light, and moved to stand directly between the pirate's spread thighs. Through the thin fabric of her chemise, Marguerite could feel the woman's heated flesh, and suppressed a shiver as her treacherous body strove to answer that heat with its own. There was no denying that her attraction to Bess was real; privately, Marguerite could admit to herself that the woman was handsome and charming when she chose, and she could not help speculating what kind of lover Bess might prove. Tender and sweet, fiery and demanding, silent but firm...inwardly shaking free of these thoughts, she spread a thin layer of salve on Bess' eyebrow. "Perchance you've lint and linens?" Marguerite asked. "I can bind up your leg. 'Tis said that I've a neat hand at such things."

"No need," Bess replied. She held still while Marguerite opened the blue jar, and began to coat her scorched face and ear.

"I think this will not scar," Marguerite said, examining the burns. "How did it happen?"

Bess frowned. "When that British pup shot his own captain over my damned shoulder," she said shortly, pushing Marguerite away and hopping off the table. "'Twas only luck that kept the ball from breaking my head like an egg."

Marguerite hastily capped the jars, and wiped her hands on the hem of her chemise. "Will you have aught to eat or drink?" she asked meekly.

"What are you become, Margo – my servant of a sudden?" Bess was irritated; her voice held an edge dipped in vitriol. "Let me be. If you're so eager to put yourself to use, lay on some clothes and go see Mistress Glasspoole on the orlop deck. She's our chirurgeon and herb-wife, and I'm sure she'll have work for idle hands."

"You mean...I can leave the cabin?" Marguerite was suddenly ill-at-ease. She did not relish the thought of moving among the *Mad Maudlin*'s rough crew. Anything could happen to an unprotected woman on a pirate vessel.

"Aye, go! If any dog claps so much as a peeper on you, squawk aloud for Dunn or Lovelock or Levalier or Mistress Glasspoole. Better yet, tell that ape of mischief Monk to escort you to the sick-bay if you're feared of goin' by your lonesome." Bess turned her back and bent over the navigation charts that cluttered the table. "Now get you gone. I've had a bellyful enough of trouble this day."

Having been so obviously dismissed, Marguerite sought the clothes she had been wearing before her ill-fated escape attempt. She removed her chemise and rummaged in the sea chest, apparently unaware that Bess was watching out of the corner of her eye.

A sweet piece of flesh, Bess thought, appreciating the nude Marguerite's plump curves and full breasts, the smooth pale skin that was livened by sprays of golden freckles. There was a nasty scar on the blonde woman's abdomen that looked to have been caused by a knife of some kind. As Marguerite lifted a pair of canvas petticoat-breeches from the sea chest, her hair shifted across her back, exposing a tattoo on her right shoulder – a wheel composed of intricate lines, spiky as a snowflake and strange to the eyes.

Bess idly wondered what the design meant. Now that her mother's dress was safely stored away, and she had bathed and dressed her hurts, the worst of her temper had cooled. She had been very angry with Marguerite, more over the girl's trespass into her privacy than anything else. Bess had a very good idea who had left the cabin door unlocked, permitting Marguerite's flight; she would have a talk with Hephzibah soon.

What intrigued Bess the most was Marguerite's sudden about-face. She had been defiant and swollen with resentment, a spitting wild-cat according to the crewman who had restrained her. *Did I prick her so deep*, Bess thought, *that she's turned meek as milk?* She shrugged inwardly. In her experience, some females clawed and bit until they were met with a firm hand, then they became purring kittens. She had not judged Marguerite to be the type, but initial impressions could be wrong.

Whate'er the cause, Bess thought, *Mistress Margo deserves a little reward. She's had a lash from my temper, now I'll give her a taste from the honey-pot.* Accordingly, Bess turned around and touched Marguerite's arm. The woman had donned a shirt and petticoat-breeches, using a blue kerchief from the sea chest as a bandeau to hold back her hair. Bess leaned forward, intending to brush Marguerite's cheek with her lips.

Instead, Marguerite's eyes closed until they were glimmering blue slits. She swayed closer, her lips parting. She captured Bess' mouth artfully, running the tip of her tongue over the full lower lip. Unconsciously, Bess tightened her grip, her body responding to the light caress. Marguerite broke off the kiss and sighed. "I'd best leave you and go to the sick-bay," she said, brushing a fingertip across the gunpowder tattoo on Bess' cheek. "Mistress Glasspoole awaits, *mijn lief*." Picking up the two jars, Marguerite exited the cabin, leaving behind the faint scent of orange flower water.

Bess stared after the woman for a long moment, her mouth tingling. Finally, she shook her head, went to the cabinet and poured herself a drink. *To success and victory*, Bess thought, raising the glass in a silent toast. *I'll soon have the wench in the palm of my hand.* She took a swallow of the fiery liquor and felt it burn all the way down. The rum did not equal the blaze that had raged through her veins when Marguerite kissed her, and Bess felt somehow cheated, her victory hollow and meaningless next to unraveling the puzzle that was Marguerite De Vries. She scowled. Bess finished the drink quickly and returned to her examination of the chart.

When Marguerite returned, Bess was determined to ferret out all her secrets – by any means necessary, including crooked ones.

CHAPTER NINE
The Herb-Wife

Marguerite walked out onto the quarterdeck, a mysterious little smile on her lips.

Ha! she thought in triumphant glee. *Pole-axed with a kiss! Aye, Bess O'Bedlam will soon be dancing to my tune. I've given her a taste, now I'll make her beg for the rest. Not too hastily, though. I've no wish to surrender myself entire till I've gained some advantage.*

The sun was low on the horizon; brassy gold and orange and magenta spilled across the darkening waters. Thin streaks of clouds like wisps of smoke trailed in the sky. Below on the main deck, some sailors were playing able whackets, a game of cards where the loser was beaten across the hand with a knotted kerchief. A few of the crewmen had unbraided their queues, combing out their waist-length hair and applying grease to keep the locks smooth and glossy. There was a man telling fortunes in the forecastle, tossing down queer square coins and reading the patterns with more wishful thinking than skill. The brilliant blue parrot was in its cage, being fed tidbits of fruit by its proud new owner; a mongoose – no doubt another pet which helped the ship's cat keep down the onboard rat population – ran along the rail, a dark furred, sinuous shape with wicked beady eyes, and a bit of dirty string tied around its neck.

The helmsman gave Marguerite a startled glance when she appeared, then he resolutely returned his attention to the ship's wheel.

Solomon Lovelock perched on the narrow gangway that ran the length of the ship's side from quarterdeck to forecastle. His legs dangled, and he sang a pretty ditty, staring out at the waves. Nearby, a pirate with a twisted lip accompanied him on the hurdy-gurdy, the instrument making an eerie droning wail that floated across the deck. Lovelock's voice was surprising sweet and clear carrying.

> *By waves we are bent, but not broken;*
> *By birth we are destined to die;*
> *By life we receive but one token–*
> *For love, we will learn, is a lie.*
> *By blades we are bled, by hearts we are led,*
> *But true love is a curse and a lie.*

Spying Marguerite, Lovelock broke off his song. The hurdy-gurdy's wail died. Lovelock smoothed the twitching ends of his luxurious red mustache, left the gangway and joined Marguerite on the quarterdeck. "What will you, mistress?" he asked, far more politely than Marguerite had expected.

"The captain wishes me to attend Mistress Glasspoole in the sick-bay," she answered. She was intimidated by the burly quartermaster with his shaven head and tattoos, but tried not to show it.

Lovelock moved to take her arm, and hesitated before his fingers brushed her skin. He pulled his hand back as though he had been scalded. "Sick-bay's on the orlop deck," he said after clearing his throat. "A moment, if you please, and I'll escort you there myself."

He summoned a sailor and issued orders *sotto voce*. When he had finished, Lovelock moved towards the set of steps that led from the quarterdeck down to the main deck. Marguerite followed, paying close attention in case she wanted to go that way again.

Lovelock went down a hatch, using a wooden ladder. He waited for her at the bottom. Marguerite climbed down into the semi-gloom, glad that the petticoat-breeches hid her from the man's upturned gaze in a way that a dress could not have managed. There were a few lamps lit, their thick glass covers shielding naked flames. Lovelock guided her aft, through a narrow corridor lined with doors that suddenly opened out into the gun deck, which was empty of personnel. The ports were closed, the cannons silent on their carriages, but everything was in order for the next time they were called upon; the neatly arranged accoutrements of sponge, rammer, powder horn, handspike and quoin flanked each gun. There was still a faint rotten-egg trace of gunpowder in the air, as well as the smells of tar, pitch and dust, and a lingering tang of oft-heated iron. The great oak beams of the ship, curved above her head like the ribs of some monstrous skeleton of the deep, were coated with greasy soot. Lovelock took up a horn battle lantern to light their way, as it was quite dark.

They continued aft until they came to another ladder that led further down into the bowels of the ship to the orlop, which was *Mad Maudlin*'s lowermost deck. There was a door at the bottom of the ladder, a lamp burning brightly beside it, but the glass chimney was filled with yellow witch-fire rather than a conventional candle. Marguerite glanced behind her, in the direction of the bow. A lightless expanse stretched out seemingly to infinity. The unrelieved darkness was oppressive and frightening. Who knew what might lurk in the thickly gathered shadows? Unsettled, Marguerite bit her lip and followed Lovelock through the door.

Sick-bay was at the very stern of the vessel. Ventilation was supplied by a wind-sail above-decks that funneled fresh air below, since the orlop was under the ship's waterline. Regardless, the atmosphere was close. Lamps hung in gimbals wherever they could be accommodated. Eight hammocks were strung on the bulkheads, four on each side. Only two were occupied with unconscious patients whose battle wounds were serious enough, Marguerite supposed, to require constant attendance. The men were secured in the hammocks with the traditional seven turns-and-a half hitch of lashing. There was a long table in the center of the space, the wooden top scarred and white from scrubbing. Buckets of sand stood underneath to catch blood, other fluids, and amputated limbs as needed.

A glass-fronted cabinet was set atop a wooden apothecary's chest with myriad small drawers; the whole piece of furniture was bolted to the bulkhead, and included a small work bench. Railed shelves held a profusion of bottles and jars, mortars and pestles, surgical instruments and other paraphernalia of the medical trade. Bundles of dried herbs and strange roots hung from pegs fastened into the overhead beams.

It was clean and neat, and the person responsible looked up after they entered. Mistress Glasspoole was a woman in late middle age, with long strands of graying black hair tumbling from beneath the lacy lawn mobcap on her head. Deep lines were graven from her nose to the corners of her mouth, and sweat sheened her face. She had an ample figure, thickened by her years, and appeared very stout and strong. Keen brown eyes assessed Marguerite with a glance, then Glasspoole's lips swept up in a generous smile, revealing false teeth made of ivory – hippopotamus rather than elephant, Marguerite thought, judging by the finer grain and faintly greenish cast of the material.

"Well, well," the herb-wife said, sweeping towards the pair. "God bless my soul! Mister Lovelock, what beauty do you bring to grace my poor sick-bay?" The false teeth lent a clack and a whistle to her speech.

"This is Mistress Margo," Lovelock replied, crouching to avoid bumping his head on the low ceiling. "Late of Antigua, aboard at the captain's pleasure. I'll be off now, for I've duties to attend." He seemed in a hurry to get away.

"In a moment, Solomon Lovelock." Glasspoole wiped her hands on the apron tied around her blue-bodiced dress. "How's your little trouble, eh?"

Lovelock seemed embarrassed. Much to Marguerite's astonishment, the big bald man – who could have broken Glasspoole in half, had he been so inclined – actually scuffled his foot on the deck like a schoolboy facing a headmaster's inquisition.

"T'ain't so bad as before," he mumbled.

"Take down your breeches, lad, and let's have a look."

"Mistress!" Lovelock blurted, rolling his eyes in horror.

Glasspoole shook her head, the ribbons of her mobcap fluttering. "Like children they are," she said to Marguerite. "Full of fanfaronade and bluster when it suits them, but the smallest matter will make a man turn green to the gills."

Turning back to Lovelock, Glasspoole told him firmly, "Continue with the salve, Mister Lovelock, and be sure to cleanse yourself with seawater beforehand. And wash also after using the seat of easement, and be gentle when wiping yourself with tow. If the trouble worsens, come see me at once."

"Aye, mistress," Lovelock choked. He turned on his heel and fled the sick-bay, slamming the door behind him.

Glasspoole returned to her workbench. "A fistula on his backside, poor lad, that gives him no end of grief. One of these days, I'll have to bend Solomon over my table and lance it. Of course, he'll be rigid with drink afore he'll face my steel, but that's the way of things."

Somewhat bemused, Marguerite walked to the workbench and placed the jars she had brought from the captain's cabin on the uncluttered surface. She stood to one side of the herb-wife, watching her select various dried leaves from the drawers of the apothecary chest and put them into a mortar. Mistress Glasspoole's hands were mannish, big-knuckled and knotty veined, but she was far from clumsy. Her fingers were nimble, her touch assured. She sounded a bit comical because of the whistle in her speech, but the woman clearly commanded respect from the crew.

"Is there aught I can do to help you?" Marguerite asked.

Glasspoole waved a hand. She wore a thick gold ring on her thumb, set with a red cabochon coral and a round white pearl. "Grind this for me, if you would. It must be fine, so put your elbow to it, lass."

Marguerite took hold of the stone mortar and began grinding with the pestle, rendering the contents to a powder. Meanwhile, Glasspoole melted a creamy white substance in a pan over a small spirit lamp. She said conversationally as she stirred, "This is pure spermaceti and sweet almond oil, for the making of salves and balms. Virgin bee's wax is as good, if mixed with oil of olives, but there's few hives at sea."

"What's in the mortar?" Marguerite asked, genuinely curious. The leaves were mostly dull green and to her, unidentifiable, but there were also bright orange petals in the mixture.

"*Sphagnum cymbifolium*," Glasspoole replied, a twinkle in her eyes. She rolled the Latin off her tongue as easily as an educated physician. "*Stachys palustris*, *symphtum* and *plantago major*."

At Marguerite's look of incomprehension and awe, Glasspoole relented and said, "That's bog moss, woundwort, knitback and waybroad for the layman, lass. And let us not forget pot-marigold, the physic's friend. All good to keep wounds clean, and ward off mortification so the flesh can heal proper. I've no time for the usual trade in unbalanced humors, in blood and phlegm and bile; I'm no physic who's bought a ticket and walked the hospital wards, but I reckon that I know how to heal a man better than some who swear to Hippocrates, then leave a man to die after they've bled him white and call it God's will."

She lifted the spoon from her pan and gestured towards the shelves. "I don't rely on quackeries, Mistress Margo. I'm an herb-wife of seven generations, and I ken my trade very well indeed. My former husband – Albert of blessed memory, God rest his soul – was a first mate. Many years I lived with him at sea, serving our masters, till the Good Lord saw fit to carry Albert off and leave me a widow with nary a mite to my name."

"How came you to serve with the captain?" Marguerite could not quite bring herself to mention Bess by name.

"Oh, that's a windy tale!" Glasspoole stirred with her spoon for a moment. "Fetch me those herbs, lass, and let me finish off this wound balm for my stores. After, we'll sit and have a spot of malmsy and talk as two women together."

Marguerite carried the mortar to the stout woman, who tipped the powder into her pan. Glasspoole let the herbs sizzle a moment, then moved the pan to the workbench to let it cool. She chose a dark glass bottle from a railed shelf, removed the cork, and measured a few spoonfuls into her mixture.

"An electuary of fresh woundwort leaves," Glasspoole explained, "to clot the blood. I've no use for bleeding, as I prefer to keep a man's life-fluid in his veins where it belongs." Her task completed, Glasspoole opened the glass cabinet, using a key that hung from a string tied to her apron. "The more dangerous simples, like spirits of poppy, I keep locked away tight. There's some fools who'd go looking for liquor and take poison in their ignorance."

Marguerite sat in a chair beside the surgical table as Mistress Glasspoole served them both with an earthenware cup of sweet wine. The herb-wife plopped down next to Marguerite, fanning her face with her apron.

"Dear Lord! With all the hullabaloo this day, I've been rushed off my feet with nary a chance to catch breath," Glasspoole said. "Later, I shall have to fill ampullae with the wound balm, but for now, have a swallow of malmsey, lass. 'Twill do you good."

"How did a Christian woman come to serve a pirate?" Marguerite asked after she had taken a drink. The wine was very good, if rich and cloying on the palate.

"I'd a small shop in Nassau, working the other side of an herb-wife's trade," Glasspoole said, draining her cup and re-filling it from the bottle. "Lust philters to stiffen a man's horn, love potions to soften a woman's heart, curse-powders to hex an enemy, salvation-powders for protection 'gainst evil. 'Twas a fair living, and I'd sometimes have an old shipmate turn up at my door wanting a cure for the Spanish pox and such-like things."

"You're a witch." Marguerite was not surprised. Many women practiced the arts, though few had real power. In her experience, those who claimed to have domination over the spirit-world were often charlatans like herself, preying on the weak-minded and desperate with their own brand of gammon. She had never gotten involved with that particular game. There had been one woman in St. John's Town with a reputation for the Evil Eye, she recalled. Certainly, anyone who crossed her soon suffered ill luck in droves. Marguerite had avoided the woman, as did most everyone else. Mistress Glasspoole seemed very different.

"An herb-wife," Glasspoole corrected gently. "Though I suppose there's some who'd call me a hedge-witch, and they'd be close to the mark. At any rate, on a black and moonless night some years ago, I was wakened by a knock at my door. 'Twas Bess O'Bedlam herself, carrying a mate who'd had his brain-pan cracked open in a tavern brawl. She thought to hold me at pistol-point till I showed her that I was no common physic. I did all I could for the lad, but in the end he died. Nonetheless, the captain appreciated my skill and asked me to join her crew, as their physician had taken a ball and lost his arm in a sea-brawl against a French sloop out of Martinique. I packed my things and left Nassau that very evening. I missed the sea, lass, and Bess had more need of me than young doxies and foolish vain men."

"But Bess is a pirate. She kills people!" Marguerite protested.

"Aye, 'tis true, but no matter where you go in the world, or how high or low your station, there's always some bugger out to cut your throat and take what's yours," Glasspoole pointed out. "I don't give a fig if a man's a pirate, a pulpit-thumper or a pasha, he deserves healing, if only for the sake of charity. Bess O'Bedlam's got honor of a kind, she cares about her people, and that's good enough for me."

Marguerite did not want to argue with the herb-wife, so she got up to examine the bottles and jars on the shelves. Each bore a paper label inscribed with spidery handwriting, but she had no idea what they meant, since she had never learned to read, and she suspected the labels might be written in Latin, anyway. Continuing her perusal, Marguerite became fascinated by a cat's skull, the bones inscribed with strange gilded symbols, the sharp little canine teeth capped with gold. The eyes were set with opals, and it appeared to be staring back at her with a hint of malice in its rainbow-shimmering gaze.

Glasspoole came up behind her. "What's this?" she asked, poking at the back of Marguerite's shoulder.

"Eh?" Marguerite whirled around, startled. She had to think a moment to understand what the woman was talking about. "A tattoo," she replied, frowning. "I've had it all my life. How can you see it through my shirt?"

"Not with the eyes, lass. There's other ways of seeing, if you take my meaning." Glasspoole stood back a pace and sucked her false teeth in and out while she considered, her eyes sunk in a nest of concentration wrinkles. "All your life, you say?"

"Aye. My mother had it done the week after I was born." Marguerite twisted her neck but could not catch a glimpse of the mark on the back of her shoulder. "'Tis a puissant charm of protection, she told me."

Glasspoole scratched her chin, her nails rasping against the wind-roughened skin. "'Tis made with charmed ink, no doubt, and by one skilled in such things. There's genuine power, but I cannot speak to its purpose. Not protection, lass. Something else."

"*Godskannonne!*" Marguerite exclaimed, exasperated. "My mother told me—"

"A mother will say anything to comfort her child," Glasspoole interrupted, "even though that comfort be a lie. Who sired you, Margo?"

"A whoreson of a French sailor." Marguerite screwed up her face in a scowl. "He left my mother to fend for herself after he swived her and planted me in her womb. She turned doxy after my birth to keep bread on the table. Mother died when I was nine."

"Well, there's more to the tale than that, or I'm a blue-bearded ape," Glasspoole murmured. She went to the apothecary cabinet, opened a small drawer, and removed a necklace of star anise and whole cloves strung together on a thin cord. "You wear this, lass. Day and night against your skin. If aught troubles you – a nightmare, perchance, or a coldness in your belly that has no cause – tell me quick."

Marguerite took the offered necklace and put it on, tucking the long string of spices into her shirt. The smell was not unpleasant, reminiscent of cakes and mulled wine. Star anise and clove points prickled between her breasts. "I have always had nightmares," she confessed. "Most nights since I was a child."

"Do you, now? The same each time?"

"Aye." Marguerite fiddled with the drawstring around the neck of her shirt. "A horrible man. He looks like death." Speaking about the nightmare that had plagued her for so long made her uncomfortable. She shifted on her feet.

Glasspoole's teeth clicked together. "Go on, lass."

"He reaches out to me. His hands are like claws. He tells me that I'm the key." Marguerite took a breath, let it out with a sound that was very much like a sob. "It frightens me down to the marrow of my bones. I don't understand anything except that I'm very afraid. When I wake up, I'm crying."

"Hmph. A curious state of affairs, to be sure." Glasspoole narrowed her eyes to glimmering slits, deep in thought. "Do your menses come on regular?"

"At the full of the moon."

"And the nightmare...does it visit during your blood-tide?"

Marguerite considered the question carefully. She had no idea why Glasspoole wanted this information, but sensed it might be important. If the herb-wife could do anything to relieve the terrifying dream that made her wake screaming, she would do everything she could to help. She trusted Glasspoole instinctively. Although they had only just met, there was something about the older woman that told Marguerite she had an ally in Mistress Glasspoole, and possibly a friend.

"Now that I think on it," Marguerite said after a long pause, "I cannot say the nightmare has ever come then. No, not when the blood-tide's upon me."

"Curious. The more I hear, the less I like."

"Have I been ill-wished?" Marguerite's heart beat faster. "Cursed?"

Glasspoole patted her arm in a comforting gesture. "Calm yourself, lass. No need to let your nerves run hurly-burly. Leave the matter in my hands. I'll do what can be done."

The sick-bay door opened and Bess stepped into the room. She was wearing a turquoise-blue waistcoat with silver buttons over her shirt and clean indigo breeches, though her feet were bare. "Good e'en, Mistress Glasspoole," she said to the herb-wife.

"Time for supper, is it?" Glasspoole let out a heavy sigh. "Do go on, lass," she said to Marguerite. "I'll think on your trouble for a while. Perchance I'll find a solution."

"Trouble?" Bess glanced from Glasspoole to Marguerite, and back again. "Is she ill?"

"Nothing to vex yourself over," Glasspoole said tartly, her mobcap quivering. "Be off with you, Captain, and take Mistress Margo with you. If you've naught else for her to do, she can turn a hand in the sick-bay each day till we come to Hotspur Cay."

Bess nodded. "Very well. I'd druther she labor here with you than run amok all over my ship. Step lively, Mistress Margo, or your supper'll get cold."

Glasspoole plucked at Bess' sleeve. She bent forward and whispered in the captain's ear, "If the lass has difficulty at night, send Jim Monk for me."

Bess raised her brows, but Glasspoole put a finger beside her nose to signify mumchance, and withdrew to her workbench. Nonplused at the herb-wife's behavior, Bess gestured Marguerite towards the door.

Shooting Glasspoole a grateful look, Marguerite left the sick-bay, the scent of anise and cloves rising up around her at every step.

CHAPTER TEN
A Night and a Nightmare

Marguerite accompanied Bess back to the captain's cabin, making no attempt at conversation. Her thoughts were occupied by Mistress Glasspoole's revelation regarding the tattoo on her shoulder. She had always thought of it as a protective talisman, the last tangible proof of her mother's love and devotion. Now that comforting belief had been ripped away, but Marguerite did not want to think ill of the woman who had sacrificed herself so that her child could live.

Mayhap she did not know what it was, Marguerite thought. *Mama was unlettered, after all, and might not have understood a charm-needler's mischief.* Still, it troubled her. She did not want her cherished memories of her mother tainted by doubt. Marguerite thrust the matter aside for the moment, unwilling to dwell upon it. She needed to focus her attention on the pirate captain who was holding her captive.

After they climbed out of the hatch and back onto the main deck, Bess turned to Marguerite and said, "I've no wish to keep you confined, Mistress Margo. If you give me your solemn word not to pester my men, and to keep to my cabin, the galley, the quarterdeck or sick-bay, I'll not lock you in again unless I must. If I ask you to stay inside, 'tis for your own good, and I expect to be obeyed. Will you so swear?"

"Aye, that sounds like a fair bargain," Marguerite replied, spitting in the palm of her hand. Bess emulated her, and the two women smacked their spittle-wet palms together to seal the deal.

"I tell you truly, Margo, that if you think to betray my trust, it will go hard on you," Bess warned.

"I'd expect no less from one with a formidable reputation such as yours," Marguerite replied pertly. "Pray tell me, I am curious – will you feed me to the sharks as punishment if I'm a naughty wench?"

Bess chuckled. "Aye, though the poor man-eaters would no doubt get the worst of it," she said, leading the way to her cabin under the poop deck. "The sharks hereabouts have never tasted so dainty a morsel and might expire from so rich a dish. Just see that you abide by our pact, mistress, for I would not give the creatures gout without cause." She opened the door with a flourish, making a courtly leg.

Marguerite paused on the threshold. The table had been cleared and set for two with snowy white linens, silver plate and stemmed glasses. There were covered dishes and a bottle of wine. Since night had fallen, all the lamps had been lit, casting a mellow glow over the cabin. Beyond the stern windows, glimpsed through the glass panes, the moon shone bright in the dusky lavender sky, surrounded by glittering pinpricks of stars.

Bess gallantly swept her arm towards the table. "At your pleasure, dear heart."

Marguerite gave her a dimpled smile at the chivalric gesture and sat down in a chair. Bess took the opposite seat. While they dined, Bess was at her most charming, pouring wine and serving Marguerite from the blue-and-white Delft platters. Hephzibah had created a spicy dish with the meat taken from the *Winchester*; the braised beef was seasoned with grains of paradise, tamarind and allspice, and had been cooked until it was falling-apart tender. The main course was potted pigeon pie, stewed cabbage and baked yams, followed by plum duff.

Marguerite pronounced everything delicious. "I've rarely eaten so well on land," she commented, taking another spoonful of beef.

Bess chuckled. "Aye, that Hephzibah's a marvel. Her beggar's pudding would raise a man from the dead." She took a swig of wine and continued, "So tell me, mistress...what was the *key* to your success back in Antigua?"

She was hoping to elicit some kind of reaction – something that might bring her closer to unraveling the tantalizing puzzle revealed by Hephzibah's spirits – but Marguerite dropped her fork, her face so pale that the freckles stood out like spots of ink.

"What did you say?" Marguerite's pupils were so dilated, her eyes appeared black in the lamp light, circled by the merest rim of blue. She had a ghastly expression, like a woman who had seen a ghost grinning at her from a grave.

Bess was startled by such a strong response to her relatively innocent query. "Whatever's wrong, dear heart?" she asked.

Marguerite pushed her plate away, no longer desiring another bite of dessert. Being reminded of the nightmare had made her lose her appetite. She was usually able to forget about her horrible dream during the daylight hours, but as it became night, her apprehension returned. She did not want to reveal this to Bess, though, lest she be mocked for it. Therefore, she forced herself to smile and shrug, saying, "Naught but too elegant a dinner on a belly unaccustomed to such fare."

"Ah, well, have a touch more claret to batten your hatch," Bess said solicitously, re-filling Marguerite's glass. That done, Bess sat back, seemingly relaxed, but her gaze was sharp. "Your mam was Dutch, eh?"

"Aye, Gertruida De Vries."

"Does she live still on Antigua?"

"Nay, *liefje*. Gertruida was a merchant's daughter in Antigua, but her widower father financed the wrong ship and lost everything in a hurricane off the Canaries," Marguerite said, deciding there was no point in lying. "He was ruined. Grandfather hanged himself rather than go to debtor's prison. My mother fell in love with a French sailor soon after, who got her with child and fled. She had no family, no fortune, no prospects. She whored till I was nine, when she died of a fever. 'Tis a common tale, I suppose."

Bess toyed with her two-pronged fork. "There's more than one man that gambled a ship and lost," she said. "Tom Carew was a hire-captain for the British East India Company when he wrecked in a storm near

Madagascar. The company men blamed him for losing the cargo. They black-balled him, which weren't but addin' insult to injury since Carew was also a financer and lost his own savings, too. He turned pirate soon after with a 32-gun Spanish xebec." She took a swallow of wine and continued, "He captured the xebec at Nombre de Dios, if you can believe that; just cut her out of the port easy as kiss-my-hand and sailed under the Spaniards very noses. Hah! He was a fierce one, all right. Fancy Tom, they say, was clever as a fox and bloodthirsty as a Jesuit missionary. Plundered the Spanish Main for years afore he disappeared with *Deceiver*."

Marguerite was not interested in the career of Fancy Tom Carew. She tossed her napkin on the table and gave Bess what she hoped was an encouraging smile. "And what of Bess O'Bedlam?" She ran a finger over the rim of her glass, looking at Bess from beneath her lashes. "Will you not share some of your own history with me?"

"There ain't much to say, mistress." Bess did not want to talk about herself. Her origins were a mystery, and she preferred to keep it that way. There was too much pain in her past to relate casually. She tried to re-direct the conversation back to the *Deceiver*. "I reckon Fancy Tom's career was a touch more excitin', what with the treasure and all."

"Have *you* never taken a treasure ship?" Marguerite asked, equally determined to learn more about the pirate despite her reluctance.

"A time or two," Bess answered evasively. "Though none so great as Carew's."

Marguerite sighed in frustration, deciding to try another tack. "You've whip scars on your back," she said, making it a statement of fact rather than a polite inquiry.

Bess did not answer immediately. Instead, she took another glass of wine as a delaying tactic. Marguerite raised her brows and sat quietly, her gaze fixed on Bess.

Finally, Bess said, "I was whipped at the tail of a thief-taker's cart in Marseilles."

"Oh? I'd like to hear that tale."

"Let it lie, Mistress Margo. There's some things that ain't to be told." Bess' tone was flat; it was clear that as far as she was concerned, the subject was closed.

There was silence between the two women for a while. At last, Marguerite leaned an elbow on the table and gave Bess a challenging look. "Truth for truth," she said. "A fair exchange. You ask me a question, and I'll answer with no flummery. Then you'll do the same. Are we agreed?"

Bess considered the proposition a moment. She nodded. "Only if I take the first turn."

Marguerite leaned back, grinned, and spread her hands wide. "I'm at your mercy, *liefje*."

"Do you know aught about Tom Carew or the *Deceiver*?"

"Naught but what you've told me, I swear," Marguerite replied. "I'm as innocent as a babe in the matter."

Bess scowled. "Are you certain?"

"That's two questions, and I've answered the first already." Marguerite's grin widened. "Now 'tis my turn."

Bess pushed her chair back and rose. "I like not this game of yours."

"You owe me a question, *godskannonne*." Marguerite, too, got to her feet. "Has your liver turned yellow, Captain? Afraid to answer a challenge when it's put to you?"

Bess' nostrils were pinched and white. She ground out, "Ask then, damnation to your soul."

To Bess' surprise, Marguerite laughed, a silvery tinkle that held genuine amusement and not a trace of mockery. "I think I'll save your debt and dun you another time," she said, blue eyes a-light. "It might be handy some day."

Jolted out of her bad humor, Bess smiled. She reminded herself that her task was to charm Marguerite, not behave like a bear with a sore paw. Even if the woman did not know about any connection between herself and the *Deceiver*, one clearly existed. The spirits had claimed it was so, and they never lied. Misdirected, mayhap, or twisted the truth into a tangle, but truth was in every spirit's tongue. It was up to Bess to get as much information from Marguerite as possible; the smallest detail could provide a link.

She brushed back her chestnut hair, wincing as scorched, brittle bits broke off the ends, and littered the shoulders of her waistcoat. "I suppose you always collect what's owed you," Bess said.

"Always." Marguerite approached the pirate. The lamplight made her hair seem like pure molten gold as it flowed over her shoulders. She came close, and reached up to touch Bess' hair. "I could trim that, if you like. Or do you not trust me with shears?"

"I've survived the sharpness of your tongue, mistress," Bess said, lips quirking. "Iron shears are dull compared to the curses you cast."

"I'm no witch," Marguerite replied, wetting her lips. Her eyes were heavy lidded, smoldering bright with desire. It was time to continue a different game – one with Bess' eventual seduction in mind. Marguerite had only pretended to be a prostitute in Antigua, but she had learned a great deal by observation. She arched her back slightly, making her full breasts appear more prominent, and wished she was wearing a dress with a low décolletage.

"No witch," Bess echoed, "but you've surely enchanted me, dear heart." She appreciated the sight of that delectable bosom, practically begging to be touched, but restrained herself from responding too boldly. She did not want to frighten away her prey, or seem too eager. It was better to let Marguerite come to her, although she fully intended to encourage the young woman as much as possible. *'Tis a merry dance*, Bess thought, *and I'll guide the steps. I'll play the tune.*

"Perchance I've cast a spell on you after all," Marguerite purred.

Bess inwardly congratulated herself. It was very gratifying to see Marguerite answer her flirtation with more of the same. "Your beauty is magical enough," she replied, letting some of the passion she felt blaze forth.

Fully conscious of the effect she was having, Marguerite swayed closer, until their bodies were scarcely a finger's width apart. She tried to make herself inviting, a cradle of bone and flesh and skin that Bess could sink into and be welcomed. "Do you deem me a sorceress?" she asked softly, staring up at the woman.

Bess' hands rose of their own accord, and settled on Marguerite's hips. "More of a temptress, I think," she said. She bent her head, intending to lay a kiss on Marguerite's mouth, but the woman slipped away, shattering the tension between them.

"Where are the shears?" she asked. Marguerite's voice was calm, but her flushed cheeks told another tale. *The moment's gone far enough*, she thought, struggling to control her involuntary reaction to Bess. Her blood was tingling, her heart painfully a-gallop, thudding against her ribcage until her flesh felt pulpy and bruised. Heat rushed through her, and it had nothing to do with the tropical weather. There was no denying that the pirate captain was attractive, but Marguerite had bigger game in mind than a simple dalliance.

"In the cabinet," Bess replied, pouring herself a glass of wine. She downed it in a single gulp, feeling the need for something to cool her ardor. The cabin seemed very hot of a sudden. Bess walked behind the table and threw open the rose-glass windows, grateful for a cool breath of air. Tension sawed at her muscles. She deliberately tried to relax.

After a few moments, Marguerite brought the shears, drew Bess to a chair, fastened a piece of linen around her shoulders, and began to snip away the fire-ruined chestnut locks on the left side of her head. Marguerite moved to the right side, a frown of concentration on her face. Cut strands of hair floated to the floor.

"Have a care," Bess said, "for I've no wish to be as bald as Mister Lovelock."

"Be still," Marguerite admonished, when a jerk of Bess' head nearly caused her to clip the woman's ear, "or you'll end with a head that's smooth as an egg." She continued trimming until she was satisfied. Carefully removing the linen sheet, she said, "'Tis done, milady buzz-about. Go and see."

Bess went to the mirror above the washstand and examined her reflection. Marguerite had trimmed her hair close on the sides, getting rid of the damage done by the flintlock's fiery explosion, and left it long in the back for a queue. Short chestnut curls framed her face. Bess was pleased by the effect. She grinned, noting that her cut eyebrow gave her a rakish look.

"You should have 'prenticed to a barber," Bess said.

Marguerite wrinkled her nose. "I've no taste for blood-letting," she replied, pointing out the typical barber's side-trade – bleeding his customers for the sake of their health. "Besides, there's few men who'd trust a woman so near his vitals with a cut-throat razor."

"At least I've no need for shaving," Bess said, rasping her sun-tanned cheeks with callused palms. "Thank 'ee kindly, Margo. That was a job well done. Perchance I'll keep you on as a fart catcher when I've made fortune enough to retire and live like a grandee."

Marguerite giggled. She had difficulty envisioning Bess with a noble lady's entourage of obsequious servants and footmen following close at her heels. It was even more hilarious to think of herself as one of that jostling crowd, called "fart catchers" from their close proximity to their mistress or master.

There was a knock at the door. Jim Monk entered the cabin, tugged his forelock at Bess, and proceeded to clear the table of their supper things. He did this by the simple expedient of gathering up the four corners of the cloth to make a bundle, which he then removed with ease, as well as much clinking of china and glass. After the door closed behind him, Bess stretched, careful not to bash her hands against the low ceiling, and yawned.

"'Tis late and I'm for bed," she said, unbuttoning her waistcoat. "Will you care for the lamps, mistress?"

Marguerite went around the cabin, extinguishing the lamps in the gimbals that kept them upright no matter how violently the ship moved. As she did so, she considered the best way to deal with the inevitable. There was only one bed. She did not want to share it with Bess, and knew instinctively that asking the woman to sleep elsewhere would produce not only ridicule, but downright disbelief. Therefore, Marguerite removed her petticoat-breeches and shirt, saying, "If you'll pass me the counterpane, I'll find a space on the floor to sleep."

Bess raised her brows. "That's hard comfort," she said. "The bed's big enough for two, and I'll not mind the company."

"Nay, *liefje*. I'd rather take my chances elsewhere," Marguerite replied, sounding prim.

"I bathed today, and I've no lice, and I cut my toenails short." Bess spread her hands apart. "What's the trouble?"

Marguerite decided to tell part of the truth. "I have nightmares," she said simply. "Very bad nightmares. 'Tis best that I sleep apart."

Bess shrugged out of her shirt and removed her breeches, draping the garments over the top of her sea chest. "Is that why Mistress Glasspoole gave you that necklace?"

Marguerite clutched at the long strand of star anise and cloves; the sharp points of the spices cut uncomfortably into her palms. "Aye," she said, which was not exactly a lie – the herb-wife could have meant the charm to prevent dreams as well as ward off any ill fortune from her tattoo. "So I may have the floor?"

"You may sleep anywhere you wish, dear heart, as long as you don't leave the cabin." Bess whipped the quilted silk counterpane from the bunk box and gave it to Marguerite, along with a feather-stuffed bolster. "Try the window seat, if you like. 'Tis padded at least. The quarter-gallery is behind that curtain, should you need to make water in the night." Without further ceremony, the naked woman climbed into the bunk box, pulling a light sheet up over her chest and turning over on her side to face the bulkhead.

Marguerite stood uncertainly for a moment in the gloom. Faint star-shine and moonlight came in through the open windows, as well as the sound of waves slapping gently against the hull and the smell of salt. The ship was running on an even keel; from somewhere above deck came three chimes – a sailor on the middle watch striking the ship's bell to indicate the hour. Marguerite could not interpret the time, but she knew it was very late. Abruptly, she yawned, a jaw-splitting exercise that made her realize just how tired she was. She stripped off her clothes, found the curved seat that followed the length of *Mad Maudlin's* stern, and curled up with the counterpane, the bolster under her head. It was not uncomfortable, although the seat was narrower than a bed. Marguerite's last conscious thought before sleep claimed her was that in rough seas, she would have to sleep on the floor or risk being thrown violently off the seat when the ship pitched and rolled in the grip of a squall.

For a while, she drifted peacefully. The nightmare, when it began, was the same as always.

Marguerite was held fast in the grip of a dread so powerful, she could not summon the strength to move. Above her loomed a hideous figure of a man, the flesh so wasted upon his bones that his appearance was more skeletal than human. Long strands of dirty white hair straggled across his seamed face. His eyes burned, black fire twisting in his pupils. His teeth were rotten stumps, and the man's breath was foul.

"My key," he said, reaching towards her with long, thin fingers. His nails were like claws. "Mine! Come to me!"

"No!" Marguerite sobbed, trembling in every limb.

"Mine!" he repeated. "My bone, my blood, my key. Come to set me free!"

Darkness swirled around her, tinged with crimson around the edges. She heard distant voices, men's unbridled screams. The earth rumbled beneath her feet. A flash of gold so bright, so searingly molten it was like a small sun, blinded her. Heat assaulted her on every side, accompanied by a sulphurous stench that seared her nostrils. Marguerite was choking on brimstone fumes. Her lungs were burning, filled with hot coals.

The skeletal man reached out, his claws brushing her skin.

There was no one to save her.

She was truly in hell.

Marguerite became aware that someone was shaking her roughly.

"*Merde*! Wake up, woman! 'Tis naught but a dream!"

It was Bess.

Marguerite's eyes snapped open. She drew a shuddering breath, and the dream receded into the depths of the night as consciousness reasserted itself. She was not surprised to find her cheeks wet with tears. Marguerite heard the scrape of flint and steel as Bess lit a lamp. The light helped; soon, Marguerite stopped shivering.

Bess stood, looking down at her with a thoughtful expression. "You've a wail like a *bean sidhe* with a bellyache," she said, then went to the cabinet and poured a measure of liquor from a case bottle into a pewter cup. She returned and thrust it towards Marguerite. "Drink that to settle your nerves. It ain't no rotgut Irish poteen but good *oloroso* sherry, stolen from a Spanish captain's own stock."

Marguerite took the cup and drank the contents down in a gulp, almost choking on the liquor, which was quite dry but not abrasively so. She passed it back, glad that her hand was no longer shaking. "Thank 'ee kindly," she said.

"Did you know that your tattoo glows with witch-fire when you dream?" Bess asked. Her expression was wary, her tone cautious, as though she was dealing with an unstable gunpowder charge that might blow up in her face.

"Does it?" Marguerite threw back the counterpane and stood, turning her back to Bess. "Is it glowing now?"

Bess cocked her head to one side. "Nay, I cannot say that it is." Indeed, the intricate tattoo appeared to be quite ordinary now, shrunk to a mere ink-stain inscribed on the skin. But Bess knew what she had seen when Marguerite's scream awakened her – thin yellow-green flames crawling and shifting over freckled flesh, the lines forming and breaking apart in strange symbols that made her heart leap into her throat. She had no difficulty with spook binders or witchcraft in general. However, such things had no place happening on her ship without her permission, and she did not like it.

A hasty rap at the door made Bess' frown deepen. Her scowl grew more fierce when Mistress Glasspoole entered without waiting for a reply.

"What's this?" Bess growled, oblivious to the fact that she was naked. Distressed by the nightmare and surprised at the interruption, Marguerite grabbed the counterpane and clutched it modestly around her body.

"Half the crew's in a mortal terror, and the other half's a-hanging on the yards, and the ship's cat is cowering in the lee scupper," Glasspoole whistled through her ivory teeth, "for there's been an almighty uproar in the foc's'le. Sickly green flames were spied running on the mast; not Saint Elmo's pallid *corpus sanctos*, mind you, but genuine witch-fire. The watch reports no other ships in sight, and you know neither Hephzibah nor myself has more than a touch of the power, and never enough to summon spirit fire."

Bess rubbed sleep from the corner of her eye with a knuckle. "Mistress Margo was affrighted by a nightmare," she said. "I'd have sworn she had no talent for magic."

Glasspoole glanced at Marguerite and said, "She doesn't, but I've a notion what does."

"The tattoo?" Bess shot an aggrieved glare at Marguerite. "Why did you not tell me the mark was charmed?"

"Margo does not ken the whole of it," Glasspoole said stoutly, drawing the captain's attention back to her, "nor do I, for that matter. 'Tis charmed, but to what purpose, I cannot tell. One more skilled than I at such matters will have to winkle out the truth. In the meantime, the lass can sleep in a sick-bay berth. She'll be well protected – the wards are as strong as can be crafted – and she'll not disturb the ship again."

Bess scowled. She did not relish the thought of having Marguerite out of her sight all night, but on the other hand, she had *Mad Maudlin's* safety to consider. Her crew gave her the respect and obedience due to a good captain, but the hands might mutiny if they believed that Marguerite was dangerous. In that situation, Bess would be forced to kill men who were otherwise an asset to her piratical enterprise. She did not want matters to go so far.

"Very well," Bess said to Glasspoole, not missing Marguerite's expression of relief. "Margo may sleep in sick-bay till we arrive at Hotspur Cay. I charge you to keep a close watch on her, Esmeralda Glasspoole. If aught happens, I'll hold you responsible."

"Aye, Captain," Glasspoole replied. "You'd best take precautions yourself."

"Such as?"

"Stuff the keyhole of your door with fennel seeds. Scatter a pinch of devil's dung about the place. I suspect the cause of Margo's trouble is a visitation – of the living or the dead, I know not, but I can smell the reek of it." Glasspoole tucked a stray lock of grizzled hair back beneath her lawn nightcap.

Bess shrugged. She left such matters to those who were competent at them. Despite the fact that she was nicknamed the Water Witch, she had no trace of occult talent herself, nor did Bess envy those who did. "I'll do as you suggest," she replied, and turned to Marguerite. "You'll bunk down in sick-bay for the nonce, mistress, but I expect you to join me for breakfast in the cabin each morning."

"Aye, I can do that," Marguerite said, giving the woman a grateful smile.

"This ain't license to do as you please," Bess admonished. "When I want you, you'd best come running, quick as kiss-my-hand. If I hear you've been makin' trouble, 'tis back to my cabin you'll go, and I'll hear no argument."

"I understand."

"Good. Now get yourself dressed, for you can't run about the place mother-naked." Bess waited until Marguerite had assumed the shirt and petticoat-breeches, then came close to her. Settling her hands on Marguerite's shoulders, Bess leaned forward and placed a fleeting kiss on her brow.

"Sweeter dreams, dear heart," Bess said, concern and a certain tenderness in her gray gaze. "Don't fret, but obey Mistress Glasspoole. There's bound to be someone at Hotspur Cay who can untangle the trouble."

"Thank you," Marguerite breathed. She felt somehow safer, as if Bess was standing between herself and an unknown but terrifying danger.

"Come along, lass," Mistress Glasspoole said, lips twitching in amusement. "An old dodderer like myself needs her beauty rest."

"I'll go and have a word with the foc's'le hands," Bess said, pulling on her own clothes. She seemed a little shame-faced, as though embarrassed by the caring display. She quickly left the cabin, nearly bumping into Henry Dunn as she reached the quarterdeck.

Glasspoole tucked Marguerite's arm in her own and led her to the sick-bay. The space seemed snug now, not claustrophobic in spite of its location deep inside the ship, and Marguerite immediately felt more at ease. She chose a hammock and climbed inside, exhausted both mentally and emotionally.

"I think you'll have no further difficulty this night," Glasspoole said. "I've a cot in yon niche beyond the curtain, should you need me. Good e'en, Margo."

"Good e'en, mistress." Marguerite settled herself on the thin flock mattress that fitted the curve of the hammock, and pulled the sheet to her chin. It was comfortable, and she was soon fast asleep, untroubled by further nightmares.

The next week flew by as *Mad Maudlin* continued her journey to the pirate haven, Hotspur Cay. Marguerite suffered no more bad dreams. However, about three days after Marguerite's initial nightmare, Bess complained of hearing something (or someone) scratching around the keyhole of her cabin door in the night. An investigation in the morning showed marks upon the wood, as though an animal had tried to claw its way inside.

Mistress Glasspoole said nothing, though her lips thinned. That very day, she locked herself inside the captain's cabin with a basket full of mysterious bottles and jars. When she emerged hours later, the herb-wife was exhausted and had to be assisted back to sick-bay by Henry Dunn. The room stank of bitter smoke and took some time to clear. Whatever she had done seemed to do the trick; Bess did not experience any further disturbances.

Marguerite's days quickly fell into a routine. After waking in the morning, she dressed and reported to the captain's cabin to break her fast. She and Bess continued to flirt with one another, although not with the same intensity as before. A light stroking of the fingers, a quick peck on cheek or hand, was all the physical contact that, by silent mutual consent, they permitted each other. Bess remained more reserved, and Marguerite took her cue from that behavior rather than risk being importunate.

After breakfast, Marguerite spent half the day in sick-bay with Mistress Glasspoole, making salves and simples and tending minor hurts. Upon learning that her protégé did not know how to read, the herb-wife prevailed upon Henry Dunn to give Marguerite lessons. The gunnery master, Levalier, took it upon himself to teach her weapons and self-defense. In the evening, Marguerite had supper with Bess, and afterwards returned to sick-bay to sleep.

On the eighth day of *Mad Maudlin*'s journey, Marguerite was on the poop deck with Levalier. She wore her customary petticoat-breeches and a shirt, untucked; a blue-spotted kerchief held back her hair. The vain Frenchman was resplendently dressed in a cream satin coat and yellow breeches, although he eschewed silk stockings and went barefoot in deference to the rolling deck. His white powdered wig was slightly askew, as always. Levalier held a broad-bladed knife with which he menaced Marguerite.

"Do not lunge so far that you lose your balance, mademoiselle," Levalier said. "Always, always on the balls of your feet – like so!" He demonstrated the technique, lashing out with his weapon at the same time as he rocked forward.

"Your reach gives an unfair advantage," Marguerite grumbled, dancing out of the way of the man's knife. She shook her head, sweat droplets splattering on the deck. There had been rain earlier in the day, but the sun had burned off the clouds, and even the wind was too heat-laden to refresh. She was hot and tired, and her resentment of Levalier was bordering on hate. It was unnatural. The man was cool and composed despite his clothing; he was not even breathing heavily, while her lungs were warped and aching against her ribs.

Levalier's protuberant green eyes bulged further. "All the more reason for you to attack instead of waiting to defend!" he said mercilessly. "So! *Regardez-vous* – the eyes, throat, belly, groin, thigh and knee, all vulnerable to the blade. Act swiftly and to the purpose. Kill your enemy before he kills you. Now the *montante*, mademoiselle, if you please."

Marguerite wiped her burning eyes with the back of her hand. Her knife felt far too heavy and clumsy, an instrument of brutality rather than subtlety. She took a step towards Levalier, her weapon held low at her side. As she came closer to him, she slashed upwards, aiming the blow at the inside of his thigh. At the last second, wanting the lesson to be over, she turned the motion into a thrust at his chest, aiming to slip into his heart.

Levalier simply brought his hand down, striking her wrist and jarring the knife out of her hand. Pain shot up her arm to the shoulder. Marguerite backed away, clutching her bruises.

Levalier tsked. "*Non*, mademoiselle. Never the chest. Too many bones. You must keep the softest flesh in mind. If your knife becomes tangled in the ribs, you will be disarmed."

"I think you've already disarmed me," Marguerite said, wincing as her wrist throbbed.

It took a moment for the Frenchman to realize that her statement was a feeble attempt at humor. He did not laugh, but the corners of his mouth quirked up. "You made a fair attempt at the *botta in tempo*," he said, tucking his knife into its sheath, "but it was very clumsy. If you fought me in truth, you would be dead, *non*?"

Marguerite answered sullenly, "*Godskannonne*! 'Tis only sparring."

"*Putain de merde*!" Levalier stomped towards her, good humor abandoned, his eyes flashing with ire. "Do you think this a jest, mademoiselle? Do you wish to slay your opponents with your wit?"

"I've no wish to slay anyone, m'sieur," Marguerite flared back at him.

Levalier put his hands on his hips and loomed over her. "That may be so, but be assured, *ma petite*, if you cannot defend yourself, someone will take advantage of you."

Marguerite turned away, bent and retrieved her knife, not at all intimidated. "I lived without killing for a long time."

"And you have a pretty scar to show for it, *non*?" Levalier smiled coolly at the look of consternation on Marguerite's face. "Spare your blushes. It is common knowledge, mademoiselle, courtesy of Jim Monk spying through the keyhole of the captain's cabin. He has the curiosity of all young boys. *Eh bien*, from the scar he described, you were fortunate to escape with your life. Next time, you may not be so lucky."

Marguerite shrugged. "According to the captain, my tongue's a dangerous enough weapon."

Levalier sighed, the sound of a put-upon man. "As you wish." He took a step away, then without warning, turned and lashed out at her with a knife that had been concealed up his sleeve.

A week of exhausting drills under the Frenchman's tutelage made Marguerite's body respond without her volition, as training supplied the response and bypassed her conscious thoughts. She bent back slightly, allowing the blade to pass over her without harm, then straightened and swept her weapon at the taller man. The tip of her knife ripped through the side of his coat. Her foot stamped hard the deck as she followed with a backswing that would have sliced through his jugular vein had he not been swift enough to avoid the blow.

Appalled, Marguerite stopped and stared at him. Levalier gave her a courteous bow of approval. "And that, mademoiselle, was an excellent *attaco responsivo*! Well executed, without hesitation – I kiss the hand. Tomorrow, we will practice the *stocatta* and the *stramazone*...after I have mended my clothing as well as my skin."

"I didn't mean..." Marguerite saw blood seeping through the heavy cream fabric of the Frenchman's coat. The stain looked like poppies blooming in a sea of milk. "Oh!" she exclaimed, eyes round and horrified. "You're hurt! I'm sorry, m'sieur! *Je suis désolé!*"

"A scratch," he replied with an elegant Gallic shrug. "It is nothing, a mere trifle." Levalier eyed her seriously for a moment, then continued, "There will come a day, *petite*, when you must kill or be killed. When that time arrives, I hope you will remember me with kindness. Until then, you may curse poor Levalier as you like, but I will continue to be a hard taskmaster. I suggest you take our play in utmost seriousness, mademoiselle, or I will give you a thrashing to help you remember the lesson."

"I won't forget again," Marguerite promised. Being attacked by Levalier in such a surprising fashion had been a vivid reminder of the time when she had acquired the scar on her belly. She decided that it would not be a bad thing to learn to defend herself more handily. The Frenchman was, she had to admit, an excellent teacher.

"*Bien mieux!*" he said. "Then I am satisfied."

Bess came up to the poop deck and leaned against the taffrail. She was carrying a leather flask, which she offered to Marguerite. "How goes the knife-work, Mister Levalier?"

"It is well," he answered, taking a lacy handkerchief from his pocket and delicately dabbing his face with it. "She will never be a great fighter, *ma capitaine*, but it may be sufficient if she acts more the *garçon manqué* and less *la belle poule.*"

Bess grinned. "I can't see our Margo as a tomboy, though she looks fine enough in breeches, but I agree that she's a pretty hen no matter the clothes."

Marguerite worked out the stopper from the neck of the flask, and tilted it towards her mouth. It was full of water mixed with fresh lime juice, warm and sour with a musty leather tang, but delicious all the same. She lowered the bottle after taking several long swallows, and wiped her mouth with the back of her hand.

"*Godskannonne!* M'sieur Levalier treats me more like a fencing dummy than a woman of any kind," Marguerite said, only half in jest, "for I swear he's broken my wrist."

Bess pushed away from the taffrail, brows knitted together in a frown. "Let me see."

Marguerite held up her hand. Bess carefully probed the site, and worked the joint around despite her gasps and flinches. "'Tis not broken but bruised," was Bess' assessment. "Mistress Glasspoole's excellent arnica ointment ought to take away the worst of the sting, and for the rest, a salt water soaking's the best remedy."

"Will *you* kiss it and make it better?" Marguerite asked archly, fluttering her eyelashes.

Levalier snorted.

Bess ignored the gunnery master. Rather than couch her reply in words, she raised Marguerite's hand to her mouth and lightly pressed her lips against the blue-veined pulse point. She could feel Marguerite's heartbeat quicken. Bess lingered a moment longer than necessary, marveling at the fragility of the bones that she held in her grip.

Marguerite swayed closer, placing her free hand in the middle of Bess' chest. "I've a need for that balm in other places," she suggested, blue eyes glimmering wickedly.

Bess was sorely tempted. She had stayed a bit aloof from Marguerite, unsure of how the charmed tattoo might affect her or the ship, yet unwilling to break off the seduction efforts entirely. Her attempt to manipulate Marguerite's affections seemed to be working, however. The voluptuous blonde woman had all but undressed and begged to be taken. Perhaps it was time for her game to advance to a new level. Before Bess could answer or even gather her thoughts, she was interrupted by a man's cry.

From high at the top of the mainmast, a hundred feet above the deck, the watch shouted, "Land ho!"

Levalier glanced towards the bow. Bess let out an oath, dropped Marguerite's hand and went down to the main deck, joining Henry Dunn. The two went to verify the look-out's report with spyglasses. Marguerite watched, her pride stung a little, as the captain turned and said something to Dunn, who nodded and began shouting orders at the crew. Levalier smiled.

"We will soon be at Hotspur Cay," he said. "*Excusez-moi*, mademoiselle. I have duties to attend. *A la prochaine fois*." Levalier gave her another bow and walked quickly away.

Marguerite stood alone on the poop deck, peering into the distance. The wind whipped her hair over her face, stinging her eyes. She put up a hand to hold back the wayward locks, her eyes fixed on *Mad Maudlin*'s bowsprit as it dipped into the waves, then rose again, shuddering off a cloud of white spray. She turned and saw *Maudlin*'s long wake trailing out from the stern like a lace ribbon, unfurling over the turquoise blue waters. The ship rolled to leeward, heeling over a strake, but Marguerite did not lose her balance. She moved more easily on the ship now, her muscles used to the motion. She had not been troubled by seasickness again.

Hotspur Cay, she thought. *I wonder what awaits me there? And I wonder if the clime will prove warm enough to finally thaw the captain's cold heart?*

Marguerite was frustrated. She *knew* Bess was attracted to her. The response to her overtures could not be faked; she could feel Bess yearning towards her, but somehow the pirate remained in control of her affections. Oh, they made a merry dance, one of coming together and breaking apart with courtly love-play. Yet that was all they did – toy with each other until both were breathless from the heat. Marguerite had done everything she could to manipulate the pirate captain with words and gestures, but it was clearly not enough.

She would have to make the ultimate sacrifice to achieve her aims.

'Tis as plain as a boil on a beggar's face, Marguerite thought. *If Bess O'Bedlam will not bind herself to me without a token, then I must give her one – my body to be ravished as she desires. I'll use a woman's softest arts to ensnare her. Once we're lovers, she'll be more inclined to trust me. Perchance she'll even tire of me after a while. Either way, I can chance an escape when the opportunity arises.*

Marguerite was aware that she was on dangerous ground. Nevertheless, she did not find the prospect of sleeping with Bess to be completely unappealing. There was a small concern that the captain might prove to be an overly rough lover, but she would not let that stop her from implementing her plan. All doubts and fears had to be swept away, for Marguerite was determined to succeed. She smiled to herself, turned towards the bow again, and spied a knotty crest of green on the horizon.

Hotspur Cay, she thought, inhaling deeply. *It may be your haven, milady pirate, but I will make it the place of your surrender, so help me God.*

CHAPTER TWELVE
Spanish Fire

Hotspur Cay was a small island, one of many that dotted the Caribbean. It was uncharted and unknown except to Bess and her co-captains. The approach to the island's snug harbor was guarded by sharp-toothed coral reefs, and there was only one safe course to avoid the certainty of shipwreck. A pilot had to know precisely how to navigate the reefs, else his vessel and crew would perish.

Bess had learned the secret years ago from an old fishing captain, who had used Hotspur Cay as a smugglers' base. Now each ship in her fleet carried at least two people, their loyalty unquestioned, who knew the hidden course. The risk of exposure was minimal. The crews that Bess commanded considered the tropical island to be their refuge, a home away from the perils of the sea, and they knew better than to lead an enemy to their own doorstep.

In the protected semi-circle of the harbor – a green eye bordered by black coral that curved like lines of kohl – *Mad Maudlin* stood at anchor alongside two other vessels, the *Mistress Moon* and the *Medusa*. These ships were sleek brigantines, two-masted and square-rigged, with rakish lines and the look of well-armed predators. *Mistress Moon* sported a small figurehead of a naked woman's torso with a trident in her hands. *Medusa* had no such adornment, but her sides were painted in a gay green-and-gold checker pattern. The ensign flying from her topmast depicted a fierce Gorgon with bared bosom and snakes in her hair.

The crew of *Mad Maudlin* went ashore in a jolly-boat in shifts, to be greeted by cries of welcome from friends, family and lovers. Over the years, a small community had developed that had permanent residence on the island – mostly wives, husbands, lovers and children, with some craftsmen and other folk who had pledged their allegiance to Bess O'Bedlam. Marguerite was bemused by the celebration, particularly when well-wishers swamped Bess. The pirate seemed very much at home here, smiling and laughing and apparently at ease. Indeed, it seemed to Marguerite that Bess shed a great deal of her normal tension and rigid control the moment her boots crunched onto the sand.

As for herself, Marguerite was somewhat out of sorts. The days aboard *Mad Maudlin* had done something terrible to her balance. She could not stay on her feet and nearly toppled over twice, saving herself only by grabbing Bess' arm. The pirate's amusement at her predicament did nothing to assuage Marguerite's annoyance.

"'Tis just your sea legs," Bess said, "so don't fret about it, mistress. You'll not need me for a walking stick much longer."

Nevertheless, Marguerite fumed. After the crowd left, moving chattering onto a trail that was swallowed up by the dense fringe of trees and plant growth, she threw off Bess' hand and took a few tottering steps on her own. A fringe of coconut palms followed the curve of the beach. Further down, a rocky promontory thrust out into the harbor like a rough-hewn finger. Fishing nets were hung on poles here, and fish scales glittered like silver coins under the sun.

Bess came up behind Marguerite and nuzzled the skin behind her ear. "Beautiful, ain't it?" the woman sighed. "A real paradise on earth, and better'n any heaven I've heard described by a pulpit-thumper."

Marguerite shrugged her off. "Leave me be," she said flatly. It was not just the lack of balance that was making her angry. She was nervous and uncomfortable; she felt rubbed raw, her nerves stretched taut and thrumming under the tension. Being pulled unwillingly aboard Bess' ship had been bad enough. Thanks to Mistress Glasspoole and others, the situation had been tolerable. Now she was expected to make herself at home among people who could be potential threats at worst, indifferent strangers at best. A lump rose in her throat. She had never thought she might miss Antigua; indeed, Marguerite had often dreamed of escaping the island of her birth, but at the moment, she would give anything to be returned there safely.

Bess was about to reply when a laugh sounded behind them. Marguerite turned and realized that her day had just gone from dreadful to hellish beyond her wildest imagining.

A woman stood there, tossing a profusion of dark curls back over her shoulders. She was petite and wiry, with flashing black eyes and flawless olive-tinged skin. Her beauty was heart-stopping; every feature of her face and body seemed to have been crafted by a master of the art of feminine beauty and allurement. Marguerite could appreciate that loveliness, even as she loathed the woman for possessing it.

"So, Lizzybetta, who's the new *puta*?" the woman asked, curling her lip in a sneer. "She looks like a spotted cow."

Marguerite's instinctive loathing turned instantly into blackest hatred.

Bess rolled her eyes at the woman's ill manners. "Mistress Margo De Vries of Antigua, this is Maria Carmela Engracia Fuego y Márquez, late of Cádiz. Carmelita, be nice to Margo. She's no whore but a guest, my very favored guest, savvy?"

Carmelita raked Marguerite up and down with a hostile look, then turned her attention to Bess. Her attitude changed; the rigid lines of her body softened, and she favored the pirate with a smile. "I've missed you, Lizzybetta," she said, her voice dripping honey.

Bess did not answer. Carmelita came closer and pressed herself against Bess' body, her manner highly suggestive. "My bed has been very cold," she said with a fetching little pout, running her fingers through Bess' hair. "I've longed for you so much. How could you leave me all alone, *querida*?"

"Lita, you've not been alone in a bed since you was rising fourteen," Bess replied, pushing the woman away firmly but gently, "and even when we made the beast with two backs, you had other lovers, so don't think to play me for a fool. I know better. Just leave off, for I'm in no mood for your caterwaulin'."

Carmelita's black eyes glittered. "Don't you remember, Lizzybetta? Have you forgotten the nights we spent together? Naked under the stars, sweating, crying out to the moon with your mouth on my—"

"That's enough, by the sweet bleedin' Christ!" Bess interrupted. "I've naught to give you, Lita. Go find some other unfortunate soul to plague with your lovemaking, for I'll have none of it."

"Bloodless *bruja*! You once had passion enough for the both of us, Lizzybetta. Has your new whore drained you to a shadow?"

"Mistress Margo ain't a whore," Bess said, weary resignation on her face.

"Oh? Tell me, in what brothel were you born, señorita De Vries?" Carmelita asked Marguerite, giving her a poisonous glare.

"The same one as your mother, señorita Márquez," Marguerite shot back, absolutely infuriated by the insults. Not only had Carmelita's initial acerbity and rudeness gotten under her skin, but the dark woman's aggressive and possessive stance towards Bess was making her long to scratch those brilliant eyes from their sockets.

Carmelita's fingers curved into claws. "I'll kill you for that, you butter-eating bitch!" she choked.

Marguerite had learned a few handy phrases by listening to sailor's talk, both on Antigua and on the *Mad Maudlin*. She made an obscene gesture, spat on the sand and said, "*Chupe mantequilla de mi culo, hijaputa cabrona!*"

Thoroughly enraged, Carmelita let out a shriek and launched herself at Marguerite, who drew her knife and waited, seething with the need to draw blood. When she had sparred with Levalier, Marguerite had not been able to imagine a situation in which she would gleefully slaughter an opponent. This attitude had altered radically where Carmelita was concerned. Her blood was boiling. Her skin itched, stretched too tightly and tingling with rage. Not only did she want to kill this prickly bitch, Marguerite planned to carve out her heart and eat it before her dying eyes.

Bess grabbed Carmelita by the arm and literally threw her backwards. The woman landed on her buttocks with a tooth-rattling thump. She let out a spate of aggrieved Spanish that made Bess scowl.

"Belay that noise and shut your bonebox!" Bess said emphatically, brandishing a fist at both women. "If you two want to go about fizzin' like two cats on a fence, I'll not stop you, but no weapons, by God! If I catch either of you damned fishwives with a naked blade, I'll beat you till you can't sit proper. Am I rightly understood?"

Carmelita made a spitting sound and tossed her black hair back over her shoulders. "*Maldita puta!*" she said defiantly. "I'll kill that cow-whore, daughter of a thousand bitches! You go to hell, Lizzybetta! *Jodete!*"

Bess paid no attention to the cursing woman. She fixed her gaze on

Marguerite. "Put away that pigsticker, Margo. I'll not tell you again."

Coldly, Marguerite thrust the knife back into its sheath on her belt. "*Krijg de pest, vuil kutwijf!*" she said to Carmelita. "Come near me again, and I'll carve you from liver to lights."

Carmelita's face was twisted into an ugly grimace. "You're dead, *coña!*" she replied, scrambling up in a spray of sand. "Some day I shit on your grave!"

"Lord God Almighty, give me strength!" Bess grated. "Lita, close that foul hatch beneath your nose or I swear that I'll kill you myself, and feed what's left to the thrice-damned dogs. Margo, come with me." She took Marguerite by the arm and dragged her away from the beach, making for the line of palm trees.

Behind them, Carmelita continued to shriek curses and promises of violence.

Once they were out of sight, Bess gave Marguerite a little shake. "What was that about, mistress? Are you so eager for bloodshed?"

"'Twas not my choice to fight," Marguerite replied, still simmering. She faced Bess, her blue eyes a-blaze. "Was she your bawd, Captain?"

"Lita and I were lovers," Bess said, her voice calm, "but that was long ago. These days, I wouldn't have her if she was served to me on a silver platter with an apple in her mouth and a fistful of parsley up her arse."

"Well, she seems to think otherwise."

"Damn it, Margo!" Bess shouted in exasperation. Abruptly, she stopped and eyed Marguerite, her curiosity evident. "Be you jealous, mistress? Bitten by the green monster mayhap?"

Marguerite was stunned by the realization that there was some truth behind the pirate's question. She hated the Spanish wench with such passion because the thought of beauteous Carmelita making love to Bess was anathema to her. The notion made her stomach twist into knots composed of equal parts of dread and longing. Despite her obvious flaws, Carmelita was lovely as a goddess and imminently desirable – how could Marguerite ever compete for Bess' attention with such perfection close at hand? Bitterness flooded her mouth.

The success of her plan to escape relied on making Bess fall in love with her – or at least, gaining her trust to such an extent, the pirate would never dream that Marguerite could betray her. With that aim achieved, she would be free to exploit any opportunities that came her way. Carmelita was a definite threat. That was why she wanted to kick the doxy to death and dance on her corpse.

She told herself firmly that there was no other reason to be upset.

Not one.

Marguerite was shaken from her reverie when Bess chuckled and continued, "'Tis mighty endearing of you to be affronted on my behalf, Margo, but you've no need to gripe your guts. I ain't interested in none other save yourself. Rest easy, for I'll not cast you off in exchange for that hot-blooded wench. You're much more to my taste."

Thinking fast, Marguerite decided not to deny the charge of jealousy, but instead use it to her advantage. She leaned against Bess, looking up at the taller woman. "I beg your pardon," she said, letting her bottom lip tremble a little. "I know not what came over me."

"Ah, Lita's enough to make a saint turn renegade," Bess said, giving Marguerite a pat on the buttocks. "Let's not dwell on the wench. She'll find someone else to sharpen her claws on. Meantime, I'll show you somewhat of Hotspur Cay."

She led Marguerite on a small tour of the island, which did not quite meet her expectations of a piratical lair. She had expected some lawless, chaotic settlement, but this was more like an ordinary small town. Hotspur Cay boasted a smithy, a bake shop, a tavern, as well as a butcher, a chandler, carpenters, a tannery, coopers, sail-makers and even a place that sold second hand clothing and notions like needles. Goat herds were tended in a rocky region to the south, while pens nearer the settlement held pigs, flocks of francolin birds transported from Africa, chickens and live turtles. She also spotted dove-cotes and supposed that the people ate fairly well here. Brightly colored parrots squawked and flitted from tree to tree in the dense tropical growth outside the settlement.

Bess was at her most charming, describing points of interest and making sly jests. By the time they returned to the settlement, Marguerite was in a much better mood and had mostly forgotten about the odious Carmelita.

There were houses and barracks for sailors dotted around the central commercial area, set on dirt lanes that were kept clear of the creeping undergrowth. For the most part, the homes were neatly crafted of tropical woods with palm-thatched roofs and verandahs, but five were more splendid than the rest. One house in particular was very grand.

It was set a little way apart from the others. Besides being low and broad, with a verandah that was shaded by frangipani vines and a proper wood-shake roof, it had a tall latticed tower attached to one side. A ladder led up through the tree canopy, ending at a platform from which a person might command an excellent view of both the island and the ocean surrounding it.

A pair of four-pound cannons flanked the bottom of the steps that led to the front door, which was painted a vivid blue. A cage hanging from a hook on the support beam of the verandah roof held several tiny fluttering birds, as colorful as living jewels. A large black cat crouched on the rail that ran around the porch and watched them intently. His tail twitched back and forth, and his gaze never wavered from the cage.

Bess smiled proudly. "I'm most at home on the sea, mistress, but this house ain't so bad to rest one's bones for a while. Yon black-hearted harbinger of doom and destruction is Master Paddyshank. The cat's a vicious old bugger, but he keeps down the vermin."

Marguerite approached the cat with caution, clucking her tongue. Paddyshank gave her an evil glare from his wide golden eyes and hissed, showing teeth like needles. The cat streaked down from the verandah and vanished through an open window.

"Pay no mind to Paddyshank," Bess said. "He keeps mostly to himself." She went up the steps and opened the door, gesturing Marguerite to precede her inside.

The interior of the house was cool and light. Dark varnished floorboards contrasted with lime-washed walls in each of the high-ceiling rooms; a punkah hung like a banner from the center of the dining room ceiling, lacking only a servant to pull the string and make the palm-woven fan sway back and forth, to keep the flies off dinner and provide a breath of breeze. There were no interior doors at all, allowing for a free flow of air throughout. The furniture was all of excellent quality, from the large mahogany dining table and glittering bronze-and-crystal chandelier, to the carved sandalwood bed in the master chamber, and the air was perfumed with the bewitchingly sweet scent of frangipani.

Bess drew Marguerite into the bed chamber first. "Here's something for you, dear heart," she said, opening an ornately painted wardrobe. It was full of women's gowns, a rainbow array of silks and satins and lighter muslins that made Marguerite gasp in wonder.

"Take your pick," Bess said, pleased by Marguerite's reaction. "If aught needs alterin', we've a tailor named Pinxt who's a marvel with needle'n thread. Does anything catch your fancy, mistress?"

"Oh, aye," Marguerite breathed, reaching out to brush her fingertips against a silver embroidered black gown. "I've not seen such fine things in my life."

"There's jewels and buckles and bows and all manner of fiddle-faddle to match. You'll be the finest lady on the whole of the island, Margo, and no mistake."

Bess moved to stand very closely behind Marguerite, so close that she could smell the orange-flower perfume on her skin. "It's all yours, dear heart," she continued, her hands coming up to grip the woman's elbows. "Whatsoever you desire."

Marguerite turned around, her hand coming up to stroke Bess' throat. "You," she whispered. Unshed tears burned in her eyes. "I desire you, *liefje.*"

Caught up in a sudden outpouring of tenderness, without feeling the need to reject or rationalize, Bess brought her mouth down to cover Marguerite's. The kiss was sweet, an exchange of affection rather than a heated tussle. Marguerite whimpered, sliding her hands up the back of Bess' coat, and tangling her fingers in the chestnut locks at the nape of Bess' neck. The pirate squeezed Marguerite's waist, and let out a choked groan when the blonde woman deepened the kiss, opening her mouth to invite Bess' tongue for a duel of slick velvety flesh that left them both breathless and light-headed.

Someone coughed.

Bess and Marguerite sprang apart, their faces coloring. The intruder was Mistress Glasspoole.

"I've brought a few things to shield Margo whilst she's on the island," Glasspoole said, showing her hippopotamus ivory teeth in a grin. "I'd meant to protect her 'gainst otherworldly powers, but perchance I had better look into protecting her virtue as well."

Bess let out a strangled cough. "I've business to attend," she said, tugging at her waistcoat. "A meetin' with captains Byng and Quittam. Why don't you take Margo to the shops, Mistress Glasspoole? No doubt there's a few faradiddles she needs." Bess smoothed her hair and exited the bedroom.

From beneath the bed, the cat Paddyshank yowled and grumbled. Mistress Glasspoole clacked her teeth together. "Well, come along, lass," she whistled to Marguerite. "Pull yourself together. You haven't had a visitation from the Virgin Mary, you know. 'Twas naught but a kiss."

Marguerite touched her lips, still entranced, and stared at the doorway where Bess had disappeared. She blinked. Slowly, her mind recovered from its haze.

You are not falling in love with Bess O'Bedlam, she said to herself, but even in this silent inner dialogue, Marguerite remained unconvinced. She tried again. *'Tis a ridiculous fancy, a phantasm made of whole cloth. Nothing more.*

A tiny part of her brain insisted that this assessment was a lie, and Marguerite crushed it ruthlessly. "I'm coming, mistress," she said to Glasspoole. Taking one last look around the master chamber, Marguerite followed the herb-wife out of the house.

CHAPTER THIRTEEN
A Multiplication of Puzzles

When Bess arrived at the meeting place, she was in a foul humor.

What in the name of God is wrong with you? she asked herself, fuming. *'Twas not but a simple kiss, as any maid might give another. Have your brains turned soft as jelly? There ain't no difference betwixt Margo and those you've taken to your bed in the past. By the sweet bleedin' Christ, all women are the same in the dark!*

Yet some small, secretive part of herself knew that this was not true. Bess refused to acknowledge her lack of conviction. She growled and yanked open the door of the meeting house, disgusted with her behavior, the way she had lost control and allowed Marguerite to burrow under her skin in such an insidious fashion.

It was difficult to forget how she and Marguerite had seemed to come to a silent understanding in their embrace. Body to body, there was no room for lies, only honesty. Bess was angry and confused, unable to interpret her feelings towards Marguerite. She wanted the woman, certainly. There was no doubt about that. As for the rest, it was a conflicted jumble that made her head ache. Not wanting to examine her emotions too closely, Bess thrust these unwelcome thoughts aside and stomped inside the building.

Captain Frederick Horatio Byng of the *Mistress Moon* and Captain Allegra Quittam of the *Medusa* were waiting for her. Byng was a small, nervous man who could not sit still without twitching or fiddling with some object. Today, he held a small jeweled dagger, turning it over and over in his fingers. He frowned as sunlight flashed and glittered on the steel blade, and drew a rainbow of reflections from the gemstones.

His long brown hair was plaited back from a sharp-featured face, and the queue was ornamented with a large black riband tied into a bow. He wore an exquisitely tailored silver satin coat with amethyst buttons, and a purple waistcoat beneath; his shoes had crimson heels and diamond studded buckles. Byng looked like a useless dandy, one who cared more about fashion than any other subject. In spite of his foppish dress and nervous habits, however, he was a ruthless commander whose civilized veneer concealed a will of purest adamant. Byng rose as Bess entered, and made a graceful leg.

"Good day, madam," Byng said, pursing his lips. "How kind of you to join us."

Bess nodded in acknowledgement of his greeting and sat down at the table. "'Tis good to be home, Freddie. How was your trip to Nassau?"

"Ghastly, madam, simply ghastly. Half of *Mistress Moon*'s crew is down with the gleet on account of shore leave, and the physics will need muckle quicksilver to treat the poor poxed bastards. In prizes, we found little satisfaction save for a Portuguese trader with a cargo of spices off the tip of Florida, though the coward surrendered without a fight." Byng sniffed in disapproval, twirling his dagger. "I further regret to inform you that Katla has left me to fend for myself once again, so I am bedded down in bachelor's quarters for the nonce."

"Katla's tossed you out on your ear, eh?" Bess grinned, her mood improved by the comic nature of her captain's predicament. Byng's Icelandic wife, who also happened to have charge of the fortune-teller's shop next door, was extremely suspicious and jealous of her spouse. When she believed that Byng had strayed from his marriage vows – which was often – she had a habit of throwing him out of her house, bag and baggage. Katla usually took him back after he had groveled enough to satisfy her.

The relationship between Byng and his cool, pale wife was a source of amusement for Bess. She found it funny that Byng put up with Katla's behavior when she knew he was not a craven. She had seen him face cannons and hurricanes without being daunted, but one icy glare from his wife sent him scurrying to placate her with presents and apologies.

Allegra Quittam snorted and took a swig of wine. "Aye, on account of Katla saw her Freddie boy cavortin' with the merry widow Thorpe."

"Mistress Thorpe is old enough to be my mother!" Byng complained. "I was merely assisting her with a package, as any gentleman might. Katla's imagination is cursed inconvenient at times." He twitched in his chair and glared as if daring them to laugh at him.

Bess exchanged a knowing glance with Quittam. The captain of the *Medusa* was taller than Bess, and perhaps a year or two older, though the pitiless tropical sun had damaged her once fair complexion beyond repair, creating deep lines and wrinkles in a face that seemed composed of saddle leather. In contrast with Byng, she was dressed in a threadbare man's shirt and a pair of old breeches, with a yellow-spotted kerchief knotted round her throat. Quittam kept her dirty blonde hair short, separated into a wild array of quiffs bound with thread, which stood up all over her head like little artist's brushes.

Quittam filled her cup from a bottle sitting on the table. Her cloudy green eyes were the same color as the jade rings she wore on every finger, including her thumbs. "As for *Medusa*," she said to Bess, "we took an East Indiaman fair wallowin' with a cargo of Chinee porcelain, tea, silk an' opium, and other heathen things. 'Tis all in the storehouse. I've paid my crew with coin for their share of the prize."

Bess noted that Quittam was sporting a new pair of earrings, jade hoops swinging from gold chains that brushed the sides of her neck. She did not care if a captain of her fleet took a share of booty before turning the rest over to the island's storehouse, as long as he or she was not greedy. *Thou shalt not muzzle the ox that treadeth out the corn*, she thought. Bess poured herself a cup of wine, adding water from a jug until the liquid was barely pink.

"Well done, the pair of you. Our tame merchant, Mister van der Steen, is due to arrive on the fifteenth of the month," Bess said, after taking a drink. There was a plate of sweetmeats on the table. She took a sugared almond and continued, "He'll have a mort of necessaries for us. Allegra, you've the charge of bargainin' with him; I trust you'll get full value of our trade-goods from that ol' purse-clutcher. Freddie, 'twill be your task to oversee the transfer of cargos. You'll meet with the merchant on neutral ground, Wilder Cay to the west."

"Lord! Must I clutter *Mistress Moon* with a hold full of Chinese rubbish?" Byng flipped his dagger into the air, and caught it by the hilt. "I'd rather sail out and take what we need by force than play this tedious game of trade. We're pirates, by God, not shopkeepers!"

"Van der Steen's useful," Bess said, giving Byng a quelling glare, "so don't be cuttin' his throat out of boredom, Freddie. The trade we do with him is what keeps Hotspur Cay alive 'n well. We've no need of porcelains or spices or tea, but we do need powder and shot and meal. Let him sell the goods as he pleases and keep the profit. He's been loyal to us over the years and reliable, besides."

"If you want some excitement," Quittam said to Byng, "why don't you go and kiss Bess' new wench outside your wife's home? 'Twill be interestin' to see who removes your man-horn first – Katla with a dull bread knife, or Bess with a bit of lead shot."

Byng looked horrified by the notion. He shuddered daintily. "I'd sooner cut my own throat and leap into a shark's maw. 'Twould be a quicker end, at least."

Being reminded of Marguerite made Bess scowl. As far as she was concerned, that subject was forbidden. "Is there aught else?" she snapped, hoping to return to business. "Or are we to gossip all day like housewives at the village well?"

"Just this." Quittam slid a sheet of paper across the table. "The accounts for *Medusa's* venture."

"And mine," Byng said, adding his own sheet. His handwriting was pure copperplate with elegant flourishes, while Quittam's was a childish scrawl.

Bess examined the documents, consuming a dried apricot as she read them through. At last, she laid the papers aside. "Now I've some news for you," she said, "concernin' the *Deceiver.*"

Instantly, both captains gave her their full attention.

"Black Harry Rye is dead," Bess said. "A fit of apoplexy is my guess, since he was about to bewray himself at the point of my flintlock. He swore to know naught of *Deceiver* or Carew, but we all know he was a lyin' dog. Anyhow, I followed his dying words to a tavern in Antigua and found a maid – Mistress Margo De Vries. Her whole purpose in this tangle ain't known yet, but Hephzibah's bones say that she's the key to unlock the treasure."

Quittam and Byng nodded in understanding. Hephzibah's skill with the speaking bones was well known. Neither of them would question the ex-slave's abilities.

"Margo has a queer tattoo that's charm-needler's work," Bess continued. "Mistress Glasspoole knows not the meaning of it, but for certain it has some power. There was witch-fire on *Mad Maudlin*, and I seen the tattoo change with my own eyes."

Quittam ran a ring-laden hand over her blonde quiffs. "Mayhap Katla can read the runes," she suggested. "Of a certain, she's got the true Sight."

"Aye, that was my thought as well," said Byng, still toying with his dagger.

"I'll do that, though 'tis my thought that Captain Speedwell might find out more," Bess said.

Byng nodded. "The *Red Queen's Revenge* isn't due for another sen'night at least. But you are correct, madam. Lettice Speedwell is a clever thaumaturge and excellently educated as well. If any person can divine the nature of Mistress De Vries' connection with *Deceiver*, I'd wager on Speedwell in a trice."

"Be that as it may," Bess said, brushing sugar crumbs off her waistcoat, "we'll try Katla first. I need not say that Mistress Margo is to be treated with respect, by God. She'll have the run of the island, but she's not to leave for any reason. If Margo tries to do a midnight flit, I want her held but not harmed. Any man or woman who offers her hurt will be sorry for it, right till the moment they meet St. Peter's judgment. Am I rightly understood?"

"Aye," Byng said sourly, echoed by Quittam, who added, "I hear she's a sweet piece, this new doxy of yours."

Bess shot the woman a sharp look. "Damn your eyes, Allegra! Don't the world know you prefer to spread your fork for the trouser trade?"

Quittam shrugged. "'Strewth, I like man's meat, but I admire a well-filled petticoat, too." At Bess' glare, she laughed. "Luff off, Captain, luff off. I'll not poach your pretty."

Bess pushed away her empty cup and rose, deciding to ignore Quittam and get back to the business at hand. "As soon as we ken the whereabouts of *Deceiver*'s grave, we'll take the full fleet on the venture. 'Twill be all-or-nothing, for if we fail to find Carew's treasure, I'm inclined to give up the notion and seek another fortune elsewhere."

Quittam nodded. "That ain't but good sense."

Byng whirled his dagger in his fingertips and said, "There are other treasures to be plundered, madam. No doubt we shall find a new target should the search for *Deceiver* prove a failure. However, I have faith in your good judgment. You've not disappointed me yet."

Bess patted Byng's shoulder. "You're a good man, Freddie."

"No, I'm not," Byng replied. He flicked the dagger into the air, caught it by the hilt, and slammed it point downward into the table top. The sound reverberated through the room. "I'm a bloody murdering bastard with a multitude of sins on my conscience," he said. "If you disappoint me too often, madam, I'll kill you and take your command. We are both cognizant of this fact. Until that happens, I'll serve you loyally. You have my word of honor, after all, and a gentleman always honors his oath...as long as it suits him, you understand."

"Aye, but that don't stop us from bein' friends," Bess replied. She knew that Byng would, indeed, kill her if she failed to perform her duties as leader of their pirate band. So would Quittam. It was a hazard of the profession that she accepted, along with the great possibility that someday, she might be caught and hanged, or killed in the midst of battle.

"Oh, we're all a bunch of jolly butchers," Quittam said, her green eyes alight with good humor. "Let's leave off the killin' for today, Freddie m'lad. 'Twould be a shame to ruin your new coat, seein' as how blood's damned difficult to get out of satin."

"Too true, madam," Byng sniffed, slouching back in his chair. His toe tapped the floor in a restless rhythm. "Now on to more important matters than murder. What can I give Katla to soothe her ire? Something sparkly ought to do the trick."

"There's a gracious plenty o' baubles in the storehouse," Quittam said. "Why don't you poke about the place? Might find sommat to spark the lady's fancy. Otherwise, you'll be po-faced for a month and the rest of us'll have to put up with your belly-achin'."

"I'm off for Katla's," Bess said. "Mind how you go with your missus, Freddie."

"As always, madam. As always," Byng replied with a wink.

Bess left the meeting house and turned her steps towards the fortune-teller's shop.

Marguerite allowed Mistress Glasspoole to take her into various shops, which were clustered around a central flagpole. Bess O'Bedlam's crimson banner fluttered from the top, a brisk wind alternately revealing and concealing the skeleton and pierced heart motif that was appliquéd onto the cloth. The shops were built like the houses, mainly wood and thatch, except for the smithy, which was made of imported brick.

First, they entered the surgery and dispensary, where her colleague, Master Janus, enthusiastically greeted Glasspoole. Marguerite stood forgotten to one side while the pair exchanged a spate of bewildering healer's shop-talk, freely tossing around incomprehensible words and phrases like, "acid of sulphur, dulcified" and "*caruncula lachrymalia*". Janus was a pleasant, middle-aged man, but his obsession with the physic and chirurgical trade meant that he paid very little attention to anything else.

Glasspoole broke off a highly technical description of her treatment of a seaman's broken leg when she observed Marguerite growing more rigid with boredom by the second. "Forgive me, Alistair, but I simply must be getting on," Glasspoole said to Janus, punctuated by whistles and clacks of her false teeth. "Why don't you come to supper tonight and we'll speak more on the matter."

Janus nodded, gave Marguerite a startled smile as if just noticing her presence, and went back to puttering around his surgery.

Next, Glasspoole took Marguerite to a notions shop run by a swarthy

Italian called Vendetti. At the herb-wife's urging, she purchased a length of white ribbon, a pretty bronze hand mirror, a bottle of *eau-de-cologne* – much better quality than she could have afforded back in Antigua – and a bundle of hairpins. Although he scowled upon learning that the goods were to be charged to Bess' account instead of immediate cash, Vendetti included an ivory comb in the package as a "welcome gift" to the newcomer.

After they left the shop, Glasspoole indicated a fortune-teller's place. The shop was marked by a glass ball full of roiling red witch-fire that hung on a pole outside. A wooden sign depicted a tree with a human eye in the center of the trunk; there were silver stars tangled in the tree's branches. The eye blinked, startling Marguerite until she realized it was just an illusion created by a minor spell such as any hedge-witch might craft.

"The proprietor is Katla Byng," Glasspoole said, "a good friend who has the rune-cunning of the North. I'd like her to have a look at your tattoo."

Marguerite swung her package back and forth, and shrugged. "'Tis all the same to me," she said. "Lead on, mistress. I've naught else to do to pass away the time."

There were strange symbols carved on the posts and lintel of the doorway, a series of interconnected lines and curves that hurt the eyes if stared at too closely. The deeply cut marks had been rubbed with pigment to make them dull red. An iron lamp in the shape of a dragon-prowed longboat hung above the strings of glass beads that shielded the entrance.

Glasspoole swept the bead curtain aside and entered, calling out over the rattle, "Katla! 'Tis Esmeralda come to pay a visit! Where are you, lass?"

Since it had no windows, the interior of the place was darker than outside. Marguerite, who had followed on Glasspoole's heels, paused to let her vision adjust. The shop was small, and simply furnished with a wooden table and chairs. There were none of the usual fortune-teller's trappings – no scrying mirrors or cards or tea pots or coins – merely a colorful box sitting on a sturdy-looking table.

Katla approached from the back of the shop, carrying a tray with three glasses and an earthenware jug. "Esme! Well met, my friend." Her voice was unusually accented. Katla was tall and willowy, wearing a plain indigo-dyed dress, but her appearance otherwise was so strange that Marguerite gasped.

Despite the fact that she was clearly a young woman, her hair was completely white, a waterfall of silver held back from her face with a leather band. Katla's skin was also colorless, so translucent that lacy networks of blue veins were clearly visible. Her eyes were the palest shade of azure imaginable. Exposed by the low bodice of her gown, Marguerite spotted a tattoo inked above her collarbone. It was an odd spiky thing, reminiscent of the symbols carved around the doorway.

"Who's this?" Katla asked, raising delicate silver brows at Marguerite.

"Mistress Margo De Vries," Glasspoole replied. "Late of Antigua. She's Captain Bess' woman."

Marguerite was about to instinctively deny this description, but Katla forestalled her protest.

"So I see," the pale woman said with a smile, putting her tray down on the table. "The signs are unmistakable. Sit and eat with me, mistresses. There are fresh meat pasties today, and fennel-seed beer to wash them down."

So I'm the captain's woman, Marguerite thought, a tiny thrill running through her at the idea. Bess was very attractive, very charismatic when the mood was upon her. She again briefly wondered what kind of lover the pirate would be – rough and demanding, tender and considerate, or wildly passionate. Suddenly, Marguerite realized that the two other women were staring at her. She cleared her throat, hoping her blushes were not too apparent.

Glasspoole showed her false teeth in a grin. "Keep your mind on business, lass. There'll be time enough for cloud-fancies and calf's eyes when the captain's about."

Marguerite blushed harder. To mask her embarrassment, she sat down next to Katla at the table. "What did you mean, the signs are unmistakable? What signs?"

Katla opened her mouth to reply, then evidently thought the better of whatever she was going to say. "The captain has a strong will, as do you," she replied after a pause. "Two such persons will strike sparks from one another, like flint meeting steel. These things leave marks to be read by those who know where and how to look."

Marguerite still did not understand but decided not to pursue the matter. At Katla's urging, she took a pasty from the platter. It was warm, filled with meat and gravy and unidentifiable vegetables. The crust was flaky and crisp. Marguerite ate two, then sipped from a mug of weak beer that tasted faintly of anise and cooked sugar.

After she had eaten, Glasspoole said to Katla, "Mistress Margo's got an unusual tattoo. I'd like you to cast your expert eye over it. 'Tis charm-needler's work, and I'm fairly flummoxed."

Katla turned a look of astonishment on Marguerite. "I sense nothing," she said.

It was Glasspoole's turn to be amazed. The ribbons of her mobcap seemed to quiver with indignation. "Yon tattoo lit up *Mad Maudlin* with witch-fire! And it changed shape, too, according to the captain, who isn't one likely to be deceived. There's power in it, no mistake. 'Tis the purpose, though, I can't divine."

Katla shook her head. "There is nothing to be read, nothing to be seen beyond the superficial," she insisted.

"Impossible!" Glasspoole whistled sharply, her seamed face screwed up in a frown. "Unlace your shirt, Mistress Margo. Let her have a peek at the damnable thing."

Marguerite obeyed and slipped the shirt from her shoulders. She half-turned in the chair, to give Katla an unimpeded view of her tattoo.

The pale woman examined it closely. "Did anything else happen aboard ship?" Katla asked.

Glasspoole nodded. "Aye, for the captain's cabin suffered a visitation. I'd stuffed the keyhole full of fennel seeds – they're good for more than flavoring beer, as you know – to keep out unwanted visitors of the spirit kind. Cleared out the place with devil's dung, too. Still, something tried to claw its way in. I had to work my strongest wort-cunning to protect the cabin afterwards. If I had to make a guess, I'd say we had a *cacothymia* on our hands."

Marguerite was worried. This sounded serious. "What's a caco...cothy...*godskannonne!* You use break-teeth words, mistress. Speak plainer, if you please."

"A malevolent spirit," Katla explained, prodding Marguerite's tattoo with a fingertip. "Could be dead, might be a living soul that wanders far from its body." She looked up and continued to Glasspoole, "I can sense nothing. I don't doubt your word, Esme, but whatever was here has vanished."

"Are you certain?" the herb-wife asked.

Katla sat back and turned her attention to Marguerite. "Did you have any trouble with the tattoo afore you boarded *Mad Maudlin*?"

"Nay, I don't think so. I have nightmares most nights, but that's been since I was a child." A shiver ran down Marguerite's spine. "Not when I was in sick-bay, though."

"And this?" Katla touched the string of star anise and cloves around Marguerite's neck.

"A charm of protection," Glasspoole said. "I gave it to her." She described the young woman's recurring dream, which added to Marguerite's mounting distress.

"I don't understand why I had no nightmares when I slept in sick-bay," Marguerite fretted. Earlier, she had plaited back her blonde hair into a single braid; now she fiddled with the ribbon-wrapped end, feeling nervous and slightly sick. The pastries she had eaten made a lump in her belly that was heavy as a lead ball.

Glasspoole clacked her teeth together. "Because there are things that prey on wounded men, drawn to the pain and the violence. Nasty things that feed on death and suffering. There's damned little of the otherworld that can get into my sick-bay, mistress, and I keep it so whether I've patients in the berth or not. Which puts me in mind of a thing. Katla, have you any myrrh?"

"Certainly." Katla rose and went to the back of the shop, which was swathed in shadows. She returned a few moments later bearing a small box that smelled highly aromatic.

"Thank 'ee kindly," Glasspoole said. "Margo, I'll make you a powder to burn before you go seek your bed. A pinch is all you'll need in the night lamp. That ought to keep any unwelcome visitors at bay."

"Rosemary and John the Saint's wort with the myrrh?" Katla asked, an interested expression on her pale face.

"Aye, and archangel's root, sandalwood and bay," Glasspoole answered, "with a touch of *sanguis draconis*. I had all else save the myrrh. Now, will you sing the runes for her, Katla? Perchance you'll See the answer to this conundrum."

"If you think it will help." Katla reached for the hornbill ivory box on the table. It was a golden yellow color banded in deep scarlet, and carved with figures that resembled writhing tentacles. "Be at ease, Mistress Margo. There's naught to hurt you here."

Marguerite forgot about her dishabille as she watched the silver-haired woman at her work. Katla pricked her finger on a sharp corner of the box. A small bead of blood welled up; she rubbed it over the tattoo on her throat, which immediately flared scarlet. The already dim light in the room seemed to darken further, until Marguerite could see very little except Katla. Her otherwise colorless face was illuminated from below by the red glow from her tattoo, landing her an eldritch appearance, like a goblin lit by hell-fire.

Katla picked up the box, shook it thrice, and a bone tile fell from a slot on the side. Again, she shook it, retrieving a second tile made of wood. The third tile was a round section of deer antler. They were all blank. She sang under her breath in a strange knotty-sounding language with trilled "r's". The red light at her throat crept downward, separating into thin filaments that groped through the air towards the table, seeking the three tiles.

Just as Katla's singing reached a crescendo and the scarlet threads of light had nearly touched the tiles, something unexpected happened.

Glasspoole had been sweating; she poured herself a cup of water from a jug on the table, adding a pinch of salt. She was sitting at Marguerite's other side, and had craned her body around, the better to witness the proceedings. As she grew more engrossed, however, the herb-wife apparently forgot about her cup. Water trembled at the rim as her hand tilted, then fell with a splash on Marguerite's bare shoulder.

Yellow-green witch-fire erupted instantly from Marguerite's tattoo, clawing up to the ceiling of the shop like a bonfire raging out of control. The whole room blazed with the sickly coruscation. Glasspoole let out an indelicate oath. Katla screamed as the explosion of occult flames extinguished her own red witch-light. Marguerite echoed the shrill scream, more frightened than hurt by the display.

Glasspoole, trained to respond calmly to emergencies by years of experience on sailing vessels, snatched off her apron and threw it over Marguerite's tattooed shoulder. She rubbed the flesh hard to dry it, ignoring the yellow-green sparks that snapped and bit at her bony fingers. The witch-fire flickered and died, completely snuffed out by her ministrations. Katla slumped back in her chair, breathing heavily, her eyes fluttering closed.

Marguerite stared, shocked speechless.

"Well, well, well," Glasspoole said, standing in the puddle of spilled water. She had dropped her cup in the excitement. "Nothing there, eh, Katla? I reckon you'll sing another tune now." Her mouth stretched in an awful grin of triumph.

Katla opened an eye. "I'd curse you if I had the strength," she said weakly. "For now, let's just say that I believe you. There's more here than I imagined. You had better make up a goodly batch of your incense, Esme. I'll want some myself after that."

Marguerite whimpered and clutched her shirt to her bosom, terrified.

CHAPTER FOURTEEN
An Uneven Course

Bess had walked into the shop while Katla was singing the runes. She had remained silent and still, even when the rune-song was broken by the appearance of witch-fire from Marguerite's tattoo. As soon as the event was over, she came forward and said harshly, "What in the name of God was that, mistresses? I'll not have such sorceries, by thunder!"

Glasspoole waved a hand. "Rest easy, Captain. No harm's done."

"That ain't my point," Bess snarled. She had not only been startled by the unexpected display of power, she had been terrified for Marguerite. The thought of Marguerite coming to harm made her belly clench and her nerves ragged. The gunpowder tattoo on her cheek writhed as she ground her teeth together. Bess continued, "'Tis dangerous to meddle in ignorance of the outcome. You know that as well as I." Her eyes were as gray as storm clouds, and just as threatening.

"It was the water," Katla said, sitting up with a sigh. Strands of silver hair clung to her pale sweaty face. "What else was in your cup, Esme?"

"Naught but a bit of salt." Glasspoole's brows shot to her hairline. "Salt water! That's the key!"

Marguerite was trembling. Bess noticed her distress and went to the blonde woman. She knelt down and took Marguerite's cold hands between her own, rubbing them briskly. "Be ye hurted, dear heart?" Bess asked, tempering her tone though inwardly, she was still simmering with rage.

"I think not," Marguerite replied, giving Bess a grateful look, "but I'm fair addled all the same. That's what he calls me, the man in my dream. His key."

Glasspoole and Katla exchanged a glance. "I wish Speedwell was here," the herb-wife muttered.

"We'll have to fend for ourselves till Lettice arrives," Katla said. She brushed her silver hair back with her palms. "First, though, I want to sing the runes again. Try to keep Mistress Margo dry," she added with a small smile.

Glasspoole nodded, her mobcap bobbing up and down, and resumed her seat. "Captain, you'll join us, I hope."

"I still haven't heard an explanation," Bess said, rising from her crouch.

"You'll get one shortly," Glasspoole whistled. "Sit down, if you please, and stop hovering over the girl like a hen with one chick."

Bess sank down in a chair on the opposite side of the table, since the herb-wife and Katla sat flanking Marguerite. She crossed her arms over her chest and scowled impatiently. When she had stood rooted in the doorway of the shop, fear on Marguerite's behalf had clenched her chest with anxiety until she could barely breathe. It was only the knowledge that she might make matters worse by interrupting that had kept her from leaping head-long into the situation. In those harrowing moments, Bess had forgotten about *Deceiver*, about her planned manipulation, about everything except the near overwhelming need to protect Marguerite from danger.

Now she bit the inside of her cheek until it bled, relishing the rusty iron taste of blood. *Damnation to my soul!* Bess thought angrily. *I must be going mad. When did I ever give a ha'penny fig for a wench? She must have placed an enchantment on me, if I cannot bear to see her harmed. The sooner I've found* Deceiver, *the quicker I can cut her loose. Aye, that's the best thing. Once I've cast Mistress Margo adrift, she'll have no further hold over me.*

This bit of self-deception made Bess feel no better. Instead, the thought of losing Marguerite made her heart give a painful thump against her ribcage. Still scowling, she turned her attention to Katla, who was repeating the interrupted ritual.

Once again, Katla pricked her finger and smeared blood on the spiky tattoo at her throat. This time, however, after the third tile had fallen out of the box, a fourth tile slipped from the slot as well. Although the rune-singer seemed surprised, she did not break off the ritual. Threads of red light crawled down towards the blank tiles as before. When the threads finally touched the bone and wood and antler tokens, there was a crackling flash of brilliant scarlet, and the light abruptly vanished.

Marguerite looked closely. Inscribed on each of the formerly blank tiles was an angular symbol, each one different from the rest. The lines appeared to have been burned into the surface, but she could smell no trace of smoke. Katla trilled something under her breath, and touched each tile where it lay, using the barest brush of her fingertip.

One by one, Katla indicated the newly marked tiles. "Raidho," she said, "Sol's chariot, the necromancer's sign. Hagalaz the hailstorm, portent of destruction and crisis, the path between worlds. Eihwaz, yew tree of the underworld, mystic link of life and death. Othala of the generations, a heritage that binds for good or ill."

As she spoke, the symbols faded away, leaving the rune tiles blank once more.

"What does it mean?" Marguerite asked, shivering. Everything sounded very dire.

"Your blood-line is linked to Tom Carew," Katla said, scooping up the tiles and placing them back into their hornbill ivory box. "So is your tattoo, mistress. A skilled charm-needler's work made for a dual purpose – to bind you to Carew, and to point the way wherever in the mortal world he may be found."

"Such a thing couldn't be done unless you've inherited his blood," Glasspoole said. "Else the bond would've broken, no matter how strongly crafted in the beginning."

"But why?" Bess burst out, her head aching with frustration. Each new bit of information gave no answers, but created further questions. "How, by God? Carew died twenty-five years ago. I doubt Margo is much past nineteen."

"I'm four-and-twenty," Marguerite said, "and I'm fairly certain my mother never knew Fancy Carew."

Katla got to her feet, retrieved a piece of paper, an ink bottle and a seagull quill from the back of the shop. Upon her return, she carefully pulled the loosened shirt away from Marguerite's shoulder, and after sharpening the end of the quill with a white-handled case-knife, drew a picture of the tattoo on the paper. When she was finished, she showed it to Bess.

"A bewitched compass of a kind," Katla said, "a variation of the old *aegishjalmar* – the helm of awe – of the long-dead Norsemen. It's active on salt water only, not on dry land. Captain, that's why she never had trouble with the tattoo afore you took her off Antigua. Once she was on the ocean, the charm acted according to its purpose." She turned her head to address Marguerite. "I take it you're not much for sea travel, Mistress Margo."

"*Mal de mer*," Marguerite answered shortly, fascinated by the drawing. She had never been able to see her tattoo before, possessing only a single cracked hand mirror whose glass was quite cloudy. The lines of the tattoo reminded her of a wheel, with spokes radiating out from the center, each crowned with a symbol. "What does it do exactly?"

"Your tattoo is a beacon, for one," Katla said. "This nightmare you've suffered so long is actually a spirit visitation – a very powerful and malign one that may be Carew himself. Whatever the spirit's origin, it's attracted by the charm, able to find you unless you're protected by more puissant magics. This is why we know that you must share Carew's blood, mistress. 'Tis the only way to work and weave such a spell. It may seem impossible, but you're related to him in some way."

"I don't understand," Marguerite said, genuinely bewildered. "My mother had no family. But I know naught of my father save that he was French."

"Carew was English and had no siblings," Bess pointed out. "I doubt his sire and dam are still alive."

"Be that as it may," Glasspoole said, "at least we've cracked part of the puzzle. I believe that Margo's tattoo can show us the way to *Deceiver*'s grave, if we can ken the working of it."

Bess recalled what Hephzibah's spirits had said through the speaking bones. "Child of bone and blood, she be. Child of kin-ties, bearing the way," she quoted.

Glasspoole glanced at her keenly. "Is there aught else of the prophecy?"

"Aye." Bess concentrated a moment, then completed the ex-slave's pronouncement, "Seek the token, gift of the false-faced dead. Beware – a black curse on *Deceiver*'s grave. She is the key."

"A curse!" Marguerite drew up her shirt and pulled the laces tight. Her eyes were darkened by fear. "I've enough trouble without adding a curse to it, *godskannonne*!"

"That part may not be directed at you specifically," Katla said, reaching for a cold meat pasty. "The spirits always answer truthfully, but their riddles may have hidden meaning." She took a dainty bite, crumbs sprinkling her bodice, which she brushed away.

"False-faced dead," Glasspoole muttered. "Could that be Carew?"

Bess was not interested in speculation at the moment. "How does this tattoo work?" she asked, laying a proprietary hand on Marguerite's shoulder. Treasure fever had taken hold of her again. Her pulse was rapid, her mouth dry with excitement. Without thinking about it, she tightened her grip until Marguerite winced and tried to pulled away. Bess barely noticed.

"I'm no charm-needler," Katla said, nibbling on a piece of crust, "and I don't advise experimenting. We should wait till Lettice Speedwell arrives. She has much more experience at spook binding than the rest of us."

"Aye, that would be my advice as well," Glasspoole said. "Don't go taking Mistress Margo off on any sea jaunts, Captain. We might lose the both of you."

Bess was disappointed but schooled herself to patience. Abruptly, she noticed that Marguerite was looking anything but cooperative. In fact, there was a stubborn set to the woman's mouth that boded very ill. "Whatever's the matter, dear heart?" she asked. "You're as sullen as a toad whose lily pad was scuttled."

"I won't do it," Marguerite declared firmly. She had had enough of spells and enchantments to last a lifetime. "You can act as you please, but I'll not help you."

"You must!" Bess said, equally determined. "We cannot find *Deceiver's* treasure without you."

"This is none of my doing," Marguerite replied, tossing her head. "I was well and happy on Antigua till you snatched me from my home!"

"Aye, a happy little thief, barely scrapin' past starvation!" Bess retorted. "You've a chance at real wealth, by God. Why toss it away like platter-scrapings?"

Marguerite's face was flushed. She forgot about her plan to seduce and manipulate Bess in order to escape. Her temper was raging, fueled by terror and resentment. She did not know why these things were happening to her, but she did not like them one bit. It further irked Marguerite to know that Bess had gone behind her back to get information about her from a spook binder. She wondered if this was the reason why the woman had been so charming and attentive. Heat seared her cheeks, and her anger flared white-hot.

"Because I'm afraid!" Marguerite shouted, eyes narrowing with rage. "I never bargained for a part in your sordid tale. You never asked me but took what you wanted. It ends here! I'll not be used by a trumped-up, peacock prancing, dirty fingered oaf of a pirate, *godskannonne!* Kill me or send me home, for I will not aid you willingly!"

Bess drew back, her own mood blazing into fury. She had been goaded enough to forget herself and her schemes to gently bring Marguerite into willing cooperation. "You'll do as I say, or by the sweet bleedin' Christ, mistress, you'll feel my belt on your backside!"

"Do your worst!" Marguerite stared at the pirate defiantly, fists on her hips and chin tilted at a defiant angle. "Kill me or send me home! Better still, cut the thrice-damned tattoo from my body, since you take such pleasure from my pain."

"By thunder!" Bess choked. "You'll not defy me twice, you hellion!"

"*Teef!*"

"Shrew!"

"Ladies, please!" Glasspoole cried, so agitated that her false teeth nearly leaped from her mouth. She sucked them back into place and continued, "It's impossible to remove the tattoo, Margo. 'Tis magic, if you'll recall, not ordinary needler's work. The charmed ink would simply reappear over the scar, and you'd be no better off. Captain, perchance 'twould be best if Margo found other lodgings than your home for the nonce."

"Since my husband's away," Katla offered quickly, "she may stay with me."

Fuming, Bess stood up, knocking over her chair. Her fingers closed on Katla's drawing of the tattoo. She screwed the paper up into a ball and hurled it savagely on the floor. "Be warned, Margo De Vries," she said, her voice cold, her eyes glinting. "When the time comes, you'll do what you're told, and there's an end to the matter."

Marguerite got to her feet, hauled her hand back and aimed a slap at Bess' face. Bess caught her wrist in a hard grip before the blow could land. It was the same wrist that had been injured earlier that day by Levalier during weapons practice on the poop deck. Marguerite did not cry out, but her lips thinned, and she turned white.

"Remember what I told you on *Mad Maudlin*, the first time you struck me?" Bess asked, leaning down to put her face very close to Marguerite's. "I'll not beat you now, mistress, but mayhap you've earned a few stripes on account." She pushed the woman away from her. Marguerite stumbled but caught herself on the edge of the table.

"Get this hussy out of my sight," Bess said to Katla and Glasspoole. "When Speedwell returns, I'll deal with her then. In the meantime, speak to no one about that damned tattoo. If Margo makes trouble or talks out of turn, you've my permission to punish her howsoever you please. Just keep her away from me, for I'm sick of the sight of the wench." With that bleak pronouncement, and a last heated glare in Marguerite's direction, Bess took her leave.

Marguerite watched Bess go, furious and hurting. Her bosom was heaving, her nails digging into the table until they threatened to splinter. Her eyes were dry, however, her tears stoppered by the rage that still boiled within her, mingled with a touch of apprehension. When Katla laid a comforting hand on her arm, Marguerite shuddered.

"I'm not fit for company, mistress," she said, making an effort to control her voice. "Is there a place where I may rest a while alone?"

"I've a cot in the back," Katla offered. "Do you need aught, Margo? Tea or brandy?"

"Nay." Marguerite cast a final glance at the doorway, where the strings of the glass bead curtain swung fitfully to and fro. "I need nothing...especially from her." She went to the back of the shop, walking slowly and cradling her painful wrist against her chest.

"Should I go to her?" Katla asked the herb-wife.

Marguerite heard the women speaking, but she did not turn back or acknowledge the conversation.

"I think not," Glasspoole replied. "The course of true love never did run smooth," she said. "These things are best left to work themselves out."

"And if it doesn't?"

"Then it ain't worth a damn to begin with," Glasspoole pronounced. "Now come and help me grind this incense, for I swear that my elbow joint's worn to a nub."

The two women walked out of the fortune-teller's shop, leaving Marguerite to sulk and stew alone in the shadows.

CHAPTER FIFTEEN
Madness

The next morning, Marguerite came out of the guest chamber of Katla's neat little house. Her eyes were dry and aching from a mostly sleepless night. She had put on her shirt and petticoat-breeches from the previous day, having nothing else to wear since she would rather go stark naked than beg at Bess' doorstep for a change of clothes.

Katla said nothing, but served bread and soft goat's cheese and fresh fruit to break their fast. Later in the morning, however, the woman went out and returned with some plain dresses, chemises, petticoats and other necessities for Margeurite.

"I had to guess at the size," Katla said, shaking out a yellow Indian cotton gown with black-work embroidery on the bodice, "but we can have anything altered at need by Mister Pinxt, the tailor."

Marguerite was grateful for the woman's thoughtfulness. "Thank 'ee kindly, mistress," she said, picking up a blue dress with bold floral stitching on the skirts. "I've no money to pay, but I swear to return the favor when I can."

"No need, Mistress Margo," Katla said, her cheeks flushing slightly with pleasure. The tinge of color in her pale face was like viewing well-watered wine through alabaster. "Would you care to refresh yourself before changing your clothes?"

"A bath? Aye, 'twould be welcome, indeed," Marguerite replied, growing excited by the idea. On board *Mad Maudlin*, as was her habit when at home in Antigua, she had made do with freshwater sponge baths to avoid salt sores. However, sweaty weapons practice sessions with Levalier made this measure inadequate for getting really clean. She was thrilled at the notion of immersing herself in a vat of hot water and luxuriating for a change.

Katla smiled. "Widow Thorpe has a bath-house. Being a formidable Christian, she runs it very strictly, so you need not worry about being molested. Men and women don't bathe together. I'll fetch some soap and linens and we'll pay a visit."

Marguerite eagerly accepted the offer.

Widow Thorpe's bath-house was located at the end of a row of shops, next to the smithy; it seemed there was an ingenious system of heating water that had to do with pipes running beneath the always-lit forge, but Marguerite did not really follow Katla's technical explanation. There were no windows in the wooden building that housed the baths, but steam puffed from a vent in the roof, showing it was open for business. Following Katla's example, Marguerite left her shoes on the verandah, washed her bare feet in a bucket of water left outside for the purpose, and entered the dim establishment.

There were plenty of lanterns hanging from the ceiling beams, but they did little to dispel the steamy gloom. Widow Thorpe proved to be a bulldog-faced woman with a white turban wrapped around her head, secured by a gold-and-sapphire aigrette. She eyed Marguerite suspiciously; her grudging smile of welcome revealed several gold-capped teeth. Katla made the introductions, but Thorpe merely grunted and jabbed her thumb to the left. She held out her other hand and received two small coins from Katla as her fee.

As they followed the widow's direction and moved further into the humid domain, Katla whispered to Marguerite, "Mistress Thorpe is always foul-humored when it comes to women. She much prefers the company of gentlemen...my husband, Captain Byng, in particular," she added in a frosty tone.

Marguerite stripped off her shirt and petticoat-breeches, leaving them in a cubbyhole along with the fresh clothing she had brought, and Katla led her into the bathing room. Wine barrels, sawn in half, were filled with steaming hot water for soaking. A long rectangular trough was fed regularly with warm water from a metal pipe in the wall. Overflow disappeared through a grate in the floor at the opposite end. Hollow gourds were provided to be used as scoops and cups.

Standing at the trough, Marguerite wetted herself and used a scrap of linen to cleanse her body. The soap provided by Katla had an unusual scent – she could detect lavender and some sort of mint, but the rest of the ingredients defied her. With Katla's help, she also washed her hair, then assisted Katla with her own silvery locks.

When they were both clean, Marguerite and Katla found a wine tub to soak in. They sat cross-legged, face to face, knees touching. The water was almost too hot to bear at first, but very quickly became relaxing rather than painful. There were a few other women in the bathing room, some with small children. Apart from some sidelong looks, Marguerite and Katla were left alone.

"What was in the soap?" Marguerite asked, leaning back against the wooden side of the tub. Her arms were stretched out along the rim, and she let the hot water drain tension from her body. "'Twas a refreshing fragrance, at least."

"Lavender, rosemary, mountain balm, hyssop and garden mint," Katla replied. "Most useful for warding off the spirits of the dead, according to Esme Glasspoole."

"Does every simple task have to be about spook binding?" Marguerite made a face. "I had no dealings with such things on Antigua. I don't care for it at all."

Katla pushed strands of wet silver hair back over her shoulders. "In a way, you've been dealing with the consequences of spook binding all your life," she pointed out. "You've not asked to be involved, but you are nonetheless."

"Bah!" Marguerite shrugged. "I've no plan to be used by anyone, mistress. The living and the dead can keep to themselves, and I'll afford them the same courtesy!"

"You really have no choice." Katla sat back and watched the ripples of water on the surface of the tub a moment. When she raised her face and met Marguerite's defiant gaze, her own expression was sad but determined. "You can't ignore what's happened, Margo. The tattoo you carry will not simply disappear. Your nightmares will become worse in time."

"So I *am* cursed!" Marguerite said bitterly. She made a fist and thumped it on the rim, feeling a stray splinter catch at her skin. "That damned pirate! Why didn't she leave me be?"

It was Katla's turn to shrug. "There are times when we cannot escape the destiny that Fate insists is our own," she said. "That tattoo was like a pricked and primed gun waiting for the slow-match. What if you had found a lover and left Antigua of your own will? The result would've been the same. Don't blame the captain too much, mistress. By bringing you to Hotspur Cay, she's no doubt saved your life and your sanity. Mistress Glasspoole and myself are doing everything we can to preserve and protect you till all is resolved."

"I wouldn't *need* your help if it weren't for Bess O'Bedlam," Marguerite said through gritted teeth. After a moment, she forced herself to be calmer and continued, "Misunderstand me not, I'm truly grateful for your aid. Yet if I hadn't been kidnapped, none of this would be happening. Therefore, I'll not stir off this island unless 'tis to carry me home to Antigua. My mind's made up on that score. When I'm home again, everything will be as it was before, and I need not concern myself further with ungodly magics."

"By the sleet-cold hell! Are you so ignorant?" Katla's voice rang out, startling Marguerite. Water slopped over the sides of the tub as the rune-singer leaned closer to her. "This spell cannot be ignored. If you do nothing about it, madness and death will come to claim you, and neither will care to hear your excuses. Self-pity will be no comfort when you're in the grave, Margo. Beside all this, Esme and I have put ourselves at risk on your behalf – not because the captain commanded us, but because our consciences demand it. Your curse is none of my business nor of my doing, yet you'll not hear me complain like a babe denied a sweet."

Marguerite was dumbfounded. At last, something of Katla's warning had seeped through her indignation. Her mouth opened and closed soundlessly. Madness? Death? Suddenly, she felt the jaws of a trap closing around her. What she had taken for an inconvenience became much deadlier than she had thought.

She wondered if her mother had known the truth and immediately banished the notion. Her mother had been a good woman, doing what she thought best. If, in her ignorance, Gertruida De Vries had been betrayed by a treacherous charm-needler, that was hardly her fault. Nevertheless, her daughter now had to deal with the consequences. Katla was right. In such a situation, self-pity and willful inaction were tantamount to suicide. If she wanted to survive, she would have to do what needed to be done.

At last, Marguerite said, "You say this tattoo will drive me insane and kill me in the end."

"Not of a certainty," Katla replied. "We must learn the whole meaning of the charm and why you are linked by blood to a dead man who is not your relation. Then we may find a solution." She pointed a finger at Marguerite. "But you *must* cooperate, Margo. Stop fighting the captain, and do as you're told. It may be that the only way to rid you of the trouble is to allow your tattoo to fulfill its purpose."

"That would mean..." Marguerite's voice trailed off and she swallowed. The thought of submitting to Bess was grating, especially since their argument the previous day.

"Aye, you will have to cease warring with Captain Bess. The search for *Deceiver*'s treasure is to your benefit. To put it bluntly, mistress, which means more – your pride or your life? Let the captain have her way, and she'll do everything she can to help you."

"To help herself to *Deceiver*'s treasure, you mean," Marguerite replied around the stone that had apparently settled in her throat.

"Listen, child...there's no surety that your tattoo has aught to do with *Deceiver* or the treasure," Kalta said craftily. "The captain believes 'tis so, but I'm not convinced. The charm is linked to Carew himself, not his ship or his cargo."

Marguerite tapped her teeth with a fingernail and considered the pale woman's statement. This would make things much easier for her to bear, if she knew that she could use Bess to her advantage and ultimately deny the pirate her prize. She dearly desired to hurt Bess as payment for yesterday's kiss that had scorched her soul and left her confused and aching. Marguerite had desperately wanted to be ravished, would have given herself then and there but for the interruption.

That frightened her. Cold-blooded seduction was one thing; her treacherous body's response another. Blaming the pirate for her troubles was an instinctive reaction to the pressures she felt, a way of keeping Bess at a distance. The thought that Bess was just using her for gain only added fuel to the fires of Marguerite's resentment. "Do you truly believe 'tis so?" she asked.

Katla looked amused. "Aye, and aye, again! Ask Mistress Glasspoole; she will tell you the same."

"No need, mistress. I believe you, since you'd hardly tell a lie that would displease the captain if she heard it."

"Lay your injuries aside for the nonce, mistress," Katla urged. "Go to Bess and let her know that you're willing to obey her and do whatsoever you can to aid the quest. You need not lick her boots; she appreciates strength and spirit, not those who act as though her arse tastes of gold. If it later proves that your charm has naught to do with *Deceiver*, the captain will not withdraw her aid, or damn you to suffer the consequences of the curse alone. She has always taken care of those who are loyal to her. You'll reap the benefit of her patronage."

"'Tis a goodly thought," Marguerite said, "and I thank you for the advice. I'd no idea that this damned tattoo could rieve away my life."

"It is more than possible," Katla said. "Once these things are set in motion, they must run their course or be broken by one more powerful than the creator, if such is even possible. Delay means death."

"How much time, do you think, before this charm on my shoulder runs amok?" Marguerite was proud that her voice came out steady and calm, since she felt entirely the opposite.

"'Tis hard to say."

"Can you not guess?"

"A moon, mayhap...I cannot tell. I haven't that sort of skill." Katla leaned over, and lightly touched Marguerite's arm. "Trust us, and trust the captain."

"Easy enough for the first," Marguerite replied, "but the second is more difficult. Still, I will try."

"Good. Now let's get out of this water, mistress, afore my wrinkles never smooth. I swear, I'm like a raisin all over!"

Despite her worries, Marguerite laughed, but the gaiety was tinged with resolve.

As soon as she had made herself presentable, she would seek out Bess. Facing the pirate would be hard. Marguerite hated the notion of groveling for forgiveness. She would do it, however. Her feelings had smarted beneath Bess' whiplash insults and threats, but pride was not as important as survival.

With a new determination, Marguerite dressed and returned to Katla's house, intending to find Bess and speak to her as soon as possible.

Bess had gotten over her annoyance with Marguerite quickly enough. She was not one to hold grudges over what she saw as trivial matters; she had issued orders and that was that. The matter was resolved. If Marguerite would not obey, she would simply be made to cooperate. There was no other choice. Or was there?

She did regret hurting Marguerite's wrist. In that first flash of anger, Bess had forgotten about the sparring injury. Marguerite's blanched face, the look of quivering reproach, the stoic determination not to show the depth of her pain, all haunted Bess now. She wondered if she had been too harsh, too unyielding, too ready to use violence to emphasize her will. Marguerite was not a toughened crewman, after all.

Mayhap I've used vinegar where honey would've suited best, Bess thought, damning her black temper. That led her back to the kiss they had shared in her house before the rune-singing fiasco. Marguerite had been eager then, a sweet armful of willing woman that had made Bess' head spin. Wrapped in that embrace, Bess had wanted nothing more than to take Marguerite to bed and make love to her until they were both sated and glowing with satisfaction. The response to her caresses, the way Marguerite's body had writhed and begged silently for more, was difficult to forget.

Her own feelings were hard to comprehend. Her interest in Marguerite was purely business, or so she had believed – a deliberate manipulation that would end in betrayal, merely a dishonorable means to an end. Yet Bess now realized that she did not want to be rid of Marguerite when the search for *Deceiver* was concluded. The voluptuous blonde woman had roused Bess' passions, but she knew that what she felt was not merely the body's desire. They had connected on some profound level that went beyond the physical, which further complicated matters, as far as Bess was concerned.

Bess' heart ached, as did her head. These thoughts were very unwelcome. There had been lovers in her past, women she had casually used and been used by, who had left no truly deep impression. Marguerite was different, Bess admitted to herself. She was exasperating, frustrating, irritating – but also fascinating, beguiling and bewitching in all her moods, from spitting hell-cat to lusty temptress.

Mistress Margo's anything but dull, Bess thought. *Aye, I may have blundered by answering her fire with more of the same. She's fretful as a Spanish grandee's lady, and prickly as a porpentine, to boot.*

In truth, Bess did not want to have to force Marguerite to cooperate. Torture was not really an option. She did not think she could bear to cause Marguerite pain, and absolutely did not want to put this resolve to the test. However, Bess could not afford to show weakness in front of her sworn officers or crewmen. There would be a bloody mutiny if she did. Bess feared that if Marguerite remained obstinate, her fleet captains would demand a swift and terrible response. Even Byng, who doted upon his wife, would not turn a hair at using the *bastinado* on Marguerite if she stood between him and a mighty fortune.

I'll go and seek her out, Bess decided, moving from her study into the bed chamber. *Margo's had time enough to chew her own liver. She'll be over the worst of her temper by now, and I'll cozen her till she's purrin'. 'Tis the only sensible way to save the wench from harm. Besides, I've used Margo hard of late. She deserves better at my hands. Perchance a pretty token will earn her pardon, though I draw the line at bending neck and knee.*

Bess took a little alabaster chest from the wardrobe, set it on the bed and opened the lid; it was stuffed full of jewelry, valuable baubles she had taken as prizes. She chose a heavy gold bracelet set with polished sapphires and pearls, and put it in the pocket of her crimson waistcoat. She meant it as a peace offering to Marguerite, thinking that the blue stones were no less brilliant than the woman's eyes.

Putting on a clean shirt, Bess chose charcoal satin breeches and a silver-frogged satin coat to match. Bess spent a moment arranging the fall of ruffles at her wrists and tying her chestnut-brown hair into a neat queue at the nape of her neck. When she had finished primping, she surveyed her appearance in a gilt-framed cheval mirror whose quicksilver glass bore only a small spider's web of a crack in the upper corner.

"You heart-breaking old sea dog!" she said to her reflection, and winked at herself, letting out a laugh at her own foolishness. Bess patted her waistcoat pocket and left her house to find Marguerite.

To her dismay, Carmelita was waiting for her on the verandah.

"Oh, *querida*," Carmelita cooed, coming to press herself against Bess. "I've decided to forgive you for being so cruel to me. I heard you sent that little blonde *puta* to stay with Katla Byng. See, I knew you couldn't forget Carmelita! I'm too much woman to be thrown away like that!" She ran her hands over Bess' shoulders, an excited light in her dark eyes.

"By the sweet bleedin' Christ!" Bess tried to avoid those frantically groping hands. "You're everybody's woman, Lita. Didn't I see you last night with Solomon Lovelock?" The bald beefy man was Carmelita's protector and sometime lover.

"He means nothing to me, Lizzybetta." Carmelita licked her lips, and gave Bess a sloe-eyed glance that was pure wickedness. "Only you have my heart."

Bess succeeded in pushing the Spanish woman away. "You have no heart, you crazed doxy. If I weren't the captain, you'd gobble me up and spit me out like you've done so many others. Seek Lovelock if you're in such need for swivin'."

Carmelita tossed her head proudly. "I am the most beautiful woman in the world. I should belong only to the most powerful, the wealthiest, the strongest...and that is you."

Bess had heard this often, more times than she could count. Carmelita was beautiful and fiery, but she was also without morals or scruples. The woman used her perfect face and body to get what she wanted, going from person to person, only caring about whatever rewards she could reap from her conquest of the moment. Carmelita used sex as currency, and she was an expert bargainer. However, Bess was tired of the Spanish woman's grasping ways.

"I'm not interested in that stale dish you're servin'," Bess said bluntly. "Go peddle it elsewhere."

Carmelita let out a wail and wound her arms around Bess' neck, rubbing her breasts against the crimson waistcoat. "Don't say such things! You know that I love you! Only you, *querida*! Always, only you!" she said, then hauled Bess' head down and kissed her violently, cutting her mouth with sharp teeth.

Bess was being smothered, eaten alive by Carmelita's hungry mouth. She put up her hands to fend off the Spanish woman, but Carmelita was stronger than she looked. Musky sweet perfume rose from her flesh, choking and cloying. Bess finally managed to break Carmelita's hold and took a step backwards, wiping her lips on her sleeve.

Carmelita was panting in triumph, holding up the gold bracelet intended for Marguerite, which she had clearly taken from Bess' waistcoat pocket while they were embracing. "A pretty gift for a kiss, but I really prefer rubies, Lizzybetta," she said loudly, as though speaking to someone other than Bess. An ugly smile stretched her lips. Sunlight sparkled from the gemstones, momentarily dazzling.

A sudden sinking feeling centered in the pit of Bess' stomach. She whirled around to behold Marguerite, who was staring at her with a cold expression. It was obvious that she had witnessed the kiss. For a crucial moment, astonishment and embarrassment left Bess speechless. She could only stare, stunned and dismayed, while the world fell around her, and the earth failed to tremble open and swallow her whole.

Marguerite's nostrils were pinched and white. She looked at Bess, then her gaze traveled slowly to Carmelita, who waggled the bracelet and laughed, sneering. Marguerite turned her attention back to Bess. She said flatly, "I had not meant to interrupt your pleasure, Captain. Please excuse me."

Not waiting for Bess to respond, Marguerite walked back down the path, blue skirts whipping about her ankles with the speed of her passage.

Carmelita blew the retreating woman a mocking kiss. "Who needs that *puta* anyway?"

I do, Bess thought, her hands clenched into fists. Heat mounted on her cheeks and in her skull until she felt light-headed with rage. *By God, Margo is mine!*

Leaving Carmelita behind without bothering to answer, Bess hastened to repair the damage done by the Spanish woman's mischief.

CHAPTER SIXTEEN
The Gathering Tempest

Marguerite had seen enough to know that Carmelita and Bess must be having a torrid affair. The beautiful woman's possessive attitude towards the captain had been made quite clear at their first meeting. Now it seemed that Bess was taking comfort – if such a violent tussle could be called that – in Carmelita's heated embrace.

I have no claim on Bess O'Bedlam, Marguerite thought, trying to calm the pounding of her pulse. *We aren't lovers, just a captive and her kidnapper. Nothing more than that.*

Yet she could not help but be wracked by the piercing ache in her breast, and the sickening pain that griped her belly and made it hard to catch her breath. Her heart felt lacerated, hemorrhaging from the wounds dealt by that Spanish harlot; she would not have been surprised to find blood gushing, though the injury was to her soul rather than her flesh. Marguerite stumbled onwards, not noticing where she was going, blinded by unshed tears. Her only thought was to get to a place where she could weep and curse in private. Someone grabbed her arm, and she spun about, her free hand raised to strike. When she recognized Bess, Marguerite stiffened.

"Is there aught you want from me, madam?" Marguerite asked, controlling herself with an effort.

"'Twas not what it seemed," Bess said, a little out of breath. "Lita's a stubborn wench, but—"

Marguerite did not want to hear excuses. "What you and señorita Márquez do together is none of my concern."

"Aye, but—"

"I came to tell you that I've changed my mind," Marguerite interrupted once more. "I'll do whatever you ask to aid the fleet in recovering the *Deceiver*. I will obey your commands, and you'll have no further defiance from me, I swear by Almighty God."

Bess smiled gratefully. She was relieved that Marguerite would cooperate without coercion, but still felt uneasy. The woman was rigid, her face pale and set in a stony expression. Bess had gotten what she wanted – the key to *Deceiver*'s treasure – but it was not enough. Startling as that realization was, she knew that she had to make things right between them first. "That's grand, dear heart," she said. "Now, about Lita—"

"As I said," Marguerite broke in, gathering up her skirts in both hands, "the matter is finished. You owe me no explanations, madam. You must act as you see fit, and I will do the same." With that, she gave Bess a sketchy curtsey and walked hastily away, head held high.

Bess stood, bewildered and not a little angry. The conversation had been quite unsatisfying. She wondered if she ought to find Marguerite again, demand that she stand still and listen, but an instinct told her to leave the blonde woman alone for now. Later, when Marguerite's temper had a chance to cool, Bess could approach and attempt an explanation.

The thought of losing Marguerite was more than she could bear. She wondered if she was sick, perhaps feverish. It was certain that she had never felt this way before. Was it love? Bess did not know. She had no benchmark against which to judge her feelings, only the ballads and poems she had heard all her life. What the poets described seemed woefully inadequate to sum up the complexity of her regard.

Bess turned her thoughts towards Carmelita and her temper began to simmer. The traitorous Spanish wench had driven a wedge between her and Marguerite. That would have to be addressed, the sooner the better. Hell and damnation! The more she considered the matter, the angrier she became.

Carmelita's voice sounded behind her, dripping with malice. "Lizzybetta, why did you run away? I wish to give you so much more than a kiss."

"Think of the Devil and she trots to your threshold, bold as brass with her tail a-twitch for mischief," Bess said tightly. "I told you to leave me be."

"But *querida*, I can't believe you don't want me." Carmelita sounded petulant.

Bess' hands curled into fists. "I'd druther tup a she-boar. 'Twould be cleaner, at least." She kept her back to Carmelita, not trusting herself to a confrontation. Why had she ever thought that Carmelita was beautiful? Worthy of her affection? Marguerite was infinitely the superior, much more to be desired than any spiteful strumpet.

"You're thinking about *her*, aren't you?" Carmelita's strident voice was filled with outrage. "That spotted cow you dragged here from some pox-ridden brothel! You were mine, Lizzybetta! You gave me presents and promises. *Madre de Dios*! You owe me!"

"I owe you nothing, mistress grumbleguts." Bess shuddered slightly from the force of her rage. Her nails dug into her palms. "You took what I had to give, and then you demanded more and more and more, never satisfied. You tried to bleed me dry. You took lovers behind my back and swore to my face that you were faithful."

"I deserve a share of *Deceiver*'s treasure," Carmelita demanded. She stepped forward, feet crunching on the dry soil. "God damn you, Lizzybetta, I'll not let you give my share to that whey-faced *puta*! She deserves nothing! Nothing, I tell you! I'll slit her throat before—"

Unable to withstand the taunting any longer, Bess turned and grabbed Carmelita by the throat, taking some satisfaction from the woman's bulging, terror-filled eyes. Beneath her palm, the woman's pulse quickened to a ragged beat. "You have no right to anything of mine. If you come near me or Margo again," Bess rasped, "I'll kill you. Am I rightly understood, Lita?"

She gave her a shake and Carmelita mewled, her nails tearing at Bess' hands. Her face was swollen, nearly purple, when Bess finally threw her down to the ground. "Go find some other addle pated fool to torment, you damnable bitch!" Bess spat. "You're not worth the scrapings from my boots. If I had all the gold in Cádiz, I'd not spare you a copper groat!"

Carmelita coughed and gagged, a hand wrapped protectively around her bruised throat. In the depths of her dark eyes burned the fires of hatred. Her lips twisted but no sound emerged. Black hair straggled across her face. She staggered to her feet, swaying back and forth, a baleful glare fixed on Bess.

"You heard me!" Bess shouted, aiming a swat at Carmelita, which deliberately missed, but made her flinch and nearly fall down. "Leave me be, or by thunder, I'll tie a rock around your ankles and drop you in the harbor!"

Carmelita took to her heels, but not before making an obscene gesture. As soon as she disappeared, Solomon Lovelock pushed his way through the foliage at one side of the dirt road. The burly quartermaster's red mustache drooped on either side of his mouth, which was drawn into a tight peevish line. He stood with his tattooed arms folded over his massive chest.

"What in the blazing hell's wrong with you, Mister Lovelock? You look as though you've swallowed a live toad." Bess was in no mood to bandy words.

"Carmelita's my woman," Lovelock rumbled, "and I don't care to see her treated rough."

"Then control her, b'God! Keep her in irons and away from me!" Bess swept back the edge of her coat, clearing the hilt of her cutlass. "Have you a wish for blood, sirrah?"

Lovelock replied evenly, "Nay, Cap'n. 'Tis not my desire to fight, but I'll not see a woman of mine abused by another and stay silent."

Bess sighed, her belligerence melting in the face of the quartermaster's reasonable attitude. "Your protest is duly noted, Mister Lovelock."

"Thank 'ee kindly, Cap'n," the man answered. "If Carmelita gives further trouble, 'tis *my* duty to see it square, and none other's." His weather-beaten face set in an expression of resolve. "I love her, though God knows she has her faults. Yet I'd rather have her for a day and let her go free the rest of the year if I must, for I know she'll always come back to me in the end. That's why she's my duty. Carmelita's got none other to protect her, or make her do right when needful, savin' myself alone."

Bess strode forward and clapped him on the shoulder. It was like hitting a solid piece of oak; her fingers stung from the impact. "I beg your pardon for gettin' betwixt a man and his duty. However, I truly meant that I'll not tolerate her bitch's ways any longer."

"Fair enough. I'll speak with the lass. She'll not grieve you further, I swear." Lovelock marched off and was quickly swallowed up by the trees.

Bess ruffled a hand through her hair. She had not known that her quartermaster was in love with Carmelita. Had Lovelock been a jealous type, the Spanish woman's behavior could have had nasty consequences. She would not tolerate Carmelita's presence on the island if she stirred up fighting amongst the men.

If that poor, lovestruck wretch is happy with Carmelita's whorish ways, 'tis no concern of mine, Bess thought. *'Tis a sad misfortune, though, that Solomon cannot find a better woman. He's too good a soul for that conniving doxy.*

Bess shook her head. She decided to return to her house, in case Marguerite came looking for her. If not, she would surely seek her out before the day's end. They had much to discuss and much to confess, at least on Bess' side.

As she made her way home, Bess sniffed the air, frowning. She was a good judge of the unpredictable weather patterns in the Caribbean. There was a certain pressure in the air, a crisp hint of the air after lightning that bespoke gales. A storm brewing somewhere at sea. Bess judged the wind and decided it would probably blow inland. She hastened her steps, not wanting to get caught in the rain.

Marguerite made her way down to the beach, her thoughts in turmoil. She ached for Bess. Carmelita's triumphant smile was like acid, burning straight through flesh and bone, eating at her soul. Seeing Bess in another woman's arms had made her realize that she loved the pirate. It was ridiculous, it was impossible, yet there was no longer any way to deny her feelings. Nor, she thought, was there any further point to self-deception. That realization had been driven home with stunning force.

What made the situation even more appalling was the certain knowledge that she could never compete with Carmelita. The woman was simply too beautiful, too perfect in face and form, too carnal and too desirable. Why would Bess choose her, a freckled and frumpy thief, over the more delectable Spanish dish? Marguerite knew she had lost Bess forever, and that broke her heart. She thought she could actually feel the unhappy organ shivering to fragments that fell into the griping hollow of her belly, cold and sharp.

The pain she felt was incredible, considering that she and Bess had shared no more than a few kisses and caresses. Marguerite could find only the smallest comfort – the knowledge that ultimately her rejection would be avenged if the pirate failed to find the treasure she craved. That did not really make her feel any better. Instead, her mind kept circling back to Bess and Carmelita. The image of their embrace was indelibly etched into her brain.

Not that I had a chance, Marguerite thought, *for surely the captain was but wooing me to find a way to* Deceiver's grave *and a mountain of gold.* She felt no anger, no spark of fury – merely a deep sadness that made her want to weep.

Marguerite could not give in to tears, however. She was afraid that if she started crying, she would never stop but merely dissolve into a puddle of salty water. Avoiding a group of sailors and their sweethearts gathering up their picnic things on the beach, Marguerite turned her steps towards the rocky promontory that stuck out into the harbor. Waves dashed against the rough black stones, but she did not care if the glittering spray wet her. Solitude was what she desired most, and the promontory was abandoned at this late hour of the afternoon.

She picked her way over the jagged surface, using her hands for balance. Her palms and the bottoms of her bare feet were scraped raw by the time she reached the top. Marguerite felt the stings, but they were as nothing compared to the monstrous ache that throbbed in time to the beating of her heart.

All the fishing nets she had seen on the first day had been taken down, leaving only bare poles thrust into the rock. A piece of frilly green seaweed fluttered from the top of a pole like a banner, then was whipped away by the wind. Marguerite went to the very end of the promontory and sat down, dangling her feet over the edge. The skirts of her dress and her petticoat provided some padding, but the seat was still hard and uncomfortable. In a way, Marguerite welcomed the physical pain as a distraction from her gloomy thoughts.

Spray flung skyward and hung as mist in the air, accompanied by the jarring boom of waves as they crashed against the rocks and were thrown back to the sea. Marguerite blinked. Her cheeks were wet with spindrift, her eyes stung from the salt, and she was grateful for this substitute for more dangerous tears. The temperature had dropped in the last few minutes; her feet and hands felt frozen despite the heat of the day. The wind freshened. From a distance came a rolling growl, the sound of distant thunder. Having lived on an island in the Spanish Main all of her life, Marguerite knew the warning signs; she had just been too preoccupied to pay heed to them. She turned her face up and squinted at the sky, which had turned a deep gray that was darkening by the moment.

The sun had virtually disappeared behind a gathering mass of black thunderclouds rolling in fast from the southeast. They seemed to skim just above the ocean's surface, big-bellied and sullen. The waters of the harbor were agitated, the surf naught but white foaming crests that tumbled in and clawed at the beach without cease. Marguerite got to her feet, dread making her clumsy. This storm would be a bad one. There was a crackling flash of light, a kettledrum rumble of thunder, and the heavens opened wide. Rain smashed down in a solid curtain, a battering force that was akin to being struck by hundreds of tiny blows. Marguerite was instantly drenched to the skin.

A howling wind whipped her sodden skirts in a tangle around her legs as she struggled to return to the relative safety of the beach. Water ran in a blinding sheet over her face, fresh rain and salty sea co-mingling and stinging her eyes. Marguerite stumbled onwards, her feet torn by the rocks but too numb to register the wounds. She grasped a pole with both hands and clung to the support, her head bent against the gale. A huge wave came surging over the edge of the promontory and threatened to sweep her away.

Only her grip on the pole saved her from being snatched off the rocks and sucked out to sea.

Marguerite peered through the rain, trying to get her bearings. Sucking in moisture-laden air, she began struggling from pole to pole. The weight of her wet skirts hampered her movements; she had to be careful or she would trip and fall. Marguerite finally reached the last pole and clung to it, her strength nearly gone. Another storm-surge leaped over the promontory and caught her in the face. Surprised, Marguerite inhaled, then choked and spluttered, bitter water running from her nose and mouth. Deep coughs racked her frame. She drew in a breath with a whoop, trying to clear her lungs.

Another wave, bigger and more powerful than the rest, swept across the rocks. It smashed into Marguerite and tore her fingers away from the pole. She fell and struck her head. Crimson light flared behind her eyelids. Her lungs convulsed, a ripping pain in her chest. She was blind and deaf. She could not breathe.

Water and foam and darkness covered her face, and Marguerite knew no more.

CHAPTER SEVENTEEN
The Ghost Whisperer's Way

Bess passed Katla on her way home. She hailed the silver-haired woman and asked, "How is Mistress Margo?"

Katla looked surprised. "Is she not with you?"

"If she were," Bess answered, letting some of her irritation show, "I'd not be asking after her whereabouts, mistress."

"Margo went to search for you," Katla said. Her brows furrowed in a frown. "Haven't you seen her?"

Bess flushed, remembering the cold expression on Marguerite's face when she had witnessed Carmelita's lusty attack. "Aye, but she took to her heels afore we could magpie much."

At that moment, there was a blinding flash of lightning, and a torrential downpour broke over their heads. Both women scurried for cover on the verandah of a nearby house. They waited a few minutes, but the rain did not seem inclined to abate soon.

"Where the Devil is she?" Bess grated, fighting panicked concern. Marguerite would be safe if she was indoors, but what if she was wandering around in the forest? Her imagination supplied a variety of scenarios, each more fearful than the last. Hotspur Cay was nothing more than a settlement in the midst of a dangerous wilderness. Worry sent pangs shooting through her stomach. Bess tasted bile in the back of her throat.

There were no large predators on the island, but pitfalls, blown over trees, cliffs and other dangers awaited the unwary. Bess thought about Marguerite injured, her cries for help unheard, the mangled wreck of her body to be found later, those beautiful blue eyes staring sightlessly up at the sky. Bess clenched her jaw until her teeth ached.

Katla put a hand Bess' arm; the muscles were rigid with tension. "We'll find Margo," she shouted over the pounding roar of the rain.

Bess nodded in acknowledgement, but did not relax one whit. She stared into the middle distance as though she could conjure Marguerite through the force of her will alone. She cracked her knuckles, fidgeted and muttered, "I like this not, mistress. I'm going after her."

"By the sleet-cold hell," Katla said firmly, "don't do anything foolish! A solution's at hand. Stay here and don't go tearing off, or you're the one likely to be hurt."

"Don't rest your ass at anchor, then. Move!" Bess snapped. "I ain't waitin' much longer upon your convenience, mistress!"

Katla hurriedly left Bess and rapped on the door of the house. Hephzibah answered the summons, her blind eye glinting blue-white as milk in the darkness of her face. "Caught out in the rain, I see," said Hephzibah, nodding to the rune-singer as one professional to another.

"We need Leviticus," Katla said, her need too urgent for polite ceremony. "Margo's missing and needs to be found afore the captain starts ripping apart the island."

Hephzibah raised an eyebrow, but clearly recognizing that this was an emergency, called over her shoulder, "Leviticus! Come quick!"

A big man loomed up behind her. Like Hephzibah, he was an ex-slave, black-skinned but with pinkish-white patches spreading across his face and muscular arms that gave him a piebald look. They were not burn scars; the patches were too smooth, seemingly healthy skin despite their odd lack of color. Leviticus was Hephzibah's husband, and he, too, had a certain talent that earned him much respect among Hotspur Cay's community.

"What's the trouble?" Leviticus asked in a smooth baritone. He towered over his wife, who was not a small woman. "Somethin' need to be found?"

Hephzibah limped aside, her face glowing with obvious pride at her husband's skill. Leviticus came out onto the verandah, his head cocked as though listening to someone whispering in his ear. Bess reflected that he was, in fact, hearing voices. That was the piebald man's talent – to hear the spirits that constantly moved in the world around him, to control that flow of information and make the invisible watchers-of-the-world tell him what he needed to know, although the ghost whisperer's talent did not extend over bodies of water such as the ocean. As it was, he could locate lost objects or people with relative ease, provided they were on land and he knew what he was looking for.

Leviticus approached Bess and laid a hand roughly the size of a shovel blade on her shoulder. "If Mistress Margo is out there," he said, "I'll find her. Hephzibah says she's a good lady, and I can see you're twistin' yourself in knots with worry."

Bess gave the man a grateful look, though she was practically vibrating with impatience. "Thank 'ee kindly, Master Levi. I don't know what she's about. The wench ran off in a snit, and God knows where she might be sulking."

"Not only God." Leviticus tapped the side of his head. "Well, let's see what may be done."

He wore a shark's tooth on a thong around his neck. Leviticus gashed his thumb open on the sharp serrated edge, then rubbed the blood into his forehead. His piebald face was set in a grimace. His hand slowly rose, index finger extended. Leviticus closed his eyes tightly, visibly concentrating. The finger wavered in the air. Blood dripped from his thumb. His feet shuffled on the wooden boards of the verandah as he turned in a circle.

Bess watched the big black man, restraining herself from shouting or grabbing him by the collar of his shirt and shaking him. These things took as long as they required, and breaking his trance could prove fatal to him. She could feel the temperature plummet, the air growing steadily colder until her breath puffed between her lips in a stream of fog. An unlit lantern beside the door began to swing on its nail – *clank-clank-clank* – the movement had nothing to do with the wind. Just beyond the range of her hearing, Bess thought she could make out a susurration of voices. She shivered, knowing better than to try and pay attention to what the spirits were saying. That way led to danger for the uninitiated.

"The beach," Leviticus finally said, his eyes popping open. "She's on the beach." He pointed in the right direction. "Better hurry. They say she needs you."

Bess did not hesitate. She had heard enough to believe that her worst fears might be realized if she did not make haste. She pelted out into the rain, splashing through puddles in the dirt track that led to the harbor and the crescent-shaped beach. Dripping branches and leaves slapped her face as she ran, but Bess did not care about such petty concerns. The rain was a constant roar in her ears, a never-ending hammer ringing on her skull, yet all she heard was Marguerite's imaginary voice calling to her for help.

She burst out through the line of palms, her boots kicking up clumps of rain-soaked sand. Bess looked in every direction, finally spotting a swatch of limp blue fabric draped over the edge of the promontory. Waves burst apart on the jagged rocks. *Damnation! Margo must've fallen, she's no doubt hurt, please God let her not be dead!* Bess had visions of broken bones and much, much worse.

Although she had a stitch burning in her side, Bess hurried towards the promontory, fighting wind and lashing rain all the way. Somehow, she managed to scramble and stumble up the rocks, moving on pure instinct. Bess fell and rose and fell again, but never wavered from her goal – a huddle of sodden blue skirts, a mass of wet golden hair streaming over the rocks, a glimpse of white that might have been Marguerite's face.

It seemed like an eternity before she reached the woman. "Margo!" Bess shouted, kneeling down on the sharp stones, uncaring that the jagged rocks tore her breeches, and split her knees open till they bled. "By God, answer me, woman!"

Marguerite let out a low moan. She had a nasty cut on her brow, bloody but not serious, and scrapes on her cheekbone. Her eyes opened, gaze confused and wandering. She lifted her hand and touched her battered face, looking dazed.

"Get up!" Bess cried sharply, both relieved and dismayed by Marguerite's condition. The woman was not as badly hurt as she had feared, but was clearly in shock. Bess needed to get her to shelter as soon as possible. She had seen men die of trivial wounds like this, when they were left cold and untreated. Bess tugged at Marguerite's arm. She was strong, but not strong enough to carry a dead weight across the promontory. Bess used her best quarterdeck voice, trained to carry across a ship from stern to bow in the midst of an Atlantic gale. "Get on your feet, you bloody useless cow, or I swear by the sweet bleedin' Christ, I'll leave you here for the fishes to feast on!"

That captured Marguerite's attention. She squinted at Bess and said, "I am *not* a cow!" Her voice was weak but filled with a familiar tartness.

Bess very nearly wept from joy, relief, and a myriad of other emotions that jumbled together inside her mind. She wanted to hug Marguerite, kiss her, give her a sound smacking for running away and getting hurt...but all of those things would have to wait. "Then rise, milady laze-about, or are you waiting for your golden carriage with the diamond wheels?" she asked, grinning.

"Ooooh," Marguerite groaned, sitting up and clutching her head. "That hurts, *godskannonne*." The ache felt as though a hundred demons had taken up residence inside her skull and were lustily pounding iron horseshoes into her brain. Her stomach was none too happy, either. She covered her mouth, let out a sour belch, and fought back a wave of nausea.

The rain slackened, turning into a dull drizzle instead of a raging tempest. On the horizon, a rainbow arced from sea to sky. Just as abruptly as the storm had blown in, the clouds parted, and the sun reappeared in a blaze of white-gold that burned through the mist. Marguerite winced as the light stabbed at her eyes.

Chafing at the delay, Bess said, "Come along now, dear heart. You need to get dry. I'll help you; just take my arm."

Marguerite resisted a moment. She did not want or need the help of a damned pirate who had broken her heart and stamped gleefully on the pieces. Unfortunately, when she tried to rise, she had difficulty staying on her feet. The throbbing in her temples intensified, and her belly heaved. She gasped and nearly fell over. Bess quickly draped an arm over Marguerite's shoulder, supporting her as she swayed.

It was difficult, but Bess managed to get them both off the promontory and down to the beach. Marguerite was panting shallowly, trying not to vomit. This was worse than *mal de mer*. She thought that she had never felt so sick in her life. It took every ounce of effort she could dredge up not to collapse and die on the spot.

Marguerite whimpered and hung onto Bess' shoulder. Her stomach flip-flopped, making her dizzy. Cold sweat covered her skin. Her gorge rose. Marguerite finally lost the battle for control. She retched violently. A gush of salt water spewed out of Marguerite's mouth, splattering the sand. The situation reminded her of being seasick on *Mad Maudlin*, and she retched again until every muscle in her body was protesting.

Bess eased her down. "Get it all out, dear heart, for sea water's mortally bad for the digestion," she said, rubbing Marguerite's back; with her free hand, she gathered Marguerite's loose hair at the nape of her neck, holding it out of the way.

Marguerite's toes curled with the force of the next explosion. It was hard to believe that a human body could hold so much water and survive without foundering. Her head pounded; she thought her skull was going to be crushed under the weight of pain. She dug her fingernails into the sand as convulsions wracked her frame. Her mouth tasted like salt and acrid bile; she spat again and again, to be rid of the nauseating bitterness.

Finding a handkerchief, Bess used it to gently wipe Marguerite's face. She was careful to avoid the cut on her brow; it had started bleeding again, though sluggishly. "Can you walk to the settlement, dear heart? It's stopped raining."

Marguerite nodded, tried not to smell the stinking sour mess in front of her. She felt empty, drained of energy and almost drained of life. With Bess' help, she rose tottering to her feet. Holding one another, they moved along the muddy track while parrots squawked overhead, and a rainbow flickered behind them on the settling sea.

CHAPTER EIGHTEEN
A Stitch in Time

Halfway to the settlement, the women met Mistress Glasspoole, who had apparently been alerted by Katla. The herb-wife had a wooden box on a strap slung over her shoulder. When she spied Bess and Marguerite, Glasspoole sucked in her false teeth and moved towards them purposely, her full skirts flying and mobcap ribbons snapping, making her appear like a galleon under sail. She clicked her tongue in disapproval at the blood-stained rents in the knees of Bess' breeches. Her seamed face puckered into a grimace when she observed Marguerite, trembling and weak and drooping like a bruised lily.

"Neither of you has sense to come in out of the rain, by God," Glasspoole said scathingly, her dark-eyed gaze running up and down each of them. She softened a bit at Marguerite's hang-dog expression. "Well, the Good Lord made fools as well as wise men, and I suppose He knew what He was doing. Come with me and get dry, ladies, afore you come down with catarrh and the ague and the falling damps, to boot."

Glasspoole took Marguerite's other arm. Together she and Bess helped the young woman to the captain's house. Marguerite would have protested, but Glasspoole gave her an exceptionally fierce glare that made her close her mouth and decide that discretion was the better part of valor where the herb-wife was concerned.

Upon reaching the house, Glasspoole took charge and bullied her patients impartially, with no regard for their dignity or position. The gray-haired woman was a consummate professional, a master at her healing craft. It did seem, however, that she was reserving some particular vindictiveness when it came to Bess O'Bedlam.

At first, she relegated Bess to the sidelines as an observer only while Marguerite was stripped, settled into the sandalwood bed, and given a noxious brew to calm her upset stomach and throbbing head. Glasspoole also mixed up a hot compress of bran and herbs and slapped it on her bare chest where it steamed like a great green pudding. Marguerite did not complain; the heat felt good, and the herbs were quite pleasant smelling. She lay back with a mug of heavily sweetened tea cupped in her hands. Drowsiness made her eyelids heavy, and she sighed, content for the nonce.

Glasspoole gave Bess a different potion, which smelled and tasted, according to her, like week-old rat. "And I ought to know," she added, "since we were reduced to four-legged rations when *Mad Maudlin* was becalmed in the Dry Tortugas for a month entire." Bess tried to ease the tension with a bit of humor.

Glasspoole was not impressed. She snorted and handed Bess a second portion of the nasty stuff. "If you mean to take up a jester's trade, you'll be starved to a dry bone in a semnight. Now take off those breeches, and let me see what's left of your knees."

Bess complied, unwilling to argue when Glasspoole was in such a prickly mood. She took off her clothes and sat down, dressed solely in a nightshirt, and submitted to an examination. Glasspoole appeared to take great pleasure in probing her cuts with a series of dreadful chirurgical implements, each more painful than the last.

"To be sure 'tis clean and will heal properly," Glasspoole said, clashing her teeth together viciously, an ominous glint in her eyes.

Bess bore the extreme discomfort in silence, with teeth clenched and her jaw aching under the tension. At last, however, the herb-wife poured a stinging solution over both knees that made Bess jump and let out a ripe oath that rang round the room. The complaint went unnoticed, for Glasspoole merely tied bandages around her abused joints and turned again to tend to Marguerite.

"Yon split in your scalp requires stitching, Margo," the herb-wife said in her no-nonsense fashion. "'Twill be painful, and you mustn't move, but I'll do my best to keep the scar small."

Marguerite sat up, extremely apprehensive. She watched Glasspoole take a needle and thread it with catgut. "Is this truly necessary?" She had always enjoyed good health in the past, never needing to visit doctors or quacksalvers or apothecaries for their dubious cures, except for the time in Antigua she had been belly-sliced. Marguerite had heard stories, though, of agonies that made her blood run cold.

"Do I seem the sort to enjoy torturing folks?" Glasspoole replied, though she eyed Bess as if daring her to answer. She laid the needle aside and took up a bowl of warm water to which she added several ingredients from her medical box. "As for you, Captain, please be so kind as to get into bed with Margo. You'll need to hold her, for her leaping about like a toad on a hot skillet will make the matter worse and delay proper treatment."

Bess climbed into the carved sandalwood bed with misgivings. The dragon's heads on the tall posts seemed to be leering down at her. Noting the way Marguerite stiffened, Bess remained on top of the blanket, although she would rather have taken off the nightshirt and joined the naked woman underneath. She cuddled close to Marguerite and brushed a lock of damp hair back from her freckled face.

"If you must scream, dear heart, there's no shame in it," Bess said lightly, trying to put Marguerite more at ease. "I've seen grown men wail like newborns under Mistress Glasspoole's knife."

Marguerite's terror grew exponentially. Despite her belief that Bess cared nothing for her, she clutched at the woman's lean form, seeking whatever scrap of emotional support she could find to carry her through the coming ordeal. She did not mind at all when Bess rubbed her collarbone and murmured soothingly.

"Oh, now that's a strange comfort, you lumbering booby!" Glasspoole gave Bess a glare. She set down a bottle of spirits with a thump. "Why don't you lull Margo to sleep with tales of amputations and inguinal hernias and cauterizations? The girl needs strength, not more nightmares. Cease your rattle-trapping; just hold her and give her your hand."

Glasspoole took the mug away from Marguerite and brought a stool and a small table which she put beside the bed. She placed a bowl of steaming, herb-scented water on the table, along with the threaded needle, the bottle of spirits, an earthenware pot of ointment, jars of powders, and a heap of clean lint. She sat down on the stool, saying, "Margo, I beg that you'll relax as much as you're able. When it hurts, squeeze the captain's hand. Have no concern for splintering bones; the captain's as tough as old boot leather."

Marguerite swallowed hard, following Glasspoole's every movement with breathless dread. The herb-wife used lint and her herbal infusion to cleanse the wound, which stung like fire. She sprinkled the cut with various powders, and finally took up her needle.

Despite being braced for it, the first stitch came as a very unpleasant surprise. Marguerite inhaled at the sharp prick and squeezed Bess' fingers. It was a very horrid sensation – the needle thrusting through skin and muscle, the point delicately scraping the bone of her skull, to be followed by the slithering thread, and another spark of pain as the needle dipped through the other side. Glasspoole drew the edges together and tied them off in a neat knot, snipping away the trailing end of the thread. She dabbed the wound with more lint and repeated the process, while Marguerite smothered her yelps and tried not to cry. It took six small, careful stitches in all to close the wound, but to her it felt more like six hundred.

Each time Marguerite bit her lip and flinched, Bess was filled with sympathy. She wished that it was herself suffering under the needle. Bess forgot about her own injuries, minor though they were, because she was focused entirely on Marguerite. The hand she held spasmed, and Bess crooned under her breath, put her face close to the woman's cheek and tried to lend what comfort she could.

Glasspoole worked silently and swiftly. Since there were no truly effective anesthetics or numbing agents, speed was the chirurgeon's method to spare prolonging a patient's agony. When she was finished, the herb-wife cleansed the area with raw spirits – causing Marguerite to let out a choked cry as the stuff burned like the flames of hell – and smeared the wound with a cool ointment that would also serve to help the flesh heal cleanly.

That task completed, Glasspoole cleaned the cuts and scrapes on Marguerite's palms and the soles of her feet, smearing them with wound balm. None of the injuries were serious enough to warrant further treatment. She tucked Marguerite back under the blanket, and slid a small hops-pillow beneath the bolster at her head to help her sleep.

"Keep your brow dry and clean," Glasspoole said, "and don't scratch the stitches, howsoever they may itch. I'll come by each morning to make sure the wound hasn't begun to fester, and I'll leave a jar of balm on my way out, which you're to use every day without fail. If there's pus or you tear the stitches, you'll come to me straight away, yes?"

She waited until Marguerite nodded her understanding, then stood, washed her hands and gathered up her supplies. She tossed the bloody water in the bowl out of the open window. A hiss rose from beneath the frangipani; the cat Paddyshank seemed to have caught some of the deluge. The vines rustled as he fled, grumbling. Glasspoole closed her medical box and crooked a finger at Bess. "A word under the rose, if you please."

Bess reluctantly got out of the bed and followed Glasspoole, who drew her to one side. "Mistress Margo's inhaled a mort of sea water," Glasspoole said with her customary whistles, "and may develop a lung complaint. If she comes over feverish in the night, send to my house at once or summon Master Janus to apply anti-pyretics."

"Aye, I'll do that," Bess replied. She thought of a question and asked, "Whyfor did not Margo's tattoo crawl with witch-fire when she was doused by waves out on the promontory? It took but a drop of saltwater in Katla's shop for the magic to come tearing out like the wrath of God Almighty Himself."

Glasspoole's brow wrinkled in thought. "Mayhap," she answered slowly, "on account of Margo's bleeding – the curse has somewhat to do with blood, I believe – but I'm no thaumaturge, Captain. My learning don't lean in that direction."

"I'll wait upon Speedwell, then." Bess studied the older woman for a moment. "It seems to me that I've done somewhat to rouse your ire, mistress."

The herb-wife drew herself up to her full height, which was still a head shorter than Bess. Nevertheless even Bess, a hardened pirate, did not wish to defy her. "I've no notion what you mean," Glasspoole sniffed, "for surely I treat all my patients the same, madam, be they sinner or saint."

"As you'll have it, mistress," Bess said, deciding not to press the issue. Whatever was bothering Glasspoole would be revealed in her own good time, and not a moment before. "Is there aught else I can do for Margo?"

"Keep her quiet, and let her rest. If she's hungry or thirsty, let her eat and drink, but nothing stronger than well-watered wine. And for the sake of our dear Lord Jesus, don't start any of your famous temper fits, Captain!" Glasspoole's voice rose; she made a clear effort to lower it again, though her tone lost none of its urgency. "Margo's in a fragile state and she needs to heal, not spend her energies fighting with you. She's had a bad shock, and if she's not allowed some peace, her condition may worsen. Don't argue with the girl, just humor her if she becomes contentious. 'Twill be but for a little while. You can tear her to pieces when she's well, if that's your pleasure."

Bess swelled with indignation. "I've never ill-treated Margo," she started to say, and stopped when she realized that this was not strictly true. She continued more contritely, "'Tis good advice, and I'll take it. You need not be concerned, mistress."

"Good. See that you follow it to the letter." Glasspoole took up her medical box and left, the ribbons of her lawn mobcap fluttering behind her.

When they were alone, Bess moved toward the sandalwood bed. Marguerite lay there, looking very small and delicate among the bedclothes and bolsters. A sharp pang shot through her breast when Bess considered that she might have lost Marguerite that day. On the other hand, now that the woman was more or less locked into place and unable to run away, she could finally have a talk with her.

Bess rehearsed what she was going to say, re-arranging the words and phrases in her head until she was satisfied. She would explain about Carmelita, and tell Marguerite that there was nothing between herself and the Spanish doxy. She also intended to reveal the innermost secret of her heart – that she wanted and needed Marguerite. If nothing else, the woman's peril that day had settled the question for Bess once and for all.

The high-spirited Dutch beauty was, to Bess' point of view, the only fitting mate for the Water Witch. She felt a sense of relief, as though some invisible chain shackling her soul had snapped and set her free. The warring halves of her consciousness united. She had committed herself, now and in the future, to Marguerite alone. It was such a simple decision, yet also the most profound choice Bess had ever made.

Am I in love? I can't swear a holy oath to it, but 'tis the closest thing I know.

She opened her mouth to speak but was forestalled by a soft, ladylike snore from the bed. Marguerite, worn out from the exertions and traumas of the day, had fallen fast asleep.

Bess smiled. She tip-toed to the side of the bed and drew the counterpane over the blanket covering Marguerite so she would not get chilled during the night. She thoughtfully left the necessary pot nearby, and put a jug of water on a stand close at hand. After that, she quietly left the room so as not to disturb Marguerite's slumber.

She paused at the doorway. "Pleasant dreams, dear heart." Another soft snore answered her.

Bess chuckled and walked out of the bedchamber.

Marguerite awoke the next morning, feeling disoriented and very sore. Every muscle in her body was stiff and ached as though she had been beaten with rods. Her feet throbbed furiously. There was a strange, rigid pain in her brow – not precisely a headache, but something else. She touched her face and recalled the stitches she had endured. The catgut knots felt rough beneath her questing fingers, the flesh slightly swollen and warm.

She lifted a lock of her hair and grimaced. The golden locks were snarled and gummed with salt. Marguerite thought longingly of the Widow Thorpe's bath-house and sighed for her own discomfort. She stretched, winced as muscles protested, and pushed back the blanket. It was too hot in the room, too humid for comfort; she was covered in a sheen of sticky sour sweat, and she did not smell very fresh, either.

Dappled sunlight filtered into the room from the open windows, which were screened by broad-leafed banana plants, frangipani and masses of hot pink bougainvillea. From somewhere outside, she heard the raucous screeching of parrots, one of the wild flocks that lived on the island. Across the room, a yellow-throated orchid growing in a blue-and-white glazed Delft pot had attracted the attention of a dusky-winged moth. The ever present, spicy-sweet scent of frangipani was joined by the smoky smell of sandalwood from the bed. The odor reminded her of Bess. Marguerite's heart thumped painfully.

Bess came to save me, she thought, *when she could have let me to die.* There was a glimmer of hope in the notion. Could the pirate really care for her?

Ah, said a more cynical inner voice, *but she needs your tattoo to find the treasure, or so she believes. Your dead body is worthless to her.*

This, too, was true. Marguerite frowned. *But she was so kind to me yester'eve, when I was hurt and needed comfort. She held my hand.*

The cynic replied, *The pirate means to keep you sweet so you'll lead her to the fortune. 'Tis not you that tempts her, but gold alone. Her wooing was false.*

So was mine, in the beginning! Marguerite argued with herself. *I sought to seduce her, to make her drop her guard so that I could escape.*

And you're the one ended caught fast in the trap! Did you not see her kissing Carmelita? the inner voice taunted. *What a lusty embrace! 'Tis clear they've been lovers for some time. How the pirate must have laughed, to see you so moonstruck that you'd swallow her tricks and let yourself be gulled like an innocent newly born!*

And that was the telling blow that won the debate. Marguerite would never forget the awful agony of witnessing the torrid embrace between Bess and Carmelita. Her heart had been rent to shreds, her resolve torn asunder. Marguerite loved Bess O'Bedlam, and at the same time, knew that the pirate captain was as far beyond her reach as the sun itself. Her grief was a fresh wound, bleeding freely, never to be healed. She could not work up any resentment over the way she had been used, since she realized that she had been an eager participant in the game of manipulation.

Nevertheless, Marguerite still had her pride. She would rather die a thousand deaths than reveal just how much Bess' treachery had hurt her. The woman would never know her secret – she would see to that. When Bess came into the room bearing a tray, Marguerite arranged her features into a mask of indifference.

"'Tis a grand day," Bess said upon entering, and halted in her tracks at the sight of Marguerite's naked body. The woman was voluptuously curved, the soft swells of her flesh peppered with freckles that Bess longed to trace with kisses. The scar on her abdomen was a slash of gleaming silver across pale skin. Tiny beads of sweat coated her skin like pearls. Even with her hair in a tangled mess, she was beautiful. Marguerite did not seem to be troubled by her nudity, so Bess adopted a casual air.

"There's ham and fresh bread and an egg to break your fast," Bess said, going to the bed and placing the tray across Marguerite's legs. "There's coffee as well, and I picked a mango for you. I hope 'tis to your taste."

Marguerite said, "Thank 'ee kindly," and nothing more. She wished Bess would go away, but knew that she would have to endure the unwanted presence, since a protest would have revealed too much of her private pain.

"You'll want to wash, so I've ordered the cook to heat water," Bess continued, wondering what was wrong. She had expected a variety of reactions, from thrown crockery and curses, to tears and defiance, perhaps even gratitude. This cool reception was disconcerting from a woman whom she knew had no difficulty expressing her feelings.

Again, Marguerite thanked the pirate. She made no move to eat or engage in further conversation.

Bess took a step away from the bed, came back and stared down at Marguerite. "Is aught amiss, mistress?" she asked with a worried frown.

"Nay, I am quite well," Marguerite replied primly.

"Be you fevered?" Bess touched Marguerite's brow with the backs of her fingers. It felt a little warm, but not alarmingly so. "In pain?"

"A trifle sore here and there," Marguerite admitted. "'Tis bearable, though, and to be expected." The smells from the tray made her mouth water. She picked up the heavy silver knife and fork, cut off a sliver of ham and ate it. The meat was salty but good, a nice accompaniment to the fried egg on the plate. Amazingly, her appetite was not at all daunted by disappointment. She was very hungry, and even Bess looming over her like a statute did not stop her from enjoying the meal.

Bess eyed her a few moments, disturbed by Marguerite's display of coolness but unwilling to push the matter or demand an explanation. Mistress Glasspoole had been very explicit – under no circumstances was she to upset Marguerite. *At least she's not spleenish*, Bess thought, although she would have preferred shouting and swearing and hurling crockery to this unnatural calm. It was almost frightening. "Well, I'll leave you in peace then," Bess said, shuffling her feet.

Marguerite swallowed a mouthful of coffee. "Good day, Captain."

The implication of dismissal was clear, yet Bess hesitated. "I'll fetch you when the bath's ready."

"Once more, I thank you," Marguerite said politely. She speared a slice of mango with her fork and bit into the fruit. Juice ran down her chin; she wiped it off with her hand.

Unable to think of any further excuse for delay, and unwilling to crack Marguerite's brittle shell at the moment, Bess took her leave. *There'll be time enough later to tell her all I wish to say*, she thought. *For now, I'll let my poor sweetheart rest.*

Behind her, Marguerite finished her breakfast, then let the fork drop with a clatter, not caring that the heavy cutlery took a chip out of the edge of the plate. She put her head in her hands, pressing her palms against her eyelids until red and silver spots danced in the darkness. *God give me strength!*

If she had to face Bess on a daily basis, Marguerite thought she might go mad without any help from the otherworld at all.

CHAPTER NINETEEN
Speedwell Interruptus

After Marguerite had bathed and washed her hair with the help of Mistress Glasspoole, who had come to examine her wounds, she dressed in a loose pink silk gown and made her way, with the healer's help, out to the verandah. The bottoms of her feet were puffy, too sore to bear much weight. Glasspoole gave her a pair of soft slippers, which helped but did not quite alleviate all the discomfort; still, it was better than nothing.

Marguerite sank down into a chair, arranging the folds of her skirt and folding back the cuffs of her sleeves. The gown's bodice dipped alarmingly, showing off an indiscrete amount of her swelling décolletage, and she could not find a shift to wear underneath. She hitched at the neckline, wishing it did not expose quite so much of her bosom.

Bess came out onto the verandah, puffing a cheroot. She smiled at the sight of Marguerite. The splendor of the woman's creamy, freckled breasts was all but revealed by the low-cut gown. She could even spy a delicate slice of rosy nipple peeping over the edge. In her opinion, Marguerite looked like one of God's naughtier angels, with her golden hair pinned up and several softly curling locks left free to brush her shoulders.

Dismayed by this intense scrutiny, Marguerite cast an imploring glance at the herb-wife, but Mistress Glasspoole took her leave, promising to return the next day. She left Marguerite alone with Bess. Unsettled, Margo picked at a ruffle of lace on her skirts and avoided the pirate's steady gaze. Perhaps if she did not acknowledge Bess, her pain would lessen. Silence stretched between them, broken only by bird-song from the hanging cage.

At last, unable to bear that quiet scrutiny any longer, Marguerite asked softly, "When will we be leaving to find *Deceiver*'s treasure?"

The unexpected question startled Bess, but recalling that Marguerite had pledged her support to the endeavor, she replied, "Captain Speedwell's due back soon with the *Red Queen's Revenge*, and Sullivan on the *Swiftsure*. I'll want the full fleet gathered together afore we go."

Marguerite nodded. She had not forgotten Katla's assessment of her charmed tattoo – that it would drive her to madness and death if not allowed to fulfill its purpose. Her time was limited. "Will Captain Speedwell return within a moon or so?"

"Aye, I expect her in less'n a fortnight," Bess said, narrowing her gray eyes. She flicked ash from the tip of her cheroot. "Are you in a tearing hurry for a sea voyage, mistress?"

"'Twas naught but curiosity," Marguerite replied. She did not think that Bess understood the seriousness of her cursed condition and was loathe to confess it. She thought she could endure the woman's pretended affection, but her pity would be too much to bear.

"How's your head, mistress?" Bess asked, leaning a hip on the verandah rail.

Marguerite looked down at her hands, folded together in her lap. "Well enough."

"I've asked Mister Dunn to continue your readin' lessons," Bess said, taking a puff from her cheroot. She was standing very close to Marguerite and took some wicked delight in her view down the woman's bodice. "Levalier's willing to teach you more knife-work when you're able. You'll have to grow some new skin on your feet first."

"I suppose so," Marguerite answered diffidently.

Baffled by Marguerite's attitude, Bess crushed the cheroot between her fingers and threw it over the rail. She had little patience with small talk; the social graces were not really among her accomplishments. Bess took a deep breath as a hideous foreboding emerged – she wondered if perhaps Marguerite had not sustained some deeper injury in her misadventure. The woman seemed changed, all her inner fire banked and turned to ash.

"Are you certain that you feel aright?" Bess asked, an almost plaintive note in her voice.

"I am quite well," Marguerite replied. She cast a sidelong glance at the woman, but did not care to ask Bess the reason for her solicitude. She already knew the answer to that question. It was a lie, a ruse, to ensnare her further into the treasure hunt. A lump rose in her throat, and she held back tears by sheer willpower. Marguerite did not understand why Bess was continuing the charade, since she had already vowed her willingness to assist. She supposed Bess simply could not rest until her conquest was complete.

"Well, then, 'tis time for a palaver betwixt me n' thee," Bess said, tugging at the bottom of her waistcoat. "There's somewhat I wish to tell you, Margo." She cleared her throat, suddenly nervous. It was one thing to charm a port-town doxy into a dalliance, quite another to express her true feelings. Especially when the object of her affection was sitting as still a marble statue with a look of stoic disinterest frozen on her face.

Bess went on resolutely, "I ain't never had a woman like you, and I couldn't wish for better. You're a hell-cat at times, but by God, I find myself wantin' more'n a kiss and a tumble." Again, she coughed, cried impatiently, "Oh, damnation to my soul! I'll speak it plain and be done with it – will you stay with me, Margo? Share my bed and my life?"

Marguerite cringed. She did not want to hear any more. She wished her feet were not swollen and painful, so she could run away into the trees and not be tempted by these sweet lies. It would be easy to believe that Bess was sincere. She would let go her resolve in an instant, fly into Bess' arms and allow herself to be taken. Nay, not a ravishment – she knew that she would eagerly participate, giving and taking with equal pleasure. Marguerite tried to formulate a reply and failed. She did not speak at all while a hundred excuses whirled around in her mind, each sounding more pathetic and unbelievable than the last.

Mistaking her silence for surprise, or perhaps shock, Bess said, "I ain't going to force myself on you, mistress. If you can't... I just thought..."

Suddenly, Jim Monk came running along the dirt path. "*Speedwell's* come to harbor, Cap'n!" the boy shouted in excitement. "*Red Queen's* home with the marks of a brawl! She's hurt, Cap'n, and there ain't no sign of *Swiftsure!*"

Bess' head snapped up. "By the sweet bleedin' Christ!" she said fervently, anger at the interruption warring with impatience to be gone. Something must have happened to Captain Sullivan and the *Swiftsure*, or Lettice Speedwell's vessel would not have returned alone. Bess had to find out – it was her duty as leader of the pirate fleet.

She took a step away from the rail, and jerked to a halt. Her hand reached out towards the seated woman. "Margo, there's aught amiss and I must see to it."

"I know," Marguerite said. She was astonished at how much relief she felt at the delay.

"I beg your pardon," Bess said hastily. "I swear, dear heart, I won't take long. When I return, we'll speak on this at length."

Marguerite closed her eyes and nodded. Bess wasted not another moment, but bounded down the steps and left at a trot, headed for the harbor. When Marguerite opened her eyes, a single tear slid down her cheek. She wiped it away with her fingertips and stared in front of her, lost in thought, trying to decide what to do.

Should she tell Bess that she knew about the lies, convince her there was no more need of them? That would be difficult without revealing her own heartbreak. Should she submit quietly and take whatever crumbs of affection, however false, fell to her from the captain's table? Doing so would mean a pseudo-feast that would starve a skeleton. Her soul withered at the thought. On the other hand, she would at least find an illusion of happiness, however long it took for Bess to tire of the game and cast her aside.

Marguerite could not make a decision. All her choices seemed equally odious. And she was tired, so very tired of fighting and scheming for survival. She just wanted to rest a little while. If she could not escape Hotspur Cay, she could leave her sorrows behind in sleep.

She closed her eyes and drowsed in the chair, her dreams haunted by a chestnut-haired pirate who owned a heart that was as cold and unyielding as steel.

Bess stood on the beach with her hands clasped behind her back, gazing at the *Red Queen's Revenge*. Teams of sailors had laboriously hauled the ship into shallow waters until her keel rested aground. The former French frigate, a 60-gun ship captured by Speedwell herself years ago, had been ravaged in some fierce battle. Her mainmast was gone, although a spare mast had been lashed to the stump as a temporary measure. A gaping wound in her side, perilously close to the waterline, had been fothered with a spare sail. There were long scorch marks, more cannon holes and wreckage to the decks, rigging and remaining masts, and evidence of lead shot in her splintered planks. The ship's stern was chewed up as well, half the gallery windows a shattered mess, though the damage was not as great as if *Revenge* had suffered raking fire from an enemy who had the weather gage.

Captain Lettice Speedwell stood beside Bess. She was propped up on a make-shift crutch, her left leg swathed in bandages. "Look at her!" Speedwell said, her face mottled scarlet and white with rage. "See what that whoreson Sullivan did to my ship!"

Bess had to crane her neck to look up at Speedwell, who stood nearly seven feet tall. Her unusual Amazonian physique was equally impressive; the giantess was capable of tearing a man limb from limb with her bare hands alone, a feat that Bess had seen demonstrated during a battle with a Dutch herring-buss in the Horse Latitudes. The only one capable of matching her in strength on the island was Hephzibah's husband, the ghost whisperer Leviticus, and even he was shorter than Speedwell by a more than a head.

"Why did he do it?" Bess asked, hardly able to believe the enormity of the treachery, in spite of the evidence in front of her eyes. "Sullivan swore a binding oath, by God!"

Speedwell gulped a breath of air and made an effort to calm herself. Behind steel-rimmed spectacles, her brown eyes seemed enormous. "Simply put, Sullivan betrayed us because of greed, damn his Judas soul to eternal torment in the ninth circle of hell!" She blinked and took another breath. Sunlight turned her red hair into a blaze of copper except for two broad silver streaks that swept back from her temples.

"We plundered a frigate off Carolina, a payroll ship loaded with silver coin that had strayed from its convoy," Speedwell went on. "'Twas a rich haul, as they were also carrying furs, tobacco, rice, indigo and cotton. *Red Queen* had a full cargo on board, so *Swiftsure* took it on. I suspected nothing, madam. Nothing! Not until he fired upon me without warning, broadsides and musket balls that killed or injured half my crew in the first few volleys, and well-nigh crippled my ship. It was all I could do to get away before he sank us entirely."

"Sullivan's crew, most of them have families here, loved ones and such," Bess murmured, shaking her head. She fingered the five gold rings in her earlobe. "I can't believe he convinced them to mutiny 'gainst me."

"I believe Sullivan abandoned his regular crew in some port – most likely Nassau – and hired dockside dregs to replace them." Speedwell gritted her teeth, shifted her weight to the uninjured leg. "We've been at sea for two months. Our courses separated us for days on a few occasions. We had a successful run; that frigate was but the last of our plunder. I imagine that *Swiftsure* has enough cargo in her hold to make Sullivan a wealthy man."

"He won't live to spend a groat," Bess promised, a savage fire burning in the depths of her gray eyes. "We'll find that son of a she-dog and call an oathbreaker's curse upon his miserable head. Jack Sullivan will be worm's meat afore the next moon, I swear."

Speedwell nodded. She shifted her gaze to watch Mistress Glasspoole and Master Janus attending injured sailors from the *Red Queen's Revenge.* "Our chirurgeon was killed," she remarked. "Poor fellow bled to death when a ball took off most of his thigh."

"You're not whole yourself, Letty." Bess reached up and patted the giant woman's shoulder. Speedwell's muscles felt like iron beneath the soiled shirt. "Let's haul you off to the surgery afore mortification sets in."

"Have Charles and Allegra meet us there," Speedwell said, glancing down at Bess. "I can't sail with you on account of this bedamned leg, but by Baphomet's beard, I mean to help you catch the bloody-handed treacher! And my crew...brave lads and lassies, every one. I'll pay them a bonus out of my own shares, blood-money that will come from Sullivan's hide."

"I'll add to that myself," Bess said. She paused. "What was the butcher's bill?" she asked softly, knowing this would be an exceptionally sore spot. Unique among the pirate fleet, Speedwell's crew was more like an extended family, with herself as the matriarch of a loyal and devoted clan. Several years ago, the giantess had pledged herself and her clan to Bess, and the two had a good strong friendship, based on mutual respect and trust.

"Twenty-five dead," Speedwell said, pain etching her face. "Thirty wounded. Among those, there are five whose injuries are so grievous, they will never go to sea again." Her lips twisted. "Sullivan will pay dearly for that as well."

"We'll see to them all. Let me send someone to fetch Byng and Quittam, then I'll get you settled in the surgery." Bess leaned over slightly and sniffed at the bandages on Speedwell's leg. "Smells somewhat corrupt."

Speedwell wrinkled her nose. "I was a trifle distracted by a sinking ship and a crew that was blasted to pieces." She adjusted her spectacles and took a fresh hold on her crutch. "Well, there's naught I can do here save fret myself into a state. Lead on, O'Bedlam. I could use a tot of rum and a dainty collation. The galley was smashed to a splinter; we've been gnawing weevil's wedding cake for eight days, and my stomach thinks my throat's been cut."

Bess summoned Jim Monk, sent him to deliver a message to Captains Byng and Quittam. As soon as the boy left on his errand, she led the giantess towards the settlement. Speedwell followed, grunting and cursing under her breath with every agonizing step.

CHAPTER TWENTY
Sauce for the Goose

Mistress Glasspoole unwrapped the rags serving as bandages around Speedwell's leg. The top layer was relatively clean, but as she got closer to the wound, blood and other, nastier fluids fouled the linens. The last layer of linen had to be soaked off with hot water. Speedwell sat rigidly upright on a bed in the surgery, her back braced against the wall, her injured limb supported by bolsters. Sweat beaded her brow, and she looked grim.

Marguerite was there as well, pressed into service to assist the herb-wife since she had a bit of sick-bay experience from her time aboard *Mad Maudlin*. Her sore feet had been slathered with a salve – courtesy of the other physician, Janus, who was busy in the next room tending to a feverish sailor – and further cushioned with a layer of felt in the soles of her slippers. Marguerite gagged at the awful stench rising from Speedwell's stained linens, and averted her eyes, not wishing to see the suppurating wound.

Bess, who was standing nearby, did not turn a hair. She had seen – and smelled, when it came to that – far worse over the years. Frederick Byng paced restlessly to and fro, worrying the gilt buttons on his splendid champagne satin *justaucorps* coat. Allegra Quittam grabbed the tails of his garment and made him sit down in a chair.

"Keep your ass at anchor, Freddie," Quittam growled, the blonde quiffs covering her head seeming to bristle even more than usual. "All that rabbitin' about is making me dizzy, by God. One more turn around the floor and I'll be tempted to cut you off at the knees." She fingered the hilt of her cutlass, scowling at the man.

Byng stayed seated but began to tap the floor with the toe of his diamond-buckled shoe. "Sullivan's defection baffles my reason, madam. Surely he realizes we will redress the insult with force. Although if you recall, I was against giving him command of the *Swiftsure* after Captain Pettyworth's unfortunate demise. Sullivan is an absolute braggadoccio who ought to have been anathematized at birth with bell, book and candle."

"Stuff that red rag back behind your teeth, Freddie. Sullivan was Pettyworth's first mate, he swore the oath like the rest of us," Bess said with a frown, watching the color drain from Speedwell's face. "There ain't no use cryin' beef after the cow's been lifted."

Marguerite made a choked sound, her lips clenched together as she tried not to disgrace herself by vomiting.

"If you're going to turn your tripes inside out, Margo, don't do it on my patient," Glasspoole muttered, peeling away the final bandage. "I'll have silence from the rest of you gogglers or I'll put a flea in your ears that you'll not soon forget."

The wound was in Speedwell's upper thigh, a deep gash that had torn through muscle but avoided the artery. It was about a hand's breath long and badly infected, oozing yellowish matter. The surrounding flesh was bright red and swollen tight; the wound itself was very puffy, the edges almost closed shut. Glasspoole probed expertly with her fingertips. Speedwell hissed. Behind the spectacles, her eyes squeezed shut.

Glasspoole held out her hand. "A bistoury, mistress, if you please."

Marguerite gave her the sharp steel instrument. At the herb-wife's direction, she held a wad of lint close to the wound, although she still could not bring herself to look directly at it. Instead, she glanced at Speedwell, who had opened her eyes and was looking back at her.

She felt herself flushing when the giantess murmured, "I must have died and gone to Paradise, for here's one of God's own angels at my bedside to attend upon my hour of need."

Bess was immediately alarmed. Like herself, Lettice Speedwell was a lover of women. Her sheer size, coupled with an erudite manner and devilishly fatal charm, were powerful attractors. Speedwell never lacked for lovers, whether at home or abroad – in fact, she was as famous for her romantic conquests as her fighting skills and intellectual accomplishments.

The last thing Bess wanted was to battle her oldest and dearest friend. On the other hand, she did not intend to stand by quietly and watch Speedwell poach away the woman she intended to make her mate. Bess did not like the way Marguerite responded to Speedwell's considerable charisma, either. That green-eyed serpent, jealousy, reared up and fastened its fangs into her breast.

She took a convulsive step forward, about to do or say something, and stopped. Objecting at this point would make her look ridiculous. Bess settled for glowering at the red-headed giantess. *One of God's angels, indeed!* In her agitation, she forgot that she had made a similar comparison only that morning.

Working swiftly, Glasspoole used the bistoury to cut a clean slice into Speedwell's thigh wound. A spurt of creamy yellow matter erupted, caught by Marguerite on the soft wadded lint. Speedwell went rigid but made no sound other than a series of grunts. Tiny muscle tremors attested to the agony she endured.

The stench was unbelievable, but Glasspoole continued working without regard for the sickening smell. She manipulated the wound, extracting more infected material. By the time nothing but clean blood emerged, Marguerite's complexion was whiter than Speedwell's, but she controlled herself and did not flinch from her duty.

Glasspoole snapped more orders. She washed the sluggishly bleeding gash thoroughly with strong wine, then with a warm tisane of marigold flowers and goldenseal. Speedwell clutched the bedclothes and gargled deep in her throat when the herb-wife thrust a thin surgical probe into the wound. A fresh spate of dark crimson blood poured out. Glasspoole's hands, with their prominent veins and gnarled knuckles, worked the probe delicately. Her seamed face wrinkled further in concentration. She pushed her false teeth in and out absently while she worked.

Unable to withstand the pain any longer, Speedwell half reared off the bed. Glasspoole snapped, "Be still, for the Good Lord's sake! You'd not thank me if I made it worse." She amended her tone at the clenched strain on the big woman's face. "'Twill be over soon, lass. There's an irritant caught within, and it must be extracted. May I continue?"

Sweating and pale, Speedwell nodded. "Your pardon," she croaked. "Pray go on."

"Jesus Christ Almighty!" whispered Quittam, her eyes huge with horror and fascination. Bess glanced at her and she subsided, rubbing a hand over her blonde quiffs.

Glasspoole continued her probing. She bent her head over the wound, absently trailing the tip of a mobcap ribbon through some of the blood. The white satin became smeared with crimson, matching the spots on her apron.

Marguerite had moved to a worktable and begun mixing up a special poultice following the herb-wife's directions. She had previously prepared a decoction of comfrey root, kept hot in a pot over the flames of the fireplace. To the mucilage, she added wound wort, lady's mantle and a good pinch of ground wood betony, being careful to avoid inhaling the last as it would cause violent sneezing. She stirred a few spoonfuls of honey into the mixture, then carried the steaming pot to the bed.

The herb-wife clacked her teeth in triumph and withdrew the probe. In its tip was a sliver of bloodied steel. "From the cutlass that bit you!" she cackled, showing the piece to Speedwell. She threw the sliver and the probe into a porcelain bowl, which rang like a bell at the impact. "Now for the last," Glasspoole said, "and I'll leave you to rest." She slathered the herbal concoction in the pot on the open wound, drawing the edges together when she had finished. Marguerite placed clean spider webs, gathered that morning, over the site of the injury. With Glasspoole issuing instructions, she put a handful of sphagnum moss on the wound, then wrapped the whole tree-trunk thigh with linen bandages.

After Marguerite tied the last knot, Glasspoole obliged Speedwell to drink a small glass of poppy spirits – the classic recipe of one ounce opium, one ounce saffron, a drachm of cassia and cloves, the whole steeped in a pint of stout Canary wine. The giantess sighed and adjusted her glasses, which had been askew on her nose. Her huge hands trembled slightly as she returned the now empty glass to Glasspoole. "My thanks, mistresses," she said.

Marguerite brought a damp cloth and used it to wipe the sweat away from Speedwell's broad brow. "You were very brave," she said, impressed by the woman's fortitude.

Speedwell gave her a lopsided grin, took Marguerite's hand – which seemed impossibly small in the big woman's grip – and laid a gallant kiss on her fingertips with the panache of a life-long courtier. "May I know the name of my ministering angel?" she asked.

"Marguerite De Vries."

"Ah! *Uw dienares, juffrouw,*" Speedwell said in passable Dutch, her smile growing more brilliant at Marguerite's gasp of surprise.

"*Uw spraakt Nederlands!*" Marguerite exclaimed. Her own accent was not as pure as it might have been, since she was accustomed to speaking only English since her mother's death, but she remembered the language of her childhood well.

Speedwell's brown eyes twinkled. "Just a trifle, mistress," she said, switching to English. "Enough to demand surrender when I've a spoils-rich butterbox under my guns. And a bit of poetry, as well." She was still holding Marguerite's hand.

"*O Venus voestervrourw, uw vlammen niet en dooft de grondeloose Zee: ghy steeckt om hoogh het hooft,*" Speedwell said, quoting a poet of the previous century.

Marguerite stared at the giantess, her blue eyes wide, bottom lip caught between her teeth. She said breathlessly, "Oh, how beautiful!"

Bess' scowl grew more ferocious. She distrusted the smooth-talking giantess, knowing that Speedwell's flirtation was not without purpose, and that purpose was a torrid dalliance could the prey be captured by charm. "What's that jabber about?" she snapped.

Marguerite attempted a translation to English, although it was awkward to catch the flavor of the original. "Lovely Venus from the sea, your flames cannot be perished by the bottomless ocean." She gave Speedwell a sidelong glance. The woman's appearance was intimidating, but she seemed astonishingly civilized. Dimpling in appreciation, Marguerite withdrew her hand.

Bess snorted. "Still sounds like ape chatter to me."

"Perchance you would prefer the Bard of Avon?" Speedwell asked. It was clear that she had noticed Bess' challenging attitude and was looking forward to meeting her in a duel of words to win Marguerite's favor. They had played this game before, though not in earnest.

"Oh, good Lord!" Byng cried aloud, twisting a button until it flew off his coat and hit the surgery wall. "Are we here to discuss Sullivan and the *Swiftsure,* or to bandy poetry about like university students in their cups? Be so kind as to dismiss yon golden-haired cherub, madam, else we'll be lingering the whole day whilst Speedwell swoons like a mooncalf, and you fret like a boar with the toothache."

Speedwell's eyes opened wide behind her spectacles. She looked from Marguerite to Bess, and back again. A sudden realization flooded her face. She glanced at Glasspoole questioningly, and the herb-wife nodded. Speedwell muttered, "I ought to have known that the most desirable prize had been claimed by another."

Marguerite, who had gone to the other side of the room to fetch a plate of food, did not hear this utterance, but Bess did. Her only acknowledgement was a brief nod. Speedwell shrugged to show there were no hard feelings on her side, and smiled unrepentantly. *All's fair in love and war,* her expression seemed to say. Bess' brows knitted together in a frown.

When Marguerite returned with two roasted chickens and loaves of bread on a platter, Quittam and Byng had already joined the others in a conference regarding the defection of Sullivan. Speedwell smiled her thanks to the young woman and began tearing into the meal, Glasspoole's chirurgical efforts not having quelled her hunger one whit. Bess interposed herself between the giantess and Marguerite.

"Go back home, dear heart," Bess said, deliberately leaning in to give Marguerite a kiss. "I'll join you when I may."

Marguerite turned her head, so that the caress fell on the corner of her mouth rather than her lips. "Is there aught else, mistress?" she asked Glasspoole.

The herb-wife shook her head, setting her mobcap bobbing. "Nay, Margo, we've no further need. You'd best go home and get off those feet afore you end a cripple. My thanks for the assistance, lass. 'Twas well done."

"I second the thanks, mistress," Speedwell said, swallowing hastily and wiping grease from her chin with her shirt sleeve. "Mayhap you'll return later and keep me company. 'Twill be a welcome change from the blight that passes as culture in these heathenish parts."

Byng broke off his muttered diatribe against Sullivan and rolled his eyes. Quittam mouthed the word, "Katla," at him, which made the small nervous man twiddle another button loose and stare guiltily over his shoulder, as if expecting the rune-singer to appear. The button fell on the floor and rolled under the bed. He glared at Quittam but was clearly unwilling to make any riposte that might further anger his wife if it got back to her – which it would, since gossip ran round the island quicker than a summer storm. Quittam laughed soundlessly, her jade earrings swinging against her neck.

"Margo, go home!" Bess said, more sharply than she intended.

Marguerite started, flushed, and began to retreat from the surgery. She paused at the door. Speedwell was urbane, intriguing, and clearly an old friend of Bess O'Bedlam's. At least *she* had no ulterior motives for her interest, other than the obvious. *It might be nice,* Marguerite mused, *to be wanted solely for myself.* She was sick of feeling miserable, and the thought that Bess might suffer was a satisfying notion.

"I'll be glad to keep you company, Mistress Speedwell," Marguerite said coyly, fluttering her lashes in a coquettish manner. She saw Bess grimace out of the corner of her eye, and decided that she liked this petty vengeance. It eased her own pain slightly, a balm to her injured pride. "I would not like to see such a handsome woman left to languish alone in her bed."

"Sweet angel, call me Letty," Speedwell said. "By Baphomet's beard, I look forward to our next meeting! You're a breath of heaven in this pestilential place."

Marguerite curtsied – giving Speedwell and everyone else in the room a stunning view of her low décolletage – and replied, "I think you'll find that my nature is more suited to a lower place than Abraham's bosom."

"Nay, that's a more splendid bosom than old Abram could ever claim," murmured Byng, his eyes fairly popping from their sockets as he stared fixedly at Marguerite's breasts.

Speedwell's insufferable grin stretched wider.

Bess was amazed that Marguerite's most prominent attributes had not fallen out of the gown which she had once found charming and now detested with every fiber of her being. She seized the woman's arm in a bruising grip, her fingers cruelly grinding flesh against bone. "If you're quite finished flashin' your udders to all and sundry," she gritted, "get your arse home. Now! Or you'll feel the flat of my hand, by thunder."

Marguerite sniffed disdainfully at Bess, flashed Speedwell a smile, and exited the room in a swirl of pink silk and lace.

Quittam cleared her throat. "Well, ladies and gent...this has been more entertainin' than High Mass with a drunken bishop and an orgy of nuns, but shall we magpie about Sullivan now?"

Bess glared at the door, her hands balled into fists at her side. She took a deep breath, turned away, and joined the conference as if nothing had happened. A few speculative glances came her way, but Bess forced herself to concentrate only on business. The threat presented by Speedwell would have to wait, since Bess did not intend to kill her oldest and dearest friend when she was unable to fight back.

CHAPTER TWENTY-ONE
Lady's Choice

Bess, Byng and Quittam decided to take their ships and hunt down the treacherous Sullivan. To aid their search, Speedwell promised to craft a charm to locate the man and his ship. They discussed strategies in detail. It was growing dark before Byng and Quittam left to organize the hunt, and Bess remained behind.

She did not mince words. "Margo is mine," Bess said bluntly.

"Oh?" Speedwell removed her spectacles and placed them on a table beside the bed. "It seems there's some little doubt in the matter." She folded her big hands across her middle, waiting for Bess' response. The twin streaks of silver in her coppery hair caught the lamplight and glowed. She was no longer smiling.

Bess shook a fist under the giantess' nose. "By God, Letty, this ain't no game! Mistress Margo belongs to me, and there's an end to the matter. Sheer off, I say!"

"I'll keep to my course, though I thank 'ee kindly for the advice," Speedwell replied. She leaned forward slightly. Sitting up in the bed, her head was still higher than Bess'. "You've had a fair run at the lady, madam. 'Tis time to luff off and make way for another."

"*Merde*! I don't want to fight you, Letty, but I will. You ain't serious about the wench, you're just anglin' for a tumble," Bess said, thrusting out her jaw belligerently. "Find a doxy to give you easement, for *I'll* give you six inches of cold iron to chew on if *you* don't luff off."

Speedwell sat up straighter. "Have you already sampled the lady's goods?" She shot Bess a keen glance, reading something that made her smile. "No, you haven't. Are you sure this isn't mere cream pot affection, a desire for the hitherto unattainable?"

"Just leave her be."

"Then your intentions are honorable."

"I reckon they are."

The two women stared at each other for a long moment. Finally, Speedwell sighed and said, "I've enjoyed our little rivalries in the past. Each of us playing to the same wench and dazzling her with our individual brilliance till the winner caught the prize. The current situation appears somewhat different. Do you truly love the girl so much?"

Bess paused. She could not, in all honestly, say that she loved Marguerite. She had no idea what it meant. The sweet sentimentalities of balladeers and poets were foreign to her. Instead of answering the question, she repeated, "Margo's mine."

"While you may believe that, my friend, the lady does not seem to share your certainty. Or is she one of those flibbertigibbet hoydens who lead a lover a merry dance? Always teasing and flirting her honeypot beneath your very nose, and snatching it out of reach again."

"Margo ain't like that." Bess fumbled for words and finally said, "Damn your eyes, she's a good woman, she ain't a lightskirted fancy, and I mean to have her – not for a night but for a good long while, if she'll have me. So keep your paws to yourself, you goddamned freebootin' poacher, or I'll send you down to the Diet of Worms sharpish."

Speedwell chuckled. "Master Cupid's barbéd arrow has struck deep, I see. Nonetheless, I see no reason to discontinue my chase." She held up a hand to forestall Bess' protest. "Unless you mean to force the wench to your bed – and since you haven't done so already, I imagine you'll stick to softer tactics – then the lady's fair game. Let her make her own choice, or no choice at all. I cannot claim my intentions are as serious as yours, but she's piqued my interest. Any woman who'd endure your ham-fisted wooing must be a very special specimen of the breed."

Bess wanted to argue, but she recalled that Marguerite had not answered her proposal that morning. Indeed, the woman had shown reluctance to speak or even look at her. The way things stood between them, Bess could not say with any certainty that Marguerite returned her affection. She had cooled considerably since those days aboard *Mad Maudlin*. Bess did not understand this reluctance, and it frustrated her.

On the one hand, Bess was inclined to simply grab Marguerite and force the woman to accept the fact that she belonged to her. On the other hand, she needed Marguerite to come to her willingly, to make a partnership that would benefit them both. Her head was aching again, as was her heart. Bess had to acknowledge that Speedwell was right.

Aye, let the wench make her choice, she thought. *If Margo falls for Letty's patter, then she ain't fit to be mine.* It was a kind of test, to judge the woman's worthiness. Bess was both gladdened and alarmed by the fact that she would not be around to witness the dealings between Speedwell and Marguerite. *Well, when I return, if Letty's coaxed Margo into bed, she'll crow about it, and then I'll know for sure, one way or t'other.*

"Done, by God!" Bess said vehemently. "Margo can choose for herself, and I'll not stand in her way."

"That's most sporting of you," Speedwell murmured.

"Afore I forget, there's news about *Deceiver*," Bess said, deliberately changing the topic of conversation. She told Speedwell about Marguerite's tattoo, the riddle of Hephzibah's speaking bones, the message of the runes. The giantess listened intently to the narrative. When Bess was done, Speedwell nodded, her brown eyes sparkling with curiosity.

"I'm even more intrigued," Speedwell said. "Charm-needler's work is rarely so powerful. Not many people are willing to bind their lives completely to a spell."

"Margo had no choice. 'Twas done to her as a babe in arms." Bess absently tugged one of her gold earrings. "She's somehow tied to Fancy Tom Carew by blood and bone."

"The mystery deepens," Speedwell said. She shifted on the bed. "I'll see what may be found whilst you're all away." Her face broke into a grin. "'Twill be a very pleasant exercise, for I think that spending time with yon ministering angel will be no onerous task."

Bess growled beneath her breath, and fought the urge to ball up her fist and punch Speedwell's injured leg. "I'll leave you in peace, Letty."

Speedwell reached for her oversized spectacles and slid them onto her nose. "There's work to be done before I surrender to the arms of Morpheus. Would you be so kind as to give me paper and ink, a quill and a good sharp clasp-knife? I'll make a list of what-nots for Jim Monk to fetch from my house."

Bess did as she was bid. As she left the surgery, she thought about Marguerite – her smile, the freckles scattered across her breasts that trailed lower down her body, the mass of golden hair sliding across her shoulders, the voluptuous curves that teased the eye. Bess shook her head, still growling. The remainder of the fleet would leave in the morning to track down the renegade Sullivan. There was very little time to speak to Marguerite. Should she go to her, reveal her feelings once again? Try to make the woman understand how much she meant to her? No, Bess decided, she was too proud to beg. She had said everything that was necessary. Her intentions had been made plain. The rest was up to Marguerite.

When she returned, their future would be fixed for good or ill.

Marguerite awoke the next morning with her mood better than it had been lately. Not wanting to prevail upon Katla's hospitality, she had slept in the guest chamber of Bess' house. The hour was quite late before she had finally gotten to sleep, with much time spent dozing only to awaken with a start at the slightest sound. The notion that Bess would return home, possibly to continue that damnable seduction game of hers, had made Marguerite nervous. However, after a blessedly dreamless sleep, she felt able to face whatever challenges the day might bring – including the perfidious she-devil called the Water Witch.

The house was very quiet. A living shadow flowed onto the bed and settled on her legs. It was the cat, Paddyshank. Marguerite stared at the animal, who blinked his great golden eyes at her. She eased her body from beneath the counterpane, unwilling to disturb him, and used the necessary pot. When she had finished and returned the china pot to its carved walnut cabinet beside the bed – there was a man who came round daily with a barrel to collect the night soil – Marguerite pulled on a wrapper over her nightgown and hobbled barefoot along the corridor, twisting her hair into a coil at the nape of her neck and fastening it in place with an amber-headed pin. Paddyshank followed, then shot ahead, low and slinky, his belly almost scraping the floor.

Marguerite went into the master chamber on tip-toe, her eyes fixed on the carved sandalwood bed. It was empty, the bedclothes undisturbed. She let out the breath she had been holding. Then Marguerite noticed the sea chest was missing. Her eyes opened wide. She spun about and opened the wardrobe door. Not the one that held the beautiful gowns and things that Bess had shown her, but another crammed full of masculine coats and shirts and breeches. There were definite gaps in the collection.

Bess was gone.

She did not know whether to laugh or cry. Bess had left without a word, had abandoned her with careless ease and not a whisper of good-bye or fare-thee-well. Marguerite took a shaky breath, clutching the collar of her wrapper close to her throat. Although she knew that Bess did not care anything about her, this blunt evidence of indifference cut her deeply. A panicked thought came unbidden – if the pirate did not return in good time, Marguerite faced madness and death because of the cursed tattoo. She wished now that she had not been so cowardly. Had she spoken to Bess, explained the circumstances, put aside her hurt feelings and pride as she had promised Katla...

'Tis too late for regrets and may-have-beens, she told herself. *What's done is done. I'll have to wait for my chance and pray that Bess comes home afore I begin to rave.*

Marguerite swallowed past the lump in her throat. Slowly, she reached for a satin *justaucorps* coat and brought the sleeve to her face. The familiar scent of sandalwood rose from the garment. She would always associate that musky bitter-sweetness with Bess. Marguerite rubbed her cheek against the fabric, realized what she was doing, and let the sleeve drop as if it were afire. She banged the wardrobe door shut with a little more force than necessary. Her feet throbbed, her scraped hands and knees were stinging and raw. She told herself that the tears in her eyes were caused by physical pain, nothing else.

"They've all sailed on the morning tide," said a voice behind her. Marguerite turned and saw Lettice Speedwell leaning against the wall near the door. The ceilings were high enough that the giant woman could stand straight, but she must have bent down in order to pass under the lintel. "I bid you good afternoon, mistress," Speedwell continued, and glanced ruefully at the crutch under her arm. "Forgive me for not making a proper leg, but I'm somewhat inconvenienced at the moment."

"There's nothing to forgive," Marguerite replied with a sigh. "Is the hour so late?"

"Aye, well past noon by the sun. Have you broken your fast? If not, might I beg the indulgence of your company at my home?" Speedwell smiled. "A pretty woman at the table is a most excellent tonic for the digestion."

Marguerite cast her a return smile, flattered by the big woman's compliment and by the interest in the sparkling green eyes behind the spectacles. She opened the door of the ladies' wardrobe. "I must dress first," she said, "but I'll gladly join you, Letty. I've a need for company myself."

"Then I shall trouble you no further, Mistress Margo, but await on the verandah in breathless anticipation. Do hurry, my angel, for I do not know which shall cause me to perish first – the gross hunger of the body, or my insatiable appetite for your divine presence." Speedwell performed a sketchy bow, turned and ducked through the door, using her crutch adroitly. She propelled herself down the corridor and was soon out of sight.

Marguerite watched her go, bemused that a formidable seeming Amazon possessed such courtly manners and such admittedly diabolical charm. The awful emptiness in the pit of her stomach, which had yawned wider upon learning of Bess' departure, appeared to have been appeased a bit by Speedwell's appearance and by the invitation. Both Mistress Glasspoole and Katla Byng respected the giantess, and she trusted their opinions. It could be that where Bess had failed to find a solution to her curse – indeed, the captain appeared to welcome it, as that was her means to a vast treasure – then Speedwell might succeed.

She told herself not to hope too much. Speedwell was a pirate, too, and presumably cared about *Deceiver*'s treasure as much as Bess. She would have to be cautious. Marguerite reached for a gown of printed Indian cotton that boasted a finely embroidered bodice. She would take extra care with her hair, as well, and sponge her body down with scented water.

Marguerite did not intend to seduce Speedwell. She had tried that route with Bess and been led to disaster. Her heart still ached for Bess, even though she was aware that her longing was futile. No, Speedwell would not be a conquest of love or lust. However, Marguerite knew that in any battle, a woman had to use whatever weapons came to hand. If Speedwell thought her beautiful, then she would be dazzling.

I've been left small choice in the matter, Marguerite thought, taking a stiffened petticoat from the wardrobe. *There's no choice at all, if the truth were told.*

She stopped as something else occurred to her. Yesterday, at their first meeting, she had been flattered by Speedwell's attentions, and also by the notion of striking back at Bess, returning pain for pain. A night's reflection had given her pause. What if Speedwell asked a high price for saving her life? The giantess did not seem the sort to make crass demands, but Marguerite knew appearances were deceptive. That gallant manner could hide a multitude of sins.

Aye, Letty's palaver could coax a virgin nun to the bed chamber, Marguerite thought. She removed her wrapper and pulled the nightgown over her head. *But I'm no innocent girl-child to fall backwards with my skirts over my head at a compliment. If she tries to force me to a dalliance, I'll defy her as I've defied Bess. No one will take me against my will, no matter the cost. I'd rather die than prostitute myself to necessity, and there's an end to it.*

Marguerite felt a soft brush against her ankles. Paddyshank had returned, and was winding around her legs, purring. His fur was silky, his golden eyes mere slits in his black face. She said aloud to the cat, "And what do you think of all this nonsense, sirrah?"

Paddyshank yowled, spat, and raced to hide beneath the bed.

"A wise decision," Marguerite said, wishing she could join him there.

CHAPTER TWENTY-TWO
Charmed and Charming

Bess stood in the forecastle, her gaze directed outwards towards the twin creamy waves that peeled back from the cutwater as the ship slipped along on a southwestern course with the wind on her quarter. *Mad Maudlin*'s bowsprit was alight with witch-fire, the charm promised by Lettice Speedwell. Droplets of spray and spindrift caught the scarlet light and glowed like embers before falling back spent to the sea. The magical flames suddenly thinned and dulled; Bess noticed the change and shouted, "Shift a point to larboard!"

The helm answered, "A point to larboard, aye!" The great white sheets curved overhead like the wings of a great predatory bird. As soon as the course correction was made, the witch-fire on the bowsprit leaped up again, its brilliance renewed. She glanced over her shoulder and saw the *Mistress Moon* and the *Medusa* sailing in escort, following *Mad Maudlin*'s lead.

You can run, you poxy bastard, but by God you can't hide from the oath you took, Bess thought savagely. Speedwell's knowledge and skill in the occult had once again proven to be a boon. All the captains – including Bess herself – were bound together by a mutual vow of loyalty to the fleet, enforced by a mighty spell. The oath did not preclude treachery, did not forbid murder or scheming against the other members, but it did ensure two things. First, that no captain could ever reveal the location of Hotspur Cay, or betray any other of their number to the authorities. Second, if they broke faith with the rest and deserted their duty, the consequences of oath-breaking would be appalling. A renegade's fate was meant to be terrible, a thing to be avoided at all costs. Sullivan had evidently not cared, or perhaps did not believe the magic could touch him.

Bess intended to enjoy every blood-soaked, agonizing second that Sullivan's error in judgment would cost him.

The charm on the bowsprit was a hunter's guide, crafted specifically to pin-point Sullivan's location. It made Bess think of Marguerite and the tattoo she bore on her shoulder, a type of magical compass that would somehow show her the way to *Deceiver*'s grave. Bess wondered what Marguerite was doing at that moment, and this led her inexorably to Lettice Speedwell. She fingered the hilt of her cutlass, feeling cold and hot at the same time.

It would not be easy to accept if Marguerite chose Speedwell as lover and companion. Bess did not know what she might do in such a situation. Kill her friend, or at least challenge Speedwell to a fight? It seemed a petty thing to do, dueling to death over a woman. And what of Marguerite? Would she take her at the point of a sword over her dead friend's body?

It was all a hellish muddle that made Bess long for simpler days and simpler solutions to her problems. *If this is love*, she thought, *I'd rather do without, by God. 'Tis a pretty pass when I'm contemplatin' mayhem and murder on account of a damned female.*

And yet, she could not forget Marguerite, could not help the jealousy that bit and tore at her heart with poisoned emerald fangs. Bess frowned and tried to push the unwelcome considerations aside. She had always lived for the day, the hour – not the future, which was too slippery to grasp with any certainty.

Bess half-turned when she felt a touch on her shoulder; her hand tightened on her cutlass hilt in unconscious reflex. Henry Dunn shrugged his massive shoulders in apology.

"We're making excellent time," the first mate said. "I reckon Sullivan's holed up somewhere in the Keys, likely a little cay with a protected harbor 'gainst the *hurricano*. Not to malign Captain Speedwell's charm, but I thought it was best if we studied your charts and log-books. Mayhap we'll find a clue to lead us to the treacherous dog."

"S'good, Mister Dunn." Bess crooked a finger at Charles Halifax, the scrawny helmsman who was currently lounging in the waist, his watch complete. "Mister Halifax, keep a weather eye on our course," she said. "Make corrections as necessary."

"Aye-aye, Cap'n," Halifax said, taking her place in the forecastle.

Bess shook off her funk. She had to concentrate on finding Jack Sullivan. The question of Marguerite and Speedwell would have to wait. She followed Dunn aft to the captain's cabin, and a vision appeared unwanted in her mind.

Marguerite. So beautiful, so soft, and yet spirited enough to defy the dreaded Water Witch to her face. Bess saw Marguerite wrapped in Speedwell's strong embrace, pressed hard against the stooping giantess, blonde hair mingling with copper and silver, tantalizing open mouthed kisses and moans. Marguerite was a porcelain doll whose waist Speedwell could span with a single hand, her spatulate fingers splayed against those ripe buttocks...

Bess snapped out of her trance, realizing that Dunn had been speaking to her. She had not heard a word. The broad-chested first mate was eyeing her curiously. Bess snapped to cover her embarrassment, "Well, pull your peepers back in from their stalks, sirrah. Charts and log-books, aye? Come on, then, for daylight's wastin'."

She stalked away, her boot heels thumping on the deck. Dunn hastened after her.

Marguerite sat with her dress pulled down from her shoulders, leaning forward with her nearly bared breasts pressed against the edge of the table. It was an uncomfortable position, particularly since Speedwell had a heavy hand on her back, forcing her down even further, until her ribs creaked. She could feel the big woman's breath puffing against her sweaty skin, warm and moist, and the sensation made her shiver.

"Fascinating," Speedwell said, holding a magnifying glass in her free hand; it looked like a toy. She examined Marguerite's tattoo, her nose nearly brushing flesh. "I've not seen charm-needler's work so fine in many a year. I'd swear it was Fowler's – him being the preeminent artist of his time – save that the last I saw of the man some six-and-twenty years ago, he was face down on a tavern floor with his skull stove in."

Marguerite asked, "Who killed him?"

"I did," Speedwell replied matter-of-factly, "for the bastard son of a misbegotten she-dog tried to sneak away without paying his half of the bill. 'Twas not the first time he'd caroused with his mates and slunk off before the reckoning. He cheated at cards, too."

"Oh." Marguerite blinked. She was disconcerted that this confession of cold-blooded murder did not make her afraid of Speedwell. In fact, it seemed almost normal, and quite understandable considering the circumstances.

Speedwell laid the magnifying glass aside and picked up a large needle that looked fit to stitch a Colossus' shirt. "You'll feel a little prick, Margo. Please try to stay perfectly still."

"I imagine most women hear that at least once in their lives," Marguerite murmured.

Speedwell laughed out loud. "And for me, that's held truer than most, considering my size! Although I've never been interested enough in a man's apparatus to attempt the experiment more than once. I love women too much to give them up."

Marguerite flinched as the sharp point of the needle thrust into her shoulder and withdrew again. "Were you and Bess...did you ever..." Her voice trailed off. She was not sure that she really wanted an answer to her impulsive question.

"Were we lovers?" Speedwell sat up, motioning for Marguerite to do the same. She placed the bloodstained needle on an odd mirror made of volcanic glass. The shiny black surface was set in a deep frame crafted of silver-gilt finger bones and semi-precious gems like turquoise, amber and garnet. "Nay, though Bess and I been friends for a good long while. I suppose that she and I are too much alike for such intimacy, although I must admit that we've sometimes shared a woman; drunken, meaningless fumblings soon forgot when sunrise comes. 'Tis a trifle hard to tell who's touching whom when you're crowded three to a bed."

Again, Marguerite blinked. She had learned more about Bess from Lettice Speedwell in the last two days than during her entire time with the woman herself. Marguerite sat up, gathered the bodice of her dress closed and watched while Speedwell proceeded with her investigation.

They were in Speedwell's workshop, which was attached to the back of her house. The air was smoky-sweet with incense, translucent amber grains smoldering in a bowl of charcoal embers placed in front of a golden idol depicting a wasp-waisted woman with eight arms. There were workbenches and tables, shelves holding strange fluids and other substances in bottles, and cupboards painted with mystical symbols. Every piece of furniture was oversized and sturdy, made to accommodate Speedwell's height and bulk.

A human skull nailed to a wall had a glittering silver-and-black opal headdress fastened to its bony dome. Marguerite swung her feet back and forth, ignoring the eerie sensation that the skull's empty eye sockets were staring straight through her skin. She sat perched in a chair that was more Speedwell's size than her own; Marguerite felt like a toddler boosted to the family table.

Speedwell rose and went to a shelf. She returned bearing a jar filled with rosy liquid and set it down. Inside the jar was a weird root that had an uncanny human semblance – head, arms, legs and torso, all formed of twisted plant fibers. Marguerite gasped when the thing turned its "head" and tapped on the side of the glass with a knotty limb. *It was alive.*

"A special mandrake child," Speedwell said, surveying the hideous thing with pride. "It must be gathered from beneath a gallows ripe with a murderer's corpse, and this during a specific conjunction of the planets, then nurtured with various body fluids – blood, sperm, bile, spittle, and so on – and brought to unnatural life by a variety of nasty ceremonies. I took this manikin from a defrocked Jesuit priest in Macao. It is quite old and very dangerous."

Marguerite stared at the root, and despite its lack of eyes, could have sworn the thing stared back at her. She started when it jumped against the glass, nearly toppling the jar over. Speedwell steadied the receptacle and shook a finger at the manikin. "Behave yourself, or by Baphomet's beard, I'll chop you to flinders for a tasty sallet."

The mandrake child appeared to shrug, although it had no proper shoulders. Thin tendrils on its head and at the terminations of its limbs floated in the rose-colored water.

Speedwell rolled up her shirtsleeves and said to Marguerite, "Do not speak, mistress. I implore you to absolute silence during the ritual we must now perform. The embodied spirit is deadly to the uninitiated, and I do not wish you harm."

Marguerite nodded.

Speedwell paused and added with a grin, "Fear not, my angel. You're under my protection, and that is formidable, indeed."

With no further ceremony, Speedwell removed the lid of the jar and plunged her hand inside. Liquid slopped over the glass sides and spilled on the floor. She grasped the mandrake child firmly and drew it up, then set it dripping on the obsidian mirror. Marguerite could only stare while the manikin picked up the needle that had drawn her blood, and flourished it like a miniature rapier. *Squalembrato! Stramazone! Affando!*

Speedwell shook her head, the silver streaks in her copper hair flashing in the lamplight. "I think not," she said. She drew a curved blade from its sheath at her waist. The weapon might have been a cutlass for a normal sized person, but she used it as an over-large dagger. "Perform your divination, child of air and darkness. For payment, I offer life." She used the tip of the blade to make a slit in her finger, which immediately began bleeding.

To Marguerite's horror, a gash opened in the manikin's head, which greatly resembled a mouth. Speedwell allowed blood to drip into the gaping maw, drop by drop. The creature drank greedily. At last, she withdrew her hand. The mandrake child made a high piping sound, almost beyond the range of Marguerite's hearing, like the squeaking of a bat, and brandished the needle in a threatening manner. Speedwell sheathed the blade and pushed her steel-rimmed spectacles back up the length of her nose.

"By Aquariel and Athanatos," Speedwell said, touching gemstones at the four corners of the mirror frame, "I command thee, O child of air and darkness, to reveal that which is hidden, the secret knowledge of this riddle of flesh. Speak, and know that Gethel, who guards the truth of mysteries, will judge your words. I conjure you to obey!"

The manikin trembled. Marguerite almost felt sorry for the creature until it leaped directly at her face, the needle aimed at her eye. Some invisible barrier around the mirror stopped it in mid-air. The mandrake child fell on its back, its knotty limbs a-sprawl. It got up and piped again, sounding angry and shrill.

Speedwell's face was thunderous. "I command you to obedience!" she shouted, her voice a rolling boom. The creature wailed, shivering until the tendrils on its head whipped back and forth in a frenzy. An awful tension sizzled between Speedwell and the mandrake child.

Marguerite held her breath. She could feel currents of thaumaturgical power riding the air, like the sharp scent of the air before a storm. The hair stirred on the back of her neck.

Finally, the manikin nodded in submission. Speedwell relaxed slightly, but did not abandon her vigilance. "I conjure and command you to obey!" she said.

The mandrake child immediately swallowed the blood-stained needle. As soon as the needle disappeared down its gullet, it began to speak.

Marguerite could not understand the manikin's words, but Speedwell apparently did. She grunted and looked surprised at one point. The mandrake child continued its piping and squeaking until Marguerite's nerves felt grated raw. That voice was akin to the unbearable squeal of steel scraping on steel, and it sent chills racing down her spine.

At last, the mandrake child was finished with its recitation. It coughed out the needle, which was now clean. Speedwell picked the manikin up – the root dangled limply between her fingers, as if exhausted – and placed it back into the jar. She put the lid on firmly and returned the glass jar to its place on the shelf.

Marguerite grew alarmed at the pole-axed expression on Speedwell's face. Deeming it safe to speak, she asked, "What's wrong, Letty? What did you learn?"

Speedwell opened her mouth, closed it again. Behind the spectacles, her brown eyes were clouded with disbelief. She ran a hand through her hair, smoothing the coppery strands. "How old are you, Mistress Margo?" Speedwell asked after a long pause.

Marguerite answered impatiently, "Four-and-twenty. Why? What does this have to do with my tattoo?"

"Everything." Speedwell took off her spectacles and laid them on the table. She looked down at Marguerite, her mouth pursed. "It seems that your father is not an anonymous French sailor after all."

"*Godskannonne*, Letty! Speak plain and to the purpose, if you please." Marguerite felt a hard lump of fear settle in the pit of her stomach.

Speedwell answered, "You were sired by Fancy Tom Carew. Or at least, you share his blood in a closer degree of consanguinity than two utter strangers can claim."

Marguerite made a sound that might have been a hiccup, but was closer to a sob of protest, and clapped a hand over her mouth, her eyes wide as disbelief swamped her senses.

CHAPTER TWENTY-THREE
Under the Guns

Mad Maudlin crowded sail in chase; *Mistress Moon* tacked to approach on the *Swiftsure*'s weather side. The *Medusa*, commanded by Allegra Quittam, came about to cut off Sullivan's escape from the stern. *Swiftsure* was a converted clinker-built lugger, not as sleek as the brigantines or as well-armed as Bess' flagship cromster. It was only a matter of time before she was caught, particularly since *Swiftsure* was hampered by the weight in her hold and showed no sign of sacrificing treasure or guns to the deep in order to gain speed. She had spread virtually every bit of canvas she owned, including topgallant studdingsails and royals, but *Swiftsure* could not flee fast enough.

To wring every bit of speed possible from the wind, Bess had earlier ordered buckets of water whipped up to the mastheads to wet the sails and help them draw. Estimating their speed, she said to the first mate, "As soon as we close on *Swiftsure*, fire a shot athwart her forefoot. Mayhap that'll induce Jack to shorten sail and surrender."

"'Tis doubtful. Sullivan's a greedy cullion, ain't he? His ship can't outpace us, not with a load wallowing in her belly and destroying her trim, but be damned if he'll lose his ill-gotten gains," Dunn replied. He cupped his hand around his mouth and shouted orders from the quarterdeck.

Bess made her rounds, checking the action stations and encouraging her crew. The bow chasers and swivel gunners were ready at their stations. The men were shirtless; many of their backs bore the scarred evidence of brutal beatings with the cat o' nine tails, for a good many of the crew were Royal Navy deserters. Most of the hands had spotted kerchiefs tied around their heads. Slow matches stood in their tubs, trickling smoke. Below, on the gun deck, supervised by Levalier, more crewmen manned the long twelve-pounder guns that had nicknames like Sully-Me-Not, No Mere Bagatelle, Jealous Kate, and Mayhem carved into the well-polished wooden carriages. Bess exchanged a few words here and there before returning to the quarterdeck, satisfied.

Mad Maudlin's bowsprit still flamed with scarlet witch-fire, licking at the white spindrift thrown up by the vessel's swift passage; the bow threw up billows of blue-green waves tinged with red. Beneath her feet, Bess sensed the rudder's susurration, the thrumming vibration from the stern sounding board. *Mad Maudlin* was like a living thing with her wings spread, her stays and double backstays and preventers as humming-taut as fiddle strings, the pulse-beat of water sliding beneath her hull. A school of dolphins briefly surfaced, running along the ship's side, their sleek grey bodies as closely intertwined as a sailor's plait, and then they peeled away and vanished under the spray.

Bess was attired for war. She had six flintlocks in a ribbon sling around her shoulders, her cutlass at her side, and a dagger in her boot. She had left off her waistcoat but tied a blue-and-white sash around her middle to support the sword sheath on her left and the blunderbuss on her right. Wind ruffled her chestnut locks to an unruly mass of curls. Only four gold rings glinted in her earlobe; Bess had removed the one representing *Swiftsure* until that ship could be recaptured.

She checked the weather glass and scanned the sky for signs of storm. It was early in the afternoon, crystal clear with not a cloud in sight except the white canvas that strained overhead. The sun blazed, a ball of molten gilt-copper set in vivid turquoise. Bess squinted against the glare; in her opinion, there was little chance of a squall.

At her order, a crewman threw out the log-line to measure *Mad Maudlin's* speed, aiming beyond the wake, while Jim Monk squatted in the forechains, held the reel and called, "Turn!" as the red rag of the fifteen fathom stray-line vanished; the knotted cord paid out swiftly until Lovelock called, "Nip!" twenty-eight seconds later, and the reading was given.

"Seven knots and a half," Lovelock reported.

"We'll range alongside *Swiftsure* on the larboard tack," Bess said to the quartermaster, "but hold fire till we're within a half pistol-shot's distance of her, save for the first warning shot. I mean to make Sullivan surrender, by God, or sink him straight to hell. Signal Captain Byng to take the weather-gage, and rake *Swiftsure* to stern if Sullivan don't surrender."

"Aye-aye, Cap'n," Lovelock replied. He went to the poop deck and removed a hand mirror from the pocket of his leather vest. Both the other ships would have watchers at the mastheads with spyglasses, waiting to receive instructions from *Mad Maudlin*. He tilted the mirror to reflect the sun, flashing a message in Bess' private code to *Mistress Moon*, then did the same for the *Medusa*. The vessels soon flashed an acknowledgement of the orders.

"When *Swiftsure's* boarded," Bess continued to Henry Dunn, "I want men sent aloft to cut her rigging as soon as practical." Her lips quirked in an unpleasant smile. "He'll not get away so easy this time."

"Aye, Captain." Dunn also grinned. "Prisoners?"

Bess snapped open her spyglass. "If they give parole, we'll take the men aboard and leave 'em at Nassau or Antigua. Otherwise, no quarter given." She put the glass to her eye and focused on *Swiftsure's* stern. The renegade ship was trying to flee before a freshening wind, but the pursuing ships were catching up quickly.

Medusa was a sleek, green-and-gold checkered hound coursing after a smaller hare. *Swiftsure* responded with cannon fire, trying to drive off the pursuit, but the crew – the ship was short-handed, Bess could tell from the set of her sails and a dozen other tiny details that experience analyzed in a wink – clearly had not much practice with the guns, which were six-pounders at that, for every shot fell far short, sending up loud splashes and causing fish to float belly-up to the surface. Bess muttered, "Damnation to your soul, Sullivan. There's the first shot fired, and now you're doomed."

Puffs of smoke from *Medusa*'s bow chasers and cracks like thunder signaled the vessel's retaliation. *Swiftsure*'s spritsail was holed and the stern exploded in a flurry of splinters and shattered planks. Another crashing round destroyed her stern chasers, crippling her ability to return fire from that quarter. *Swiftsure* tacked to south-eastward, but her foretopmast suddenly gave way, shrouds and stays parting. Canvas billowed down to cover the foredeck guns. Slippery crimson poured in a solid sheet from *Swiftsure*'s scuppers; the waist and poop were cluttered with bodies but no disorder yet, no mad scramble of a leaderless crew in panic.

Bess thought it was too bad such excellent officers' lives should be wasted, but if the ship did not heave to, there was nothing else to be done. She watched through her glass and marked a ball from *Medusa* that disintegrated *Swiftsure*'s wheel. The helmsman was cut in two; the upper half of his body jerked backwards to smash against the remains of the taffrail.

Meanwhile, Byng on *Mistress Moon* cut across *Swiftsure*'s stern, loosening a hail of shot that chewed the other ship to pieces. Eddying smoke raced ahead of both ships, quickly dissipated by the breeze. Bess put her spyglass away as *Mad Maudlin* closed in on the fray. She took her blunderbuss from her sash and made ready to board, her feet braced on the deck. Henry Dunn, his gaze narrowed in calculation, gave the order to luff up; he did not want to overshoot his target.

Swiftsure fought back, peppering *Medusa* with more shot from her intact guns. Quittam's ship suffered some slight damage and a hole in her forecourse, but not enough to force her withdrawal from the engagement. *Mistress Moon* presented her larboard cannons – nine pounders taken from a French sloop – and waited for an upswell before firing, in order to inflict maximum damage. The jagged case-shot tore through *Swiftsure*'s remaining masts and rigging, and obliterated the cross-yards as well as the top-men who had stood upon them.

Heavy guns on both sides pounded the lugger. Wreckage scattered across the ocean surface, some of it aflame. Under Dunn's expert guidance and the sure touch of the helmsman, *Mad Maudlin* nudged her way under *Swiftsure*'s lee. Grapples were flung out, and crewmen lashed the two ships together, yardarm to yardarm. At Levalier's direction, the broadsides ceased. *Swiftsure*'s crew, running mad in panic, abandoned their guns. A small group of them struggled to lower her jolly-boat into the water, but they fought too much amongst themselves to make an efficient escape. On the larboard side, *Medusa*'s crew grappled Sullivan's vessel, too. Bess ran like a cat along the rail, then jumped over to *Swiftsure* with the rest of the boarding party.

Sailors from *Mad Maudlin* swarmed up the masts, slashing through the remaining rigging to drop what was left of *Swiftsure*'s sails. Others hastened to cast loose the ship's sea anchors. Although outnumbered, Sullivan's crew seemed willing to fight, and a chaotic battle broke out. Three sailors came at

Bess. She coolly waited until they were in point-blank range, then braced the stock against her hip and fired the blunderbuss. Heavy grape-shot scattered from the bell-shaped muzzle, a blizzard of destruction that chewed through flesh and bone. Blood hazed the air, and Bess blinked it from her vision.

She discarded the blunderbuss, drew a flintlock in her left hand and her cutlass in the right. A savage grin stretched across her face. Bess stomped down the deck and saw Allegra Quittam with slow matches tied to some of her blond quiffs. The smoking serpent locks and soot-stained complexion lent her the dreadful appearance of a demon straight from hell. The tall woman kicked a foe out of her way and shot him as he lay sprawled on the deck. The body jerked once and was still.

A movement in the corner of her eye caught Bess' attention. She avoided a cutlass thrust and shot the man in the face with her flintlock. His features disappeared in a blur of blood and shredded flesh. Another sailor screamed his defiance and ran at her with a boarding ax. Bess tossed her spent flintlock towards his eyes, making him flinch, and sliced his throat with a powerful backhand slash of her cutlass.

Before long, those of *Swiftsure's* crewmen who survived the initial attack surrendered by throwing down their arms and begging for mercy. While Quittam supervised herding the prisoners below decks to await their judgment, Bess went in search of the traitor Sullivan. She found him in the captain's great cabin, drinking a fine port and smoking a cheroot.

Jack Sullivan was a handsome man, one of the Black Irish breed with dark hair and vivid blue eyes. He rolled the cheroot around in his mouth and gave Bess an insolent nod. "Had I known you'd be paying a visit," he said, straightening the ruffled cuffs of his lawn shirt, "I'd have asked the cook to bake a sea-pie in your honor."

"You poxy bastard!" Bess grated. She had drawn a fresh flintlock and held it aimed steadily at the man. "You damned cross-grained cowardly rapparee! Where were you when the fightin' was hot?"

"Here, of course. I'm much too fond of my own skin to risk it for a load of quayside trash. Have you killed 'em all, then?" Sullivan smiled slightly. His face was a rugged example of masculine beauty from his broad brow to the cleft in his square-cut chin, but his lips were plump, almost womanish. "I told the men to fear Bess O'Bedlam's justice, that you'd weigh them down in chains and send them to a watery grave."

Bess sneered. "What have you done with the crew you took from Hotspur Cay?"

"Too loyal to you to subvert, too many for me to murder quietly. I left them on Hispaniola." Sullivan rose, and Bess cocked her flintlock. "I'm quite willing to surrender peacefully," the man chided. "Further violence would be unseemly."

"You've not yet seen violence, m'lad." Bess ground her teeth in rage. "By thunder, the captains intend to call an oathbreaker's curse upon your miserable head."

Sullivan removed the cheroot and pursed his plump lips. "Byng and Quittam won't condemn me. Neither will you, for that matter."

"Oh?" Bess raised an eyebrow. "Why not, milord cock-o-the-walk?"

"Because I know where *Deceiver's* grave lies." Sullivan smiled wide at the expression of consternation and frustrated anger on Bess' face. "You don't dare kill me now, you black-hearted bitch. If you do, the secret dies with me."

"You're lying," Bess said flatly.

"Am I? Can you afford to take that chance?" Sullivan tweaked his blue satin waistcoat to settle it more comfortably. "Will you let the greatest treasure in the Spanish Main be lost forever because you couldn't control your itch to hang me? I'll tell you the secret in exchange for my life and a share of the treasure, as well as your vow to let me be."

Bess grimaced. She did not believe the man, but as long as there was the slightest chance that he was telling the truth, she had to let him live...for now. "Come on and face your betters, traitor," she said, motioning with the flintlock. "We'll soon see what's what."

"As you wish," Sullivan said. He put on a cocked hat made ostentatious with ostrich feathers and preceded Bess out of the cabin, seemingly at his ease.

Byng had rowed over to the *Swiftsure* on his jolly boat and boarded the ship along with his coxswain and several crewmembers. He paced the deck restlessly, while Quittam watched with barely contained irritation. Upon catching sight of Sullivan, Byng cried, "You motherless son of a Barbary ape!" and drove his fist into the taller man's stomach. Sullivan bent over, gasping in pain. His hat fell off and rolled away into the scuppers.

Quittam grabbed the back of Sullivan's hair, forcing him to stand up straight. "If I had my way," she growled, "I'd peel the skin off your worthless bones an inch at the time!"

"I know the way to *Deceiver*," Sullivan wheezed. His bottom lip was smeared with blood where he had bitten himself at the impact of Byng's blow. "Tell them, Bess!"

"So he says," Bess replied laconically. She was not inclined to stop the others from beating him. As far as she was concerned, no matter what Sullivan knew or did not know, he had earned a drubbing as the very least of his punishment for treachery and desertion.

Quittam let go of Sullivan and backhanded him hard across the face. The slow matches were gone from her hair, but her features were still covered in soot and gunpowder residue. Cloudy green eyes, hard as the jade they resembled, stared out from a black, greasy mask. "Think that'll save your hide, Jacko?" she snarled. Quittam looked at Bess. "Give me a brazier of hot coals and a meat skewer, Cap'n. I'll soon have the bastard singin' a pretty tune."

Sullivan gaped in disbelief and turned to Byng. "Freddie, you won't give me to the women, will you?" he pleaded. "They ain't human!"

"Jack, you never were a very good liar," Byng replied coldly. He drove the heel of his boot into Sullivan's knee. The bone cracked audibly. Sullivan turned white and sagged to the deck, a thin whine coming from his throat.

Byng continued, ticking off points on his fingers, "*Primus*: if you truly knew the location of Carew's lost ship, you'd have gone after the treasure yourself instead of lurking about the port islands like a damnable burglar seeking a safe place to dispose of his ill-gotten goods. *Secundus*: how did you expect to load the treasure onto your vessel when the hold is already full and fit to burst? You could have taken *Swiftsure* out on a venture and slipped away with none the wiser instead of attacking Captain Speedwell after taking a rich prize. *Tertius*: only an crack-headed fool – which I know you are not, circumstances notwithstanding – would trust this lot of villains anywhere near a fortune of that size and not expect to get his throat cut the moment his back was turned. No, Jack. 'Tis a poor tale. The facts do not bear it out. You know no more of *Deceiver* than the rest of us."

"I can make sure of that." Quittam gave Sullivan an evil grin. "He'll be beggin' to speak afore I'm done with him."

The man mewled in agony, his forehead pressed to the deck. Around him, sailors muttered and fingered their weapons. Everyone watched Bess sidelong, awaiting her decision.

Bess considered the options. She had trusted Jack Sullivan because he had been a good first mate to the *Swiftsure's* former captain. That confidence had been betrayed. Byng's points were logical ones and made sense to her. Sullivan had turned renegade because of greed, taking his prize and running with it. Had he possessed any knowledge whatsoever of *Deceiver*, he would not have bothered to defect with a hold full of cargo.

The most telling factor was that Hephzibah's spirits had not mentioned Sullivan at all, only Marguerite De Vries. She was the key, not this cowardly traitor who spun moonshine in a vain attempt to excuse his sins and save his own skin. He knew nothing. Mercy was not an option when it came to those who broke faith.

"Take him to *Mad Maudlin*," Bess said to the others. "He'll suffer the oathbreaker's curse, by the sweet bleedin' Christ, and may the Devil accept him into a roasting hot hell."

The assembled sailors cheered. Quittam leaned down and said to Sullivan, "Ah, m'lad, you should've let me have you. 'Twould have been an easier death." She cuffed the side of his head, grabbed his arm and hauled him to his feet. Sullivan let out a muffled shriek as his weight came down on his shattered knee.

Hands reached out to take him, dragging Sullivan roughly over the rail to be passed hand to hand like a parcel until he reached the flagship. He screamed denials and curses at his captors, but he stopped struggling when some of the sailors offered to drop him overboard. Like most sea-faring men, Sullivan could not swim.

"Handsomely, boys, handsomely!" Bess called, putting the unfired flintlock back into its sling. "He'll be wounded sore enough and soon enough to slake your thirst for vengeance. Freddie, Allegra, let's see to the dog and get it done. I've had a mort of this poxy business."

Byng whipped a perfumed handkerchief from his pocket and patted his forehead with the dainty scrap of lace. "Indeed, madam. I, too, am eager to return home. This filthy Iscariot has occupied too much of our valuable time."

Bess returned to *Mad Maudlin*, followed by Byng and Quittam. The crew had dumped Sullivan on the deck. He stared up at the circle of grim-faced sailors, panting. Blood smeared his face; there was a cut on his cheekbone, courtesy of Quittam's rings. He had been stripped naked. Sullivan's skin was white where the sun had never touched it, and his lax manhood nestled in a thatch of coarse black pubic hair. "You can't do this!" he said, his hands going to cup his genitals protectively. "I earned that prize. 'Tis mine!"

"You made a vow," Bess replied, "as did we all. You could've had your share."

"Oh, aye!" Sullivan hawked and spat; the wet gobbet landed just shy of Bess' boot. His face was gray with pain but otherwise defiant. "Why should I risk my skin for a paltry share of a fortune when I could have it all? Why should I take orders from a thrice-damned bitch who thinks her arse is made of gold? I'm no lickspittle, by Christ! Jack Sullivan's a man, unlike some who've had their pricks removed along with their pride."

Byng said dryly, "My wife has no complaints, sirrah. My prick's intact, and my pride as well, for a gentleman takes satisfaction in honoring his oaths."

Sullivan stared back but said nothing further. The contempt in his eyes spoke volumes.

Bess nodded to Byng and Quittam; they took their places at the North and South cardinal points. She moved to the East point and laid down a long lock of coppery hair, bound with a silver ring, that represented their missing captain, Lettice Speedwell. After taking care of that detail, Bess went to stand in the West.

The spell itself was simple. None of them needed talent or skill to invoke it, since the magic they called upon was part of the oath that bound them together. The charm required the presence of all the other captains, in spirit if not in body, as well as their unanimous agreement. Together, Byng, Quittam and Bess chanted:

> *Cold steel and fire and ice – work the fate upon him thrice!*
> *Ice and fire and cold steel – for the traitor, no appeal!*
> *Cold steel and ice and fire – body and soul to death entire!*
> *Broken on oathbreaker's wheel – by fire, ice and cold steel!*

Each of the captains took a dagger and placed it at their feet with the blades pointed towards Sullivan. Bess waited a long moment. Nothing happened.

Sullivan sneered. "Your magic ain't naught but charlatan's gammon, you damned worthless jackeens!"

The wind suddenly died.

Rigging creaked overhead, but the great white sails did no more than shiver along their length. No one spoke or moved. Bess' skin crawled. She braced her feet on the deck as if in preparation for a squall. Black clouds boiled overhead, driven from the north and blotting out the sun in their thickness; the temperature dropped by degrees until every breath issued from between her lips like a fog, and ice sparkled on the stays. The long rounded swell of the sea made *Mad Maudlin* and *Swiftsure* rise and fall in tandem.

Without warning, a ball of azure witch-fire burst outward from the ship's bowsprit and ran along the rails and up the masts until it covered *Mad Maudlin* in eldritch light. The sailors moaned; some crossed themselves, while others made signs against the Evil Eye. Bess had not known exactly what to expect, since they had never performed this ritual before, but she stood firm and did not betray her startlement lest the men begin to panic in truth.

Tendrils of witch-fire snaked towards Sullivan, who had screwed his eyes shut and was mouthing what Bess thought might be prayers. Slowly but steadily, the thin streamers crawled through the air, like blind worms seeking their prey. He cracked open an eye, then flinched back but found himself pinned to the deck, unable to move a muscle. Sullivan sucked in a breath, and let it out in a shrill scream as the first tendril touched his bare chest.

Real flames blossomed from his skin, an eruption of red and yellow and hotter blue that sizzled and crackled loudly. The horribly unappetizing smell of cooked human flesh – so much like roasting pork, sweet and smoky – rose like sacrificial smoke. Sullivan screamed again as more tendrils touched him, and more flames spurted from his body. He jerked in their embrace, uncontrollable spasms that threatened to tear muscle from bone. Sullivan soon had a web of fire wound about him, his body embraced by crisscrossing lines that burned merrily.

A fork of lightning split the clouds asunder, followed by a rolling crash of thunder. Great lumps of hail began to fall from the sky, but only within the circle that surrounded the wailing man. This was no ordinary hail; shaped like razors and just as sharp, the ice sliced down into Sullivan, opening up long bloody cuts. They did not extinguish the flames that ate away at his flesh. His screams were terrible to hear.

Sullivan's skin hung off in strips, his whole body covered with blood. His chest heaved; he let out a hoarse cry, and a fine scarlet spray hissed from his throat. Bone showed in his arms and legs, shockingly white against the darker red muscle. One eye was gone, nothing but a weeping empty socket. The other stared at Bess, the pupil so distended that the blue iris appeared black.

"For God's sake, finish it!" he moaned.

The daggers at the captains' feet vibrated, the blades tapping the deck.

As one, the weapons shot towards Sullivan, impaling him through his remaining eye, heart and kidney. The man keened and fell over, nails clawing the wooden planks. After a moment, he stiffened, then relaxed. The flames died; the hail ceased and a fresh salty breeze drove away the black clouds. Witch-fire ran in reverse, sucked back to the bowsprit, flickered and was gone. The sun came out, illuminating the smoking, ruined corpse of the traitor.

Byng sniffed and applied a lacy handkerchief to his nose. "By God, that's good riddance to bad rubbish!" he said.

"Too true, Freddie," Bess replied. She turned to Henry Dunn, who was standing behind her. "Remove this trash from my deck," she said, pointing to the mutilated corpse, "and I want every plank holystoned till there's no trace left, for I'll not have *Mad Maudlin* polluted by traitor's blood."

"Aye-aye," Dunn replied crisply. He sent some men for round shot from the ship's stores, as well as a length of canvas. There would be no prayers said for the oathbreaker, no ceremonies, no mourning. Sullivan would be dumped overboard with little ceremony save the traditional stitch through his nose as he was sewn into a shroud by the sailmaker's mate.

"Who's to sail *Swiftsure* back?" Quittam asked, seemingly not the least bothered by the horror she had just witnessed.

Bess turned her back on the dead man. "Solomon Lovelock's my choice. Aye or nay?"

"He's a good man, unlikely to betray us," Byng said. "You've my vote."

Quittam ran a sleeve over her soot-blackened face; the cloth came away covered with dark grease. "Mine as well. I'm off to *Medusa* with my men. With any luck, if the winds are favorable, we'll make it back to Hotspur Cay in a few days." She nudged Bess with her elbow. "Wonder what mischief your mistress is getting up to whilst you're away, eh?"

Angered, Bess clenched her fist. "Shut your bone box, Allegra, to keep your guts warm. Don't you know the Devil loves hot tripes?"

Quittam laughed heartily. "Damnation to my soul! Sounds like you love the wench!"

Bess turned white, then crimson. She put her hands on her hips and said, "Belay that nonsense! Get off my ship, you pestiferous doxy, or I'll give you the merry rope's end!"

Still laughing, Quittam took her leave. Byng lingered a moment, a speculative gleam in his dark eyes. Touching his handkerchief to his lips once more, he bowed to Bess and clambered down the accommodation ladder, where his boat waited to carry him back to *Mistress Moon*. Bess scowled after him. She had not missed the knowing little smile he had tried to hide behind that scrap of cambric and lace, and it made her burn. The fangs of jealousy bit deeper.

What were Speedwell and Marguerite doing on Hotspur Cay?

Bess would have sold her soul for the answer to that question.

CHAPTER TWENTY-FOUR
A Question of Desire

Marguerite avoided Speedwell after the unwelcome revelation of her connection to the murderous Fancy Tom Carew. She still liked Speedwell, who never failed to be courtesy itself and who was quite charming, full of dainty compliments and graces, but... *No one craves the company of an ill-omened bird*, she thought as she gathered her hair into a long plait that hung between her shoulders, fastening the end with a bit of ribbon. Besides, witnessing Speedwell's thaumaturgical might had so intimidated Marguerite that she had quite abandoned her plan of cold-bloodedly seducing the big woman. Anyone who commanded an enchanted mandrake child would no doubt be immune to her charms.

Today, she was supposed to aid Mistress Glasspoole, who was performing a chirurgical operation with Dr. Janus – a lithotomy, in fact, the removal of a troublesome bladder stone from one of Hotspur Cay's inhabitants. Marguerite was to wield a soporific sponge soaked in a devil's brew of opium, black nightshade, henbane, water hemlock, lettuce seed, mandragora, and climbing ivy whose application would render the patient insensible, thus foregoing the need to lash him down with leather restraints and gag him lest his screams disturb the chirurgeons as they plied lancets and bistouries and needles.

She wended her way to the surgery, deciding that she ought to avoid breakfast in case sickness overtook her. According to Glasspoole, Marguerite was becoming a fine chirurgeon's assistant, and truth to tell, she did not mind such work, although the blood and the sight of the wounds themselves took some getting used to.

After the grisly operation was done, Marguerite was free to wander the island, since her friend, the rune-singer Katla, was fasting on account of some obscure Icelandic custom. She found herself on a small hill, shaded by trees whose limbs were heavy with the brittle-skinned fruits called *mamoncillo* or Spanish limes, although they were similar to actual limes only in gross appearance. It was the large nut inside, rather than the thin layer of sour yellow pulp, that made the fruit desirable. Marguerite's stomach rumbled with hunger and she considered returning to the settlement to purchase a snack to appease her growing appetite.

She thought about an old, toothless black woman – doubtless an ex-slave – who spoke only a garbled mixture of Portuguese and French. The woman squatted over a fire in the square and roasted *mamoncillo* nuts on an iron griddle. She also sold skewers of mutton brushed with a fiery sauce, to be eaten with slices of ripe paw-paws. Another vendor near Katla's shop always had a cauldron full of little crabs, conch, shrimp, dabs, plantains and calabaza gourds all boiled up together in coconut milk turned orange-gold with annatto seeds. He served the stew in empty coconut husks with an oyster shell for a spoon.

Marguerite's mouth watered.

Below in the hollow of the hill, she saw a herd of floppy-eared goats tended by three small boys, one of whom was completely naked save for a thin piece of string knotted around his waist. The string supported a square, foreign coin with a hole in the middle, an amulet to ward off the Evil Eye. The boys waved cheerfully at her before chivvying their herd onward, alternating shrill whistles with prodding the bleating goats with a stick to encourage them to trot together. Marguerite watched them go, then turned and walked in the direction of the settlement, using a palm frond to wave away flies and other insects attracted to her sweat.

While she walked, Marguerite considered Bess O'Bedlam, who was never very far from her thoughts these days. She found that she missed the pirate and regretted that Bess had been forced to leave Hotspur Cay in such haste. She remained troubled by the question of whether Bess was sincere in her affections or not. For her part, Marguerite had spent some time examining her own feelings. She would no longer deny that she wanted Bess in her bed. Holding herself aloof had not dimmed desire one whit, nor had their unexpected exile from one another.

Truly, Bess' absence had only caused Marguerite to revise her opinion. A woman's prerogative, as men said in jest, but it was true. Being granted time and sufficient space for rational consideration, her temper having long since cooled, Marguerite came to realize that her fit of jealousy over Carmelita was naught but folly.

Discreet inquiries among some of the more gossip-prone members of the community revealed that Carmelita was Solomon Lovelock's woman, and it was well-known that he would brook no cuckolding. Carmelita flaunted that damnable sapphire bracelet and boasted of its being a gift from Bess, but Katla and Mistress Glasspoole had assured Marguerite that this was impossible. Bess was too wise to make an enemy of a good man over a woman, even a prime article like Carmelita. Yet Marguerite had seen them kissing – this was undeniable. The more she thought about it, however, the more she wondered if she might have been mistaken. Oh, Carmelita *had* been kissing Bess, but it now seemed to her as if Bess had been taken aback, unwilling to return the embrace.

A hummingbird shot past her ear, startling her out of her thoughts. It was a tiny iridescent jewel that hovered among the spiked flowers of a coral tree. Marguerite paused to watch it dip its long, slender beak, moving from scarlet flower to flower, its wing-beats so swift as to be near invisible blurs of motion. Absently, she fanned herself with the palm frond, scattering a cloud of miniscule fruit flies.

When Bess came home, Marguerite wanted to talk to her, to allow an explanation to be made, for she now regretted her haste. The islanders had been at pains to tell her about Bess, her generosity, her kindness to those she considered her own, as well as her fierce protectiveness. Every soul on

Hotspur Cay had a story to tell about Bess O'Bedlam, and Marguerite had listened. She came to understand that Bess was more than a bloodthirsty pirate; she was the chieftain of an extended clan and the founder of a thriving colony.

I'll crave her pardon, Marguerite thought, still watching the hummingbird as it darted among the tree branches. *I am in the wrong, after all, and was the first to give offense by assuming Bess was insincere in her affections.* She scowled. *It's all that Spanish bitch's fault! Aye, what I wouldn't give to sink a cloth-yard of well-sharpened steel into her gullet!*

Having been warned off by Speedwell – who had assumed an easy command of Hotspur Cay in Bess' absence – Carmelita had made herself scarce where Marguerite was concerned. Still, if Marguerite caught the hated vitriolic wench, she was inclined to...

An errant breeze carried with it the smell of hot oil and fish. Marguerite broke off her war-like thoughts as her stomach growled. She was close to the harbor; shading her eyes with a hand, she saw a huge kettle had been set up on the strand, apparently to fry a catch of fish being brought in by some of the men. Children had gathered mangoes and pineapples, and a special press had been dragged to the beach for the purpose of crushing sugarcane, harvested from fields on the other side of the island. The islanders mixed the sweet, foamy liquid with rum and fruit juices to create a kind of delicious punch.

Marguerite tossed her palm frond down and hurried along the path, her resolutions forgotten in the rush to silence her complaining belly.

Once Bess returned to Hotspur Cay with her fleet, events clipped along at an unbelievably swift rate. Carpenters swarmed over *Swiftsure*, repairing the damage done during the fight and replacing lost masts with solid greenwood; sail-makers and their mates plied needle to acres of canvas. The other ships were also titivated and re-supplied; freshwater casks rolled aboard, sloshing and wet, followed by tuns of salt pork and soused pork, pigeons preserved in fat, ship's biscuit – thrice-baked and hard as stone – portable soup cakes, rum, wine, and powder and shot, as well as four-legged rations that were harried bleating into the holds, to be later transformed into roast mutton and goat sausages.

Bess herself was too busy to deal with non-shipboard concerns, although to be fair, Marguerite had tried to seek her out twice; it was unfortunate that Bess had been forced to rebuff her. Every cask, every tun, every hogshead had to be placed just so to avoid throwing *Mad Maudlin* out of trim; there were a thousand details that needed her attention, and since she had lost Solomon Lovelock to his own command, she had to oversee the work herself with Henry Dunn's able assistance. Bess was up before sunrise and did not seek her bed until many wearisome hours after dusk.

At last, though, all was ready; the other captains – including Speedwell, her injured leg now able to bear her weight – were also finished with their preparations. Bess was determined to sail on the morning tide. There was one last piece of business that required tending, however, and she went to her house at supper-time, not surprised to find Marguerite already at the table and dining on roast pork, yams and leafy-green callaloo, with a platter of ripe custard apples for dessert. Bess had not bothered to send a message ashore, deciding that the element of surprise might serve her better than allowing the woman time to marshal her defenses. Enough time had been wasted, and besides, Speedwell had been looking uncommonly smug of late. Bess' instincts told her that nothing untoward had happened between the red-haired giant and Marguerite, but she did not intend to hesitate any longer.

Marguerite looked up from her plate, her fork poised, wide blue eyes fixed on the resolute Bess, who was conscious of her bedraggled appearance and now wished she had taken the opportunity to bathe and change out of her grease-spotted shirt. Still, Fortune favored the bold, and Bess O'Bedlam had been born with more than her fair share of nerve.

"Stay," Bess said, when Marguerite made to rise. "I've somewhat to say to you, Margo, and my feeling is 'twould be best swallowed with your ass at anchor."

Marguerite continued to stare. Bess cleared her throat. Declarations of love were things to be slurred around a mouthful of coarse *aguardiente* to a tavern slattern perched upon one's knee; a farrago of drunken, bombastic vows and promises, easily made and easily forgotten when night faded into morning, and sensibility overcame the brandy fumes. Before Sullivan's perfidy had become known, she had asked Marguerite in so many words to be her leman. Now she wanted an answer. There was very little poetry in Bess' soul, and for once she felt the lack. Nevertheless, she pressed on.

"Margo..." Bess hesitated; Marguerite's regard was piercing. She swallowed, and tried again. "I've had...that is to say, I'm..." Bess paused once more, and becoming angry at this hesitation – was she a virgin laboring under a first calf-love? – spoke out bluntly. "I love you, Margo. At least, I think 'tis love," she was compelled to admit, then, growing angrier still, "By the sweet bleedin' Christ, woman, have you naught to say, or will you sit there, dumb as a herring and staring like a shatter-brain?"

The fork dropped, clattering against the plate. Marguerite inhaled deeply; a scarlet blush mounted in her cheeks. She had wanted to apologize and try to make things right between them, but two abrupt rejections by Bess were two too many, for she retained some degree of pride. Resolutions aside, this sudden fit of nonsense was more than enough to arouse Marguerite's ire.

"*Godskannonne!*" Marguerite cried, stung. "I can't say that I love you, either, and still less now, for your ragabash lack of manners has quite put me out of color!"

Bess stomped over to the chair, seething, her good humor vanished. "You seem a lively enough wench," she retorted, and took hold of Marguerite's upper arm, jerking her to her feet. "Damn you! Damn you for a witch, and a temptress, too!"

Marguerite's eyes grew bigger and bigger. Unwilling to delay another second, Bess dipped her head and crushed her mouth against those tempting lips that yielded beautifully beneath her insistence. Marguerite's tongue touched hers. Bess was jolted into immobility by that sweet burning touch. She was dimly aware that Marguerite was clutching her shoulders, splayed fingertips digging hard into her muscles. Bess broke the kiss and opened her eyes, staring down at Marguerite's face.

Candlelight blurred the beautiful features and created a golden, saintly aura around her head that was belied by a besotted, pleasure-dazed expression that no holy martyr ever bore. Tenderness swelled in Bess' breast. If what she felt was not love, then the poets and balladeers were black-hearted liars. She leaned down again, her movements for once unsure, and was met half-way by Marguerite, who surrendered with a ragged moan.

Bess kissed her way along the woman's jaw, and carefully, delicately, ran the very tip of her tongue along the shell of Marguerite's ear. Marguerite groaned and collapsed against her, heavy and warm and soft. Bess tightened her grip; the blood pulsed in her veins like waves under a full moon's tide. Marguerite turned her head and kissed Bess hungrily, stabbing into her mouth with a hot velvet tongue. Passion flamed higher, escalating into an inferno that swept through them both.

Marguerite tore her lips away; she was panting and flushed, her eyes wild, but she never slackened her grip on Bess' shoulders. There were no words that could be said; no language was adequate to explain the fierce, blazing desire that drove them inexorably towards one another. The feeling spread like molten gold beneath her skin and settled between her thighs. Marguerite burned. Her flesh tightened against the bone until she felt as if every hair on her body stood to attention; her mouth felt bruised. Her head spun, leaving her light-headed. Anger had turned so abruptly to desire that suddenly, shockingly, in the grip of a longing that shook her to the core, Marguerite thought that if could not have Bess O'Bedlam, she would die. Nothing else mattered. She touched a knuckle to the soft indentation in Bess' upper lip and shivered.

As if she read her mind, Bess nudged Marguerite until she was backed against the table, the wooden edge digging into the small of her back. Bess' pupils had dilated until only a thin edge of grey could be seen around the black. "Margo," she whispered. "I need...I need you." Impatiently, she cleared the table with a sweep of her arm, sending platters, cutlery and glasses smashing to the floor.

"Oh!" Marguerite breathed. Of their own volition, her hands reached up and pulled the black ribbon from Bess' hair, loosening the chestnut locks so that they brushed, feather-light, against her face. Bess' lips echoed the caress, nuzzling her throat with such teasing touches that they maddened Marguerite beyond her capacity to endure. Bess urged her to lie back. She squirmed beneath Bess' weight, aching and wanting nothing more than to ease the fire that raged within her.

Bess licked a long wet line over Marguerite's collarbone; the taste of her skin was deliciously spicy and salty, verging into musk as she followed the plump, blue-veined curve of the woman's breast, pushed into a quivering mound by her bodice. Marguerite whimpered and arched her back. Bess buried her face in the musky décolletage to hide her grin, then with great reluctance, released Marguerite and stood on shaky legs, refusing to support herself on the table lest she yield once more to temptation.

"Come and share my bed, Margo, please. I need you," Bess repeated, relieved and gloating all at once when Marguerite lay there stunned with her breath coming in great heaving spasms, then suddenly scrambled to her feet. Marguerite had never looked so beautiful. Bess' heart swelled; she choked on words, and gently touched Marguerite's hand instead.

Marguerite tugged Bess' hand to her mouth and began sucking and licking the woman's fingers in the lewdest manner possible, while watching Bess with hooded eyes.

"Almighty God!" Bess blurted, so filled with desire that it was physically painful. Slippery heat bloomed, and her clothing seemed to have drawn strangling tight. Without wasting another moment, Bess pulled Marguerite out of the dining room and along the passage to the bedchamber.

The bedchamber was cool and dim, scented with sandalwood from the great four-poster bed that commanded the space. Bess tore off her waistcoat, not mourning or even missing the two ruby-and-gold buttons that ripped off in her haste and pulled her loose linen shirt over her head. Marguerite hissed frustration between her teeth and muttered ripe Dutch curses as her shaking hands fought with her gown's knotted laces. Bess watched a moment, amusement warring with passion, and finally snapped her arm down; the hilt of the knife strapped to her forearm smacked into her palm.

Marguerite looked at her, but there was admiration rather than consternation in the depths of her blue eyes. Bess flipped the knife up – the blade was a good six inches long and honed needle-sharp – and in a single expert, explosive movement, slit the recalcitrant laces without touching the chemise underneath. Marguerite shrugged; the gown slithered off her shoulders, slid down her arms and puddled on the floor. The chemise and petticoats followed. She posed, chin raised, hands on her hips, proud and unashamed.

"Well?" Marguerite asked, cocking an eyebrow, not at all shy or afraid. "Do you fancy what you see, madam all-a-mort?" She and Bess had been headed for this point since their first meeting in the filthy shed behind Fiddler's Green in St. John's Town; even then, there had been an attraction, though well denied by both parties. Whether Bess truly loved her or was merely toying with her affections seemed like an unimportant question at the moment, one best contemplated in the morning after a night spent in delicious transports. There were no regrets, no hesitation. She might not live to have this opportunity again. Marguerite wanted Bess, and she meant to have her.

Bess snapped her wrist forward; the knife flew across the room and embedded itself in the wall, the hilt vibrating from the speed of its flight. Her face flushed with lust; she wetted her lips with her tongue, her gaze devouring the sight of Marguerite's nakedness. "Aye," she said, "I fancy you, indeed." Bess' breeches joined her shirt, tossed on the floor, then she joined Marguerite on the bed.

They surged together, skin against skin. Bess sank the length of her body in the cradle of Marguerite's spread thighs. Where they touched was satin and velvet, sweat and fire, and spreading slippery heat. Marguerite gasped and shuddered, her breath hitching as Bess braced herself and let her free hand wander between their bodies. There was no need for words; open-mouthed kisses and caresses were the language they used to communicate desire.

Maddened by a wanton need that grew hotter by the second, Marguerite clawed at Bess to spur her efforts on. The long flat muscles of Bess' back were hard as tiles beneath the woman's whip-scarred skin. This reminder of past hurts eased Marguerite's desperation; she glided her fingertips over the latticework of scars, the softer patches of clear skin, the solid bumps of vertebrae that formed a long archipelago of bone. Bess slicked her tongue into Marguerite's mouth, heavy and slow. Her hand moved with deliberation, then she broke the kiss and slithered down to use her mouth, her lips, her tongue. Waves of pleasure crashed through Marguerite until she arched her back and let out a choked cry of completion, bursts of light like a St. Catherine's wheel sparkling behind her closed eyelids.

When she wandered back to herself, languid and sated, Bess was watching. Her eyes were hooded, her countenance shiny with Marguerite's juices. Still unwilling to speak, Marguerite guided Bess to lie down on her back.

Bess let herself be pliant, obeying Marguerite's unspoken commands. As the voluptuous woman moved above her in the half-gloom, a shaft of light from the window cast a chiaroscuro of gold, amber and shadow over her skin, the patterns suggestive of a navigation chart that Bess followed from the peaks of the sun-gilded north to the shadowy tangle in the south between Marguerite's legs. Her hands reached out and traced the curving lines, her callused fingers and palms catching on womanly softness. Her fingers stroked Marguerite's flanks where the sweat was already cooling.

Marguerite's expression was rapt and greedy. She leaned down and sucked Bess' lower lip into her mouth, her tongue flicking the sensitized flesh until Bess squirmed. Marguerite smelled of *eau-de-cologne* and fruit, and the scent drove Bess near to the breaking point.

Bess loosely fisted Marguerite's hair, using careful pressure to guide the other woman's head to where it needed to be, forcing herself to be gentle when her body clamored for release. Tension thrummed through her, tight and near painful. Marguerite's touches were bold, piercing Bess to the core.

She trembled, her body straining after the sweet, sweet friction that would send her flying. When Bess finally convulsed, the pleasure was almost too intense to bear. Her heart beat wildly, and she caught her tongue on the rough edge of her teeth. The momentary sting was lost in the raw sensations that overwhelmed her and left her out of breath, wheezing like an ancient beldam while Marguerite crooned and curled around her, a warm soothing presence at her side.

It was a while before Bess realized that the wetness on her face was tears, although she was not crying. She sighed, listened to Marguerite's drowsy love-talk, and let herself fall asleep, utterly relaxed for the first time in years.

CHAPTER TWENTY-FIVE
The Sighting of the Isle

In the captain's cabin, Marguerite stood by the curved stern windows, rinsing the night's sweat from her body with cool water and a sponge when Bess awoke. Like most sailors, she had the admirable ability to drop off to sleep and awaken to full consciousness almost instantly. Looking over at Marguerite, naked and covered in water droplets, her skin dappled with bright sunshine that was filtered through the mullioned rose glass, Bess felt such a swelling of fondness that she could not help grinning like a fool. She settled back in the bunk box as Marguerite turned and regarded her with affectionate asperity.

"Do you plan to lie abed all the morning, like a shiftless, frowzy old fussock?" Marguerite asked, but her smile took any sting from the words. Bare feet thundered to and fro on the deck in answer to the muffled roar of officers' shouted orders. It was the second week of their journey, and to Bess' gratification, Marguerite had gotten over the worst of the *mal-de-mer* in a few days.

"Old?" Bess flipped off the sheet and stretched, her spine popping. She ran a hand over her flat belly down to the juncture of her thighs, provocatively fluffing her dark pubic curls with her fingertips. "I'll give you a good Spanish doubloon for every gray hair you find, madam, either below-decks or at the masthead!"

Marguerite sat down on the edge of the bunk box, her glance filled with tenderness. "How do you fare?"

"I could ask the same of you, dear heart." Bess trailed her fingers up Marguerite's arm; she felt an impulse to use her lips and follow the blue vein from elbow to wrist, to taste the skin covering Marguerite's pulse, but refrained, feeling as idle as Marguerite had implied. Satiated good humor filled her to the brim with a warm glow. At that moment, all was well in Bess' world, and she basked in the perfection.

Marguerite sighed and shrugged. "I would rather have stayed on Hotspur Cay than undergo this errand to God-knows-where for the sake of mere treasure."

"'Tis more than treasure that draws me on," Bess asserted, sitting up and scooting over so that she could pull Marguerite into an embrace. With her lover's blonde head snuggled beneath her chin, Bess continued, "*Deceiver*'s a legend in the Spanish Main, a tale told among the fo'c'sle hands, growin' bigger each time in the telling. To be the one who finds *Deceiver*'s grave...that's the closest to immortality I'll ever be."

"So you do it for glory?"

"Aye. Is that wrong?" Bess sniffed Marguerite's hair, enjoying the closeness and the warmth of her body.

"I suppose not." Marguerite closed her eyes. She had not yet told Bess about the curse that afflicted her, about the possibility of madness and death if they failed to find the lost ship. There were only a few days remaining till the new moon. Fortunately, the ships had managed to stay on course, avoiding the deadly Calms of Cancer in the Horse Latitudes and the equally dangerous Sargasso Sea whose monstrous denizens devoured the unwary. *Mad Maudlin* now sailed before a brisk northeasterly wind, achieving a rate of speed that made foam fly back from the bow, the spray breaking as far aft as the gangway. In the last fortnight, Bess had talked to her about many things, including the misunderstanding with Carmelita, but Marguerite had difficulty unburdening herself in like fashion since there was nothing Bess could do to avert her destiny. It was better, in her opinion, to simply enjoy what time they had together, and not think on what evils that tomorrow might bring.

Marguerite loved Bess, her Bess...the expert sailor who took her out on deck at night and patiently named the constellations and the stars; the lover who was, by turns, tender and fierce, possessive and sweet; the woman who might be crude and sometimes mannerless, but who was also unexpectedly affectionate and playful. Marguerite could not have asked for a better companion nor a more passionate one, and she wondered at her own foolishness in denying the possibility of their bond. Bess made her feel precious in a way that was outside her previous experience, and she cherished every moment of that regard.

She disentangled herself with some regret, stood and went to her sea chest, which sat beside Bess' own. Taking out a shirt and a pair of canvas petticoat-breeches, Marguerite dressed herself while Bess watched with narrowed eyes.

"What's amiss, Margo?" Bess finally asked, getting out of the bunk box and pulling on her own clothes – a loose shirt and a pair of nankeen breeches, for she intended to spend the day aloft in the cross-yards, searching for any sign of land.

"Why, naught that I can claim, sweetheart," Marguerite answered pertly. She pursed her lips, begging for a kiss, and Bess obliged eagerly.

Before Bess could question her further, Marguerite slipped out of the cabin and went on deck. The crewmen were used to her; other than a few politely murmured beg-your-pardons, she passed unmolested to the bow. Waiting for her was Mistress Glasspoole, a lacy mobcap secured to her head with a scarf that tied under her chin. The sun's reflection off the foamy waters threw the older woman's face into sharp relief. In her hand was a vial of some lurid green substance that had been concocted by Lettice Speedwell.

"Are you ready, lass?" Glasspoole asked, whistling through her false teeth.

For reply, Marguerite pulled her shirt up and turned her back, exposing the charmed tattoo on her shoulder. She had grown used to the thrice-daily ritual, though it was still unpleasant, and she had learned no liking for it.

The wind whipped at her plait and stung her eyes, drawing tears; overhead, the jib sail flapped loudly for a moment before a cross-breeze filled it. She gripped the rail and set her teeth, waiting.

Glasspoole unstoppered the vial and poured the tiniest amount of viscous liquid onto the spiked wheel tattoo. Instantly, yellow-green witch-fire sprang up, licking down Marguerite's arms. The sensation was not unlike insects crawling on her skin, and she tried not to wriggle too much, although a muscle twitched uncontrollably in her jaw. At least with Speedwell's cobbled-together brew, the activation was more controlled than mere salt water, and Marguerite remained conscious.

Henry Dunn came to stand next to her; beads of sweat glistened on the dense mat of hair that covered his bare torso. At his nod, Marguerite pulled her cramping fingers off the rail with some difficulty. As her hands flew into the air, a thin web of witch-fire formed, growing thicker and larger and finally ballooning outward, two tendrils anchored to her wrists but the rest shaped into a fat cone that vibrated strongly. Marguerite struggled to maintain her balance; it was like trying to control a clumsily constructed kite in a storm. Gingerly, Dunn reached over the rail and touched the tip of the cone with a flattened lead tablet. There was a blinding flash and a shower of yellow-green sparks, a yelp from Marguerite as one of the sparks brushed her cheek and left a trail of brief, burning pain, and the witch-fire snuffed out as suddenly as it had formed.

Exhausted, Marguerite slumped to the deck, tilting her head back and looking at the sky. An albatross kept easy pace with the ship, gliding on invisible air currents; the bird's outspread white wings seemed as big as sails against the hot blue sky. She absently wondered what the albatross was doing so far outside its usual Pacific waters, but she was too tired to speculate.

Mistress Glasspoole's face appeared in her line of sight, a hovering gargoyle with a kindly expression. "Will you rest here, Margo, or return to the captain's cabin?" she asked.

"Oh, I'll stay here for the nonce," Marguerite replied. Her muscles felt rubbery, and she had a feeling that if she tried to walk, she would simply fall over, never to rise again.

It was Dunn's turn to be solicitous. "I can order some of the hands to carry you below; if not, we'll rig an awning with sailcloth and fetch you tea from the galley." He seemed sincere in his wish to see to her comfort, being a former Royal Navy officer and possessing a certain grim gallantry now that her place as Bess' woman was assured.

"That's very kind of you, Mr. Dunn. The sailcloth and the tea, I mean." Marguerite leaned back. Each time the tattoo was made to yield its secret, it sapped her strength. She rubbed sweaty palms on her breeches – her fingertips were tingling, and she knew from experience that the pins and needles would last a while – and watched the albatross coast along, imagining that it was watching her, too.

She fell into a troubled sleep, although she was not tormented by her old nightmare. Instead, Marguerite wandered through a fog where vague and amorphous threats waited at every turn, all of them too pale, too inconsequential to give much countenance. The experience was disquieting but not terrifying.

When she woke, Dunn had indeed arranged an awning to protect her from the sun, which was somewhat past its noon position, and there was a flask of cold tea next to her. Bess stood above her. She had assumed a bottle-green broadcloth coat and tied a dull scarlet kerchief around her head. She looked down at Marguerite, frowning.

Marguerite's neck was stiff. She sat up and rubbed at the tightness with a hand, trying to ease the pain that threatened to turn into a full-blown case of the megrims.

"And you accuse me of laziness," Bess grumped. "Drink your tea." She was not angry but she was growing increasingly concerned. Dunn had shown her the new navigation tablet, the lines and directions engraved upon the lead's surface by the enchantment; nothing had changed since the last time. She was beginning to wonder if they were chasing an illusion, a magical *fata morgana* crafted by a long-dead man.

Marguerite took a swig from the flask. The tea tasted like the finest ambrosia and refreshed her wonderfully. She continued gulping until most of the liquid was gone and stifled a delicate burp behind her fist. The tannic astringency lingered in her mouth.

Bess squatted down next to Marguerite. Her good mood from earlier in the day had evaporated. Apart from the damned tattoo business, she had found that someone had left the sweetening-cock open, and near six feet of water had gotten into the well before the carpenter's mate reported the problem, which meant the crew manning the chain-pump to much grumbling. Shortly thereafter, a crewman on the *Red Queen's Revenge*, which was sailing close to *Mad Maudlin*, had toppled from the yard, bounced off the mainsail, and been catapulted over the side, where the crack-polled idiot had to be rescued amidst much hullabaloo. Another fool on her own vessel had gotten drunk on rum and Alicant wine taken clandestinely from the spirits-room, stolen a flintlock from the arms locker and taken shots at a sea bird. His aim proved as unsteady as his balance, though, for he nearly took off another man's head and was on the point of toppling over the rail before a furious Dunn ordered him clapped into bilboes and stowed in the crew's forecastle quarters until he sobered.

Bess was about to let spill this litany of woes, this Iliad of ills, when the look-out at the masthead sang out, "Land! Land, ho!"

She shot to her feet. "Where away?" she called.

"Two points to larboard!"

She took her spy-glass from her coat pocket and beat Henry Dunn to the larboard rail by a half-breath. Holding the glass to her eye, she scanned the horizon, her heart in her throat, her flesh goose-pimpled with excitement, everything else forgotten except the greed to be the first to see the long lost *Deceiver*. *There!* Bess focused on a green ridge, a barely noticeable hump above the line of silver-shot waves in the distance.

"Keep her dyce!" Bess roared at the helmsman, then she lowered the spy-glass and grinned at Dunn. "Well, sir, I believe we have found it."

"Aye, that's my thought as well." He shook his head. "I've no recollection of an island laid thus on the charts. Yon reef will have to be mapped careful."

"I've no wish to gut our *Maudlin*, Mr. Dunn, nor strand her on a sandbar. We'll lie off and send a jolly-boat with a good leads-man. I'd druther find a protected harbor; 'tis the season for storms, but needs must." Renewed happiness bubbling in her veins, Bess went to share her joy with Marguerite, but the woman was gone.

Bess squinted against the salt spray. *Mad Maudlin* bucked over a rolling wave, plunged into the trough, and rolled back to an even keel. The wind was freshening. Bess stepped to the foremast and laid a palm against the smooth wood, warm from the sun, slick with grease and sticky with melted pitch. Bess assessed the tension traveling down the mast from the straining sails, then cast a professional glance at the sky. "Take in the topgallants," she ordered, sensing a potential squall. The swarthy Bostonian boatswain, Toby Falconer, echoed her command. Checking the other ships in the convoy, Bess noted with approval that the four vessels were lying as close to the wind as possible, under all the sail they could prudently carry with a tropical storm threatening.

She ordered Dunn to send messages to the *Swiftsure*, *Medusa*, *Red Queen's Revenge* and *Mistress Moon*, to alert them about the sighting of the island in case their own look-outs had not spotted it. Spray from the bow wetted her face, and Bess stuck a hand into her coat pocket to find a handkerchief. Her fist closed around something cold, hard and metallic. It felt like a coin. Curious, she withdrew the object and held it up for inspection, instantly recognizing it as the coin she had taken from Black Harry Rye while he lay dying in a stinking alley in St. John's Town an eternity ago.

No civilized nation on Earth struck currency so odd, she decided, wondering if it might be some heathenish coin from the Orient. A circular bit of silver, the front was stamped with thirty-two lines radiating out from a smallish red stone very like a ruby. The coin resembled a compass card. Bess absently rubbed her thumb over the gem, and a glint of scarlet winked back at her. Intrigued, Bess turned so that her body shielded the coin from the sun, and rubbed the ruby again. Once more a whisper of scarlet scintillated on one of the compass lines, and only one. Bess raised her eyes in the indicated direction and saw Marguerite standing in the ship's waist, staring over the side at the creamy water hissing swiftly by.

Bess had always possessed excellent instincts, and they told her this silver talisman was bespelled in a way that involved Marguerite. However eager she might have been for an explanation, she was not willing to put any further burden on her lover. Marguerite was already suffering because of the tattoo; there was no need to upset her with a new and unpleasant revelation. Bess believed that Harry Rye had been on Antigua for the express purpose of finding Marguerite, and *that* was no doubt connected with *Deceiver*'s treasure. Resolving to speak about the matter to Speedwell at her earliest opportunity, Bess thrust the coin back into her pocket and decided to say nothing to Marguerite.

The jib sail, improperly braced and strained to its limit, suddenly tore loose and hung by a corner; the confused thunderous flapping set her teeth on edge. "By the sweet bleedin' Christ!" Bess cried, distracted and furious. "Is this a sailing ship, Mr. Falconer, or a goddamned lubber's cruise? Secure that sail!"

She watched while the hands jumped to the task, spurred on by the hideous curses spewed by both Bess and Falconer, who was extra vicious by dint of his being held up to blame before the crew. By the time the damaged jib sail was taken down and a replacement brought up from the hold, Bess had forgotten about the talisman and only wanted her dinner.

CHAPTER TWENTY-SIX
Discovery!

The reef proved navigable after a safe route was established, and the harbor, while small, was deep enough to accommodate the ships without any danger of their running aground. The captains decided that *Mistress Moon* and *Swiftsure* would anchor outside the reef as a precaution, while *Medusa*, *Mad Maudlin* and the *Red Queen's Revenge* would take the harbor.

All five captains and their officers set about ferrying supplies over from the ships, and quite soon a respectable little camp had been set up above the tide-line. Hephzibah commandeered the cooking tent – she got no argument from any of the other cooks – while Falconer took a cutter out with a few crewmen to go fishing for bonito and barracuda, which were plentiful in the waters. A shore party set out to go hunting for wild pig or birds. Katla Byng, who had finally forgiven her husband for his supposed infidelity, took Mistress Glasspoole and a group of well-armed sailors into the interior to gather edible plants including the guavas, coconuts, tamarind, sea grapes and sugar apples that had been glimpsed from the shore. Marguerite wanted to go with them, but Bess refused to allow it.

"God forbid you should be lost or hurted," Bess said, taking Marguerite by the arm and guiding her to a seat made from a sea chest with a blanket draped over it. "It would give my heart no easement whatsoever to think of you wanderin' about the wilderness, even in such stout company." A flock of little green parrots scolded them from a nearby calabash tree whose limbs were heavy with both birds and oblong fruits. Bess scooped up a shell and flung it at them. The entire flock exploded into the air with loud shrieks and much whirring of wings.

Speedwell stumped over to join the women. The giantess' leg had nearly healed, and she had only a trace of a limp. Her knee-length blue velvet *justaucorps* coat, with its silk embroidery, gold buttons and heavily decorated turned cuffs, as well as her splendid breeches, were far more suited to a royal court than a tropical island. She cleaned the lenses of her wire-rimmed spectacles with a lacy cambric handkerchief, saying, "If conscience does make cowards of us all, then love must make us simpering idiots."

Bess scowled. "Letty, what is it to you? The lady's made her choice, so I'll thank you to back your sails."

"What are you talking about?" Marguerite broke in, looking first at Bess, then craning her neck to glance at Speedwell.

"Oh, naught but a gentlewoman's wager," Speedwell said airily, shoving the spectacles onto her nose, and tucking the handkerchief up her coat sleeve.

Marguerite's eyes narrowed dangerously.

Bess rounded on Speedwell, aggrieved. "Why don't you keep your bonebox shut, you damned blatteroon, for I tell you, Letty, that you're diggin' your grave with your tongue!"

Speedwell's only response was a shrug and a smile.

Marguerite chose to ignore the by-play, as well as the implied contest between Bess and Speedwell. She had, indeed, made her choice, and the past was in the past, where it belonged. "What next, Letty?" she asked.

"Oh, you mean the treasure, eh?" Speedwell's broad face creased in a thoughtful frown. "I had hoped that your tattoo would continue to point the way."

"In what fashion?"

"If I knew that, sweet angel, I'd have come to the island and taken *Deceiver* for myself." Speedwell chuckled. "Be not fretful, Margo. The matter will either resolve itself, or I'll craft a spell to ease the way."

"Aye, the crew will enjoy a short time on dry land, though I'm sure they'd prefer some native girls to play the beast with two backs," Bess said. "In the meantime, though, we'd best see that the men don't overindulge in rum, otherwise there'll be broken heads and worse."

"*Red Queen*'s in need of a careening," Speedwell said. "Her bottom's fouled with weed, and I can feel the stuff dragging at her."

"My *Maudlin*'s due for a scrapin', too, otherwise she'll be wallowing like a hog in mud." Bess' gray eyes twinkled. "The men won't thank us for such a dirty, nasty job, but idle hands are the Devil's delight, as the parson says."

"Indeed. I'll recommend the same to Byng, Lovelock and Quittam." Speedwell took Marguerite's hand and bowed over it. "Fare thee well, angel, till the evening, at least." She went away over the sand, a magnificent velvet-clad figure shouting for her first officer.

Marguerite sat on the improvised chair, watching Bess. The woman's face was half in shadow, haphazardly cast by a tall palm; the gunpowder tattoo on her cheekbone seemed darker, like a flourish of quill-brushed ink. In repose, standing silently and looking out at the sea at the boats ferrying back and forth from the beach to the anchored ships, Bess' lean, black-clad figure reminded her of a Toledo sword, the brilliance and keen deadliness hidden in a plain scabbard but ready to flash forth at a moment's notice, dazzling the eye.

"I'm sorry," Marguerite said after a pause.

"For what, dear heart?" Bess asked.

"For all the trouble I've caused. All the fights, all the pain..." Marguerite sighed and rested her head against Bess' thigh; the breeches' nankeen fabric felt rough against her cheek. If her fate was to die on this island, she wanted to do so with a relatively clean conscience. "I was afraid, you see...dreadfully afraid, and I didn't dare show it."

Bess stroked Marguerite's hair with the back of her hand. "Do you still fear me, Margo?" She had to speak around a lump in her throat; the pensiveness in her lover's voice nearly broke her heart.

"No. I love you, and I trust you. I've given myself to you, and I trust that you'll not toy with my affections." She touched Bess' leg, suddenly, achingly aware of the woman's body, of the slide of her flesh beneath the clothes. There was little privacy in the camp; even less when Bess might be summoned at any time to deal with some trouble. Nevertheless, Marguerite could not help thinking how easy it would be for Bess to lean over and let their lips meet. Her skin remembered the feel of callused palms gliding on shoulder, waist, hip and thigh; she would never forget more intimate touches, either, explorations that left her weak and shuddering, begging shamelessly for more.

Bess noted the mottled flush spread over Marguerite's countenance and guessed the cause. Marguerite was quite the wanton, as she had learned, and that passion pleased her. Bess' pulse quickened. "There's no need for apologies betwixt us, dear heart. We both schemed and plotted and caught each other in the end, aye? So let there be no pardons sought. That part is over. We ought to be thinkin' of the rest of our lives."

Marguerite glanced up and was startled when Bess bent swiftly and caught her half-open mouth in a kiss that was sweet rather than intense; a gentle meeting of moist softness and light pressure, a mingling of breath. Bess straightened and ran a hand through the loose curls that hung over her brow. She said with studied casualness, "Shall we go exploring ourselves, Margo?"

There was a gleam in those steel-grey eyes that Marguerite recognized. She hopped off the sea chest, already anticipating a passionate interlude. It was with a degree of impatience that she waited for Bess to arrange a ribbon sling under her coat to hold a brace of loaded flintlocks, and to stuff her pockets with shot, powder and a packet of sandwiches wheedled from Hephzibah. Thus accoutered, Bess cocked an arm in invitation; Marguerite took it, and the pair of them set out to seek some privacy.

While they walked, Bess and Marguerite took turns identifying the flora of the island – flamboyant pink bougainvillea; hibiscus flowers; poisonous but beautiful oleanders; the straggling, blue-flowered plumbago; white cedar trees entwined with pretty coralita vines; and tall dildo cactuses whose long thin arms branched vertically from the base. The branches vaguely resembled a man's most intimate part, and sharp spines protected the red fruits. Marguerite also recognized a yellow orchid called Dancing Lady, growing on fine stalks that waved wildly in the breeze, like amber-and-gold jewels set *en tremblant*. Bess found a passion-fruit vine; once the wrinkled, purple orbs were sliced open with a knife, both of them sucked on the headily perfumed, bright orange pulp and spat out the seeds.

The two women followed no trail but simply wound their way through the trees and bushes, sometimes helping each other over obstacles or uneven ground. It had been a long while since Bess had been able to drop her guard and simply enjoy herself; it was a measure of how much she trusted Marguerite that she was able to do just that. *Mad Maudlin*, the other ships, and her responsibilities were laid aside in favor of this leisurely exploration with her beloved at her side. Bess realized that this was what

Marguerite had become – her beloved. She opened her mouth, about to confess as much, when Marguerite let loose a scream that fairly made her hair stand on end and her heart turn into a choking knot in her throat.

Bess drew a flintlock and cast around, seeking the threat. "What is it?" she half-whispered, expecting a wild pig, or a poisonous snake, or a naked savage at least.

Marguerite whimpered and crouched down, covering her head with her arms. "Up there!" Her face was white with terror. "Bats! Don't let them get in my hair or I'll go bald!"

Bats?

They had stopped in a small clearing that was surrounded by kapok and loblolly trees. Bess saw velvety brown bats, less than the size of her forefinger, with a thin, mouse-like tail about half its body length long. The bats clutched the branches and trunks of the trees; they seemed harmless, and she thought they were either insect or fruit eaters. When she drew nearer to have a closer look, a tiny green lizard on a kapok tree flashed its red dewlap at her in warning, and she stepped back, putting her flintlock away.

"Margo, these little creatures can do you no harm," Bess said, laughing. "Come along, dear heart. We'll go and leave the bats in peace, and they'll do likewise, I'm sure."

She had spoken too soon, however. A glossy black bird with bright yellow eyes – a Carib grackle – swooped down with an ear-splitting squawk and boldly took a swipe at Bess' head, making her duck. The grackle squawked again, and this time, the bats took exception. Flapping in erratic flight, the soft brown bats wove through the branches and away from the clearing, spurred on no doubt by Marguerite's horrified screams. Bess finally went over and took the woman by the arm, pulling her to her feet.

"That's enough, Margo! Belay that noise, woman! They're gone!" Bess shouted, trying to be heard. When Marguerite did not respond, she assumed the woman was hysterical, and gave her a gentle smack across the cheek.

The sound cut off at once. Marguerite opened her eyes a crack, checked to be sure the horrid vermin had indeed disappeared, and turned to Bess. "You hit me," she accused. Her cheek did not hurt at all – the blow had been insignificant – but she was nonetheless outraged.

As soon as Marguerite stopped screaming, Bess' attention was distracted by the direction in which the bats had taken flight. She had an excellent sense of direction; as far as she could tell, those bats were headed for the shore, to a part of the island that she had viewed through the spyglass during the *Mad Maudlin's* approach. There was a sheer cliff face there, the exposed rock white and crumbly, veined with darkest green like an old cheese. Bess automatically checked the height of the sun. High and low tides at this latitude and at this time of year were approximately six hours apart. By her quick calculation, it was low tide now, with high tide due in roughly three hours.

Bess turned to Marguerite and made an apology, sealing it with a series of light kisses on the woman's eyebrows, cheeks, nose and jaw. "I am most heartily sorry to have offended thee," she said. "Bats won't turn you bald, dear heart, though you may deafen me by roaring like a Bashan bull with his ballocks caught in a fence."

Marguerite flushed. "I'm sorry. I just hate bats! When I was a girl, my mother and I had a room in a house where bats roosted in the attic. Ugh! The smell was enough to make a maggot lose its appetite. The woman who kept the place, she used to tell me tales about the bats, how they would crawl to my bed and suck my blood, and if they touched me, all my hair would fall out..." She shuddered.

"Cruel tales to frighten a child," Bess said, putting an arm over Marguerite's shoulders. "Come along then...I'll show you there's naught to fear. Them bats is harmless to all save insects, or maybe fruits." She began to tug the woman along.

"Are you sure they won't..." Marguerite stopped speaking and wrapped her arms around Bess' waist. It was awkward to walk so closely together, but they managed because Marguerite would not have relinquished her hold for anything.

"Nay, dear heart. Harmless, as I said. Here, beware of that manchioneel tree; the whole thing's deadly poison, and the only cure's seawater, of which we haven't any at the moment." Bess kept up a line of chatter as she herded Marguerite in the right direction.

It was not too long before they reached the cliff. Bess balanced on the extreme edge and peered down. Marguerite kept hold of Bess' wrist and braced herself against a tree. The pirate leaned out – making Marguerite gasp and tighten her grip – and chuckled.

"What is it?" Marguerite asked through a fear-dried mouth; she was terrified lest Bess should slip and fall to her death.

"See for yourself," Bess replied. She swung away from the edge, bits of rock crumbling from beneath her heel, and anchored herself to allow Marguerite to cautiously peek over.

The drop had to be a hundred feet, at least. Marguerite watched the waves that dashed themselves against the rocks, throwing up a glittering arch of spray. The sound was a clashing roar, dulled somewhat by distance but still loud enough to give her gooseflesh. Sleek monk seals rollicked in the surf beyond, chasing a school of darting, silvery fish. Marguerite noted an unusual rock formation to one side at the bottom – it was tall and shaped like an upside-down "J" to her perception, with the long arm of the letter attached to the cliff face, and the hook curving out to sea. A few seals broke off from the chase and swam around the J-shaped rock to the calmer waters that were within the sheltering hook, and continued towards the cliff, where their dark brown bodies disappeared. Marguerite supposed there must be a tiny beach there, hidden from view. She found nothing humorous, however, and signaled for Bess to help her back in, only relaxing when her feet were planted solidly on *terra firma*.

"Well?" Bess asked, grinning.

Marguerite shrugged. "There's naught to see save some seals and surf and rocks."

"'Tis thought that *Deceiver* tore her guts out on a reef," Bess said, "but we've seen no sign of the ship in the natural harbor, so Mr. Lovelock sailed round the island in *Swiftsure* as close as he dared, looking for signs. Unless there are more uncharted isles in these parts, this must be where *Deceiver* lies, yet her grave ain't obvious. Damnably difficult to hide a ship the size of Carew's *Deceiver*, d'ye ken?"

Marguerite nodded.

Bess took a deep breath. "Well, then...Lovelock saw this cliff and reported it solid; I seen it, too. That can't be so; the water's rushing in and out, gentle-like, with no turbulence though the sea outside is churned up fierce. My wager's that the rocks – that high curve there – hide the entrance to a cave that can't be seen from sea. If Carew was a good sailor – and he was, dear heart, one of the best of his generation – then he could have sailed *Deceiver* into the cave if there was room for his mast-heads to pass unscathed, and if the wind was favorable."

Marguerite thought about what she had seen, the waves and the deeper water within the hook, darker blue and tinged with shadow. If Bess said it was possible for a very good navigator to thread a ship around the hook and into a potential cave, she had to believe it. "What do you want to do?"

"I'm tempted to climb down and see for myself, exceptin' I'm not sticky-fingered like a spider, and would likely break my fool neck in a fall," Bess said. She reached out and brushed a few strands of stray hair back behind Marguerite's ear. "*Deceiver* can wait; she's waited these twenty-five years, and she's a patient old lady. I, on the other hand..." She let a blaze of desire show in her eyes, and was smugly satisfied by the answering passion in Marguerite's heated gaze. "I've no wish to wait another moment."

"*Mijn liefje, mijn duifje*," Marguerite murmured, the Dutch endearments spilling over her lips as she was pulled into Bess' arms. "Love me..."

"Aye, for now and ever," Bess said, licking Marguerite's throat. She pulled back, breathing hard, then sucked lightly on Marguerite's lower lip, nibbling the delectable flesh while Marguerite shuddered and moaned. They tumbled down to the earth, kissing more deeply now, each drinking life from the other's mouth, sharing their bodies as well as their souls. Soon, the women rocked to a shared rhythm drawn by clever fingers, their kisses exploding with heat, no room for thoughts save "more".

Afterwards, Bess and Marguerite slept, curled together and warm.

It was not long after that the bliss faded and the nightmare began.

CHAPTER TWENTY-SEVEN
Nightmare Made Manifest

Held fast in the grip of powerful dread, Marguerite could not move; her strength was completely drained, leaving her able only to watch as the hideous man loomed over her, cackling with what she supposed was an insane sort of glee. As always, he was a wasted, skeletal figure with long, dirty white hair, and eyes that burned like black fire.

"My key!" he crowed, his breath stinking like bilge-water. Filthy, jagged fingernails skittered over her face.

"No!" Marguerite shouted in denial.

"Aye, my blood, my bone, my key! Come to set me free!" he crooned.

The man bent and scooped her into his arms; despite his thin, unhealthy appearance, he was strong and able to bear Marguerite without a tremor. She could not resist him at all, though revulsion made her want to vomit. A languid torpor, insidious as spirits of poppy, weakened her limbs. He mashed her face into his shoulder; he stank of the grave, a sickeningly sweet taint of corruption that made her stomach heave. His bony fingers sank deep into her flesh, so that she could feel the bruises forming as well as the pain. He carried Marguerite away while he continued to babble a sing-song about keys and blood that she could not comprehend.

Was this Fancy Tom Carew, the man reduced to a gibbering ghost? A spirit whose evil was scattered by madness? He called her the key to his freedom, but what did it mean?

"Set me free, my key," he whispered.

Marguerite bit into the man's mildewed coat, hoping to reach the withered flesh beneath, but the taste was so foul she spat the cloth back out again. How long they traveled, she did not know; time did not exist in that grey, formless place, where only she and her abductor had substance, and the rest was fog. At last they stopped in a place where Marguerite could hear the rushing of the sea; where the man's stench was lessened by the smell of salt in the air. She heard gulls screeching, and booming surf, but the sounds were oddly distorted. Marguerite turned her head and opened her eyes.

Then she screamed.

Bess sensed that she was alone in the moment just before she awakened. Instant alarm had her scrabbling at the abandoned sling of flintlocks and lurching to her feet with her eyes still shut. Where was Marguerite? She opened her eyes. There was the ribbon from Marguerite's hair, left abandoned in the grass; both shoes, too, and stockings as well. Bess cast about, knowing full well that Marguerite had not been attacked by a wild beast; the noise would have drawn her out of sleep, as it would have if her lover had rolled off the cliff, impossible as that seemed. They had fallen asleep well away from the edge, and she knew from experience that neither of them was overly restless in bed.

"Where's the wench got to?" she muttered, then raising her voice in a shout, "Margo! Sing out and answer, dear heart, wherever you may be!"

A crashing in the nearby bushes came as a great relief. Bess kept hold of the flintlock, though – she had not survived a dangerous profession for so long by being credulous – and called, "Were you seeking nature's easement? B'God, I wish you'd have stayed a mite closer, Margo, for you've frightened a year off my life with this peep-bo game."

To her astonishment and fury, the person who appeared was not Marguerite, but Allegra Quittam. "Well, ain't this a pretty sight!" Quittam said, cackling and waving a ring-laden hand at Bess. Her thread-wound blonde quiffs stood up like little paintbrushes on her head. "There stands Bess O'Bedlam, flummoxed by a doxy."

"Don't speak so of Margo, you dog, or by the sweet bleedin' Christ, I'll send you to the Diet of Worms in a snap," Bess growled. "Have you seen aught of Margo?"

"Nay, I've seen neither hide nor hair of the butterbox baggage," Quittam said, her jade green eyes filled with amusement. "Are you so caught, then, by the honey-snare? I thought I'd never live to see the like."

The reply that Bess made was short, savage and blasphemous. "Don't stand there bein' clever, Allegra...help me find the wench. She wouldn't go a-wandering without her shoes; her feet's too tender."

Although still amused, Quittam checked the ground, moving in a widening circle, and soon called out a halloo. "It ain't nothing to do with Margo, but plant your peepers here...we're not the first to set foot on this isle."

Several scraps of mildewed black cloth were caught on the bark of a West Indian pine; below, in a small patch of damp ground, was a single footprint. Bess examined the print and the cloth scraps, frowning. "It don't signify," she said at last, brushing aside a clump of spindly, spidery white lilies and finding a second footprint. The man who made it was missing the littlest toe of his left foot. "Mayhap there's some poor sailor been marooned a time past, but if so, he couldn't take Margo. She'd have struck up a fuss."

"What if he knocked her on the head?"

Bess' scowl turned blacker than a thundercloud. "I was sleepin', by God, but I weren't dead! D'ye think any rapscallion could come upon me unawares, you thumping great beetle-brained booby?" Suddenly, her face cleared as she thought of the unusual talisman, lying forgotten in her coat pocket. Bess found the silver tablet and rubbed the central ruby with her thumb. One of the graven lines flashed scarlet, and she followed the course with her eyes, at first disbelieving, then angry beyond anything she had felt before.

The scarlet line indicated that Marguerite had gone over the edge of the cliff.

"What is it?" Quittam asked, leaning over Bess' shoulder. "Oh, a talisman. Put not your trust in such gimcrackery, m'lass. Thaumaturges don't truckle with poor magics like that, and a hedge witch's work is more likely to point you to the nearest dung-heap or brothel than any treasure."

"Not this'n," Bess answered shortly. She went to the edge and glanced down. Marguerite would not jump of her own accord. Could the woman have been pushed? Bess held up the talisman; sunlight glinted from the silver surface, straight into her eyes. She grunted and blinked away the dazzle. When her vision cleared, to her astonishment she saw the scarlet line had stretched out from the talisman. It was drawn through the air and bent at a downward angle between her feet. Bess turned around; the line straightened and stabbed downward again, this time at the ground about ten paces from her position.

Understanding dawned.

The cave.

Marguerite was under her feet, somewhere in the ground. How she had come to be there, Bess did not know. Some witchery was afoot, and there was only one person who could provide the answer. "Clap on sail, Allegra, and we'll beat back to camp," she said, "for this is work more fit for Letty Speedwell than we two, without an ounce o' power betwixt us."

Quittam grasped her upper arm, halting Bess in her tracks. "Why concern yourself with a wench? There are plenty more where she came from. Margo's usefulness is done, less'n you've such a taste for that woman's beef."

Bess wrenched herself away and put a hand on the hilt of her cutlass. "Are you challengin' me, Allegra?" Hot rage stirred in her belly till she could have choked on it; she welcomed the sensation, as it overrode the cold clench of fear in her chest.

Quittam eyed Bess oddly but kept hands away from her weapons. "You've led us a profitable venture. I've no quarrel with you."

"Then I'll have goddamned silence on the subject of Margo unless you've somewhat useful to say."

"As you wish." Quittam bowed her head in acquiescence.

Bess turned on her heel and tracked back to the beach encampment, not bothering to see if Quittam followed her.

"Letty!" she called upon reaching the tree-line.

The giantess sat beneath a royal palm, sketching in a notebook. At Bess' call, she raised her head and, perceiving that something was wrong, put away her work and rose to her feet. "What's amiss? Where's Margo?"

"Lost," Bess said. "Look, you, here's the tale..." She gave Speedwell a recitation of the bare facts, including her supposition as to the cave. By the time she was done, excitement was mingled with concern in Speedwell's expression.

"That would explain *Deceiver*'s absence," Speedwell said, taking the silver talisman and examining it. "A cave would serve admirably to hide the ship from casual view. Now tell me again...what signs did you perceive by yon cliff's edge?"

"A few scraps of broadcloth and two footprints," Bess said, striving to reign in her impatience, "with the smallest toe missing on the left."

Speedwell opened her notebook and murmured something arcane. Bess caught a glimpse of writhing ink and an impression of something nasty blossoming on the page before she averted her gaze. "Damnation, Letty, that fair makes my flesh crawl!"

"That's as may be, my friend, yet bear up a while longer," Speedwell said. At last, she snapped the notebook closed, but not before a tendril of orange witch-fire escaped and puffed out of existence. In her other hand, the silver talisman looked like a miniature snuff-box, capable of holding only a single pinch of tobacco. "Aziel, whose aspect is the Sun ascendant," Speedwell said as though lecturing an apprentice, "who is first of the Grand Dukes of Hell, Overlord of the Infernal Counsel, and commands nine upon nine legions of lesser demons, has dominion over the hidden treasures of the Earth."

"Pray tell, what's *that* to a blind baboon's arse?" Bess asked, biting back far harsher words.

"Why, naught for you, captain damn-your-eyes. As for me, I'll require a moment to craft a puissant protection, and then I suggest we find this cave of yours, for there lies Margo and the *Deceiver*, and the answer to our questions. Yes, by Baphomet's beard," Speedwell continued, putting aside notebook and talisman so she could pull her silver-laced red hair back and tie the queue with a ribbon, "choose a crew of hardy, black-hearted souls who aren't afraid to spit in the Devil's face."

"I'll do that," Quittam said. She fled down the beach, where her barked orders caused a flurry of activity.

Frederick Byng came over. Dressed resplendently in a gold-frogged green satin coat and shoes with emerald buckles, he toyed with a quizzing glass whose single lens was a flat piece of golden-green shimmering peridot. "What's this I hear about an expedition?" he asked, his features sharper than ever and his nose a-twitch like a rat's that scents the bait.

"Margo's been taken by God-knows-who or what," Bess said grimly. "She's in the same place as *Deceiver*."

"And where's that, pray tell?" Byng fiddled with his quizzing glass, flipping it around and around his slender fingers.

"In a cave round about the island," Bess replied, not trusting Byng an inch more than necessary. He might have appeared to be civilized, but the man had the soul of a murderer born, and would not hesitate to sacrifice anyone – with the possible exception of his wife, Katla – to get his well-manicured hands on *Deceiver*'s treasure. "You stay here, Freddie, and take charge of the camp whilst we're away. Let Allegra be your second. Solomon Lovelock is to continue patrolling the waters, in case of unwanted callers."

Byng looked faintly suspicious but agreed in the face of Bess' urgency. "Aye, that can be done easily enough."

Quittam returned. "I'll stay with Freddie," she volunteered before Bess could say anything to her. "Did you know that Carmelita is here?"

"What?" Bess' head whipped around and she pinned Quittam in place with a glare. "What did you say?"

"I just saw that Spanish doxy, Carmelita, with Solomon Lovelock, there by the cooking tent," Quittam said, jerking a thumb over her shoulder.

Bess ground her teeth together. "I've no time to see to the señorita. Mr. Lovelock's been warned to keep her away from me; all else is his own business." She saw that the jolly-boat was ready and tugged Speedwell's sleeve. "Come along, Letty. Let's see to Margo."

"And the *Deceiver*, of course?" Byng cut in, his brows raised.

"Naturally, Freddie." Bess gave him a mocking bow and led the way to the waiting jolly-boat. Once she and Speedwell were aboard, the crewmen shoved the boat into the blue-green billowing surf and jumped in themselves, swiftly taking their proper places with Henry Dunn acting as coxswain. His deep voice sang a rhythmic chanty as the men worked the oars in unison, putting their backs into the work to shoot the jolly-boat over the surface of the sea.

> *Naught we care for wind or weather,*
> *Naught we care how blue the sea;*
> *Heel, haul, and heel-o! my boy-o,*
> *'Tis homeward bound for me n' thee;*
> *Aye! Naught we care, for we are free!*

The water was so crystalline clear that it was possible to see all the way to the bottom, where black coral and star coral stood alongside elephant ear and orange rope sponges and other weird sea creatures, the whole surrounded by fine white sand. Colorful fish, turtles, stingrays and sharks swam in groups, or as solitary predators seeking to eat and avoid being eaten in their turn. A school of slender, silver, sharp-toothed barracudas cruised beneath the jolly-boat, scattering other fishy denizens from the area; their formation was as precise as an Army regiment on parade.

Speedwell sat in the stern, muttering to herself.

Bess was uncomfortable around magic; she preferred to rely on flintlock and cutlass and her own rough courage to see her through, no matter the situation. Spook-binding was best left to those with the talent for it. Worry fisted her heart; she gnawed the inside of her cheek until she tasted blood, then she spat over the side to avert bad luck.

Ah, Margo, dear heart...if aught's happened to you, I'll see the world burn for it!

She huddled against the gunwale, her gaze on the green hummock of the island, while above their heads, black storm-clouds gathered, rushing in fast from the sea.

CHAPTER TWENTY-EIGHT
The Devil His Due

It was with some degree of trepidation that Bess' party rowed around the hook of the rock formation that concealed the entrance of the cave. At their approach, a number of seals, agitated by the arrival of strangers, fled scolding, their barks ringing and echoing in the shady hollow of the "J". Sooty-winged petrels that had made their nests in irregularities in the cliff face above, took to the air in squawking flight. Henry Dunn stopped singing his chanty as the jolly-boat slid deeper into shadow. The cave mouth yawned agape before them, tall enough to accommodate a ship, but the blackness beyond was impossible to penetrate with eyes too accustomed to the sun. The crewmen worked their oars silently, dipping and lifting with hardly a splash. In the last crescent of a sunbeam, water droplets dripping from the raised flat blades glittered like strings of diamonds, and then the boat glided into the cave's gloom.

A soft, grey, ambient light filled the high-ceilinged opening and revealed the bare-masted ship which loomed there, the curve of its rising keel exposed to the upper edge of its copper clad-bottom. Broken stays and sheets hung limply from the yards and crosstrees. The futtock shrouds and ratlines were thick with bird and bat droppings. A beautifully carved figurehead on the bow depicted Satan himself, complete from the tips of his horns to his hairy goat's feet; the face was androgynously beautiful, that of a fallen angel with mother-of-pearl eyes. The scroll of the escutcheon bore the silent wreck's name – *Deceiver*.

"*Deceiver*'s grave," Bess whispered, half to herself. It took an effort of will not to clamber to her feet in the jolly-boat, so strong was the urge to board the derelict.

Speedwell nudged her with an elbow, nearly toppling her over anyway. "See there," she said, pointing a finger off to the side.

A wide swathe of white sand and rock bordered the quiet circular pool where *Deceiver* still rocked at anchor after twenty-five years, her mastheads just clearing the ceiling. Bess followed the line of Speedwell's pointing finger and saw Marguerite lying on the sand. The woman's eyes were closed, but whether she was asleep or dead, Bess could not tell. Her mouth went dry as dust; unshed tears burned in her sinuses like acid.

Speedwell's huge hand, hastily clapped on her shoulder, prevented Bess from leaping over the gunwale and swimming straight towards Marguerite. Instead, sick with apprehension but not daring to show the depths of her fear, Bess was forced to wait until the jolly-boat's prow crunched onto the sand. She jumped out, ignoring the water that poured into her sea-boots and made every step squelch unpleasantly.

"Margo!" Bess cried, falling to her knees beside her unconscious lover.

She ran her hands over the woman's body, relieved beyond words to find that Marguerite was still breathing. Bess could detect no injuries, but she was no chirurgeon. A sound alerted her that the jolly-boat was moving away. She surged to her feet. "Letty, what in the Devil's name are you doing?"

"Boarding *Deceiver*," Speedwell called back. "Just for a moment, madam, I assure you. Any plundering will have to await a bigger boat and a larger crew to ferry the goods around the isle to the harbor. I simply wish to take Carew's logs back with us."

"Damnation to your soul, Letty! There ain't no time for that!" Bess shook a fist at the departing jolly-boat. Marguerite's low moan brought her attention swinging back to her lover's plight. "There, dear heart, come back to me; handsomely now, handsomely," Bess crooned, kneeling beside Marguerite again.

A sharp piece of shell cut into her knee through her breeches; she shrugged aside the pain. She swung between relief at finding Marguerite alive and breathless concern over her continued unconscious state. Bess brushed damp hair back from the woman's deathly pale face. A faint yellow-green shimmer surrounding her lover's body spoke of witch-fire barely contained or recently loosed. Marguerite's light silk gown was dry, but the hem was water-stained a hand's-breadth deep and stiff with salt. However she had gotten here, Marguerite had been wetted in the sea.

A chill invaded Bess' bones. What if Marguerite was injured internally? She had seen sailors receive a knock on the head that left them stupefied, incapable of functioning. Sometimes they never recovered their wits. If that happened to Marguerite... Creeping horror covered her flesh and tightened the skin until it tingled with cold; her stomach lurched and left a sour taste of bile on the back of her tongue.

Even focused as she was on her lover, Bess registered loud creaks and explosive cracks from the direction of the ship. She dismissed the sounds as unimportant. Twenty-five years of neglect had no doubt left *Deceiver* less than watertight and prone to making protests. Another creak nagged at her attention, and another, and another. Finally irritated by the noises and wondering if the ship was going to fall apart, Bess swung her gaze away from Marguerite and onto the *Deceiver*'s profile.

The figurehead was looking back at her.

At first, she did not comprehend what she was seeing. That ignorance lasted only a heartbeat before Bess leaped to her feet, shouting at the crewmen she could see meandering about on the deck: "Clear off! Clear off, by Christ!"

None of the sailors paid her any real heed. Bess was too far away to inflict immediate retribution, and all of them had heard the legends regarding *Deceiver*'s treasure cargo. Meanwhile, the Devil's head was turning further; its left horn scraped the bowsprit, causing the ship to shudder under the minor impact. A wrench of its shoulders, one at a time, freed the upper part of the figurehead's torso; the oaken planks of the prow let out a groan under the strain, sounding like souls tormented beyond their capacity to bear. The Devil held a long-shafted trident in one hand; the carved muscles of its torso and arms shifted as it continued to turn at the waist to regard the crewmen with its mother-of-pearl eyes.

Bess shouted a moment longer and waved her arms, trying to attract the figurehead's attention, but it was focused on the sailors that sullied the ship's deck. One of the men finally noticed the Devil's wooden face had turned to look at them and called out a warning, but too late. Reaching back its arm at an angle that a human would find incredibly awkward, the Devil's wooden fingers grasped the now screaming crewman by the middle, and squeezed.

The man's body was pinched between massive fingers crafted of seasoned hardwood that was as unyielding as iron. His mouth gaped wide, but no sound emerged. Alerted to the danger, one of the others found a rusty boarding axe and hacked at the hand; the steel made no impression at all, save a few small splinters that chipped loose from the figurehead's knuckles. The Devil's face was an indifferent, beautiful mask; utterly serene as it continued to squeeze the crewman in its grip. A door banged open under the break of the ship's poop, and Speedwell appeared on deck. Bess could not tell what Speedwell was saying, but the big woman's mouth was moving, and the silver streaks in her hair glowed purest white as power poured forth in the form of lavender witch-fire – a sign of the highest thaumaturgical working that could be crafted.

Witch-fire lashed at the figurehead, a coruscation of brilliant lavender, plum, violet, amethyst and heliotrope. The figurehead paid no heed. The victim's spine snapped with sound that echoed in the cavern. A great gout of blood arced from the crewman's mouth, a pulsing crimson fountain that carried his life with it. The Devil dropped the dead man on the deck and reached for another, paying no attention to Speedwell's magics at all. The crewmen scattered, backing away in a group to the starboard entry port where the jolly-boat had been secured at the bottom of the ladder.

Bess was torn between swimming out to *Deceiver* and defying the hellish enchantment that was killing her men, or staying on the little beach to defend Marguerite in case the figurehead decided to attack them as well. At her feet, Marguerite moaned again; a flare of witch-fire spilled over her skin, yellow-green and glistening like liquid peridots. Whatever spell had brought *Deceiver*'s figurehead to life seemed to be affecting Marguerite as well. Bess chewed her lower lip, enraged by her own helplessness.

"Lord God Almighty!" Bess said, barely able to get the words out around the lump in her throat. Her voice rose. "Abandon that hulk! Shift your asses and *move!*"

The crew scrambled down the ladder and tumbled into the jolly-boat in a confusion of elbows and knees; Dunn roared among them, cuffing heads and organizing the men to the oars, while Speedwell cast a spell that sent tendrils of blue witch-fire whipping around the figurehead's legs, binding it lest it should break off completely to follow and wreak havoc. The

Devil continued twisting around; it was far more flexible than a human, not bound by the constraints of flesh. Cracks sounded like guns-shots as the figurehead pulled its torso entirely free from the prow, allowing it to bend forward from the waist.

The jolly-boat pulled for the little strand where Bess waited impatiently. Two of the crew helped her load Marguerite aboard, and they rowed for the cave entrance at speed. The men's faces were ashen; cold sweat beaded every brow, and their eyes were bright with terror. Nevertheless, they sculled with a will, each rise and dip of the oars in time to Dunn's bull-voiced commands. Bess was in the stern, facing front; she saw the moment when the boat had to pass within the Devil's reach, and she crouched protectively over Marguerite. Speedwell was beside her, a constant stream of arcane syllables pouring out of the giantess' mouth. She seemed to have aged five years in a moment; deep lines showed on her brow and at the corners of her eyes. The twin silver streaks in her red hair had broadened a good finger's width, and still Speedwell chanted, witch-fire guttering on her spread-apart hands.

Creaking wood was all the warning they received; that, and Bess' half-strangled shout. The trident plunged down among them; one of the points pierced the bottom of the jolly-boat, and water bubbled from the splintered hole. There was a bucket on board; Bess immediately started bailing. Marguerite was propped between two benches, her back against the gunwale. The unconscious woman's unbound hair trailed in their wake like a mat of golden weed, and her head lolled back and forth as the crewmen redoubled their efforts.

Dunn's brazen orders reverberated from the stone walls: "Lively, lads, put your hearts into it, damn your eyes!"

They pulled away faster; another few feet and the boat would be beyond the cavern entrance into the sheltered hook, and from there to the open sea. Outside, rain was hissed down in a solid iron-grey sheet, and thunder rumbled in the distance. Bess continued to bail, her back and shoulders aching. *Creak!* The trident swept down again, this time impaling a crewman. The spade-shaped point burst through his back and out his chest, lifting him screaming into the air, his legs kicking futilely. Blood pattered down, echoing the rainfall; the water was stained with muted scarlet. The Devil figurehead's inhumanly beautiful face showed no animation as it shook the trident, sending the crewman sliding further onto the shaft. His screams abruptly cut off and he went limp, though blood continued to drizzle from his body until the Devil's hand and arm were sheeted with wet crimson.

Bess bailed for her life, and Marguerite's life, and the lives of everyone aboard the jolly-boat. She could not stop to think that she might be next, wriggling on the trident like a worm on a fish hook. If she paused to consider the three-pronged weapon that might, even now, be aimed at her back, then terror would surely overwhelm her and all would be lost. Bess forced herself to keep moving. Dunn's voice dwindled to a harsh croak, but the men obeyed at their oars. The acrid stench of fear could not be drowned out entirely by the scents of rain, lightning, and salt. It was only discipline that kept the crew working in concert when if left to their own devices, every one of the sailors would have abandoned the jolly-boat and fled into the sea in a blind panic, though few of them could swim.

Dunn kept the incipient hysteria at bay, as did Bess; when a crewman faltered, Bess cried out, "I'll kill you myself, Daniel Honey, if you don't clap hands to that oar and row like hell-hounds are nipping at your heels!"

Creak! The trident plunged down, missing the stern of the jolly-boat by inches. Water billowed over the stern in a blood-tinged wave. Bess glanced over her shoulder and saw the dead crewman. His name was Preservation Meldrum, she recalled, a Navy deserter with a common-law wife in Portsmouth. His body remained impaled, dripping mingled water and blood as the trident rose into the air once more. Meldrum's eyes were fixed open, but they were blank and soulless, unknowing and uncaring. He hung on the shaft, limp as a discarded puppet. When the figurehead shook the trident at the escaping boat, Meldrum's arms moved in an illusion of waving them good-bye and God-speed.

On *Deceiver*'s deck, Bess thought she saw the figure of a man. He wore a tattered black greatcoat, and his colorless face was framed in a spill of silver hair. She blinked, and he vanished. Bess shook her head, dismissing the vision, and bent to her work, bailing water to keep the jolly-boat afloat until they should come back to the harbor on the other side of the island. Around Marguerite, the yellow-green witch-fire that had surrounded her suddenly died as the boat shot past the entrance, guided around the J-hook and took to open water where mist and rain shrouded the skies.

Speedwell collapsed, falling into the bottom of the boat. Bess turned the giantess' head so that she would not drown. Speedwell's blue velvet *justaucorps* coat was singed around the edges; her face was ghastly pale and pinched with exhaustion. Bess thought it best to leave the woman to recover on her own. Even minor spook-binding was mortal hard work; only the Lord knew how much it took from a body to perform such awe-inspiring feats of thaumaturgy as Speedwell had demonstrated in the cave.

Having seen to her friend's comfort as best she could, Bess ducked her head to avoid inhaling rain, fixed her gaze on the bottom of the boat, and bailed as fast as she was able.

Once back at camp, with Mistress Glasspoole to attend them, both Speedwell and Marguerite awoke. It became clear that Marguerite did not remember much of her ordeal and had no memory at all of how she had come to be in the cave that sheltered *Deceiver*. She had a wad of mildewed broadcloth clutched in her hand, torn from some rotting garment, but could not tell how it had come to be there. Glasspoole clucked, forbade further interrogation, and poured herbal draughts down Marguerite's throat until the woman rebelled, refusing further treatment except a glass of straw-colored hock to take the taste of the draughts away.

Lettice Speedwell remained drawn and haggard. After a while spent in her own tent, she emerged and sought out Bess, who sat at the fire near the cooking tent, wielding a stick to poke at *malanga* tubers roasting in the embers. A big ship's copper pot held stock made from portable soup in which was boiling the edible flower buds of the spike-leafed water-fat agave, together with chayote, arrowroot, plantains, white guinea yams, dasheen stalks and canna lily roots to make a thick stew. Marguerite stirred the stew with a wooden spoon, humming to herself. She had changed into a white cotton dress, the bodice decorated with a complex pattern of white embroidered wheels and arabesques, repeated on the skirts. The color made her face seem less pale.

After Speedwell sat down on the sand, folding her legs tailor-fashion beneath her, Bess scooped a *malanga* out of the embers and offered the potato-like tuber to the giantess on the point of her knife. Speedwell took it, juggling the hot roasted root until she could get it wrapped in her handkerchief.

"At least we've come away with the logs," Speedwell said after taking a bite and hastily swallowing air to cool her mouth.

"Aye, we have, though it cost me two good men," Bess replied somewhat bitterly. She made a stab at a stray *malanga* that had rolled clear of the fire and come to rest near her booted foot. "You could've warned me that there was foulness afoot."

"True, I sensed something of a magical nature, but without performing certain conjurations..." Speedwell broke off and crammed the rest of the root into her mouth. "I'm sorry, Bess," she said after she chewed and swallowed, "I am truly covered in chagrin, and know not what else to say."

Bess shrugged and offered the big woman a handful of ruby-red *acerola* cherries, a deliciously perfumed *cherimoya* fruit, and a star-shaped yellow *caimito* apple. Speedwell shared the *cherimoya* with Marguerite, whose eyes closed in almost orgasmic pleasure at the blended flavors of strawberry, mango, pineapple, coconut and banana that permeated the soft, sweet, custard-like flesh. After sucking the juices from her fingers, Speedwell took a finely carved walrus-tusk case from her coat pocket, removed two cheroots and lit them at the fire.

Bess sniffed in appreciation and accepted the cheroot which Speedwell offered. The tobacco was redolent of tamarind, jaggery and spices, and the smoke that rolled around on her tongue was bittersweet, suiting her mood. Both of them spent a few moments silently puffing, then Speedwell said, "I've spent an hour or two studying *Deceiver's* logs."

"And?" Bess almost snapped but tempered her voice at the last moment. She studied the glowing end of her cheroot. She and Speedwell had been friends for many years; there was no need to take out her frustrations on the woman.

"And I'd rather wait until all the captains are assembled, so I don't have to tell the tale twice or more," Speedwell answered. She blew out a cloud of smoke that hung in the humid air like a tattered veil and knocked the ash off her cheroot.

Bess frowned, but her impatience was short-lived; within a few moments, Byng and Quittam joined them at the fire, taking bowls of stew ladled out by Marguerite. Hephzibah limped over from the cooking tent with a wooden platter of soft tack and took her leave without ceremony. Lovelock showed himself soon after; lurking in his shadow, Carmelita looked lovely in a deep red gown with a scandalously deep décolletage. On her wrist was the sapphire bracelet she had taken from Bess, a piece of jewelry that had been meant for Marguerite.

Marguerite scowled at the sight of the woman she loathed, and Carmelita returned the expression with much malicious interest. Lovelock wrapped a beefy hand around Carmelita's arm and spoke to her under his breath. She flipped her red skirts, aimed a rude gesture at Marguerite, and fled down the beach, her high-pitched mocking laughter trailing after her. Lovelock flushed, but sat down when Byng urged him to do so.

Marguerite subsided, although her hackles were still raised. She took a piece of soft tack and bit into it savagely, imagining it was Carmelita's neck.

Speedwell cleared her throat. She took a final puff from the cheroot and threw the stub into the fire. Taking a large leather-bound journal from the inside of her coat, Speedwell said, "Here is the sorrowful tale of Fancy Tom Carew, lads and lasses. Pay heed and listen closely, for the truth of the matter is somewhat different than we've been led to believe."

"Speak plain and to the purpose, Letty," Bess said. "You ain't no market story-teller."

"Well, then...here's the gist of the thing as plain as a pikestaff," Speedwell said. Her bespectacled gaze swept round the assembled company, lenses flashing in the firelight. "Tom Carew isn't dead," she said. "How's that for a nasty surprise, eh?"

The captains stared at each other, speechless, while Marguerite dropped her spoon in the fire and swore a blasphemous curse that summed up everyone's feelings succinctly: "God *damn* it!"

CHAPTER TWENTY-NINE
The Truth Revealed

"Twenty-five years ago," Speedwell said, settling herself more comfortably on the sand, "in a tavern in Port Royal, Fancy Tom Carew met a weather-witch named Kat Spenser. Carew had earlier paid to have the demon Aziel summoned by a spook-binder; it was from Aziel, who has dominion over the riches of the earth, that he learned of a Spanish treasure galleon plying the Straights. The *Concepcion* was her name, under Captain Esteban Ramirez. Carew had no taste to challenge a 74-gun galleon with his 40-gun *Deceiver*, most especially since *Concepcion* was part of a convoy protected by other ships, so he planned to take her by deceit. For that purpose, he made the acquaintance of Mistress Spenser."

Quittam nodded, setting her jade earrings swinging. "Those Spanish captains may be arrogant sons-of-she dogs, but they protect their own. I'd not like to go into battle alone against those odds, by God."

Speedwell went on, "Carew cold-bloodedly seduced Mistress Spenser and convinced her to weave a storm-spell that would cut *Concepcion* out of the convoy, to leave the galleon stranded on a reef that he knew – this very isle, in fact, the secret of which he'd kept close and never shared. Besotted by his charms and filled with more love than sense, Mistress Spenser did as he asked, though the witchery was almost beyond her skill.

"The storm she crafted was a mighty one with heaving seas, and high-blown waves, and winds that tore *Concepcion*'s masts to flinders. Those poor souls that the tempest failed to kill, Carew's crewmen did for when he brought *Deceiver* to take possession of the foundered ship. Carew transferred the treasure to *Deceiver*'s hold. Once the task was done, he poisoned his crew."

"The greedy scapegallows," Bess said, putting more driftwood on the fire. "How did he think to manage sailing *Deceiver* home with no crew?"

"With a weather-witch on board to assure his winds were favorable, Carew could've sailed *Deceiver* to London if he wished, with only himself to mind the wheel...but I get ahead of the tale," Speedwell said, bending a disapproving glance on Bess.

Bess shrugged. "Go on, I'll keep my bonebox shut."

Speedwell tapped the log-book with her forefinger. "Alas for Carew, Mistress Spenser partook of the doctored water, which he'd spiked with crushed rosary peas, a deadly poison according to our good Mistress Glasspoole. As she lay dying, believing he had betrayed her, Kat Spenser summoned the last of her power to lay a death-curse on Tom Carew. The gist of the curse lies thusly – that Carew is neither alive nor dead in truth, but dwells in the twilight betwixt, his flesh rendered insubstantial save to himself and those who bear his blood. He can see the treasure he coveted, for he is bound to the isle, but Carew can never touch it."

"A murrain upon Carew's addle-pated inattention to detail. He ought to have kept a weather eye on Mistress Spenser, since she was paramount to his plans; a dying witch's curse is the most potent kind of enchantment that exists," Byng commented, fiddling restlessly with his peridot quizzing glass. His long brown braid was fastened at the end with an emerald-studded slide; the gems caught the firelight, winking bright as the arch of stars above. "'Tis but one of the reasons I remain wedded to my shrew of a wife."

Speedwell ignored Byng's comments and said, "And as for our sweet angel Margo's role in the curse..."

Marguerite clasped her hands and leaned forward eagerly; a little too eagerly for Bess' liking, as she had to hasten to rescue the woman's plait from slipping off her shoulder and dangling in the flames. "Yes! You said that I'm his blood, but *godskannone*! It's impossible! I'm only four-and-twenty," Marguerite said.

"You aren't Carew's daughter, sweetheart...but I believe your mother was."

"*What?*" Bess echoed Marguerite's shocked exclamation.

"I've no evidence as such, but 'tis certain that you're of Carew's close blood. 'Child of bone and blood...child of kin-ties, bearing the way...'" Speedwell quoted from Hephzibah's prophecy. At Marguerite's blank look, she turned to Bess. "Have you not told Margo?"

Bess had the grace to look uncomfortable. "It ain't come up."

Marguerite laid a hand on Bess' arm. "Tell me what?" A column of sparks drifted skyward while she waited for the pirate's answer.

Briefly, Bess explained about Hephzibah and speaking to the bones; about the spirits' early prophecy that called Marguerite the key to finding *Deceiver*. When she was done, the weight of the woman's gaze made her squirm a little. At last, Marguerite said thoughtfully, "We'll speak of this later, *liefje*. Go on, Letty."

Bess did not know whether to be relieved or apprehensive at the delay.

Speedwell swallowed an ill-timed smile and continued, "Carew and his treasure are trapped on this island by the curse, which is tied to his blood, for only by spilling his heart's blood can Carew escape; only by death may he be freed. Mistress Spenser meant to drive him to self-destruction with despair, thus assuring his place in hell. But Carew is clever as a Jesuit, though, and here's where Black Harry Rye enters the tale.

"It seems that Black Harry was the sole survivor of the holocaust because he'd hidden a bottle of rum in *Deceiver's* hold and drank that instead of the poisoned water when thirst came upon him. Carew plied Harry with good French gold from a cache he had hidden in the great cabin, and Harry's task was to scour the islands in search of any bastard who shared common blood with Carew, him having swived many a wench in his youth. 'Twas Harry that had the silver talisman made, and it led him to newborn Marguerite De Vries, the babe that was kin to Carew. In guise as a good Samaritan, Harry convinced Gertruida to put the tattoo on her child as protection against evil, but in reality, the charmed tattoo was meant to draw Marguerite to the isle where *Deceiver* and Carew waited."

"Why?" Bess asked.

"Because only Carew's heart's blood can set him free of Kat Spenser's revenge." Speedwell adjusted her spectacles. "Marguerite shares his blood – this connection means if Carew kills her, he'll resume his flesh, and she'll be cursed to take his place. He can touch her because of their kinship; he can influence her as well."

"Pardon me, but why did Carew wait so long?" Quittam asked. "If the tattoo's purpose was to draw Margo to the island, how did it happen that he squandered the chance for so many long years?"

"Because Harry Rye was a drunkard, a liverish specimen whose head was cracked once too often in brawls. Taking Carew's gold, he went on a monumental debauch of rum and bum. He forgot Gertruida's name, and Marguerite's, and where they both lived. When the tattoo did not draw Marguerite to her grandfather, and Harry returned to the isle for more gold, Carew tasked him with locating Margo again, using the talisman. For more than twenty years, Harry ate and drank and whored his way over the Spanish Main on Carew's coin."

"I'll wager that with such patronage as Carew's, Black Harry did not seek the wench too hard," Byng said.

"No doubt," Speedwell answered. "I believe it was Carew that abducted Marguerite today and took her to the cave. He has some power here on his home ground, at least where Margo is concerned. He's invaded her dreams for years. Now it seems he may reach her flesh as well as her mind and do as he wills."

"Carew will try to take me again," Marguerite said. "He'll try to kill me." Once, this news would have dismayed her utterly; now she found that she was calm – not resigned to her fate so much as welcoming the answers to questions that had eluded her for such a long time.

"Aye, he will try," Speedwell said, laying a big hand on Marguerite's knee. She took no notice of Bess' glare at the familiarity. "But fear not, sweet angel; you've my protection, and I'll spare nothing to see what may be done to break the tattoo's spell."

"Why didn't he kill me before, when he took me to the cave?" Marguerite asked.

Speedwell shrugged. "I know not. Mayhap his strength proved insufficient at the time. He is no doubt marshalling his forces to make another attempt."

Bess growled, "*Mad Maudlin* will catch the morning's tide and leave Carew to rot with his ship. He'll not have Margo, not while I yet breathe."

The fact that she would abandon the treasure without a second thought did not register at first; when it did, Bess did not betray herself but grew even more resolved to protect the woman she loved. *Aye, I love her*, she admitted silently, *for I know what love is now. I've chosen Margo, and the rest may dance to the Devil's tune in hell*. Rather than be astonished at this revelation, Bess felt a sort of peace steal over her, unknown even in her rough-and-tumble childhood. She only wondered why Marguerite gazed at her so guiltily, like a child who has been caught in mischief and anticipates a clout around the ear.

Speedwell looked at Marguerite. "Have *you* not told *her*?" she asked, jerking her chin at Bess. At Marguerite's chagrined expression, she chuckled. "Seems the two of you have somewhat to discuss. Come along, then. I'll craft a seal of the Second Solomon round your tent; be sure to stay within the circle and do not stray from it, no matter the temptation, for to do otherwise will mean disaster." She rose, brushing off sand. The moon had risen high, round and white as a pearl against indigo night. Tall as she was, Speedwell's head seemed to brush the moon, nearly blotting out its softly blurred light. "Are you sitting there, dumb as fishes, or bidding the rest good e'en and seeking your bed?"

Bess stood and offered Marguerite a hand. "What's to tell, Margo?" she asked, pulling the woman to her feet.

Marguerite flushed. "I'll tell you soon enough."

"I'll not brook a long delay," Bess warned.

"'Tis only till we're alone!"

"As you will, dear heart." Bess' easy acceptance was a sham; inwardly, she champed at the bit, wanting at once to shake the truth out of Marguerite. Peace was gone, turned into disquiet. Why could they not simply sail away from the island and return to Hotspur Cay? Carew's evil spirit could not touch his supposed granddaughter there, especially since Lettice Speedwell, Katla Byng and Mistress Glasspoole would help keep him at bay. If that proved ineffective, there were other spook-binders in the world who could be persuaded – or bought, or forced with threats – to make charms and counter-spells and what-not against the curse. Speedwell's hint that something was amiss did not sit well with her.

Still, she waited, chafing with impatience, while Speedwell fetched a long rowan wand topped with a chunk of rock crystal banded with copper that she used to draw a seal of the Second Solomon in the sand around Bess' tent. First, she made a pentagram, with the tent in the center, and connected the five points of the star with a circle. On the outer curve of the circle, she made the fourth and fifth pentacles of the moon, the third pentacle of Jupiter, the third and fourth pentacles of Mars, the fifth and sixth pentacles of Saturn, and the seventh pentacle of the Sun; lines connected them to the Great Seal and the symbol called the Breastplate of Moses.

To this geometric tangle Speedwell added an object taken from a jar that she removed from her coat pocket. It resembled a human eye, though the pupil was slitted like a cat's, and it was too large to have been cut from any child of Adam's head. The iris was muddy yellow, but that brightened to pure flake gold when Speedwell, stepping delicately over her work and being careful not to smudge any lines, placed the eye into the center of the Great Seal. The giantess touched the Seal with her crystal-tipped wand and intoned an incantation in a rippling language that seemed mostly vowels. To

Bess' private disgust, the eye blinked as if had come alive, and the pupil expanded as a fierce inhuman consciousness invaded the disembodied orb. The eye shifted in its sandy orbit, glaring here and there.

"That ought to confound Carew for the nonce," Speedwell gasped. She was shaking slightly; it was clear that she was near the end of her strength. "The Presbyopia of Argus isn't easily eluded or obscured. 'Tis as potent a guardian as I can craft."

Bess grasped Speedwell's wrist. "Thank 'ee kindly, Letty," she said, meaning every word. Magic was not to be trusted, but Lettice Speedwell had long since proved her loyalty.

Speedwell straightened. Strands of red and silver hair stuck to her sweaty face. "'Twill come out aright, my friend, I swear."

"That's my thought as well." Bess bade Speedwell good-night and led Marguerite into the tent, stepping over the lines drawn in the sand.

The tent was as luxurious as time, effort and *Mad Maudlin's* stores could make it. A thick mat of carpets covered the floor. Instead of a cot, kapok-stuffed mattresses were piled on one side, along with fresh sheets, a coverlet, and plenty of bolsters and cushions. On the other side was a long table and two chairs. On one end of the table lay a writing box. A pair of lanterns and a heavy silver candelabrum sporting beeswax candles instead of the more ordinary tallow dips stood in the middle of the linen cloth set with dinnerware for two. The women's sea chests were at the foot of the bed. Behind a cunning screen rigged with sailcloth sat the copper hip bath. An additional horn battle lantern hung from the central tent-pole. It was very cozy and comfortable for a temporary dwelling.

Bess lit a lantern with flint and steel; it was a Bengal light, used for signaling aboard ship. The flame burned behind blue glass, creating an oddly chilly atmosphere inside the tent that reminded her of diving deep into the sea, swimming beyond the sun-warmed surface and into the icy current that streamed beneath, imagining the further depths where Leviathan dwelled. Her flesh pebbled with the illusion of cold. Bess said, "So, milady mute-as-mumchance...why can we not sail on the tide and tell Fancy Tom Carew to kiss our arses?"

Marguerite sat down on the edge of the bed. She had not wanted to make this confession, and had hoped that once upon the island, she would not have to. It seemed, however, that Fate conspired against her again. "I'm cursed, too," she said reluctantly. "The tattoo...they said it would kill me."

Bess sank onto the floor, sitting close enough to Marguerite's leg to lean on it. She felt the heat of the woman's flesh though her skirts, but that could not warm her. Her voice roughened with a combination of anger and concern. "Tell me, Margo."

Marguerite did, explaining why she had withheld the information. "I've avoided madness and death for the moment," she concluded, "but if I leave the island..."

"Is this certain?" When Marguerite did not answer, Bess repeated the question, jiggling the woman's knee.

"I don't know," Marguerite admitted, "but I feel 'tis so."

Bess relaxed marginally. "Don't work yourself into a fret, dear heart. We'll have Katla sing the runes for you on the morrow. If it happens that you must sojourn here a while, I'll not abandon you." She reached up and cupped Marguerite's cheek. "If needs must, Speedwell can sail the *Red Queen* to many a port, seeking a cure, or mayhap the means to put paid to Carew once and for all. Freddie and Allegra and Solomon can do as they please."

"You'd...you'd give up *Mad Maudlin* for me?" Marguerite's throat closed; she swallowed hard, near to tears at this proof of Bess' love for her.

"Aye, I would," Bess said. She shifted onto her knees, so she could tilt her head and lay a butterfly-brief kiss on Marguerite's mouth. "For you are my dearest, my joy, my heart, my soul, and I love you."

This declaration took Marguerite's breath away. Trembling, she touched Bess' face with her fingertips. "I love you as well."

"Well, then...'tis settled," Bess said, her lips quirking in a smile. "Let us put out the light, Margo. Trouble may wait upon the morrow."

"Come to bed," Marguerite whispered.

A tender lassitude weighted her limbs. She kissed Bess, savoring the muted sweetness of the woman's mouth. Her breath quickened; rising need made her suddenly urgent, languid movements changed to frantic clutches. If this was all she was allowed to experience before dying – this single moment of connection – then Marguerite intended to grasp every single nuance, and cherish the memory in her mind forever. Blazing desire shattered her resolve when Bess' strong, callused hands ruffled up under her skirts and seared her flesh, tracing invisible love letters that she could read through her skin.

Neither woman remembered to blow out the light.

CHAPTER THIRTY
Things That Go Bump

"*Grietje...doe je ogen open, liefje...*"

Marguerite obeyed, her eyes fluttering open at her mother's soft-voiced command. She had been awakened thus every morning in her childhood, as long as she could remember. Happiness suffused her; she felt the tropical humidity on her skin and smelled the lingering traces of the night blooming cereus that grew outside the window of their little set of rooms. Her mother never allowed the tall cactus to be cut, no matter how it blocked the light; the spines deterred thieves from climbing inside and stealing their paltry possessions.

"*Kom es hier...*"

She flipped back the coverlet and rose at the summons, scooting to the edge of her cot and letting her legs dangle a moment before putting her feet on the cool floor. Marguerite wore a threadbare white chemise that had belonged to her mother; the garment was far too big for her little frame, the ragged hem brushing her toes, but putting it on made her feel like a grown woman, though she was only six years old. Wisps of hair fell into her eyes. She yawned and rubbed her face; her flesh was sticky with dried sweat.

"*Kom es hier, Grietje...*"

Marguerite shuffled towards the door to her mother's bedchamber. She was never to go inside, she remembered, unless her mother gave permission. Sometimes, Marguerite heard noises – groans or hoarse whispers; choked-off babble or sometimes muffled screams. This was different; Mama was calling her, so she went to the door. The wooden panels were scratched with a patchwork of signs and symbols and graffiti; there was a particularly crude drawing of two figures engaged in an act with an octopus in the lowermost panel. The bottom edge of the door was ragged, as if an animal had chewed it. Marguerite's breath hitched. Vague foreboding made her heart beat faster. The thought suddenly entered her head that she should not do this. Something terrible was behind the door, something with big sharp teeth that ate up little girls in a snap and crunched their bones. No, it was a *thing* made of crumbling cemetery dirt, eyes like shiny beads that glittered with greed, clods of earth dripping from an arm that extended to pull her in, pull her under...

"*Kom es hier...*"

Compelled by her mother's command, Marguerite reached for the tarnished knob, and a second voice shouted, "No!"

Marguerite woke a second time, and found herself standing outside the tent, a foot poised over the line of the circle. It had been a dream. She snatched herself back and nearly fell, until Bess wrapped arms around her from behind. Marguerite was shaken and confused. She leaned against the bulwark of Bess' body, glad of the solid warmth that helped dispel the chill that still embraced her to the bones.

"Your soul to the Devil, Carew!" Bess cursed loudly.

Outside the inscription in the sand stood a black-clad figure with long, dirty white hair that whipped over his shoulders in the salt-scented breeze blowing in from the beach. Fancy Tom Carew's face was a network of scars over bleached white skin; twisting flames burned in the depths of his dark eyes. His lips parted in a sneer. When he spoke, his voice was a drawn-out sigh that could nevertheless be heard as clearly as a scream.

"Give me my key," Carew said. He pointed a long, skeletal finger at Marguerite, who shuddered and pressed herself closer to Bess.

"Go to hell!" Bess exclaimed.

Carew took a step closer. "Damn you for a sneak thief, O'Bedlam! Give over my key and I'll spare the rest of your crew. Otherwise..."

"What will you do, eh?" It was Bess' turn to sneer. She was not afraid; indignation, anger, and a fierce protectiveness for Marguerite filled her with a heat that would admit no apprehension. "You impudent old dog! Your teeth were drawn by Kat Spenser and you've no flesh to speak of, just a collection of ill-favored wind. Hah! Why am I to be a-feared for my crew? A good fart would blow you stinkin' back to the grave!"

At these insults, Carew howled and launched himself at the women. No sooner had the spirit crossed the arc of the circle than there came a blinding flash of light, and he was thrown back as though launched from a catapult. Carew vanished and reappeared on the other side of the drawn lines in the sand. An expression of fury and sheer hatred settled over his scarred face. "Give me my key!" he demanded.

For answer, Bess made an obscene gesture.

Each of the lines of the Second Solomon seal began to glow with pure blue witch-fire. Granules of sand danced as a subtle vibration rose to the surface from far beneath the ground. Carew bared his teeth. "My key!"

Carew howled again; the sound was shrill, climbing up the scale until pain lanced through Marguerite's ears. At her feet, the golden Argus eye swiveled madly in its place; it might have been a single orb lacking any other feature, but the eye's anger was unmistakable. Marguerite stumbled back, forcing Bess to retreat as well or risk being pushed over. At the same moment, the witch-fire exploded, clawing upward in ragged banners of power that illuminated the night like a Beltane bonfire. All over the camp, crewmen ran from their shelters, most of them armed with hastily snatched weapons; the scene resembled an anthill stirred with a stick, a confusing, flustered commotion. Clad in a knee-length nightshirt that seemed as broad as a sail, Speedwell came charging towards Bess' tent; the giantess juggled a bronze bell, a candlestick and a thick ivory-bound book whose cover was studded with cabochon garnets and onyxes.

"Thou hast strayed from thy true course," called Speedwell somewhat breathlessly as she ran. Her spectacles had slid down to the end of her nose, and she had not a hand to spare for pushing them back. Loosened for sleep, her silver-streaked red hair spilled to her waist. "I have discovered thy trespass. I abjure and command thee, O spirit, to depart and resume thy proper place, by the Secret Name of God, which thou art constrained to obey..."

Bess grimaced. The exorcism ought to have been attempted by twelve priests, in the presence of an innocent child and an ancient beldam. Bell, book and candle had the power of Church tradition behind it, but even Bess knew that thaumaturgical operations were only effective if one followed the properly established forms. Bess appreciated Speedwell's prompt response to the threat; she just did not believe that it would work.

Blue witch-fire continued to burn on the sand. Carew paid no heed to Speedwell; he continued to howl and point at Marguerite. In his exasperated fury, he shifted too close to the Great Seal where the Presbyopia of Argus spun. As soon as the toe of his boot crossed the inscribed line, a roar split the air and a monstrous, golden-scaled hand burst from the sand, fastening its claws onto Carew's leg. He surged backwards, snarling, but jerked to a halt when the grip on his leg remained unbroken. Suddenly, Carew sank down to his ankles in sand. Scraps of black broadcloth shivered and fell to the ground. Another strong pull, and he was submerged to the thighs. Dirty white hair standing on end, crackling ectoplasmic sparks of ill temper, Carew cursed and vanished, and this time, he did not reappear.

The sand shivered once more and was still. The witch-fire fizzled out, and nothing remained save the drawn lines and the golden eye, now closed as if sleeping after its labors.

Speedwell sank to her knees, panting.

Marguerite started to go to her, but the giantess put up a hand. "Nay, sweet angel...you and Bess ought to remain within the protective circle, at least till the dawn. We'll speak further in the morning."

Bess had no inclination to return to their tent, and neither did Marguerite. They sat down at the entrance, Marguerite in the cradle of Bess' thighs, and held each other until a blood-red sun burst over the horizon and chased the last of the night's shadows away.

"He tried to trick me," Marguerite said at breakfast. She and Bess, along with Speedwell, Katla Byng and Mistress Glasspoole, sat around a table in the cooking tent, with calico-turbaned Hephzibah puttering in the background, tending a pot of burgoo bubbling over a fire. With the burgoo, she served them soft tack, cheese, fruit, and pewter mugs of blood-warm canary sack. Crewmen came and went, helping themselves to platters of food set out on sea chests laid side-by-side.

"By twisting your dreams to the semblance of youth past," Glasspoole said, nodding. She slurped a spoonful of burgoo, paused, and added more molasses-rich sugar to her bowl. "If you had walked past the Second Solomon's protection, Carew would have had you."

"He won't get a second chance," Bess said darkly, drinking wine and wiping her mouth on her shirt sleeve, leaving a stain behind on the linen. "Letty, what must be done to rid us of this troublesome whore-son of a ghost?"

"Yon's a bit of business that has no simple solution," Speedwell replied. At Bess' glare, she added, "Put away that grim expression, my friend. Have I not sworn to see Mistress Margo made free of Carew's influence? 'Twill take time, though, no matter how you swear and fling yourself about like the veriest petulant creature in creation."

Katla touched Marguerite's hand to get her attention. "I sang the runes this morning," she said. "The outcome was thus – Fehu, reversed, which speaks of bondage and slavery; Nauthiz, the need-stave, tells of a need to face one's fears, and summon the will to defeat them; and finally, Algiz, the elk of protection, tells you to follow your instincts."

"So I must face my fears and follow my instincts, or remain in bondage." Marguerite looked into the woman's near colorless eyes, then her gaze dropped to the wheel-like tattoo at the base of Katla's throat, one of the outward symbols of her power. Katla's colorless skin and hair were the marks of a magic user, the same as the silver in Speedwell's red hair, Hephzibah's blind white eye, and the ghost-whisperer Leviticus' piebald flesh. The spirits gave much to those who were born with the talent to use their power, but they also demanded a heavy price that usually manifested itself in physical terms.

"The runes' council is not the clearest kind," Marguerite continued, trying not to sound ungrateful.

"I'm sure it will become clearer in time." Katla sighed and shook her head; her silver hair was unbound, held back from her face with a leather band. "A second inquiry has confirmed one thing – you may not leave the island. If you do, you will surely die."

Marguerite drained her wine cup. "Damned if I do and damned if I don't. I had a feeling 'twas thus," she said. Pushing aside her untouched bowl of burgoo, she announced, "I've a wish to sit on the beach and watch the waves for a while."

Bess hastily finished her breakfast, cramming a slice of mango into her mouth and stuffing her pockets with hardtack. After swallowing, she said, "I'll accompany you, Margo. 'Tis my thought we might collect a pail of clams. Have you never done so as a child? No matter...you'll learn to dig with your toes."

Once on the beach, Marguerite allowed Bess to do the actual digging; the woman pried at dimples in the wet sand with her toes until she uncovered their shells, whereupon she dug down and scooped the clams into a pail she borrowed from Hephzibah. Marguerite preferred to walk barefooted in the surf, bunching up her skirts and petticoats to avoid them being wetted. The tide was going out, though, so she sought another occupation. There was a little round tide-pool set among some rough black rocks; Marguerite walked the few steps necessary to reach it and sat on the edge of the pool watching a starfish, a few spiny sea urchins, and a fringed anemone among the waving ribbons of kelp. Three small crabs scuttled under the water, chasing tiny fish that had been stranded by the outgoing tide.

Marguerite's mood was uncertain. She appreciated that Speedwell and the rest wanted to help her; she was also grateful for Bess' offer to remain on the island with her. Certainly, if left alone, Marguerite would quickly succumb to Carew; she had no defenses against his spiritual, mental and physical attacks. She shifted her gaze to Bess, who had been joined in her clam hunt by Hephzibah. The dark-skinned woman's limp did not deter her from vigorous digging. The lesson-by-example was clear — no matter the danger, life went on.

What else could she do except wait and hope for a solution? Any other course seemed folly, no matter what Katla's runes had revealed.

A loud scream from the other end of the beach drove every other thought from her head. Marguerite hurried from the tide-pool, her heart in her throat, and caught Bess by the shoulder. "What is it?"

Bess' gaze was cold. "Stay here with 'Zibah," she snapped. Dropping the pail, she sprinted away in the direction of the screams, which were impossibly rising in both pitch and volume, and then cut off without warning; the subsequent silence was well-nigh deafening. Marguerite shielded her eyes with a hand but could make out nothing on account of a high-piled heap of boulders that separated this part of the beach from the other. While she continued to peer, a brown pelican dived from the top of the boulders and splashed into the sea, no doubt after a school of sprats or fry; it was closely followed by a scavenging hook-billed gull, whose "ha-ha-ha" cry sounded like mocking laughter.

Hephzibah picked up the half-filled pail and limped over. Her blind eye turned towards Marguerite, but Marguerite had the feeling that Hephzibah could perceive her just the same. "Do you know what's happening, mistress?" she asked.

"Nay," Hephzibah said, "I've no more idea than you, but I suspect it ain't a cause for celebration."

Unintelligible noises came from the direction of the camp. Marguerite would have gone forward alone, but Hephzibah warned, "Stay close. My thumbs are pricking; there's wickedness about."

The camp was in turmoil when they arrived. Bess and the other captains had sequestered themselves inside her tent. The flap was laced closed; Henry Dunn and his powdered and patched lover, Levalier, had been set to guard. Crewmen gathered in knots of three or four or five, whispering together and dividing their attention between Bess' tent and the cooking tent. Carmelita moved among them, from group to group. The beautiful Spanish woman looked like unadulterated malice in a brown silk gown. Marguerite's uneasiness grew.

Hephzibah grunted and took Marguerite's elbow, guiding her to the back of the cooking tent where a slit had been made to allow easy access. Within, they found Mistress Glasspoole tending an injured sailor; a second man had not been as lucky, and his body was laid out on the same table where Marguerite had breakfasted not an hour earlier.

Marguerite clapped a hand to her mouth, feeling ill. The dead man had been savaged; most of his face was missing from brow to chin, leaving a raw, red, gaping hole in the front of his skull. Glasspoole said without turning around, "If you're to turn your stomach arsey-varsey, Margo, I'd take it as a kindness if you were to do so outside."

"What happened?" Marguerite asked, quelling her nausea with an effort of will.

"Traps," Glasspoole said shortly. "Lend a hand with that bottle of styptic."

Automatically, Marguerite obeyed, removing the stopper from the bottle of alum and lime, and handing it to the waiting herb-wife. Glasspoole applied the styptic generously to the groaning man's shallower wounds. He was bleeding from a number of gouges in his chest and arms. Marguerite could not begin to imagine what sort of trap might make those kinds of wounds, or what animal the trap had been intended to capture or kill.

After Glasspoole finished smearing her patient with various balms and bandaging him, she gave him a dose of poppy wine and left him to sleep. Hephzibah provided warm water for the herb-wife to wash her hands free of blood. When she was done, Glasspoole sat down and took the cup of sercial wine offered by Marguerite.

"I know not what other foul magics are hereabouts," Glasspoole said after drinking half the cup, "but I do know this – every day that is spent here, someone will die."

"What happened?" Marguerite repeated.

Glasspoole finished the wine; the lines in her face had deepened, and anger thinned her lips. "Greed for gold is what happened, with not a jot of common sense to temper the temptation. Whilst hunting agouti, Richard Jones and his brother, Albert, found a few doubloons under a bush. It was Jones that bit into one to test the purity of the gold, and the ensorcelled coin exploded his face and half his brain-pan away. Poor Albert was injured in the blast. Ah, Margo, 'tis not Carew's doing; at least, not directly. I suspect Carew's creature, Black Harry Rye. Any hedge-witch of modest talent will craft such spells for a price. Rye likely scattered the island with the things in case an unwelcome visitor paid a call and thought to disturb his master's hoard."

"That's no good," Hephzibah said, shaking her head. She was clearly concerned. "You know sailors, Esme. If they see the glint of gold, no warning is enough. 'Twould be the same as if we forbade them the pleasures of the flesh, and sat them before a brothel with the naked bawds on promenade day and night."

Glasspoole inserted a finger beneath her lacy mobcap and scratched her scalp delicately. "Aye, death is no deterrent. Every feather-witted one of them will figure that he's the lucky one meant to snatch the lot and suffer no consequences."

Marguerite glanced around. "Where's Bess?"

"Speaking to Lettice Speedwell and the rest. The conference is strictly under the rose," Glasspoole said, "hence Mr. Dunn and Monsieur Levalier's presence outside the tent to ensure privacy."

From outside came the clash of raised voices. Over the noise Henry Dunn shouted, "Belay this riotous assembly, God damn and blast you all!"

Hephzibah's dark skin turned an unhealthy shade of grey. "Mutiny," she whispered.

Glasspoole grimly poured herself another cup of wine, while Marguerite dashed out of the tent, fear for Bess' life lending wings to her feet.

"We wants our fair share!" shouted a near-toothless sailor.

Another man – scarred and bewhiskered, an unappetizing specimen wearing breeches with faded ribbons in the seams – shoved his way to the front of the mob that had gathered before Bess' tent. "We know there's gold," he growled, poking a finger at Henry Dunn's hairy chest, "and if any damned bum-boy thinks to cheat us, b'God—"

He broke off as Levalier grabbed his finger and bent it violently backwards, sending the man to his knees, squealing with pain. Levalier snapped, "*Fils de bas*! Do you dare? *Merdaille*!" He released the fellow and kicked him in the stomach as the sailor groveled in the sand. Levalier spat on him and kicked him once more for good measure.

There were about three dozen crewmen in the mob; many more hung about the sidelines, watching to see what would happen before they committed one way or the other. The tent flap remained closed. A muttering arose from the mob. Marguerite was about to push through when Toby Falconer appeared, blocking her way. "Pardon me, but you ought not to get involved, ma'am. The men's blood is high," he said in his nasal Boston accent, "and there's likely to be violence. Captain will skin me alive if aught happens to you."

"Let me go!" Marguerite cried, twisting free of his grip.

Falconer made as if to grab her again, and she slipped away to the edge of the crowd. She was only armed with a dagger – an eight-inch blade, wickedly sharp – but it was nonetheless a weapon. Marguerite reached under her petticoats to the sheath strapped to her thigh and drew the knife, determined to fight her way to Bess if necessary. The ear-splitting crack of a gunshot and a cloud of brimstone-tinged smoke only served to increase her resolve.

If she stood on tip-toe, Marguerite could just see over the heads of the men in front of her; they formed a solid barrier that she could not easily cross. She heard Bess' shout, and another shot, and someone cursing vehemently. *Bess!* Marguerite used her elbows without discretion, fighting her way through the assembled sailors by using every nasty trick she had ever learned on the quays of Antigua. She glimpsed Levalier's powdered wig sailing through the air; it disappeared into the heave and press of bodies. Gritting her teeth, Marguerite struggled to stay on her feet. She knew that if she fell, she would be trampled.

Bess' voice suddenly resolved from the general muttering: "Stand down, by the sweet bleedin' Christ! Stand down, or all you'll get from me is lead shot, six feet of earth and a stone for a pillow! I'll send every man-jack of you to the Diet of Worms!"

The mob parted to reveal Bess standing in front of the tent. The dark blue kerchief was missing from her head; chestnut curls framed her scowling face. The blunderbuss in her hands gave weight to her words, and the authority in her bearing helped quell the rebellious men's grumbling.

"For shame!" Frederick Byng cried, coming to stand beside Bess. Behind him stood the wigless Levalier, a trickle of blood at the corner of his mouth, and squat Henry Dunn, who looked furious as he fingered a flintlock. Trickles of smoke escaped the pistol's bore.

"Fie upon you!" the dandified captain continued. He also carried a blunderbuss – the best short-range weapon for dealing with a crowd. The ostrich feathers in his tricorn hat shivered in the wind. "Ungrateful sea-dogs! Have we not given you plunder beyond the wildest dreams of ordinary seamen? Have you not caroused in the most sordid ports, had your fill of the most depraved whores, drunk deep of the richest wines? Have your purses not been lined with silver, and aye, good French and Spanish gold?"

"And 'twill be so again!" Quittam added, coming to stand with the other captains.

Speedwell loomed behind them all, a mountain of plush robin's egg blue velvet. "My wits must be softening," she rumbled, "for I'd swear upon Baphomet's beard that I spy *Red Queen*'s people amidst this unlawful throng, imponderable as it may seem."

Several men who had gotten caught up in the excitement now slunk off, shame-faced. Speedwell's crew was more like an extended family, with herself acting as the ultimate authority and matriarch of the clan. Like any other family, betrayal from its members was not expected and was doubly hurtful if it occurred. Speedwell watched them go and said nothing further. A lance of sunlight caught her spectacles' lenses, turning them opaque; no one could read the expression in her eyes, but she frowned deeply.

Carmelita appeared, her black hair disheveled, a satisfied smirk on her lips. Hatefulness radiated from her in near palpable waves. Marguerite's grip tightened on the hilt of her dagger. The Spanish woman had no doubt been stirring the pot, tossing in spice by the handful and telling God-only-knew what tales of gold and greed to the sailors to fire their mood. She was the sort to enjoy a riot as long as someone else ended bleeding. Besides, Carmelita had a grudge against Bess as wide as the whole world; from what Marguerite had heard from others eager to tell the tale, Carmelita was not used to being rejected and had been seething with resentment over Bess and Marguerite's love affair.

"Out of my way, *coña!*" she said to Marguerite, brushing past her.

Marguerite controlled the urge to execute a perfect *botta segrete* – a secret attack – and stab Carmelita through the heart from behind. The woman's brown silk skirts rustled as she moved to the front of the crowd; men parted before her like waves retreating from Moses' staff on the shores of the Red Sea. Carmelita did not so much walk as she swayed invitingly, a tempting morsel meant to entice any man's appetite. When she reached a point about an arm's length from Bess, she stopped and put her hands on her hips.

"What do you want?" Bess asked bluntly.

"My share," Carmelita answered, equally blunt. "Don't think to cheat me, or any others here, of our rightful share, *querida*."

Bess bared her teeth in a not-smile. "No one's bein' cheated," she said with forced patience. "Did you not hear of how Preservation Meldrum and Lazarus Bullock were killed by *Deceiver*'s enchantment? I know Daniel Honey's been tongue-flapping the sorry tale to any who'll spare an ear to listen."

Color mounted in Carmelita's cheeks, lending a touch of pink to her olive-hued complexion. "*Dios!* Let Captain Speedwell deal with the curse. Is that not why she came here?"

Renewed grumblings among the throng showed the crewmen's approval of this proposed solution.

"You speak of the problem as though 'twas easy as kiss-my-hand," Speedwell said, drawing herself up to her full and daunting Amazonian height. "This is a death-curse; even those most ignorant of thaumaturgical matters have enough wit to understand that it is no light hex, simply remedied. The curse upon *Deceiver* may be beyond my ability to crack, but 'tis early days yet, and I've only begun to study its complexity."

Lovelock appeared at Bess' side, his face flushed as red as his flamboyant mustache. "Your pardon," he rasped, "for my tardiness."

Bess acknowledged the bald man with a nod, setting the five gold rings in her earlobes swinging. "I'll thank 'ee kindly to control your doxy, Solomon," she said. "If we were a-sea, conspiracy to mutiny is worthy of a keel-hauling."

"*Maldita puta*! You would not dare!" Carmelita was clearly scornful.

"I dare much," Bess replied. She gave a shove to Lovelock's meaty arm. "Go on, then, sirrah, afore I add incitement to riot to the grievances."

Lovelock reached for Carmelita, and she resisted, whirling around to face the assembled sailors. "Cowards! Take what you want! Are you not men? Your fortune is on the other side of the island. Take the gold and to hell with them!"

"I've no wish to meet my end on the Devil's trident!" cried one of the men. There were mutters of agreement. Everyone had heard Daniel Honey's account, as well as the tales told by the other survivors of the ill-fated expedition to *Deceiver*.

Bess said, "Then patience you must have till we've kenned the thing entire, for none of you wishes to be brought to the lee and be buried on land like a common lubber. You'll have your gold, mates – I swear by the Virgin and Child, and you all know that Bess O'Bedlam's word ain't never been broke."

At last taking hold of Carmelita, who hissed like an offended cat, Lovelock raised his voice to address the crowd. "The captain's right; 'tis patience that's needful here. If any man wishes to forfeit his claim on *Deceiver*'s gold and return to Hotspur Cay, then I volunteer my *Swiftsure* to carry the poor pitiful sons-of-bitches home."

Not surprisingly, no one accepted Lovelock's offer.

Bess' jaw firmed. A steely glint entered her eyes. "So we'll have no more talk of mutiny," she said, hefting the blunderbuss in her hands to punctuate the command. "The next goddamned assembly had better be in answer to a captain's summons, or by thunderin' hell, I'll string up the ring-leaders and leave 'em hanging on a yardarm!"

Carmelita wrenched herself out of Lovelock's grasp. Her gaze wandered over the rapidly dispersing crowd and lighted on Marguerite. "*Puta!*" she spat.

"Enough, 'Lita," Lovelock cautioned. "You promised me most faithful that you'd start no brawls, else I'd not have brought you here."

Quittam, who had gone inside the tent, now emerged with five mugs of wine. "Good Rhenish hock," she said, "from Bess' private stock, thank 'ee kindly. Who'll drink with me – to *Deceiver's* gold, by Christ's wounds!"

Byng took a mug. "To the frustration of Tom Carew!"

"To lifting the curse!" Speedwell said, also accepting a mug of sloshing liquid.

Lovelock and Bess said nothing, merely accepted their share of the wine in silence.

Bess was the first to drink; after she had raised her mug to the other captains, she took several long swallows and let fly with a satisfied belch. Speedwell and Quittam were next, followed by Byng; but when Lovelock made to drink, Carmelita dashed the mug from his hand, retreated to a safe distance and watched the others intently.

"What are you about, woman?" Lovelock asked. The tattoos on his arms writhed as muscles shifted beneath the skin.

Marguerite's flesh prickled. She did not like the odd look of triumph on Carmelita's face. Approaching the woman, she asked, "What did you do?" When Carmelita did not answer, Marguerite repeated the question more forcefully. The tone of her voice caught the Spanish woman's attention. She turned a black glittering gaze on Marguerite.

"They're dead," Carmelita said, sneering.

"Who's dead? What do you mean?" Marguerite's stomach plummeted as foreboding struck, leaving a cold and hollow void in her middle.

"I poisoned the wine." Carmelita tossed her head proudly. "I'd meant only to kill Lizzybetta...and her spotted cow of a whore," she continued, glaring pure hatred at Marguerite. "Now my Solomon's the head man, for the rest are dead. Dead, dead, dead!"

"Almighty God!" Byng exclaimed, dropping his mug and clutching his throat. "Poisoned? Where's Mistress Glasspoole? She must come at once!"

"I'll fetch her," Lovelock said. His leathery face had gone pasty with horror. Without looking at Carmelita, he took off at a run, stumbling a little over the sand.

Carmelita laughed; it was an ugly sound. "You'll be sleeping with the crabs, and I'll have my revenge, and my gold, too. You chose that cow over

me, Lizzybetta...now you can die in her arms, slow and painful. She can kiss
your cold lips and weep over your corpse. You deserve each other! Me, I'll
sail away with Solomon and the treasure. That's what I deserve!"

"*Jij Spaanse tyfus hoer!*" Marguerite gritted. She slapped the Spanish
woman hard across the face with her free hand, putting her shoulder into
the blow. Carmelita fell down in a flurry of brown silk, the imprint of
Marguerite's hand already showing crimson on her face.

"*La coña de tu madre!*" Carmelita got to her feet, shaking sand out of
her skirts. "You'll die for that, bitch!" She drew a knife almost identical to
Marguerite's.

Galvanized to action despite the suspicion that she had been poisoned,
Bess tried to intervene. "Belay that!" she shouted. "Goddamn it, Margo..."

Marguerite did not answer, nor did she look away from Carmelita.
Rather than be consumed with grief and weeping, one word beat through
her mind, clamoring like a brazen bell – *poison*! Rage pulsed beneath her
ribcage, echoing the pounding of her heart. She held her dagger in a tight
grip and planted her feet solidly, as Levalier had taught her, one foot slightly
ahead of the other. Quickly gathering her skirts and petticoats, she tucked
one side of the mass into the belt that encircled her waist, to leave her legs
free for action. Her lips drew back into a snarl as the most profound anger
of her life surged through her veins. Marguerite waited for Carmelita to
make the first move in what she knew would be a fight to the death; this
moment had been brewing a long while. The Spanish woman had finally
gone too far; if Bess was to die, Marguerite intended to send Carmelita to
hell. The hilt of her dagger was solid in her palm, the blade well-balanced.
She took a deep breath, nostrils flaring, and watched Carmelita settle herself
into a guarded position.

Bess swore and moved towards them, but Byng seized her arm. "This is
not your fight," he said. She began to protest, but the words died on her lips
at the unexpected compassion in his eyes. "Mistress Margo's revenging your
murder," he said. "We've few rules in our society, but that's one of them –
never interfere in an honor brawl."

Quittam nodded; her face was mottled red and white with apparent ire,
but her jade green eyes were clear. Speedwell paid no attention; her
attention was fixed on a chunk of turquoise in her fist. When Quittan poked
her with an elbow, Speedwell started, then took in the scene and said, "A
hundred *moidores* on Mistress Margo. And think not to renege on the wager,
Allegra, for if we die, I'll collect my due even amongst the everlasting
flames."

Quittam's grin showed the skull beneath the skin. "Done, b'God."

Byng tightened his hold on Bess' arm. "Don't interfere," he warned
again.

"If Margo dies, you die," Bess told him matter-of-factly.

"If señorita Márquez does not lie, I'm dead already, madam," he
replied, giving her a mocking little bow.

Marguerite shifted slightly, watching Carmelita's eyes. It was there that intent could be read – in the subtle drift of her gaze, the expansion or contraction of the pupils, and in the slow sweep of eyelashes in a blink just before Carmelita lunged, shockingly fast, her arm extended with the glint of the knife at the end of it. Marguerite moved just enough so that the blade skimmed her side without damaging flesh and dealt a return stroke aimed at the other woman's throat. The point of her dagger tore a bloody scratch in Carmelita's neck, near her collarbone. She and Carmelita were engaged too closely for effective blows unless one or the other broke away. Carmelita's unbound hair lashed across Marguerite's cheeks, drawing tears, then the Spanish woman was dancing backwards, her nose bleeding from a lucky strike delivered by Marguerite's elbow.

"I'll gut you like a herring, you butter-eating bitch." Carmelita flicked a lock of black hair back over her shoulder and wiped her bloody nose on her sleeve. She had lost none of her arrogance; it was clear that she believed she was better and would easily win.

"I doubt that," Marguerite replied. She circled to the left, trying to maneuver the Spanish woman to face the setting sun, but Carmelita refused to cooperate, staying where she was and grinning nastily to show she knew the trick.

Marguerite sensed rather than saw the sideways motion of Carmelita's bare foot. Sand flew into Marguerite's face; she put up an arm to shield her vision. In that instant, Carmelita came at her, knife held low for the belly thrust called *stocatta*. Marguerite remembered her lessons; she blocked the blow, jarring her wrist, and shoved Carmelita back a bit; at the same time, she swept her dagger around in a feint. At the last possible moment, Marguerite reversed her blade, sending the tip slicing through the underside of Carmelita's raised arm. Hot wet pain traveled unexpectedly over her own shoulder where Carmelita had managed to inflict a messy wound on her. The injury was not serious, though it bled heavily. Sucking air into lungs that felt two sizes too small, Marguerite disengaged, ignoring the runnels of blood that formed a lacy scarlet network over her arm and down her breast.

"So, *puta*, you think to harm me, eh?" It was Carmelita's turn to circle. She tossed the knife from hand to hand; a dazzling flare glinted from the steel. Marguerite followed the woman's movements, alert for an attack. "I was tutored by Domenico Angelo himself."

"Save your breath to cool your porridge, blatteroon," Marguerite replied, although inwardly, she wondered if this boast was bluff or truth. Domenico Angelo was a fencing master of the greatest fame; his *salle d'arms* in the Haymarket was one of the landmarks of London. She could not imagine why the *maestro* of the sword would give lessons to a woman and a harlot at that, but he was a man and perhaps Carmelita had paid his fee in kind.

"The wench lies," Byng said, loud enough to be overhead. "Angelo's Haymarket room never degraded itself to host the likes of that hellcat. She learned from Levalier, same as you, Mistress Margo, though I've not seen her practice as diligently."

Carmelita spat on the ground, her contempt clear.

The sand was warm beneath Marguerite's feet; above her head, a flock of parrots wheeled and screeched before disappearing into the palm trees. She licked sweat from her upper lip. Heat-haze shimmered in the air. Carmelita lunged, but it was a feint. Marguerite stilled the instinct to respond, realizing that if she did so, she would place herself in a potentially fatal position. Between two skilled fighters, a serious combat was akin to a game of chess; one always held part of one's mind on the current situation, but another part ranged ahead, analyzing patterns and formulating strategies.

"You're dead, *cabrona*," Carmelita said, her voice pitched low so that Marguerite strained to hear. "A dead cow. Your body will rot on this island, as your soul rots in hell." Her mouth looked soft, her lips full and poisonously crimson. It was easy to understand why men and women were attracted to Carmelita; she exuded an intoxicating, well-nigh irresistible combination of sex and danger as easily as breath.

Distraction was deadly. Marguerite came back to herself as Carmelita sprang forward and made a feint at her throat. She met the Spanish woman and locked their blades; for a long moment, they stood toe-to-toe, straining and glaring, then Carmelita jumped back, her knife screeching shrilly against Marguerite's dagger. At a safe distance, she sucked a small cut on the heel of her hand; there was torturous death promised in the woman's black-eyed gaze.

After a few more passes, Marguerite had gained a slice across the knuckles – fortunately, not her knife hand – and a nick in her ear that bled freely down her neck. Carmelita had suffered a few very small injuries, including a nose that was swollen from the blow she had taken at the beginning of the fight. Marguerite knew that time was on Carmelita's side. Although none of her own wounds was immediately incapacitating, it would not be much longer before the combination overwhelmed her with sheer blood loss. Weakened, she would be easy meat for Carmelita's blade.

She decided to attempt a prime condiddle, for had she not been a successful counterfeit crank, as used to acting as any that trod the boards? Marguerite had sometimes seen mother birds pretending to be injured, dragging a wing on the ground to draw predators away from her nest. What if she pretended to be already weakening? Might that not trick Carmelita, possibly lure the other woman into making an error? Marguerite would have to commit herself totally; this was an all-or-nothing move.

Accordingly, she allowed her shoulder to droop, as if she no longer had the energy to adopt proper posture. Marguerite swiped the back of her hand across her brow; there was no need to fake the sweat that stung her eyes. Carmelita watched her avidly. Marguerite could feel the weight of the woman's assessing gaze crawling over her skin. When Carmelita sidled to the right, Marguerite followed, pretending to stumble and catch herself.

At that moment, when she was presumably off her guard, Carmelita lunged.

Marguerite had been waiting for it. She executed the *volte*, counter-thrusting at the woman with her right foot foremost. Simultaneously, she shifted her left foot so that her body turned, her torso no longer facing her opponent but presenting itself sideways, so that Carmelita's blade slipped harmlessly behind her, and Marguerite's continued lunge took the Spanish woman in the armpit, severing the artery.

Carmelita's dark eyes widened in disbelief. Marguerite had not loosened her hold on the dagger's hilt; when Carmelita staggered backwards, the blade pulled free from the wound, which gushed dark blood. The woman sank gracefully to the ground, her blood-stained skirts billowing out around her. Bess tore free from Byng's hold and went to Marguerite, who stood over the dying Carmelita with an unreadable expression.

"Bitch," Carmelita breathed, bloody foam bubbling over her lips.

Glasspoole came bustling towards the tableau, the ribbons of her mobcap flying behind her. Solomon Lovelock followed on the herb-wife's heels. He fell to his knees. "Oh, God!" he choked, reaching out to touch Carmelita's hair.

Carmelita's eyes blazed once last time, filled with hatred, and then they glazed over, dull as unpolished onyx. Her face went slack; drained of animation, she was drained of beauty, too. Marguerite was shocked to find that Carmelita was actually quite an ordinary looking woman. It was her snapping temper, her vitality, the sheer magnitude of her lust and greed that had lent an attractive gloss to otherwise plain features.

"My poor 'Lita," Lovelock whispered. His gaze traveled from the dead woman to Marguerite, and he got ponderously to his feet. "You..." he whispered. "'Tis your doing." His hand crept to the hilt of his cutlass.

Bess put a hand on her cutlass hilt also, ready to defend Marguerite to her last breath.

CHAPTER THIRTY-TWO
Freedom's Key

Before Lovelock could sign his own death warrant by drawing steel, Levalier interposed his body in front of the grieving quartermaster. "Blame me, *mon ami*," the Frenchman said. His graying hair was cropped close to the skull; he looked old and tired without his powdered wig. "Blame me, for I never taught Mlle. Carmelita the *volte*. She was too impatient for such tricks. And also, I taught Mlle. Margo too well, *non?*"

"This fight was not of Margo's choosing," Speedwell added, laying a big hand on Lovelock's shoulder. "Solomon, you know Carmelita was spoiling for snickersnee."

The big bald man glowered.

"I reckon Mistress Margo had provocation, since it was your doxy what poisoned us all." Quittam cast a glare at the lifeless corpse sprawled upon the blood-soaked sand.

Glasspoole shoved out a bony fist, and opened it to reveal a handful of vividly red seeds that sported black at the tips. "Rosary peas," she said, "taken from the cask of Rhenish in the captain's tent."

Byng blanched. "B'God, we're dead in truth."

"Don't go digging a grave just yet, Frederick," Glasspoole said, her false teeth clacking. "'Tis known that rosary peas are deadly, aye, but they must be crushed first, to release the poison. Whole, they're not near as mortal. Most times, if swallowed whole, they pass straight through the body and do no harm."

Speedwell nodded, tucking the turquoise stone into her coat pocket. "'Tis known that turquoise turns black in the presence of poison," she said, "and my stone retained its own pure color, so our danger was not mortal. However, I did not know what had thwarted Carmelita's plot, only that it had failed."

Bess turned an aggrieved glare on Speedwell. "And this you couldn't share with the rest of us, you damned moon-eyed wretch, but must instead keep mum!"

Speedwell shrugged her massive shoulders and said nothing. Bess snorted in disgust.

Quittam let out a bark of laughter that had no humor in it. "Well, it seems Carmelita's plan went awry twice, for she failed to kill us, and she failed to kill Mistress Margo."

"I can't say that I sorrow overmuch at the wench's loss," Byng said, twiddling a button on his *justaucorps* coat. He staggered when Quittam planted an elbow in his ribs and told him to be respectful of the dead.

Lovelock grimaced. "I did love her," he said. He drew a deep breath; his paunch strained against the leather vest he wore. "I know she had her faults, but I loved her."

"Will you bury her here or at sea?" Speedwell asked, not unsympathetically.

"On the isle, I think. She never was one to relish the waves." Lovelock turned to Bess. "You warned me once to keep 'Lita out of your sight; mind you do the same with your woman, for I'm likely to forget myself if I see her once too often."

"Aye, Solomon. I'll do that." Bess gave a sympathetic pat to his burly shoulder. "You go and grieve, and none will say you nay or seek to mock you. Allegra will tell you what's decided about the treasure, and if a captain's vote is needful."

Casting a final angry look at Marguerite, Lovelock turned on his heel and left.

"Will he stay loyal, do you think?" Byng asked, nodding at Lovelock's retreating back.

Quittam's eyes narrowed to slits. "Solomon? Aye, if he has a scrap of sense. He witnessed Sullivan's punishment for treason."

"Aside from the oath-breaker's ceremony," Speedwell said, shaking her hand to adjust the fall of lace at her shirt cuff, "I believe Lovelock will not betray us. He'll recover from Carmelita's death, though 'tis my feeling that he'll never befriend Mistress Margo."

"So be it. I've bigger fish in my frying pan of the moment," Bess said.

Glasspoole was already at Marguerite's side, ripping the torn sleeve to expose a shoulder wound. "'Tis deep," was the herb-wife's verdict. "You'll need stitching, I fear."

Remembering the last time Glasspoole had plied the needle on her, Marguerite shuddered.

Bess walked over to join them. She took in Marguerite's injuries with a jaundiced expression. "Damn your eyes, madam!" she snapped. "Did I not tell you to belay this brawl? Look at you! As if you'd wedded and bedded a catamount!"

"I thought you were murdered!" Marguerite blurted, sickened by the very notion. The pain of her wounds was nothing compared to the agony that had split her heart when she had believed Bess would die of being poisoned. She evaded Glasspoole's fussing and caught Bess around the waist, burying her face in the woman's neck. "I thought she'd killed you," Marguerite murmured. The smell of blood wafting from the sand, and from her own wounds, nauseated her.

"Ah, Margo...'twill take more than a sip of poison to kill me," Bess said. "My life's nailed firm to my backbone." Her irritation melted away as tenderness took its place. The body in her arms was soft and yielding, if reeking of blood; Bess paid that no mind. Suddenly alarmed when Marguerite sighed and sagged in her arms, she bellowed, "What's amiss?" and shifted her grip to keep the unconscious woman from sliding to the ground.

Glasspoole clucked and said, "Why, Margo's lost a mort of her life's fluid, and is rendered a-swoon. 'Tis common enough after a wounding, as you well know, so stop bawling like a cow with an injured calf and be useful by taking Margo into the cook tent."

Leaving Quittam, Byng and Speedwell to their own company, Bess half-dragged, half-carried Marguerite to the tent, where Glasspoole took advantage of the woman's unconscious state to put eight stitches into her shoulder and treat her other wounds as well. In the middle of the operation, Hephzibah limped away to start a pit for roasting a brace of wild piglets, brought in by a group of foragers. When Glasspoole finished stitching Marguerite's injury closed, she took Bess out of the tent to talk to her regarding the injured crewman.

Bess listened to Glasspoole's cautions about the magical traps impatiently. At last, she said, "I'll issue orders, mistress, but you know that such warnings will do no good. 'Tis a hard cruel fact, but gold draws sailors as honey draws bees. Let a few more of the bully-boys lose life or limb to ensorcelled doubloons and mayhap they'll take the lesson to heart."

Glasspoole clucked some more, until Bess' patience was at an end. "Enough, mistress, I beg!" Bess said, holding up a hand. "By the sweet bleedin' Christ, I can't play nursemaid to the sons-of-she-dogs! Now I must beg your pardon, for I've business of my own to attend." With that, Bess swept back into the cook tent, eager to see her lover.

She stopped dead in her tracks, horror clawing at her heart.

Marguerite had vanished, with not a trace left behind save bloodstains.

This time, there was no seduction of sleeping senses, nor was there a headlong flight into nightmare. Marguerite simply opened her eyes and found herself an unwilling participant in a scene of gruesomeness that struck her dumb with terror.

Somehow she had returned to the cave where *Deceiver* rotted at anchor, where the air was musty with salt, old timbers and mildew, cut with occasional sharp, ammoniac whiffs of bird and bat droppings. Above her hovered the stick-thin figure of Fancy Tom Carew. His long, dirty white hair brushed her face as he bent over her; the stench of his breath made her turn her head to the side. It was the only movement she could make. Marguerite found that her limbs and the rest of her body were somehow pinned in place, though she could feel no ropes or other ligatures binding her.

"My key," Carew said in his whispery voice. The ends of his hair felt like spiders skittering over her brow and cheeks and chin. "Made to set me free."

"Let me go!" Marguerite fought the fear that threatened to strangle her. Her bowels were a howling wasteland; she twisted against her invisible bonds to no avail. "Let me go, *godskannonne!*"

A few scraps of moldering broadcloth fluttered down like bonfire ash, then a knife appeared in her vision. It was her own dagger, the hilt held fast in Carew's scrawny fist. Marguerite vaguely remembered sheathing it after her fight with Carmelita; she thought that Levalier would have been furious to see the line of dried blood crusting the tang, evidence that she had not cleaned the blade properly after...

Carmelita's blood.

Marguerite bit her bottom lip until it twinged. She had taken another woman's life – a serious matter, indeed – but at the moment, Carmelita's death on the beach seemed a merciful end compared to what she faced now. Marguerite could not find it within herself to feel a morsel of regret. Their deadly clash had been inevitable. Her own problem took precedence, and a very nasty problem it was, too.

A gust of foul breath on her cheek made Marguerite close her eyes. She struggled against her bonds; the fresh stitches in her shoulder pulled painfully. Her eyes opened, and she stared into Carew's dark gaze, almost mesmerized by the tiny flames that burned in his oily black pupils. Her pulse quickened.

"As you die, my pretty, I will live again." Carew caressed her face with a fingernail that was more like a talon. "Life! My flesh will return! I'll be free of this godforsaken island at last! 'Tis five-and-twenty years since that stupid bitch cursed me...would that I could dance a merry jig upon her bones, the black-hearted wench!"

"Who are you to me?" Marguerite gasped, trying to avoid his touch but not succeeding. There was a sharp tug on her shoulder and a stitch popped with an almost audible sound; she felt a warm trickle of blood on her skin as the rent re-opened a trifle.

"Does it matter? You're mine, girl...that's enough." He kissed her brow, his lips dry and rough, and she gagged. Carew chuckled; the sound was like beetles clicking behind walls. From outside the cave came the barking of seals and the wash and slap of waves against rock. "I'd have had you sooner, save that fool Harry Rye, having discovered you as a suckling babe, was too ale-mazed to recall where you could be found again!" Carew said. "But though he flitted from isle to isle seeking you out, Black Harry yet put the charm-needler's mark on your soft infant's skin. No escape for you, my girl. You were born to be my key."

"No!" She would deny him with everything within her.

"Aye," he crooned, leaning even closer so that their noses touched. His breath was an open grave. "Mine, all mine...flesh and blood and bone. Mine!"

The cords stood out in her neck as Marguerite strained away from him. "Leave me be, you spiteful old monster!"

"Monster, am I?" His lips stretched in an awful grin. "I suppose it must be so, girl. I've been so long steeped in the Devil's works, you could say I'm fair pickled in evil." His finger wandered across her throat, to her breast and scratched at her nipple, which hardened under the rough treatment despite her will to the contrary. Revulsion wracked Marguerite. She spat at him; the gobbet of spittle struck his cheek. He wiped it away.

"Enough, my poppet," Carew said, still showing his yellowed teeth.

"'Tis long enough I've waited, and there's no time to taste your charms, more's the pity."

Defiant, she spat at him again and missed.

He hefted the dagger. "Have you said your prayers like a good girl ought?" His voice was mocking. "'Twould be a shame for you to end in hell."

Marguerite's mouth was too dry for further spit or speech. Nevertheless, she poured all the scorn and fury she felt into her gaze defying the hideous creature – her own grandfather – that sought her death. She would not weep or beg for mercy; she knew that it would be futile. Instead, she firmed her jaw and waited for the dagger to pierce her flesh.

Silently, within her mind, she said to Bess: *Forgive me. I love you.*

Like a miracle, Marguerite heard Bess' voice calling aloud, "Hold fast!"

Hope sparked within her breast. She bit back a sob. Turning her head, Marguerite saw Bess in the prow of a jolly-boat rowed by stout seamen. In her sober garments, her hair hidden beneath a black kerchief, holding the shining steel of a cutlass aloft, Bess O'Bedlam looked like vengeance personified. Ruby witch-fire played on the cutlass' curved edge, turning the sword into a ragged battle-banner. Behind Bess sat Speedwell, light glinting from the lenses of her spectacles, and more light playing on her spread fingers as she conjured further witch-fire.

Booming surf sounded loud as a gunshot in the cavern. Speedwell's chanting could not be heard over the rushing hiss of water, but her mouth was moving. Marguerite's gaze fixed on Bess; her lover's face was filled with grim determination. Relief flooded Marguerite. She would be rescued, and she and Bess would leave this accursed isle, never looking back. Lettice Speedwell would find a cure for her tattoo. Fancy Tom Carew would rot here forever, together with his hell-damned ship.

A dull thud against her chest, hard enough to knock the wind out of her, drove away Marguerite's brief fantasy. She tried to inhale and found that she could not do so very deeply. Her lungs began to burn. There was a queer fluttery feeling, as though her heart was following a butterfly's irregular beat. She sought the cause.

A dagger hilt sprouted from beneath her breast.

Marguerite's eyes went wide when the pain belatedly struck.

The last thing she saw before darkness claimed her vision was Carew grinning like a skull, and the last thing she heard was his chilling laughter that followed her into cold oblivion.

CHAPTER THIRTY-THREE
The Devil in the Details

After stabbing Marguerite, Fancy Tom Carew vanished, leaving only the echo of his demonic chuckling behind.

Bess did not care. She had eyes only for Marguerite and the dagger whose hilt stuck up from the blonde woman's chest. The worked ivory hilt throbbed grotesquely, keeping time to the ever-slowing beat of her impaled heart. Bess leaped out of the jolly-boat the moment the prow crunched on sand and fell to her knees beside Marguerite.

The sense of *déjà vu* was strong. In the recent past, she had knelt upon these same sands, hovering over a Marguerite that she feared was dead. Then, her fears had been unfounded. Now Bess clenched her teeth against a wail of protest, until her jaw threatened to crack under the strain. Breathing harshly, she laid the flat of her palm on Marguerite's cheek. The flesh was warm but pale as paper except for the violet smudges beneath her eyes; the woman's complexion had gone waxy, the skin cleaving to the bones of her skull. Bess picked up Marguerite's limp hand; it felt fragile and delicate as a bird's wing. Was this the same hand that had stroked her so boldly, so cleverly, bringing pleasure so strong, it was akin to pain? It was hard to believe that this colorless, waxen doll transfixed by a dagger was the vibrant, maddening, enthralling woman that she loved.

A hand settled between her shoulder blades. Bess did not acknowledge the touch.

"Come quickly," Speedwell said. She had crouched down at Bess' side. "We may yet save Margo, but time is not our ally."

Speedwell's words cut through the veil of dullness that muffled her mind. Bess snapped back to herself, tearing her gaze from the throbbing hilt that jutted from Marguerite's breast. She could count the heartbeats... "What do you say?" she asked.

"Margo's life may be saved, but we must hurry." The giantess spoke gently, as if to an injured child.

Bess reached out her free hand and took hold of the lacy jabot at Speedwell's throat. Her eyes blazed with a fury that was a hair's breadth away from madness. "Don't you dare lie to me, Lettice! D'ye hear? Friend or no, I'll kill you where you stand."

"'Tis naught but the truth—" Speedwell broke off and looked over her shoulder. "Oh, ye gods and monsters of the Seven Sacred Spheres!"

Deceiver was preparing to sail.

A man stood on the quarterdeck. He was tall and lean, his white hair pulled back into a queue. The tails of his black broadcloth coat flew behind him as he turned, shouting incomprehensible directions at an invisible crew. Fancy Tom Carew lived again; with each faltering beat of Marguerite's heart, he was healed of the weather witch's curse that had taken twenty-five years to resolve.

Bess craned her head around in time to see pristine white sails unfurl on *Deceiver*'s twin masts. A fusillade of crackling accompanied the hull timbers shoring themselves up, and she heard whip-strokes of new ropes lashed into proper ship's rigging, from re-knit shrouds to dead-eye strops. "God *damn* him for a pox-riddled whore-master!" she gritted. Somehow, through magical means, *Deceiver* was resurrecting itself from a neglected hulk to the full glory of a sloop-o'-war. Compared to *Mad Maudlin*, the ship was small and carried eighteen six-pounder guns on the single deck, but she would be fast and highly maneuverable, especially since it seemed that Carew did not have to depend upon the inherent frailties and limitations of a human crew.

Speedwell scooped Marguerite into her arms and stood, cradling the unconscious woman easily. "If Tom Carew escapes, Margo dies," she said. "Quickly!"

The giantess sprang for the jolly-boat, jumping adroitly over the gunwale to a seat on the central thwart. Bess followed, blessing the foresight that had caused her to have *Mad Maudlin* and the other ships brought around to this side of the island instead of leaving them in the harbor near the camp; *Deceiver* would not get too much of a head start. The Devil figurehead on *Deceiver*'s prow plied its long trident to pole the ship out of the cave. Gunshot pops and groans of tortured wood accompanied the effort; the figurehead's blind mother-of-pearl eyes remained fixed on the yawning cave mouth, where several seagulls flirted in the air, their shrieks distorted by rock and water.

Speedwell held Marguerite draped across her lap. The silver streaks in the big woman's hair glowed like moonlight over embers. "Row!" she cried, her voice raised to a quarterdeck shout that caused dust and bits of rock to shiver down from the cave's ceiling. "Row, by Baphomet's beard, or suffer a thaumaturge's wrath!"

The crewmen heaved at the oars with a will, and Bess took the tiller herself; the solid oak bar beneath her hand was comforting in its way. Someone missed the oar stroke, which sent the rest into a momentary confusion. Speedwell roared, "Row, you miserable apes!" and the rhythm was restored, the jolly-boat flying smoothly over the dark waters.

They were headed toward *Deceiver*, which was already edging out into the J-shaped alcove, propelled by the figurehead. Every moment the gap between *Deceiver*'s hull and the rock wall was lessening. Bess added her shouts of encouragement to Speedwell's and shoved the tiller over hard. Collision seemed imminent, but the jolly-boat shot past the opening, so close that the barnacles on *Deceiver*'s hull scraped a long curl of paint from the boat's side. Bess worked the tiller to negotiate the hook, and they were in open water at last.

The slightly rounded tulip-bulb shape of *Mad Maudlin* seemed far away, hardly more than a miniature ship hull up on the sun-drenched horizon, yet Bess knew that they would achieve the vessel in a few minutes. The crewmen were strong; rock-hard muscles bulged in every forearm and rolled in every shoulder as the oars worked. She took the opportunity to ask Speedwell, "What did you mean by saying Margo could be saved?"

"As her life drains, the energy enters Carew, breaking the curse and giving him flesh once more." Speedwell had a blunt finger pressed to Marguerite's throat, measuring the woman's pulse. "The more flesh is restored to Carew, the more vulnerable he becomes. 'Tis near impossible to harm a ghost, so the trick is to catch him when he's solid enough to be killed, but afore he drains poor Margo to the last drop of her life."

"Then what?" Bess asked, squinting her eyes against a lance of sunlight.

The lenses of Speedwell's spectacles flashed. "And then we see, my friend. My counsel is thus – first catch Fancy Tom Carew and sink him; aye, and his cursed vessel, too. Yon figurehead's possessed of a demon; I surmise that costly bit of magic pre-dates Carew's curse. Mayhap I can craft a conjuration to free the creature, so that it turns upon its former master. That's the trouble with demons and why thaumaturges rarely use them – the hell-beasts are unreliable servants, tending towards nasty and vengeful temperaments. More than one Master of Sphere and Wand has been dragged down into hell by a former slave."

Bess paid little attention to Speedwell's rambling; her concentration was focused behind them, where *Deceiver* had edged out of the cave. Her neck ached from the unnatural angle, but she watched the corvette's sails shudder, and a long, scarlet serpent of a pennant that unscrolled from her main topmast. The decidedly French rake of *Deceiver*'s stern grew smaller as the ship set her topgallant sails and ran close-hauled. Bess estimated that Carew's vessel was at least a league away. Fortunately, there was a cat's paw wind at the moment, sufficient to stir the surface of the ocean but not as strong as the *brisote*. Carew would not get far, not even with all his canvas aloft. She sniffed the air and scanned the sky for storm-sign.

"Tell me one thing," Bess said as the jolly-boat finally surged alongside *Mad Maudlin*, creamy-topped waves swelling and foaming between the two vessels. Before continuing, Bess stood and seized the jolly-boat's grapnel; she whipped the long line around her head, then flung it expertly upwards; the grapnel caught on the rail. Hands appeared to seize the line and belay it to a cleat.

"Tell me one thing," Bess repeated, bracing herself against the thwarts and gazing at Speedwell. "Can you save Margo or not?"

Speedwell hesitated, then said, "I will do my best, Bess. No one can say more."

Bess touched a lock of Marguerite's hair. "Aye, none can say more, Letty. Thank 'ee kindly for speakin' the truth. Ahoy, Mr. Dunn! Fetch Mistress Glasspoole and a bosun's chair, if you please. We've grievous wounded aboard."

While the operation was being carried out, she turned her attention back to *Deceiver*. Having reached open water, the ship had a stroke of luck when the variable wind shifted and grew stiffer, allowing Carew to beat to windward and head rapidly towards the horizon. Bess cursed, hawked and spat to avert any bad luck. She stroked a fingertip over *Mad Maudlin's* black-tarred strake. "You'll catch him, my beauty," she whispered, "for you've not disappointed me yet."

She turned to her crew. "Let's be on our way, there's not a moment to waste," she said shortly, and leaped for the mizzenchains on an upswell.

Glasspoole supervised the hauling of Marguerite in the bosun's chair; getting the injured woman on board was accomplished gingerly, as if she might fall to pieces if jarred in the slightest. Bess chafed at the delay but bowed to Glasspoole's expertise in the matter. If Marguerite died before they caught Carew... Exercising a formidable will, she turned her thoughts away from that notion, and focused instead on harrying the crew to prepare *Mad Maudlin* for pursuit. Every second lent more time to allow *Deceiver* to slip away.

"Bear those backstays!" Bess ordered, her commands echoed by Henry Dunn and the boatswain, Toby Falconer. To the men marching round the capstan to bring up the anchors, she said, "Haul away, boys, and wake the dead! Haul, I say!" The crew bent their backs to their labors, and soon the anchors were a-cockbill at the larboard and starboard bows. White canvas billowed out overhead with a crack like summer thunder, fresh and loud enough to rattle the teeth in a man's head.

Bess was not surprised when Henry Dunn approached her. He would need to know her plan. "Carew will make for the Windward passage, I wager," she said, going to stand by the binnacle box and forestalling whatever statement he was about to utter. "We'll make our course thus till we spy that bastard whore's get. I want the convoy to stay close, Mr. Dunn...close as a Countess' fart-catchers, eh?"

"Aye-aye," Dunn said. "I'll relay the orders."

Mad Maudlin slipped forward through the water, her movements sweet and lively. Crewmen set the topgallant sails and the courses. The wind freshened further. "Steer her sou'west by west," Bess said to Halifax, the helmsman, then to Dunn she added, "and I want the ship kept close-hauled."

"Aye, Cap'n." Dunn hesitated, and finally said, "What will we do with *Deceiver* when you catch her?"

Bess knew this question would be coming. "If possible, we'll board her, but if not, we'll come to half a pistol's shot and settle her hash with canister shot." She put a hand on the hilt of her cutlass. "Speedwell tells me that *Deceiver* is demon haunted; there's no telling what that ill-begotten bitch will do when her master's dead. You know what the figurehead did to two of our men already. Will you risk the rest of the crew? Are they willing to risk themselves for scant reward? There ain't no question of killin' Carew, Mr. Dunn. I'll slit his throat myself if needs be. As for the treasure..." Bess shrugged. "Consider it lost."

"The men won't like that," Dunn warned.

"The men can bend their knees and kiss my lily white arse," Bess snapped. She took a deep breath and calmed herself. "'Tis more than a matter of Spanish gold, as well you know. Are you loyal, Henry, or need I fear mutiny from your quarter?"

"Nay, I'll not mutiny." The finality in his voice was a relief to Bess, who carefully showed no sign of emotion. "What shall I tell the men?" he asked.

"Why, that *Deceiver*'s as cursed as her master," Bess replied. "That any sailor who sets foot on that deck will die, his soul torn from his body and sent to a harrowing hell, willy-nilly, and none of our magics can counter this enchantment. Give out that I'll pay a bonus from my own purse to the crew and allow a sen'night in Kingston to spend it."

She waited while Dunn considered; although an officer, she knew he had come to her as a representative of the forecastle hands. If he accepted her offer and the other men were unsatisfied, he would likely find himself knifed and shoved overboard on a moonless night. *Mad Maudlin* and the other pirate vessels were not a democracy – each of the captains had supreme authority, yielded only to Bess herself – but their men had ways of making their displeasure known, and it often involved murder.

Dunn's face creased in a grin at last. "Aye, that'll do," he said. "I'll see to signaling the convoy." He turned to go, and Bess saw Mistress Glasspoole headed for the quarterdeck. The herb-wife's face was set, her mouth drawn into a taut line.

Her heart sinking, Bess tried to prepare herself for the worst.

CHAPTER THIRTY-FOUR
In Pursuit of Death

"Here's an un-pretty pickle," Glasspoole said without any ceremony. Behind her, a few silver-blue flying fish arrowed out of the water, rising to the height of the rail before falling back to the sea again, the minute splashes lost in the vibration of timbers as *Mad Maudlin* gathered passageway.

"What is it?" Bess asked.

"I ain't one to use perfumed lies when the stinking truth will do, so I'll just tell you clear that Margo's in a bad way," Glasspoole said, every word accompanied by whistles. "The blade did not pierce her heart – otherwise, she'd be doomed, for as you know, magic cannot heal injured flesh. However," she continued, overriding the elation that bloomed unbidden in Bess' expression, "the wound is still very serious. Very serious, indeed. Captain Speedwell informs me that a spell is also taking her life."

"Only till I wring Tom Carew's neck," Bess growled.

"At the moment, I dare not extract the dagger, not till the spell's been broken – otherwise, she'll die all the quicker – but each moment it remains in place, the danger is that some roll of the ship or other movement may cause the sharp edge of the blade to shift and cut into her heart. I tell thee plain, such a wound will mean her death, and there's naught that can be done." Glasspoole paused; she looked old and tired, her eyes sunken into their sockets. "I'll say also, for honesty's sake, that each moment I must delay is another moment towards Margo's eventual death, if the dagger be not removed and the wound treated."

Bess nodded once. "Time's not our ally – this I already ken," she said. "Do what you can, mistress. I'll not blame you if the treatment goes awry."

She stalked off the quarterdeck, leaving the herb-wife behind, and went to stand on the foredeck. Bess did not know what to do with the emotions that boiled and seethed inside her, a mixture of helpless rage and anxiety and blood-lust. She wanted to strike something; had it been within her power, Bess would have played the part of mighty Jove and lofted a lightning bolt at Carew, smiting him instantly to cinders. She put a hand on the rail. Foam streamed back from either side of the cutwater, dark blue-green tipped with lacy streamers of white. *Mad Maudlin* began to fly, impelled by a wind that smelled faintly of lightning – the forerunner of a storm still miles away. The vibration under her hand reminded her of the knife throbbing in Marguerite's breast, and Bess snatched her hand back.

A keen humming note from the rigging caught her ear. Bess turned and heard Falconer ordering the sails trimmed to woo the utmost power of the wind. The crisp storm scent grew stronger. Spray burst over *Mad Maudlin*'s bow in a dazzling rainbow arc. Bess thought about the possibility of a white squall and checked the water for the trademark whirlwind-formed whitecaps that were a precursor of the storms that could blow out of nowhere in the tropics. On the quarterdeck stood the squat, bow-legged figure of Henry Dunn, his hands clasped behind his back, a kerchief tied round his head. While she watched, the damask-clad Levalier came from below-decks and joined Dunn. The gunnery master's powdered wig had been repaired and sat slightly askew on his head.

After a moment, Levalier approached her. The Frenchman wore a small, star-shaped beauty patch near the corner of his eye, in the position called *la passionée.* "Captain Lovelock has not acknowledged your orders," he murmured.

"What of Byng and Quittam?" Bess' hand clenched into a fist at her side. There was no need to ask after Speedwell; she had seen the giantess rowed to the *Red Queen's Revenge* and knew that Speedwell would not abandon her, or Marguerite for that matter. The other two captains...their loyalty was trickier to predict.

"They have signaled us to lead," Levalier said, "but *Swiftsure* is turning to leeward."

Sourness bubbled in the back of Bess' throat. "So he thinks we'll be too busy chasin' *Deceiver* to treat his treachery as it deserves, eh? Well, go back to Mr. Dunn and tell him we'll deal with the Judas another time. 'Tis Carew I'm after, and I ain't one to change prey in mid-stride, so to speak."

"*Oui, ma capitaine.*"

When he had gone, Bess opened her spyglass and trained it on *Deceiver.* The corvette was still beating to windward; the great white rectangles of her sails belled out tight as drumheads. She wheeled away from *Mad Maudlin* on a starboard tack, the straight line of her wake becoming a graceful curve in the water. Unreasoning fury suddenly struck Bess like a blow. It took a real effort not to draw her cutlass and lay about her with the flat edge to spur the crew to greater effort as well as release some of the anger that pooled inside her like black poison.

She drew a breath through her nostrils and let it hiss out of her mouth. Instead of killing everyone on board, Bess shouted, "Set royals! Brace sharply!"

Falconer shot her a disbelieving look, but what he read in her face made the swarthy Bostonian pale. He rounded on a crewman. "You heard the captain!" he roared. "Brace the courses lively, and set royals! You, there! Jack Watt! Get aloft, man, or you'll feel the merry rope's end, damn your hide!" He twirled the length of tarred rope that was used to "encourage" sailors to bend more diligently to their work. "Fill the mains'l!"

Following a mad scramble on the decks and in the cross-trees, *Mad Maudlin* raced after the *Deceiver,* carrying every scrap of sail that the brisk wind would allow without wringing the masts. The ship lay over steeply, her larboard chains smothered in foam, with spray bursting aft in sheets, water hissing away beneath the keel, and the sound of the rigging rising to a screech. Bess was wetted from head to toes and did not care a whit. She held onto a stay, exhilarated despite her fury.

Dunn was keeping close watch on *Deceiver* from the quarterdeck. "She's weathering," he rumbled. "Mr. Halifax, bear us up a point!"

"Aye, sir!"

"Hands to the braces!" called Falconer.

Satisfied that the ship was running at its best possible speed, Bess turned her attention back to *Deceiver*. She estimated that Carew's vessel was running at six knots, but he had not lofted all possible sail. Indeed, his course seemed leisurely. That made her suspicious. Was he trying to draw *Mad Maudlin* into a trap? Bess gnawed her bottom lip, considering, then put the spyglass to her eye once more. Beads of water speckled the lens, hugely magnifying and distorting the image. Nevertheless, Bess made out Carew himself, perched upon the main cross-yard like a vulture, watching her through *his* spyglass.

She spat over the side. "Mr. Dunn!"

"Aye, Cap'n!"

"Make your course four points to starboard!"

"Four points to starboard, aye!"

Bess waited a moment while her ship responded to the change. This alteration brought *Mad Maudlin* more in line with *Deceiver*, on a collision course that would drive her bowsprit through the other ship's vulnerable stern if it continued unchecked. She studied *Deceiver*'s progress through the spyglass. Carew had put on more sail, setting his topsails and topgallants. She wondered where he had learned the trick of forcing spirits to do his bidding, and thought it must be because of the demonically-possessed figurehead, the Devil with the angel's face. Bess snorted. She would not attempt such a foolhardy act, no matter the desperation of the situation or the convenience of not having to put up with a mortal crew and all their tendencies towards error. Summoning demons was tantamount to making war on hell; the denizens of that fiery place took vengeance on those who were bold enough – or foolish enough – to pierce the veil and drag them willy-nilly to the human realm.

That reminded her of Speedwell's promise to look into breaking *Deceiver*'s possession. If the demon was freed, it would turn on Carew – they all did, the untrustworthy buggers – but having dealt with its master, would it attack *Mad Maudlin* as well? She sent a glare at the ship they were chasing, praying that when the time came, she could deal Carew as messy and painful an ending as possible, though a necessarily short one if Marguerite had any chance of being saved.

Deceiver coursed like a hare pursued by a pack of hounds, but slowly, surely, Bess' convoy of ships was overtaking her, *Mad Maudlin* poised to take the weather-gage. Carew piled on more sail, even to the moonrakers and skysails; he was in danger of losing his topmasts and yards, not to mention the rudder pintles. *Deceiver* had to be under the sort of stresses that ripped a keel apart under normal circumstances. If the corvette was not taking on water...well, Bess supposed that his supernatural crew could likely man the pumps day and night if necessary, but it would still slow him down. No helm responded well when the ship's timbers were sprung and gushing seawater with each rise and fall of the waves.

Had Carew any sense, she thought, *he'd abandon the treasure that's weighing him down like a grain-blown horse's belly*. If *Deceiver* had not been filled with tons of Spanish silver and gold, Carew could easily have out-sailed them.

Bess made a wolfish grin as *Mad Maudlin* heeled further, imagining the winking pink flash of her exposed copper-clad bottom as it caught the light. The ship was gaining in the race. Being a cromster, *Mad Maudlin* was the bigger vessel, which meant that her keel bit more deeply into the water below the surface turbulence and could maintain a better hold to her course, whereas *Deceiver*'s smaller size caused it to be battered by waves and pushed more to leeward, so that Carew had to luff up, sacrificing speed to correct his course to windward. She looked through the spy-glass. As she had thought, his forecourse was torn to ribbons, unable to withstand the strain. Carew was crippling his ship...but even as she watched, the mutilated sail lashed itself whole again.

"Hellfire and damnation!" Bess swore. She lowered the spyglass, then whipped it back up to her eye when a motion from *Deceiver* caught her attention. The foretopsail was shivering. She knew what that meant – Carew was going to come about, taking a new tack. If they did not follow suit, the gap between the ships would widen irrevocably, and he might be able to slip away. "Mr. Dunn!"

"Aye!"

"Prepare to come about!" Bess snapped the spyglass closed and tucked it back into the wide leather belt cinched low on her hips.

"Handsomely, Mr. Halifax," Dunn said to the helmsman at the wheel.

"Helm's alee!" came the warning from Falconer as the bow turned. Crewmen snapped to take their proper places, every man alert and ready to act upon orders.

Dunn's face might have been carved from stone. Bess understood why; this was a tricky maneuver that would leave *Mad Maudlin* dead in the water if the operation was not completed perfectly. There was no margin for error. Woe betide anyone who failed his duty, for that poor, benighted son-of-a-sow would feel his shipmates' wrath.

Mad Maudlin came into the wind.

"Hard over!" Dunn roared. Together, he and Halifax handled the wheel. At the same time, Falconer bellowed, "Mains'l haul!" Crew cast the bowlines off, and the yards came ponderously round at the same moment that the ship pointed directly into the wind. All hands braced on the heeling deck. *Mad Maudlin* had sufficient steerage way to prevent her being taken aback; the rudder dug deep, but not too far over.

Falconer's call rose above the wind. "Haul off! Haul off all!" and *Mad Maudlin* went from one tack to the other without losing a single yard or hourglass grain of time.

Bess looked at *Deceiver* from the larboard quarter – Carew was maintaining his current heading – then she went to check the traverse board that recorded *Mad Maudlin*'s course and speed, updated during each watch. It was very beautiful of its kind, made of *lignum vitae* with an elaborate compass rose inlaid on the front in lighter woods. Eight holes radiated from each of the thirty-two compass points with eight pegs to mark the course, each placed on the board every half-hour. Below the compass rose were more holes arranged in four columns with eight more pegs to record the ship's speed, estimated via the log-line on the half-hour of each watch. The whole thing hung on a hook from the side of the binnacle box, within convenient reach.

Checking *Mad Maudlin*'s progress by this rough log, Bess estimated that as long as wind and water remained in their favor, they would have *Deceiver* under their guns within an hour. Putting the traverse board back on its hook, she took a sextant and measured the angle between *Deceiver*'s masthead and waterline; by this observation, she confirmed that they were gaining on the other ship. Bess turned to find Jim Monk standing behind her. The cabin boy held a pewter mug and a plate of lobscouse, the well-beloved sailor's sea pie made with fish, lobster, salt meat and vegetables layered between crumbled ship's biscuit.

"Compliments o' Mistress Hephzibah," Monk said. A gust of wind flapped the tails of his coat and almost knocked him off balance. Bess quickly knotted a fist into his lapel and hauled the young boy back on his feet. Hot tea slopped over his hand, and he bit back a cry.

Bess took the cup and plate from him. "Go below to the orlop and ask Mistress Glasspoole to tend your fingers, lad," she said, not unkindly. "And remember the rule next time: one hand for yourself, and one for the ship."

"Mistress Hephzibah said I was to wait till you was finished," Monk said, sucking the edge of his scalded hand.

"Get along with you, Jim Monk!" Bess cuffed him lightly. "I'll have no ape of mischief clutterin' my deck. Should Mistress Hephzibah ask, give her my compliments and she'll not take you to task. Besides, ain't you needed by M'sieur Levalier?"

"Aye," Monk replied. In battle, he acted as one of the ship's powder monkeys, if he was not assisting in the chirurgeon's cockpit. "Only I was s'posed to take the cup and plate back to the galley."

"Be off!" Bess cried, aiming a kick at his buttocks as the boy turned and ran. When he had gone, she gulped the tea – hot as it was, the tea was also strong and sweet, and she needed the stimulation – and scraped up lobscouse with the provided wooden spoon until the plate was clean, although having no appetite, she did not taste a single bite. Her thoughts wandered, following Jim Monk down to the orlop deck where Marguerite lay dying in the sick-bay.

By the sweet bleedin' Christ! Bess swore savagely, though silently. In an hour, her lover might be dead. Would be dead, in fact, unless she caught Tom Carew and got back the life he was stealing. How she hated spook binding! Dabbling in magics caused naught but misery, and she wished Carew to the Devil. Bess thrust the empty plate and cup at a passing crewman; he was startled, though he took the items and tugged his forelock in token of obedience. She ignored him and ordered Dunn to have the main topmast staysails set.

He made no protest, but Bess did not miss the disapproving glance he sent her way. The wind was really too fresh for so much sail; she was risking a great deal. Bess was confident that she or Dunn would sense warning vibrations in the deck before the mast tore loose, or the sails threatened to come apart. At the moment, the planks beneath her bare feet hummed with the unique pulse that belonged to *Mad Maudlin* alone.

"Come along, my darlin'," she whispered under her breath in sing-song fashion, as though to a shying horse instead of a ship. "Sa, sa, darlin', come along lively now, with the wind in your teeth and the wave beneath your forefoot. Swiftly, swiftly, carry me cross't the waters, my beauty. Carry me and mine."

Her gaze shifted to the other vessel, Carew's corvette.

Soon, Fancy Tom, Bess promised, a cold coil of hate unspooling in her belly. *Soon, 'twill be me n' thee, and there'll be a grand killing, I swear.*

The thought of seeing Marguerite's colorless face made her queasy, and in her anger she was no fit company anyway, so Bess went to her cabin to await the moment when the slaughter would begin.

CHAPTER THIRTY-FIVE
Under the Guns

A flash came first, a long tongue of red-and-orange flame, then an ear-splitting bellow accompanied by a puff of sulphur-scented smoke. The long twelve-pounder guns jumped with the recoil, and the gun carriage jerked backwards violently on its wheels, kept from careening loose about the deck by an arrangement of rope tackles.

"Prime your guns!" Levalier shouted. Like the crews who attended each of the guns, he was coated in a thin film of smoke-grease; even his powdered wig was dirtied by it. "*Garçons de la poudre*! Bring fresh charges!" he ordered Jim Monk and the other five crewmen who were acting as powder monkeys, running back and forth between the aft magazine and the gundeck, fetching gunpowder cartridges.

"Swab that gun out proper, damnation to your soul!" Bess ordered. "Do you want to lose a hand if the charge cooks off and misfires?" She had come below to the gundeck to witness the operations and now watched the shirtless number four man of the six-man crew who tended a gun named Sully-Me-Not. He used a wet sponge to cool the gun's barrel and damp down sparks in the bore, and a double-corkscrew iron worm to scrape out any left-over gunpowder. Muscles shifted beneath his sweaty, soot-streaked skin as he worked.

The other men in the gun crew each had their own number – names were not used to simplify the gunnery master's orders – and their own specific task to fulfill, including the number one man, the gun-captain. Bess kept a critical eye on the proceedings.

A crewman rammed in a new charge and wad and inserted an iron ball into the gun. Bess noted with approval that the ball had been coated in red ship's paint to ward off the rust that distorted the cannonball's smooth lines, and otherwise had to be laboriously chipped away by hand lest it cause the shot to go awry. *A Gift from Bedlam* was painted on it in white.

The number three man pushed a wire pricker into the breech-hole to puncture the gunpowder charge brought by the powder monkey. He tapped fine-grained powder into the firing-hole from a horn, his motions quick and deliberate. The man's face was set into a stony mask of concentration, his tongue poking between his tobacco-yellowed teeth.

"Run out your guns!" Levalier bellowed.

Number three leaped out of the way when his task was complete. Wasting no time, the rest of the crew put their weight into hauling the traces to bring the muzzle of Sully-Me-Not nosing out of the port. In the confined space, the timbers multiplied and flung back the sound of the wooden carriage wheels rumbling over the deck planks until the sound was deafening, like being caught inside a kettledrum.

The gun-captain stooped to squint out of the open port, a slash of sunshine falling across his face. He then stared down the V-shaped notch on the gun's muzzle and began to bark instructions. The number two man, assisted by number five, used a long handspike to turn and raise the barrel, which was then held in place with a wooden wedge-like quoin. Clearly satisfied with the gun's aim, the gun-captain took a slow-match from the perforated wooden tub on the deck and prepared to fire. He held the smoldering length of hemp clamped in the jaws of his linstock, held poised over the gun's touch-hole.

The operation took approximately ninety seconds and was repeated by the other crews who labored at their own guns.

"Fire as you bear!" Levalier ordered the gun-captains.

Boom! Sully-Me-Not went off in a cascade of flame and skull-rattling noise. The other guns fired in a continuous hellish crash, the wheels of their carriages grinding on the sand-sprinkled deck, which heaved and trembled with the shock of multiple discharges. Acrid smoke pooled thick under the beams. The heat was merciless in its intensity. All of the men were grimy with soot; the sweat that poured down their faces was black with it.

Moving adroitly to avoid getting in the way as the well-coordinated dance of reloading commenced, Bess went to peer out of a gunport at the *Deceiver*. She had to wait, blinking her watering, stinging eyes until the smoke cleared somewhat and her vision adjusted from the gun deck's gloom to the blazing sunlight outside. The sight that greeted her made her grind out blasphemies between her clenched teeth. *Mad Maudlin, Mistress Moon* and the *Red Queen's Revenge* were wreaking severe damage on *Deceiver's* hull, masts and sails; an ordinary vessel would have been sunk already from so much devastation between wind and water, but the same magic that had revitalized *Deceiver* in the island cave was still at work. The ship simply repaired itself, leaving *Deceiver* intact as if no damage had been done at all. On the other hand, the fire that Carew inflicted on each of their ships was severe enough to have caused *Medusa* to drop out of the fight already or risk being holed beyond the vessel's capacity to bear.

"This ain't goin' to do," Bess muttered. She marched back to the maindeck, refusing to duck as a screech and a thumping crash signaled a shot from *Deceiver* smashing into *Mad Maudlin*. She stumbled, regained her feet, and cursed again. There was blood on the deck where injured men had lain before being dragged to the cock-pit to be tended by Mistress Glasspoole. Sharp wooden splinters littered the boards. The foretopmast hung at a crazy angle, and both the main and mizzen sheets were as holed as Emmental cheeses.

Bess turned her head at an unintelligible shout from the bow. The starboard chaser had been dismounted and was threatening to plummet down an open hatchway. Unless it was checked, the gun was a lethal weight of solid iron that would continue its plunge straight through the cromster's bottom and deal *Mad Maudlin's* death blow. Without waiting to call for help, Bess snatched up a line and sprang for the chaser, fighting the slope of the deck. Grapeshot from *Deceiver* howled through the rigging, sending blocks into the splinter netting that was rigged overhead. Bess whipped the line around the chaser's muzzle and made it fast to a stanchion just as the ship lurched and rolled to the other side. Several hands came to assist with handspikes and more lines. Cast loose from the shot garland, a series of cannonballs grumbled across the deck and down the gangway with crewmen in hot pursuit.

"Where's the carpenter?" Bess asked the carpenter's mate, a sallow man whose forearms were covered in sprawling tattoos.

"Dead, Cap'n," the mate said, his voice as hollow as his eyes. His shirt was bloodstained and torn. "Master Nowland, 'ee took splinter in throat, God rest 'is soul."

Bess had no time to waste. "Well, go aft and sound the well, master laze-about!" she ordered, certain that *Mad Maudlin* was taking on water; the ship answered the helm a trifle sluggishly. Another thunderous booming of cannon shot from the *Deceiver* filled her ears, as well as the shrill whistle of a passing ball that skimmed over the deck. She turned her head, batting irritably at wet spray that had doused her hair. The wetness proved to be blood; her palm was coated in wet crimson. She looked and saw the carpenter's mate was gone, carried away by the shot except for a single severed arm lying incongruously on the deck, the black tattoo patterns somewhat obscured by blood but recognizable.

She made her way aft to the pump where the sounding line was coiled. Inserting the three-foot weighted rod into the well aperture, Bess let it drop, paying out the line until the rod struck the bottom of the ship, then she hauled it out. A rough estimate showed there was about a foot of water in the well – not serious, and not worthy of assigning a pumping crew yet. Bess made a mental note to find a new carpenter, provided they all survived.

Henry Dunn joined her, his eyes bloodshot and glazed with fatigue. A cut on his muscular shoulder oozed scarlet, the wound likely caused by flying splinters. "We can't take much more of this pounding," he told her.

"I've a notion on that score," Bess said, raising her voice to be heard over the roaring bellow of fire from the gundeck. "There's naught to be done with *Deceiver* till her master's dead in truth. Agreed?"

"Aye, it seems sense to me," Dunn said. "What's your orders, Cap'n? Should we try for a broadside?"

Bess shook her head. "I think not, Mr. Dunn, for that's akin to shootin' a may-fly from the air with a fowling piece. 'Tis too inexact, d'ye ken? Short of blowing her to flinders, she'll heal her timbers and courses, easy as kiss-my-hand. So I'm headed for the source of our troubles, b'God – straight to the source." Having conceived the idea, she set her jaw resolutely, determined to save not only her lover, but her friends, her crew and the ships in her pirate fleet at one stroke aimed at Carew's throat.

"What do you mean?" Dunn shot out a hand and gripped a belaying pin in the main fife rail as another loud roar came from the gundeck, and the planks shook beneath their feet.

"I'm going over to *Deceiver*," Bess said, "to meet Carew blade-to-blade."

The surprise on Dunn's face almost made her chuckle despite the seriousness of the situation. His expression changed to a thoughtful frown. "That might do it," he said. "'Twill mean putting *Mad Maudlin* within direct range of his guns."

"Can you do it, Henry?" Bess rarely used the man's first name, and for a second time, he appeared surprised. She went on, "Carew will broadside you again – there's little doubt of that, for *Maudlin* will have to sail close enough for me to jump aboard *Deceiver*. He'll not heave to and wait for me to row across."

After a brief pause, Dunn replied, "It can be done, Captain. It *will* be done." He did not look happy, but purpose shone on his perspiration-wet face. "Shall we transfer the men to one of the other ships and leave a skeleton crew to sail *Maudlin*?"

Bess nodded, relieved that Dunn was going along with her plan. "That's a good thought if it can be done sly. I'd not like Carew to catch wind too quick."

"We'll be slick as purser's slush," he said, nodding. "I'll signal *Medusa* to heave to and take on injured crewmen. 'Twill be true enough, for there's scarce a man aboard that hasn't spilled blood this day, and *Medusa's* out of the fight anyhow."

Bess scrubbed at her stinging eyes with the back of her hand. Even on the main deck, smoke from the guns eddied in curling waves from the hatchways and the open gun ports below, hovering long enough to fill the back of her throat and irritate her eyes before being whisked away by the wind. "I'll make ready."

Dunn hesitated, then touched her wrist. "Good luck attend you." He seemed sincere, so Bess patted his back.

"Wish luck upon yourself as well, Mr. Dunn, for you'll need it."

While he saw to the semi-evacuation, Bess prepared herself to face Carew. She did not know how close *Mad Maudlin* could come to *Deceiver*; she might end up having to swim part-way to the other ship. That meant no flintlocks – wet powder was useless – and a light cutlass instead of a heavier saber. She removed her coat, waistcoat, boots and stockings, leaving herself barefoot, clad only in a linen shirt and a pair of black breeches. Bess found a long red scarf in her cabin that she wound around her waist, to use as an improvised belt to hold the cutlass scabbard securely. She strapped a knife in its sheath to her forearm, then she tied a kerchief around her head to keep her blood-clotted hair out of her eyes. As a final act, Bess removed the five gold earrings that she habitually wore, laying them side-by-side on the writing desk. If she returned, she would resume command...if she failed, Bess would have no use for finery because she would be dead. She glanced at her reflection in the mirror. The gunpowder tattoo on her cheek stood out starkly against her worry-paled skin.

'Tis the only way, Bess told her reflection, the words unspoken but felt nevertheless. *This will be over, one way or t'other, and either Margo will be*

saved, or we'll both be dead.

The finality suited her. Bess had never been one to harbor fantasies of slipping away peacefully in her sleep, in her own bed, surrounded by mourners; she had always known that the end would come in pain and blood, dying alone, clinging to life until the last agonized breath. The chances were good that even if she managed to kill Fancy Tom Carew in the end, she would be too wounded to escape *Deceiver*. Would the ship sink when her master was dead? Bess imagined drowning – every sailor did, even those who, like her, knew how to swim. She shuddered at the conjured horror of a gush of cold water pouring into her nose and mouth, filling her spasming lungs, weighing her down even as she struggled desperately to claw her way to the surface, her body refusing to surrender life with grace.

Bess shuddered again and spat to avert bad luck.

When she returned to the quarterdeck, Bess saw that the *Medusa* had hove to, and a gig was plying back and forth between the vessels, ferrying crewmen. Allegra Quittam herself was on *Mad Maudlin*, speaking to Henry Dunn. Spotting Bess, Quittam hurried over.

"He says you're going over to *Deceiver*," she said without preamble, jabbing a finger in Dunn's direction.

"Aye," Bess replied, adjusting the knot of the sash around her waist. "What of it?"

"Naught, save that I'll go with you."

Bess glanced up in surprise. The woman's gaze was cool, but there was an air of determination about Quittam that was unmistakable. "Why, Allegra! I'd no notion that you cared to die this day, for surely this is a fool's mission."

"And you're love's fool," Quittam said, grimacing. "Damnation, Bess! Is she worth your life, this Marguerite of yours?"

"She is," Bess said, untroubled, for it was the unvarnished truth. Somehow, Marguerite had become more important to her than any other consideration. She did not resent this state; it seemed natural and inevitable. "Besides, Allegra, will you have Carew sail off unscathed, biting his thumb to disgrace us? Nay, it must be done, and I'll be doin' the deed alone, though I thank 'ee kindly for the offer of help."

Quittam's grimace became a scowl. The wind ruffled her thread-wound blonde quiffs; if not for the fan of wrinkles at the corners of her eyes, she would have looked like a young spoiled woman denied an especial treat. "So be it!" she said after a short pause. "You're stubborn as a she-camel, b'God, and deserve whatever happens...but I hope you'll see the color of that scurvy bastard's guts afore he cuts you to pieces."

Bess let out a hard bark of laughter. "Again, 'tis a kind notion, and I thank you for it." She thrust out a hand, and Quittam took it. Bess continued, "If Carew sends me to the Diet of Worms, 'twill be Speedwell who takes command of all."

"That suits me," Quittam said, squeezing Bess' hand, "and 'twill suit Freddie as well..." Her voice trailed off as she spotted something over Bess' shoulder. "Oh, sweet suffering Christ!"

Bess whipped her head around in time to see *Swiftsure* bearing down on them. The sturdily-built lugger carried all sails save the royals close-hauled on her two masts and moved before the wind with the swiftness of an arrow shot from a bow. The sea was flat calm, a long peaceful swell that scarcely impeded *Swiftsure's* progress. The lugger plowed through the water, seemingly aimed at *Maudlin's* bow. At first, Bess thought Lovelock meant to ram *Mad Maudlin* – truly the action of a madman, for his ship was smaller and lighter than Bess' cromster – but she soon realized that he would miss them entirely.

Swiftsure loomed closer until Bess could see Lovelock standing in the forecastle, sunlight glinting from his cleanly shaven head. There was a series of bright metal flashes from the silver buttons on his leather vest. The lugger sailed past *Mad Maudlin* with a sound like tearing silk, close enough to be hit with a thrown ship's biscuit had anyone been so inclined. *Maudlin* rocked in the other ship's wake. Bess rushed to the side, wondering what in God's name had possessed Solomon Lovelock; there was no place for skylarking in a sea battle.

Deceiver's guns roared and spat flame. The ranging shots fell short of *Swiftsure*; jets of foam-fringed water leaped into the air as the balls skipped on the ocean and finally sank without penetrating their target. *Swiftsure* retaliated with a full barrage from the eighteen-pound carronades on her upper deck. The carronades were shorter-barreled than the long cannons that Bess preferred, and subsequently had less range, but *Swiftsure* had closed much of the distance before firing. The sound of the broadside was shattering, as was the splintering crash of shot chewing through *Deceiver's* side. The devastation ought to have sent the corvette to the bottom of the sea. Instead, the hull repaired itself, and as *Swiftsure* curved away, *Deceiver* let loose with another round of fire.

When the smoke cleared, Lovelock still stood in the forecastle, hanging grimly to a stay. *Swiftsure* had taken some damage, but it did not appear to be serious. Dunn joined Bess at the side. He said, "Now's the time, Cap'n, whilst Carew's distracted. We'll slip up to his blind side."

"Make it so, Mr. Dunn," Bess said. She did not understand why Lovelock had decided to enter the fray, but she would not argue with the heaven-sent opportunity. With Carew's attention fixed on *Swiftsure*, *Mad Maudlin* might be able to close in on *Deceiver* and get away without being broadsided.

Mistress Moon, commanded by Byng, swept in from the west, the brigantine attracting *Deceiver's* fire. His path intersected Lovelock's, their ships' wakes crossing; the *Red Queen's Revenge* joined the two vessels, all three harrying *Deceiver* like a pack of hungry wolves. *Red Queen's* sails blazed with witch-fire; Speedwell stood in the waist, her unbound hair flying behind her. Only *Medusa* remained out of it; Quittam's crew was fothering a hole below her waterline with a spare sail. Bess could see that her pumps were working furiously, and ax men cut away a tangle of shrouds and stays that trailed over the side.

"Now!" Dunn ordered the helmsman. *Mad Maudlin* swung about in a wide arc, then corrected her course to bring her alongside *Deceiver*. If she failed now, there would likely not be another chance; sailing this close to another vessel took a combination of skilled seamanship and luck that she could not count on twice. Bess leaped onto the rail and squatted there, maintaining her balance easily. The ship passed through a cloud of smoke – the sulphur smell was thick and clung to her lungs – and then Bess saw *Deceiver*, a phantom that materialized in the swirling, dissipating cloud. The Devil figurehead's nacre eyes gleamed subtly; it flourished its trident and was gone, slipping past her in silence.

She timed it in her mind, her attention focused on a narrow slice of *Deceiver*'s deck that widened as the ship drew nearer. Her muscles coiled in anticipation; her mouth was dry, tasting of gun-smoke and sour fear. A rough patch on the rail dug into the ball of her bare foot. There was a persistent itch between her shoulder blades; sweat trickled from her underarms, like insects tickling her skin. Bess paused, counting, and finally hurled herself outwards in a single convulsive movement. She hung in space for a long, awful moment, then time speeded up, the deck came hurtling at her, and she smashed into it with enough force to turn the edges of her vision black and scarlet.

Bess rolled to her feet despite the savage pain in her shoulder, ignoring the vertigo that threatened to turn her stomach inside-out. She blinked. There was no sign of Carew, and no sign of any crewmen for that matter. The ship appeared to be working itself, or perhaps was under the command of invisible spirits as she had speculated. The hairs on the back of her neck prickled. Bess warily made her way to the break of the quarterdeck, a hand wrapped around her cutlass hilt. The pounding pulse of her heartbeat and the rasp of her breathing sounded astonishingly loud in her own ears.

A thump sounded on the deck behind her.

She froze in mid-step.

"Welcome aboard, Captain," said Fancy Tom Carew.

Her grip tightened on the cutlass hilt and she turned to face the murderous dog who was stealing the life of the woman she loved.

CHAPTER THIRTY-SIX
A Life for a Life

Bess drew the cutlass; the metallic *shing* of steel sliding from the scabbard made goosebumps rise on her skin. "I mean to kill you, old man," she said, her voice harsh.

Carew threw back his head and laughed; the clicking sound that came from his throat only increased her uneasiness. "You can try, O'Bedlam. Your betters have, yet here I stand."

"You're naught but a thief and a killer!"

"Aye, the same as you," he retorted. A breath of breeze blew his long white hair forward, into his eyes. He did not push it back but continued to regard her steadily. "How many innocents have dyed your hands with their blood?"

If Carew hoped to make her feel guilty, he was sadly mistaken. Bess had long ago accepted the consequences of her decision to abandon her life ashore and become a pirate; her heart and soul were blackened by the cruelty of kill-or-be-killed, and she regretted nothing. Murder was necessary to guarantee her survival. Bess remained highly protective of those she loved, like Marguerite, like Speedwell and the others who served in her fleet, but she did not give a tinker's damn about the rest of the world.

Her reply was blasphemous, as well as physically impossible. Carew made his clicking laugh again. "Good," he said. "I'd hate to waste my time with a weakling."

He drew his own cutlass, holding it in the guard position with an ease born of long practice. Bess mirrored his stance. All she heard was the creaking of timbers, the rising whine of the standing rigging's tension, and the snap of sails. Since Bess was aboard *Deceiver*, the other ships had ceased firing. A sudden grating sound, like pieces of wood grinding together, warned Bess in time to jump out of the way as the figurehead's hand swept through the place where she had been standing.

Carew lunged at her, his blade extended for a cut that would have skewered her through the chest if Bess had not moved to one side, avoiding the thrust, and countered with a sweep of her own cutlass. Their blades clashed together and they sprang apart, the shock of contact numbing Bess' arm to the elbow. She circled to the left, trying to stay out of the figurehead's reach while maintaining guard against Carew. The last wisps of white gunsmoke had cleared, revealing an endless stretch of turquoise sea that turned to molten silver where it met the horizon. A pitiless sun beat down overhead, turning the air hot as a blacksmith's forge, but the heat could not dispel the chill in her bones.

He cut at her again, this time at her face; she winced away but responded, and her answering blow took him in the neck. Bess exulted savagely, thinking that she had dealt a fatal wound, but it proved to be hardly more than a shallow scratch. Carew backed away, the fingertips of his free hand touching the cut that gaped like a tiny mouth and coming away red. "I bleed," he said, a flicker of wonderment crossing his face. "See? I bleed!"

Bess snarled; her sword swept down as she stamped forward, but the blow missed. She recovered and spat, "Come closer, damn your eyes, and you'll bleed in truth!"

He grinned, showing the rotting stumps of his teeth, and suddenly launched a frenzied attack, his cutlass whirling into a gleaming circle of steel. He pressed Bess hard; she blocked one strike after another, part of her mind on defense against Carew's cutlass, the other fixed upon her location on the deck. If she came within reach of the figurehead, it would no doubt crush her to death in its great wooden fist.

Sweat poured over her face. The shoulder she had injured during the jump aboard *Deceiver* was a burning brand, every movement sparking deeper pain. She clenched her jaw and twisted aside to avoid Carew's blade, then brought her own swinging around to counter the blow. The shriek of metal on metal seemed to slice straight through her skull. Bess clenched her jaw against the jarring impact and held her position, muscles straining, bare feet braced on the deck. Carew bore down on her cutlass, relentlessly pushing her down and back, while the pain in her shoulder worsened, and the sweat ran down, and she could feel her left foot slipping.

Bess gathered her strength and shoved, allowing the momentum to send her backwards at the same time, disengaging their blades. A sharp crack sent her staggering to the side, just in time to prevent being caught by the figurehead that had made a grab at her. Carew's mocking laughter followed her. Bess lost her footing and fell, rolling on the deck as *Deceiver* lurched and heeled over. She slammed into the mainmast, knocking the breath out of her lungs. Through watering eyes, Bess saw Carew approaching.

Up! Get up! she screamed at herself, and somehow managed to get to her feet. Bess stood there, wheezing; the hardened oak mast had caught her across her back, and she could already feel bruises forming. She swung at Carew, knowing the wild strike would miss but needing to show him that she was capable of more than just defending herself. She needed to take the fight to him, not merely react to his blows.

Her body adjusted to accommodate the moving ship, a habit learned over years of living and working on a seagoing vessel. Carew stood carelessly, his legs parted, holding his cutlass at his side. Bess panted, every intake of breath scorching like hot coals inside her chest. She remembered watching Marguerite's fight with Carmelita on the beach at Hotspur Cay, and how Marguerite had used a ruse to draw her opponent into a trap by pretending to be weaker than she actually was. At the time, Bess had been too furious to appreciate the trick, but now she wondered if Carew would prove as gullible as Carmelita.

There's naught to lose, Bess thought, eyeing the tall, gaunt, black-clad figure. *It's been five-and-twenty years since Carew fought one to one; mayhap he's forgot such feints.*

Bess moved away from the mast, exaggerating her stiffness and pain, though not by much. She let her heel drag a little; the point of her cutlass wavered when she lifted it. Concentrating solely on Carew, Bess felt as if she had become unstuck from the world, as if time had moved forward in a sparkling blur, leaving her misaligned and alone on *Deceiver*'s deck, facing a man who had been all but dead for more than two decades. She stared at him down the length of steel in her fist, and prepared to live or die.

Carew's head tilted to one side. Bess knew he was studying her, and she let her injured shoulder droop. In an instant he was upon her, cutlass striking at her stomach, arm and head. Bess countered; steel flashed and sparks flew, and once again the powerful shock of their blades scraping together nearly sent her to her knees. She scrambled away, towards the rail. *Come, little fishie, take the tasty bait...*

He was almost within sword reach when there was a muffled roar, an explosion of violet-blue witch-fire, and the ship yawed wildly. Bess dropped her guard and her cutlass to grab the rail and save herself from pitching overboard. The deck angled as steeply as a church roof, and the masts were nearly horizontal. Her weight dangled from the one hand that clutched the rail. Carew clung to the mizzenmast, his long white hair falling over his shoulder, the ends trailing in the heat-softened pitch that covered the wooden surface. Glancing forward, Bess saw the figurehead had craned itself around, and was staring directly at Carew. Flames burned in its nacreous eyes. The beautiful angel's face twisted into a hateful snarl.

"No!" Carew shouted, dropping his cutlass. "You're bound to obey me!"

The ship righted itself suddenly, slamming the copper-clad keel back into the water and sending spray flying in a glimmering arc. Bess' body lifted with the force of the ship's movement, then she was crushed against the deck at *Deceiver*'s impact on the ocean. The whole hull shuddered like a dog shaking off fleas. The vibration carried up the masts, and the sails shivered. Bruised and breathless, Bess climbed slowly to her feet. A glance over the side showed her dead and stunned fish floating on the surface, white bellies gleaming under the sun. One of them, a blue-and-silver striped skipjack, struggled feebly to right itself.

Letty must have freed the demon, she thought, wiping a trickle of blood from her nose. Her entire right side ached, and she suspected that she might have a broken rib or two. Bess leaned against the rail, wary of attracting the figurehead's attention.

Something moved beneath the carved wooden form, something that bulged and twisted as though the solid oak was merely the thinnest of skins. There was terror in Carew's black eyes. He edged closer to her. "Protect me, O'Bedlam, and I'll spare your woman's life," he said, trying for bravado and failing miserably.

"You'll shed this stolen life and turn ghost again? Hah!" Bess hawked and spat on the deck, a blood-tinged wad of sputum that narrowly missed his boots, and supported her broken ribs with a hand. "I'd not trust you to honor a good bargain, Fancy Tom. Why should I believe you'd keep a bad one?"

The crackling scream of tortured wood made them both wince, Bess doubly so as pain stabbed her side. Carew balled his fists and faced the Devil figurehead that was tearing itself apart. Whatever his faults, however grievous his sins, Bess knew from the legend that Fancy Tom Carew had never lacked courage.

"I defy you!" he shouted. "Go back to the Fallen and be damned to you, hellspawn!"

A second explosion ripped through the ship, accompanied by a blizzard of splinters as the figurehead blew apart. Acting on pure reflex, Bess fell to the deck, letting out a grunt as her ribs protested. The air felt as if it had gone thick, sticking in her lungs. The planks were hot beneath her – too hot, she thought, glancing up and immediately wishing that she had not.

A monster clung to the prow where the Devil figurehead had once reared. Its massive chest heaved; its soulless eyes glared sullenly. Black iridescent scales covered it entirely, from the raised crest on its smooth head to the spiraling fish tail that writhed and slapped against the hull. Wisps of steam curled in the air. The inhuman gaze slid over Bess and fastened onto Carew, whose sun-bronzed face turned an unhealthy shade of gray. The demon's webbed hands twitched, claws scoring the *Deceiver*'s catheads.

Flames erupted and licked at the base of the mainmast. Not witch-fire but true fire, the kind that lapped at the dry, pitch-soaked wood, wafting a thin tendril of black smoke into the air that quickly grew into a dense cloud. Bess curled her hand tighter against her ribs – she thought she could feel the broken ends rubbing together, which was disconcerting as well as painful – and suppressed the urge to fetch a sand bucket or man the forecastle pump. On any ship, fire was the greatest danger, since the materials used in building were incredibly flammable. All her instincts screamed at her to douse the fire, but she bit her lip and waited, wondering which menace Carew would deal with first – the flames, which had eaten their way half through the mainmast; the demon that had been trapped inside *Deceiver*'s figurehead and was now unconstrained by any enchantment; or herself.

His mind evidently made up, Carew snatched his cutlass from the smoldering deck and charged towards the demon.

Bess watched in mesmerized fascination as the demon hissed, showing a mouthful of needle-like teeth. Carew swung his sword and connected with its arm, inflicting a bloodless wound that closed within seconds. The demon's tail uncoiled like a serpent and slapped the deck with enough force to bowl Carew over. He fell heavily, rose, and fell again as the demon flexed its arms and slithered over the rail, landing with a thump and a wet squelching sound. It balanced there a moment, then came towards Carew, dragging itself along with its hands.

"You'll not take my treasure!" Carew cried. "'Tis mine, I tell you!

Mine!" A torrent of filthy blasphemies spilled out of his mouth as he hacked at the demon. It ignored his blows and continued its slow advance, leaving a trail of slime on the deck. The demon hissed again, its heavy tail lashing back and forth. Carew spewed a truly horrible oath and turned to flee.

The demon's hand wrapped around his ankle, jerking Carew to a stop.

Bess pressed herself against the smoothly polished rail as Carew screamed. The sound was wild and high, followed immediately by loud retorts, moans and bangs as *Deceiver* began to fall apart. All of the damage the ship had sustained – from twenty-five years of neglect as well as the attack by Bess' fleet – reasserted itself at once. Swathes of green-black mildew swept over the canvas sails, followed by rips and tears that left the courses in tatters. Stays popped from their places and hung, unraveled and useless, covered in a renewed layer of dust. Next to her foot, a ragged hole opened in a plank. *Deceiver* lurched, the fire burned, and still Carew screamed, as though the damage done to his vessel was manifested within his own body as unbearable agony.

A topmast that had been severed in the original attack crashed to the deck.

Deceiver was falling apart around her. The fire had spread; smoke stung her eyes. Bess considered the treasure sure to be crammed within the ship's hold, silver and gold in glittering heaps, the metallic gleam laced with colored jewels and ropes of pearls. She thought about the fire and the reversal of the magic that had sustained *Deceiver*, and how easy it would be to order a crew to row over from one of her ships, to fight the conflagration while salvaging the treasure. Perhaps Speedwell could persuade the demon to—

Carew's howling broke into her thoughts, and Bess realized that there was no time left. The ship was literally rotting beneath her feet; the rail she leaned against sagged, and she almost lost her balance.

On *Mad Maudlin*, Marguerite's life was slipping away.

Resolve tightened her mouth into a thin line. *To hell with it, and to hell with you, Fancy Tom Carew.*

Bess scooped her cutlass off the deck. Her arm snapped back, then forward, sending the blade whirling end-over-end through the air to land with a solid *thunk* in the back of Carew's head. His body went rigid, his heels vibrating on the smoldering planks. Blood stained his white hair, turning it wet and crimson. He convulsed in the demon's grasp; there was a pattering of blood on the deck, drizzling from the hilt of the cutlass that cleaved his skull. His eyes were half-closed, showing crescent curves of whites. The demon's hiss turned into a *basso* roar that flapped the burning sheets, sending winking ruby embers and flakes of ash floating away from the charred edges, dancing on air.

Carew was dead. She had cheated the demon of its prey. How would it react? She did not wish to stay and find out. Bess jumped overboard as another huge roar resounded behind her. The water was warm on the surface but cool underneath, chilling her skin. The sea surrounded her as did the shattering silver bubbles that her passage had ruptured from the green and blue depths. Above her, bars of sunlight slanting through the ocean layers lightened the water. A faint current tugged at her legs. It was blessedly quiet here, the sort of silence that Bess imagined might only be found in cathedrals or other sacred spaces. A burning in her lungs reminded her of the need to breathe. Reluctantly, she kicked upwards and broke the surface into harsh sunlight, gasping and blinking salt from her eyes.

Deceiver was falling apart; chunks of the corvette simply cracking off and dropping into the ocean. Bess trod water for a moment before spotting *Mad Maudlin*; the tulip-bulb silhouette of the cromster was unique. It seemed to be the closest ship to her, but that determination was difficult to make as she rolled with the waves and sank into the troughs. There was no chance that Bess could actually swim fast enough to catch up with it. The best she could do was stay afloat until the look-out at the mast-head spotted her and a jolly-boat came to pick her up. She fixed her concentration on the distant sails that looked like bird's wings soaring against the bowl of the sky.

The roaring behind her cut off and there was a loud splash. Bess did not have to look around to know that the demon had abandoned *Deceiver* and was likely coming after her. Cold clenched her gut. The water seemed to lose its blood-warmth and turn icy in a moment. Somewhere below her, a *thing* with claws and teeth could be swimming, every stroke of its tail bringing it closer and closer...

Her heart banged against her sore ribs. Bess started to swim in earnest. She had two options, neither of them good: to face the demon in its own element and fight for her life, or try to flee. Escape did not seem possible. Water slipped over her skin like silk, heated by her exertions, but it did not have the power to warm her chilled body. Years ago, during a swim off the island of Hispaniola, Bess had felt something brush against her legs a number of times. She had thought the sensation was due to sea grass, or a turtle, but after returning to *Mad Maudlin*, she had been told by that it had been a large tiger shark, perhaps twelve feet long, circling her in the water. Bess had felt the blood rush from her face and been forced to flee to her cabin lest she betray her fear; tiger sharks had indiscriminate appetites and were known man-eaters. That close call had left her shaking for a good long while.

Now she wished it was only a tiger shark sharing the waters with her.

Bess registered the cold and slimy touch slithering over her waist in the split-second before she felt sharp teeth nip at her ankle. She yelled, swallowed bitter water, retched, and sank under the waves. Her eyes were open, although the salt made them feel dry and scratchy, as if she was swimming in sand rather than the sea. Her momentary panic was over. She pulled the knife from her forearm sheath and hovered in the water a moment. Bubbles slipped from her mouth and nose; her lungs began to ache from holding her breath. The tear on her ankle burned. She swam to the surface, gulped air past the raw knot in her throat, then jack-knifed and dived. Her decision was made – she would fight.

Her eye caught movement, and she spun around, kicking her feet and waving her arms to prevent her body from bobbing to the surface. A flash of opalescent black caught her attention; she focused and saw the demon was undulating gracefully about ten feet away. Her skin was suddenly sensitized; Bess could have sworn she could sense that soulless gaze traveling over her body, like an unwelcome ghostly caress that left her feeling unclean. The demon flicked its tail and shot off, vanishing into the murk that her vision could not penetrate.

Bess surfaced again, squinting against the blaze of sunlight.

"Captain!"

The water in her ears dulled the voice. Nevertheless, Bess turned to greet the owner, Solomon Lovelock. The burly bald man sat in a small jolly-boat, shipping the oars. He tossed a line towards Bess. She swam over and grasped it, relieved beyond measure to see her former bo'sun. The man smiled tightly, his teeth gleaming white against his splendid red mustache. "With bait like this," he said as he reeled her in, "who knows what we'll catch?"

Bess grinned at the old joke despite her apprehension; the expression changed to shock when a hand wrapped around her leg and yanked her under the surface.

She slashed at the demon with her knife, scoring a hit along its arm. Needle-like teeth snapped at her. Bess whipped her body backwards and forwards, trying to break the demon's hold before it dragged her down so far she would drown before she could reach air and light again – presuming she was able to get away. She let go of the line that Lovelock had tossed her.

A gleaming streak of silver at the corner of her eye proved to be a fishing gaff swinging down from the surface, through the foam their thrashing had stirred up, to pierce the demon's flat black eye. It released Bess, and she hastily made for the jolly-boat, knowing that any safety provided by the little vessel was an illusion, yet compelled to seek that illusory refuge anyway. The demon seemed equally at home in air or water, and could capsize the jolly-boat. Nevertheless, Bess could not help but feel gratitude when Lovelock seized her fumbling hand and hauled her dripping and gasping over the gunwale.

Lovelock took the oars, the muscles in his shoulders rolling beneath bronzed skin. A thump sounded on the hull, and another. Bess scrambled to her feet, trying not to breathe too hard against the agony in her side. She still had her knife, which was a minor miracle.

"Solomon, row like the Devil himself was after you," Bess said, "and you'd not be far wrong." She glanced over her shoulder, estimating the distance to *Swiftsure*. The ship had hove to, as had *Mad Maudlin*, and both vessels were waiting for them. Bess recognized *Mistress Moon* in the distance, headed for the wreckage of *Deceiver*; bits of wood, canvas and other debris, some of it still burning, floated on the surface in an ever-widening circle. She wished Byng good luck in salvaging anything from that accursed ship. The treasure was gone, and good riddance to it as far as she was concerned.

Red Queen's Revenge headed towards them on an intercept path. At the same time that Bess realized this, a webbed and clawed hand appeared over the side and clamped down on the strake, rocking the jolly-boat. Her knees flexed to accommodate the movement, and she grunted as it jarred her broken ribs. Lovelock released the oars and drew his cutlass as the boat rocked again, tilting so far that water slopped over the edge. He reversed the blade and gave it to her, hilt first. Bess looked into the man's eyes and nodded, then took the cutlass and brought it down upon the demon's fingers, severing them.

There was no blood, merely four black-scaled fingers rolling around the bottom of the boat. Bess chopped down again, at the demon's head as it surfaced. It had no nose, just two slits above a wide, lipless mouth. The cutlass opened horrible wounds, but they closed as quickly as Bess' blade made them. She hacked and hacked, while the demon hissed and the boat rocked as though caught in a heavy swell, water slopping over the gunwale in sheets. Lovelock put his back into working the oars to bring them closer to *Swiftsure*; the man grunted with each dip and dig.

Brilliant violet-blue witch-fire suddenly erupted from the wave-caps, blinding Bess. Surprised, she lost her balance and fell backwards, striking her head on the gunwale.

Darkness rushed at her, and she had no time to cry out as oblivion engulfed her, and she knew no more.

CHAPTER THIRTY-SEVEN
Dragged to the Depths

Bess roused, groaning. At first, her mind was a confused jumble of thoughts and images, none of which made much sense. Her head throbbed; a deep breath caused an explosion of pain in her side, and she remembered broken ribs. That recollection sparked more memories – Marguerite, *Deceiver*'s sinking, Tom Carew's death, the demon – *the demon!* – and she sat straight up, her hand reaching for a weapon. The jolly-boat pitched about, and sea water slopped into her face. Bess spat out a mouthful and checked her surroundings, thankful when her questing fingers found the hilt of Lovelock's cutlass.

The man himself still worked the oars, a grim expression on his face. Bess surmised that she had not been unconscious very long. "What's to do?" she asked, not surprised to find her voice was a feeble croak.

"Yon demon's circlin' round for another pass," Lovelock said, blowing out a breath with enough force to make the fringes of his mustache shiver. Biting back a groan, Bess levered herself to her feet and scanned the surrounding ocean. The *Red Queen's Revenge* was still closing, and would cross their boat's bow in a few minutes. She thought the demon was toying with them, as a cat plays with a mouse before breaking its back with a single well-placed blow. If she had been able to communicate with Speedwell, they might have arranged something. Even now, Bess believed she knew the other woman well enough to expect a rescue attempt of some kind. Perhaps a thrown grapple or line that could be lashed to the jolly-boat as the *Red Queen* passed, to tow them to safety...if that was the plan, she would have to catch the line and tie it off quickly, or risk being jerked out of the jolly-boat by the ship's momentum, and tumbled willy-nilly in the *Red Queen's* wake.

Another eruption of blue-violet witch-fire blinded her; she threw up an arm to protect her eyes. Bess blinked rapidly to dispel the floating after-images. When her vision cleared, she saw Lettice Speedwell walking on the water as calmly as if she performed this miracle every day. The red-headed giantess chanted loudly, holding a burning dagger aloft; each step she took measured and deliberate, her feet hardly sinking at all beneath the waves that shimmered with brilliant witch-fire.

The demon surfaced and blew a stream of true flame at Speedwell, a liquid curl of crimson and orange with a fierce blue heart. Several arm's lengths away, Bess felt the heat on her cheek, hot enough that her eyebrows sizzled. Speedwell deflected the flame with a gesture. Lovelock slowed his oar-work. If the giantess got into trouble, they were the closest to attempt a rescue. Bess almost told him to go on, diverting their course to *Mad Maudlin* and abandoning Speedwell; she was impatient for the sight of Marguerite, and the suspense of not knowing if her lover lived or died nibbled at the edges of her sanity.

Bess wished she had a flintlock, or a blunderbuss, or – since she was wishing, and as likely to get what she wanted as suddenly flying to the moon – a squat "Smasher" carronade, with plenty of black powder and grape-shot, and a solid deck to fire from. Instead, she had a cutlass and a knife. Glancing around the jolly-boat revealed no other items that could be used as weapons except the oars, a leather bailing bucket and a bight of tarred rope tucked under the stern thwart. She bit the inside of her cheek, longing for action, for a fight, anything to distract her from the sick feeling in the pit of her stomach.

Speedwell's chanting was like distant thunder, a deep and guttural booming just on the edge of hearing. Turbulent violet witch-fire spread over the ocean's surface, covering the water with its crackle and snap. A wind sprang up from the north, sharp and cold, tainted with the nauseatingly sweet smell of decay. Bess gripped the cutlass hilt until it creaked.

When the demon appeared again, its black-scaled body was wound in a net of sparkling magic. It struggled and shrieked something in a strange, bubbling tongue that made Bess' flesh creep. Slowly, inexorably, the demon was pulled out of the water by Speedwell's chant to hang suspended in mid-air, writhing and twisting, uttering shriek after shriek and billows of true fire that did not harm the net at all.

A lightning bolt split the heavens, a forked brand of purest light that seared the eyes. The ocean turned to leaping blue-violet witch-fire as far as Bess could see. Overhead, the sky darkened to near black, and clouds covered the sun, plunging the scene into false night. One lightning flash after another illuminated the demon, which appeared as a collection of glittering black opal scales and needle teeth, its writhing length twined round with purple bonds. The colorless streaks in Speedwell's hair shone like molten silver, and the spectacle lenses that hid her eyes had a moonstone glow.

It grew eerily quiet, save for Speedwell's guttural incantation. The demon had stopped shrieking and hung silent in the net. The ocean's surface roiled, churned from below by something huge and unknown, a leviathan whose intentions could not be guessed. Bess' breath caught; the pulse of pain in her side grew into a throb that kept time to the beat of her heart. Behind her, Lovelock stirred, and she heard the rasp of an oar being drawn from the oarlock. She nodded in approval; an improvised weapon was better than nothing at all.

What broke the surface came as a terrifying surprise. "Letty!" Bess cried, her voice hollowed by the heavy silence. "'Ware kraken!"

A nest of huge tentacles exploded from the ocean, dripping globules of witch-fire. A row of suckers the size of dinner plates lined each tentacle, each sucker outlined in sharp tooth-like hooks. The giant squid's mantle breached and a pair of enormous unblinking eyes looked straight at Bess – an alien stare that reflected no emotions at all, not even anger or greed. A tentacle twisted in her direction, the rubbery suckers working like mouths, eager to grasp and rend. She pressed a fist against her aching side and hefted the cutlass in her other hand. There was very little that could be done if the squid took hold of her, Speedwell or Lovelock; the hooks would settle into their flesh, much like cat's claws and as difficult to escape. They would be drawn towards the mouth, the snapping parrot beak ready to slice tender flesh into gobbets and crunch up their bones... Bess gagged on the notion of being eaten alive and prayed that she would die first.

The kraken's gaze shifted to the demon, still struggling in its magic-woven net.

The vast tentacles twitched.

Speedwell continued to chant and gestured with the burning dagger. Once, twice, three times she drove the blade towards the demon; each time, the giant tentacles twitched again. At last, her face engorged with blood, the harsh consonants and short vowels Speedwell had been uttering reached a howling crescendo. Witch-fire blazed anew, the glowing flames leaping upward as if to devour the stars themselves. Sullen black clouds boiled in the sky. Speedwell threw her head back and screamed.

The kraken's long tentacles shot out and seized its prey. A renewed shriek came from the demon as the sharp hooks drove deeply into its flesh. Flame erupted from the demon's mouth, aimed at the giant squid. The witch-fire winked out in an insant, and to Bess' consternation, Speedwell toppled backwards and disappeared beneath the waves.

At the same time, Bess caught blurred movement out of the corner of her eye. A voice called, "Captain!" and a rope hit her shoulder. She caught it and secured the end around an oarlock as the *Red Queen's Revenge* slipped past the jolly-boat's bow, leaving the smaller boat bobbing as the much larger vessel passed. Bess put a hand on the line; when she felt the tension increase, she jammed her feet beneath a thwart and leaned out over the gunwale, both arms extended in front of her. She felt Lovelock's strong hands wrap around her calves, anchoring her in the boat. Connected to *Red Queen*, the jolly-boat slewed around when the connecting line went taut and jerked along in the bigger vessel's wake, the bottom of the boat bumping up and down on the waves.

Bess kept her gaze fixed on the place where Speedwell had vanished. There would be only one chance; if she missed, Speedwell – her closest, dearest friend – would be lost. Silver-streaked red hair spread over the surface of the water. As they were dragged past the spot, Bess blinked spray out of her eyes and grabbed a double handful of that hair, knotting her fists and bracing herself, her muscles coiled in anticipation.

Despite these precautions, nothing could have prepared Bess for the sudden, powerful wrench that seemed likely to rip her arms off at the shoulders. Her joints burned as Speedwell's weight and the water's resistance were pitted against *Red Queen*'s wind-driven speed, with Bess taking the brunt of the dueling forces. If she had been a rope, she would have snapped. Instead, she ordered herself not to let go. After what seemed an eternity – but was, in fact, mere heartbeats – the terrible stress on her joints eased when the ocean yielded its grip on Speedwell, and the giantess was towed alongside the jolly-boat. Even so, Bess felt that her poor wrists would never be the same.

It was Lovelock who hauled Speedwell into the jolly-boat, although that task took every bit of strength the man possessed. Bess huddled next to her friend, relieved by the steady rise and fall of Speedwell's chest. She splayed a hand on the large woman's throat, comforted by the pulse that beat against her palm. Bess glanced behind them and saw the demon sinking into the sea, still wrapped in the kraken's unbreakable embrace.

Once the demon had been dragged into the abysmal depths, leaving only an eruption of foam and oily scum on the ocean's surface, the black-bellied clouds broke apart and scattered. The artificial gloom lightened, and the sun burst into its accustomed place in the now clear blue sky. Bess squinted against the glare and sought *Mad Maudlin.*

If Marguerite was dead, she was going to dredge Carew's sorry corpse out of the sea, pay a resurrectionist to bring his soul screaming back from hell, and kill him again, and again, and again...as long as she still had money to pay for the privilege.

A little while later – and a meeting too long delayed for Bess' peace of mind – Glasspoole stopped Bess outside the sick-bay. "Why, you're sulled up as a toad deprived of its fly," Glasspoole said, her tone disapproving, "and by thunder, you'll not disturb my patient with your damnable megrims."

"Is she...?" Bess could not quite believe it, not until she heard the words.

"Aye, Margo's alive, though her wound is serious." The lines around Glasspoole's mouth deepened. "The blade did not touch her heart, but it cut deep all the same. If the injury doesn't fester, and if the fever doesn't take her, she'll likely survive. I give no long odds, mind you. Death is just as likely."

Bess' hands clenched into fists. To lose Marguerite now! She managed to swallow the obscene epithets that crowded her throat, although a red-tinged tide of rage rose within her. When she thought that she could speak without giving offense to the herb-wife, she said, "Do whatever must be done, Esmeralda. I won't blame you if Margo dies...but in that case, 'twould be wise for you to seek service on another ship."

"I'll bear that in mind," Glasspoole said. She rubbed her temple with the heel of her hand; light from a nearby lantern caught the pearl on her thumb-ring, making it shine like a miniature moon. After a moment, she continued, "Now compose yourself and come inside, for those ribs of yours need treating, and your shoulder, too, if I'm not mistaken."

Bess brushed past Glasspoole and stepped into the sick-bay. The smell struck her first – a slaughterhouse reek of spilled blood and sickness that made her want to add her own vomit to the stink. Her gaze sought and found a small, pale form bundled into one of the hammocks, lashed in place with seven turns of a line so the patient might not be tipped out on the floor when the ship heeled. Only the spill of dirt-tarnished blonde hair told her that the unnaturally quiet person covered to the chin in a thin blanket was Marguerite De Vries.

She wanted to go to her lover, to hold Marguerite's hand and kiss her bloodless brow. She wanted to pound her fists against the bulkhead until the agony of crushed knuckles and splintered bone was enough to drown out the horror that gibbered inside her soul at the sight of those beloved features, waxen in stillness. Instead, Bess obeyed Glasspoole's instructions, managing to pull her shirt over her head and not scream aloud at the sharp bite of pain that followed each movement. Still clucking like an outraged hen, Glasspoole bound her torso with bandages and treated her strained shoulder with a healing salve. Bess welcomed the hurt even as she chewed her bottom lip.

Afterwards, Bess stood beside the hammock, afraid to touch Marguerite but equally afraid not to touch her, lest the woman slip away without warning. She counted off Marguerite's breaths, not taking a single inhalation or exhalation for granted. The slap of waves on *Mad Maudlin's* hull sounded abnormally loud in the otherwise quiet space. A soft hiss caused Bess' head to whip around, pin-pointing the source of the noise – it came from a spirit lamp, where a little kettle of water boiled, steam slipping from the spout and joining with the tropical humidity in the air to form a ragged veil that hung suspended a moment, and moved slowly towards the bulkhead where it vanished. Under her fingertips, Marguerite's hand trembled. Glasspoole poured hot water into a bowl and left the room, probably headed for the cock-pit, where the men wounded in the battle with *Deceiver* would be treated until the worst cases were ready to be transferred to the orlop deck and sick-bay.

Bess might have stood there for hours, possibly even days, had it not been for the appearance of Lettice Speedwell. The giantess had to crouch down to enter the sick-bay and once inside, simply knelt on the floor, her big hands rubbing her thighs. Bess took in her friend's appearance. Speedwell was haggard; her eyes were swollen and bloodshot, set in bruised circles of puffy flesh, and there was dried blood at the corner of her mouth. There was more silver than red in her hair now, and she looked as if she had lost weight. *The consequences of spook binding*, Bess thought, and for once was grateful beyond words that she counted a thaumaturge among her most loyal friends.

"Wind's freshening," Speedwell said.

Gratitude vanished like a popped soap bubble at this unwelcome reminder of a world beyond the sick-bay, and the responsibilities of a ship's captain. Bess made a half-hearted shrug, just a hunching of her shoulder that said she did not give a damn, not while the better half of her lay pale and unresponsive, close to death. "Dunn will take care of such matters for the nonce. How fare you, Letty?"

The wry twist of Speedwell's lips spoke volumes. "Blunt and burred, and weary to my soul besides," she said. "So much magic done in so short a time takes a heavy toll. Ask me not to summon so much as a flicker of witch-fire for a handful of fortnights at least, for by Baphomet's beard, I'm fair ready for the knacker's hammer."

There was silence between them a moment, then Bess sighed. "There ain't no treasure, no reward for all our searchin', just loss and more loss." A sob clawed at the inside of her chest, trying to get out. She stifled it and went on, her voice thickened and made harsh by unshed tears, "*Deceiver's* curse has undone me, Letty. I've lost more than a treasure..."

"You've lost your heart." Speedwell completed the sentence, then reached out and put the palm of her hand flat on Bess' back. "Margo's strong, and she's willful, and I doubt she'll go gently hand-in-hand with Sir Death. Nay, she'll fight the Reaper tooth and nail, and spit in his eye as well. Don't mourn her yet, my friend. Not till you hear the death rattle, and even then, I'd not be surprised if she rose again like the Christ, for she's too lusty and life-filled to surrender easy...and too much in love with you to leave you behind."

Bess bit her ravaged lip, refusing to give in to the rising emotions that were close to making her weep. She had to remain strong, but the question came out of her mouth before she could stop it: "What will I do without her?" To her own ears, it sounded plaintive and weak, and she cringed.

"Ah, you'll go on," Speedwell answered softly, "and you'll thrive, for you can do no less...but I think 'twill be difficult, if not impossible, for you to find happiness again."

"I've never known love, 'til I met Margo," Bess confessed. She looked down, taking note of the faint tracery of blue veins in the unconscious woman's eyelids. Marguerite seemed delicate and fragile, like a piece of porcelain that had been shattered and put back together with such skill, it was difficult to tell where the damage was done. Yet a careful examination would show the crazed lines, the mended cracks, the evidence of breakage. Bess wondered if the woman who woke up would be the same spirited hell-cat who had earned her respect and admiration. It did not matter, she decided. If needs must, she would spend the rest of her life catering to Margo's needs and desires, and anyone who objected could go to hell.

"It will be well, Bess. I promise." Speedwell sounded so sincere, so gentle, that Bess' fiercely shored-up controls crumbled in an instant. She turned to bury her face against the woman's broad shoulder and sobbed as if her heart was broken.

CHAPTER THIRTY-EIGHT
Running the Hoops

Mad Maudlin was becalmed when Marguerite awoke.

She had briefly surfaced from unconsciousness a few times already, registering not much apart from pain until Mistress Glasspoole appeared to administer the drug that sent her floating back to strange but not unpleasant dreams whose details she could not now remember. Marguerite blinked her crusty eyes, glancing up at the deck beams. She was in sick-bay. Bundles of dried herbs on their pegs were still, with only a hint of sway. It was so quiet, the faint groan of the tiller ropes could be heard through the bulkhead.

Her chest hurt, but it was at a remove, as if the ache belonged to someone else and she could only feel the drug-softened edges of it. Marguerite lay still, trying to gather her thoughts. She became aware of a raging thirst; her mouth was dry as dust, and her throat felt raw. A drink of water would be good. In fact, the more she considered it, the more she desired a long draft of fresh water. *It would be heavenly going down,* she thought.

Marguerite turned her head and realized with a growing sense of shock that she could not move her arms or legs. Was she paralyzed? A lump of flesh fated to lie abed for the rest of her days, dependent and defenseless? Panic beat at her, a clang of brazen notes inside her head. She coughed to clear her throat and... *Godskannone!* Agony lanced through her, sharp as a sword point.

The fresh blaze of pain only served to increase her agitation. Prickling sweat sprang out on her skin. Marguerite remembered being stabbed by Fancy Tom Carew. The sensation of the blade driving through muscle was a visceral memory that would haunt her nightmares for a long time to come. She whimpered and hissed between her teeth.

"Handsomely, dear heart!" said a familiar voice from nearby. It was Bess. Marguerite sobbed in relief at seeing her lover. "Handsomely, there," Bess continued, her warm palm stroking Marguerite's brow. "'Tis well, Margo. You're safe aboard *Mad Maudlin*. Carew is dead, d'ye hear? Dead as a shotten herring and safely clapped in hell, never to return."

Marguerite's body instinctively tried to curl around the gnawing pain. She strained to move, to roll over on her side, to do *something* to escape the hurt that crested higher and bit deeper into her flesh with every shuddering breath she took. Finally, Marguerite heard another voice through the agony-haze. She recognized Mistress Glasspoole by the whistle in her speech, though the actual words meant nothing at the moment. Firm hands helped her shift in the hammock until she was sitting up, her body propped at an angle by several pillows and a bolster. Panting harshly and gripping the sides of the thin mattress, Marguerite could only wait for the worst of the torment to pass. Apart from pain, she felt weak, her limbs heavy, her body sore as if she had been beaten all over with a rod.

Marguerite heard Bess' furious cry reverberating around the timbers, "Be damned to you, woman! Give Margo a dose of the poppy or by the sweet bleedin' Christ, 'twill be the scold's cure for you and the Diet of Worms for certain!"

Glasspoole's reply was cool. "Calm yourself. Mistress Margo must be weaned from the drug, for overuse of 'something-to-be-praised' is as much a danger as the wound that nearly took her life." At Bess' further protest, she added, "Would you make your woman crave poppy spirits instead of you? Would you see her vital spirits sucked dry, leaving naught but a husk behind? I vow 'twill be the case. I've seen it happen, poor opium-eaters so far sunk that they care not a bum-fiddle for aught else."

"But Margo hurts so." Bess' voice cracked.

Marguerite could not stand to hear Bess sound so broken. "'Tis all right, *liefje*," she croaked, forcing the words out past the stricture of her dry throat.

"I've a tea that will help. Poppy tea made with the dried seed heads. 'Tis less strong than the wine," Glasspoole said, her skirts rustling as she walked away to her work bench.

Bess took Marguerite's hand. The woman's complexion was near colorless; her hair hung in greasy strands around a face that was still febrile, the bones too prominent. She had developed a fever a sen'night ago that had left her raving deliriously; the result, Glasspoole said, of an infection in the knife wound in Marguerite's chest. Certainly, the swollen hot flesh had been drawn so tightly that the line of catgut sutures almost disappeared into the inflamed tissues. Bess could only watch with sick terror while Marguerite raved about monsters and fought the lines that restrained her in the hammock. The ship, her crew, her fleet... Bess had dismissed all of that as unimportant beside Marguerite's illness.

Glasspoole had applied every one of the available cures – affusions of cold seawater poured over the woman's head and body, fresh water enemata, a decoction of tamarind, a mucilaginous preparation of lime-tree buds and marshmallow root. The herb-wife had opened a few of Marguerite's sutures to let the pus out and cleansed the deep wound with a variety of herbal infusions as well as spirits of turpentine and spirits of rectified wine. Marguerite's cries had been terrible to hear, at last driving Bess out of the sick-bay and onto the deck lest she do something regrettable, like drive eight inches of steel through Mistress Glasspoole's gullet.

To complete her escape she had finally climbed to the foretopgallant masthead and squatted with her bare feet braced on the cross-tree, the sea a shining silver shield stretching from horizon to horizon. Bess had allowed some of her impotent rage to bleed away while she studied the geometric patterns of light and shadow cast by the sun onto the deck a hundred feet below, focusing her mind on the rectangles, triangles and curves. It was there in the quiet with only the wind for company and the great bowl of the sky above her that she regained a portion of her self-control. When Bess returned to sick-bay, she was calmer and better able to bear Marguerite's agonies as well as Glasspoole's seemingly brutal treatment of her beloved.

In the lonely middle watches, in the dark oppressive hours before dawn, Bess had stood by Marguerite's side mumbling half-forgotten prayers she had learned from the priest who had visited her mother in the incurable ward of Bethlehem Royal Hospital. She did not believe in a merciful God, but she bargained with Him anyway. Three days ago, when Marguerite's fever had broken in a torrent of sweat, Bess had been thankful beyond words. She had sponged the sweat from the other woman's body, cleaned up vomit, helped Glasspoole change the piss-soaked linen pads...anything Marguerite needed, any service that had to be performed, however distasteful, Bess had done because nothing else mattered except her lover was alive.

When Glasspoole returned bearing a pewter mug and pressed the rim to Marguerite's lips, she drank thirstily; the liquid was warm and bitter as gall – in fact, the flavor was akin to what she imagined decomposing goat droppings might taste like – but it was wet and that was what her body craved. After she swallowed the last mouthful, she sat back and tried to smile at Bess, who practically vibrated with tension.

"I do feel a little better," Marguerite said after a moment, hoping to soothe Bess' anxiety. The statement was not a lie. As the herb-wife's medicine began its work, a portion of the hurt she felt receded to a more comfortable fuzziness. Glasspoole was right; the tea *was* weaker than spirits of poppy – which also had a more palatable taste, being sweetened with syrup – but Marguerite was not going to argue for stronger measures when she was capable of handling a twinge or two.

"I wish you hadn't been fevered at all," Bess said, taking Marguerite's hand once more. Her thumb rubbed back and forth across the knuckles.

Marguerite's scalp and skin itched like fury; she was sure there were sweat galls in the creases of her groin, and the sour odor of her unwashed body was unpleasant. She could smell herself with each inhalation. In spite of her discomfort, she could see in Bess the tell-tale signs of exhaustion and worry, and she asked, concerned, "Is the ship becalmed?" although she thought she already knew the answer.

"Aye, 'tis the Variables," Bess said, raising Marguerite's hand, turning it over and placing a dry kiss on her palm. "Naught but light and fickle airs for all that the hands are whistlin' wind charms till they're blue as baboons." Another kiss and she continued, "Is there aught I can do for your present relief, dear heart?"

Marguerite sighed and used her free hand to tuck locks of her dirty hair behind her ears, hating the oily feel of the strands against her face. "I don't know how you can stand to kiss me. I've a confounded *haut goust* that would make a maggot cast up its accounts."

Bess' eyes crinkled at the corners as she smiled. "You could smell like a blast from the very guts of hell, and I'd not care a jot. That's a trifle next to your life."

"Oh, aye, but I'm more than a trifle rank," Marguerite replied. "Frankly, madam, I stink. Might I have a bath?" She was not eager to attempt getting out of the hammock – indeed, she was not certain she could – but the idea of being clean was appealing enough to override a degree of her tiredness and pain. Marguerite thought she could manage with help, and pushed aside the voice of common sense that told her she was being overly optimistic.

From her workbench across the sick-bay, Glasspoole said, "I think not, mistress! You've only just survived wound fever. 'Tis rest you need the most."

Marguerite was about to argue when she surprised herself by making a jaw-splitting yawn. Bathing was important, but she was so very, very weary...her eyes fluttered closed. She could not fight the compulsion; it was too overwhelming. With a sigh, she slipped from wakefulness and slid away into the sleep that beckoned irresistibly.

Bess stared in apprehension at the woman who had been conscious one moment, and unconscious the next. "What's amiss?" she asked, touching Marguerite's shoulder. She got no response. "Mistress Glasspoole!"

Galvanized by the alarm in Bess' voice, Glasspoole fairly flew across the intervening space, the round airy crown of her mobcap flattened by her speed. Reaching the hammock, she performed a swift examination of Marguerite while Bess hovered anxiously. At last, Glasspoole's solemn expression cleared, and she said, "Healing takes a mort of the body's energies to accomplish. This is naught more than sleep."

"But Margo just woke up!" Bess could hardly believe that Marguerite's behavior was normal. "Be you certain, mistress?"

"Aye, and aye again, and yet a third time to make it truth," Glasspoole replied, not unkindly. "Get you gone from here. She'll sleep a while yet and wake the better for it. 'Twill do her no good to know you've been standing about fretting yourself to a collapse." When Bess hesitated, Glasspoole pushed her bodily away from the hammock and continued, "Get you gone! Margo is well and should aught occur to the contrary, I swear I will send for you. Now go!" She flapped her hands like a housewife shooing chickens from the yard.

Bess cast a glance at Marguerite, whose slack mouth and bruised eyesockets gave her more the look of a corpse than a peaceful sleeper. "What can I do for her?" she asked, shivering. It was only the knowledge that the herb-wife would surely smite her senseless for fouling the sick-bay that kept Bess from spitting to avert bad luck.

"Leave her be for the nonce is my advice," Glasspoole said.

"Give me an occupation – anything! – or I vow I'll run mad," Bess whispered, unable to tear her gaze away from Marguerite. Only the rise and fall of the woman's chest assured her that Marguerite was still alive. Of a sudden, Bess could stand sick-bay no longer. She needed fresh air. She needed to be away from this place of death and suffering. Her heart began to hammer hard against her ribs. She swallowed, her eyes burning though she viciously denied herself the relief of tears.

Glasspoole looked sympathetic. "She'd do better on land. If somewhat could be done to break the calm and get the ship to Hotspur Cay as soon as could be managed..."

"I can do that." Bess grasped at the herb-wife's suggestion. "It can be done. By God, it *will* be done!" She turned and fled, her feet slapping against the planks. Bess hurtled up the ladder and popped out of the hatchway onto the maindeck, then moved to the rail to catch her breath and consider her options. She looked out over the lifeless sea and the brilliant sunlight shimmering on the surface until it dazzled her, and spots swam before her eyes. Heat poured on her head, wave after wave of molten incandescence that soaked straight through her skull. *Mad Maudlin* rocked on swells so tender, the motion was barely perceptible. Water lapped against the hull. The masts were burdened with idle drooping sails that shivered and flapped but could not catch a breath of wind sufficient for the ship to make headway.

Henry Dunn came to the rail and nodded at her. "The men wish to run the hoops to flog up a wind," he said. "What say you, Cap'n?"

Bess glanced at him out of the corner of her eye. There would be no help from Speedwell and her thaumaturgery to raise a wind; the giantess had not yet recovered from her prior ordeal, and Bess did not need a spyglass to see that *Red Queen's Revenge*, currently lying off their starboard quarter, was as becalmed as *Mad Maudlin* and the rest of the fleet. Dunn waited for her answer, crossing his arms over his muscled chest and slitting his eyes against the glare. Bess decided the suggestion suited her current mood very well.

Marguerite's wounding and subsequent illness had left Bess stretched perilously thin. She was light-headed from sleep deprivation. Nothing – not food, nor wine, nor even the ship she commanded – had held any savor while Marguerite's survival had been so uncertain. Now that the worst was over, Bess needed a release for her pent-up emotions. She disliked spook binding, but running the hoops was an ancient sailor's charm. To her mind the hoops had the weight of tradition behind them, and the ritual was, therefore, more acceptable to her.

"Tell the musicians they may play on the quarterdeck," she said to him. "For the rest, let the sea-dogs draw lots, all save one."

Dunn nodded, apparently unsurprised. Bess supposed that so much time serving together meant that when it came to the workings of her mind, Dunn knew her better than anyone, including Marguerite. "So mote it be," he said, moving away to speak to the hands congregating in the forecastle and ship's waist.

Bess removed her silver-buttoned waistcoat and worked on the laces of her cambric shirt, finally pulling the garment over her head and letting it drop on the deck, leaving her bare from the waist up. She was a good healer; her injured ribs ached and it hurt to take too deep a breath, but she was in better condition than Lettice or Marguerite. Her skin puckered although the air remained oppressively hot, unrelieved by any breeze. Bess was unconcerned about her semi-nudity. The crew did not regard her as female, not even with her small breasts uncovered; if any man did, he kept it to himself to avoid becoming the focus of Bess' much-feared wrath.

In the meantime, Jim Monk went to Dunn's belowdeck berth to fetch a bag full of small round ivory balls – the lots that were as much a part of the ship as her keel. No one, not even Bess, knew the origin of the lots; she had found the bag and its contents tucked into a forgotten corner of a locker in the tin-lined bread room after taking *Mad Maudlin* for her flagship. The bag was old, the leather dark and greasy with age and much handling. Inside were one hundred balls made of ivory carved in dainty lace filigree that was likely Indian work; most of the balls were white, but twelve were stained the color of blood. There was also a black ball that matched the rest but as its appearance signified death in the lots, Bess kept it in her own cabin unless the crew wished to vote to "black ball" one of their number.

Another crewman went through the hatchway and down to the orlop, returning with three iron hoops from the cable tier. As barrels of provender were emptied, it was the practice to knock out the hoops and stow the loose staves in the lowermost part of the ship both as a space-saving measure and for the bosun's convenience, so that he did not have to constantly shift empty barrels to get at victuals or fresh water. The crewman set the hoops on the foredeck and joined the others in choosing lots, thrusting his hand inside the bag held by Jim Monk and withdrawing his closed fist. When he opened his hand to show a red ball, he was seized by his mates and stripped of his shirt, then sent stumbling with a shove towards the other ten men who had already been selected by chance. Bess joined them, making their number twelve.

The sounds of hurdy-gurdy, drum, fiddle and pennywhistle commenced, the musicians beginning the *Hangman's March* in *andante*. The stamping of the crew's bare feet upon the deck and the clap of their callused hands echoed the slow walking pace pulse-beat that anchored the dirge-like melody. The music and the stamping thudded in time while Bess and the rest divided into three groups of four, and each group picked up an iron hoop, spacing themselves equidistant around the circumference. Dunn bound each person's left wrist to the hoop with a bight of rough hempen rope. Bess rolled her shoulders, loosening muscles that had been too taut for too long; the bruise she had gotten on Carew's ship was hardly noticeable. She checked the sky; it was smooth and cloudless, the horizon glinting so brightly it seared her eyes and made her blink.

Dunn gave them each a length of line that had three knots at the end. Bess took hers, trying to empty her mind of everything save the beat. The music rose in tempo and volume. The knotted line she held cast a thin, straight shadow on a deck nearly white from daily holystoning. Bess started to move as the music spoke to her, at first just rocking back and forth on the balls of her feet. Soon, she and the three men bound to the hoop with her were marching around in a circle while the other crewmen clapped and stamped.

When the first blow struck her on the shoulder, Bess sucked in a breath, surprised by the fierceness of the sting. It was no light tap; this was a swing with the strength of a man's arm behind it. The knots dug painfully into her skin. Her captain's status did not matter here; she would receive no mercy and be spared not a moment of suffering, nor would she have accepted anything less. Goaded, she swung her own line and struck the man in front of her, sparing him nothing, either. Another blow struck her, this one curling around her waist and leaving fire in its wake, followed by a lash to her scarred back, and another, and another, and Bess flogged her own victim in earnest, too.

The *Hangman's March* continued, insistent and undeniable, *presto* then *prestissimo* as the musicians played frantically, faster and faster, caught by the charm they were weaving. Bess marched, the soles of her feet scorched by the hot deck planking, and laid on her knotted line with a will. The welts on her back and shoulders, the near constant rain of blows, and the rasp of the hemp around her wrist drove her to a frenzy. The iron hoop was heavy, and she strained to keep it level as they marched in the suffocating heat.

Pain lifted her higher, her mind a-whirl, her thoughts consumed by the ache that spread through her skin and struck into the very heart of her. Bess laughed, the sound lost in the wild skirling peal of music that filled her blood and lent her wings. Her face was wet, and she neither knew nor cared if it was tears or rain. The instruments reached a crescendo that mimicked the crash of thunder, then the hurdy-gurdy, fiddle and pennywhistle broke off in a clash of final wails. The drum was like the heartbeat of a Colossus – one! two! three! – and the taut drumskin split in half. At the same time, the strength ran out of her and she collapsed to her knees, the knotted line falling from her nerveless fingers. The men tied to the hoop with her also fell, one of them sobbing harshly.

There was a long moment when Bess was deaf to everything save the buzzing in her head and the blood that throbbed in her veins. It was otherwise quiet, as if the world held its breath. A drop of sweat shivered on the end of her nose and fell off, splattering on the deck and leaving a dark mark. Bess forced her cramping lungs to take in air.

From abaft the ship's stern came a sigh, a soft susurration almost below hearing. Bess sat back on her heels. She felt tired and aching but cleansed, her troubles no longer festering within her because they had been purified in the crucible of pain. Whatever happened from this point forward, she thought she was better able to bear it.

Her left hand was still bound to the hoop, restricting her movements. Dunn approached, and she waved him off, wanting no distractions while she looked and listened, trying to stretch her senses. Hope grew to certainty when the wind freshened. The sails stirred. The breath of wind grew stronger, and stronger still. Under *Mad Maudlin's* bow came the sweet slide of a slight progress in the water.

Bess grinned triumphantly at Dunn. "Square the topsails, Mr. Dunn," she said, smiling so broadly that her face hurt worse than her bruised and welted back. "Take us home."

"Home it is," Dunn answered, also grinning.

Eager hands reached for Bess, to cut her free from the hoop, to set her on her feet, to pour salt water over her back and send her laughing back to sick-bay to keep her lover company while top-men scampered to the yards to tend the sails.

Mad Maudlin was homeward bound.

CHAPTER THIRTY-NINE
In the End is the Beginning

A little more than a month later, Marguerite shaded her face with an upraised hand, gazing out over the pale stretch of sand and the shimmering ribbon of blue-green water that met it. The sun was pure gold in the sky, without a cloud to mar the perfection of the day. From further down the beach came the sound of several male voices raised in song. With a little effort, she could make out what they were singing.

> *Oh, if the babe's a daughter, she'll bounce on daddy's knee,*
> *But if the babe's a son, why then, he's destined for the sea.*
> *No man will earn his blood-money for he'll have a coat of blue,*
> *And he'll ride the highest top-sail yards like his daddy used to do.*

Marguerite sighed as a shadow fell across her, blotting out the sun.

"Where's your hat, dear heart?" Bess asked, sitting beside her in the sand. The woman's chestnut hair was wet and hung in dripping tendrils around her face.

"Don't fuss," Marguerite answered sharply, but softened the admonition with a smile. An errant breeze brought the delicious smell of pig roasting in a pit, glazed with spices and wine in a way that Hephzibah had perfected. Her stomach growled and Marguerite flushed at this noisy and indelicate evidence of appetite.

"You know what Mistress Glasspoole said." Bess rummaged among the miscellaneous items scattered here and there near Marguerite's chair. She came up with a woven banana leaf hat that she promptly clapped on Marguerite's head. "Too much sun ain't healthy."

"Nor too much of anything," Marguerite growled. "*Godskannone!* I'm mortally sick of lazing about, for if I so much as lift a handkerchief to my nose, you or Letty or Katla or Esme or even Solomon Lovelock, Levalier and Dunn scurry along to stop me." She suddenly halted and pressed the heel of her hand against the deep pain in her chest. Her wound was taking its time to heal completely. Marguerite chafed under the necessary restrictions, but even she could not deny the breathlessness and pain that accompanied many exertions.

"Lie easy, dear heart," Bess crooned, reaching over to run a damp kerchief over Marguerite's sweaty brow. "Lie easy."

"'Tis a simple thing for you to say," Marguerite answered through gritted teeth, but the awful clench in her chest eased, and after a moment, she was able to relax. "Oh, but that's no jest!" she whispered.

"'Twill become better, so Esme says, and I've no reason to doubt her." Bess caught and held Marguerite's gaze. "You're doin' fine, m'love. And I care not a whit nor a tiddle if I must wait upon your pleasure for the rest of your days."

Marguerite sat back and unbuttoned her shirt. The angry red scar that curved under her breast marred her torso. She thought it was ugly, but Bess saw the scar as a symbol of Marguerite's survival. Even as the thought entered her mind, Bess placed a series of light kisses along the disfigurement carved into Marguerite's flesh by her grandfather's dagger.

"Beautiful," Bess murmured, and Marguerite allowed herself to be soothed by the familiar, worshipful touch. She appreciated her good fortune in having found such a communion of souls with Bess, who loved her and was so well beloved in turn.

She closed her eyes, and felt Bess move away from her briefly before returning, a warm presence at her side. Something greasy and cool was smeared on her healing wound; it was a balm concocted by Glasspoole, to keep her scar supple. It smelled fairly pleasant, although not as nice as the roast meat scent still drifting on the salt-tinged wind.

Bess' mouth descended, brushing her own but moving away when Marguerite tried to claim it for a kiss. "I love thee," Bess said, "and naught will change that, ever."

"I love you, too. *Mijn liefje, mijn duifje*," Marguerite said, finally managing to brush Bess' lips with her own. Her stomach chose that moment to howl in protest. Bess chuckled, and Marguerite's blush turned fiery.

"Right now, I'll wager you'd love a plate of pig more," Bess said teasingly.

Marguerite opened her eyes and found herself dazzled by the sheer weight of affection she saw reflected in Bess' face. Had there truly been a time when she had accused the woman of having no heart? How foolish she had been! How blind not to see that Bess was a worthy person, honorable in her own way, and certainly capable of absolute loyalty! Marguerite thought about the person she had been when she first laid eyes on Bess O'Bedlam and how far they had come since, and her smile grew wider.

"Never will I love another as much as I love thee," Marguerite said. She quoted from the Book of Ruth, "Where you die, I will die, and there I will be buried."

"Shhh, speak not of death and dying, or you'll wring me to tears."

Marguerite touched her fingertips to Bess' brow, to the shadowy curve of the gunpowder tattoo on her lover's cheek. "Don't cry, my sweet pirate lass. 'Twill cause my poor heart to crack in twain, I swear. And besides, if you dissolve into weeping," she said, grinning, "who will fetch me my dinner?"

Clear and loud, Bess' laugh rang out, startling a seagull. The bird shrieked its raucous displeasure and flapped away, becoming a rapidly disappearing dot in the blue Caribbean sky. Marguerite stretched and settled into Bess' arms to watch a lone cloud scud across the sun. From a distance, she could see a silver-headed figure approaching and identified it as Katla Byng, the rune-singer; the woman was carrying a platter of food and headed in their direction. Marguerite made a sound of contentment, nestling her head in the crook of Bess' neck.

Bess hid her smile in Marguerite's hair. They moved from strength to strength; it would not be much longer before *Mad Maudlin* could sail with her captain aboard once more, and Bess intended that Marguerite should be at her side. Together, they would journey the seas, under sun or stars, for as long as it pleased them.

When the travails and battles were done, Bess would bring Marguerite home to Hotspur Cay, to their house with the vivid blue door, and lay her beloved down in the bedchamber on a feather mattress and love her sweetly till dusk deepened the shadows around them, softening their little world to indigo and mauve. It was a dream, but the fantasy was also a reality, so long as Bess held Marguerite in her arms. Their love could withstand any tempest, and would only deepen and grow as the years went by.

The Water Witch had found her mate. All was well, and that was as it should be.

We who were born to baser things; we who were born to die,
Our lives are built 'pon blood we've spilt, with nary a pang nor sigh;
For sins we know, and we must go through lead and smoke and flame,
We roaring boys who live and die in the Water Witch's name!

Death rides on her shoulder, the Devil at her side,
She'll fight the wide world over, for she is hell's own bride!

~ Bess O'Bedlam's Song

Bibliography

Among the volumes of great usefulness in the compilation of this glossary, and in the writing of this book, were:

The Dictionary of the Marine by William Falconer (1830)

The Seaman's Grammar and Dictionary by Captain John Smith (1691)

Dictionary of Sea Terms by R.H. Dana, Jr. (1851)

A Dictionary of Sea Terms by Darcy Lever (1863)

The Naval Chronicle (1799-1819)

Mast and Sail in Europe and Asia by H. Warington Smythe (1906)

The Voyage Alone in the Yawl 'Rob Roy' by John MacGregor (1867)

Boat Sailing in Fair Weather or Foul by Captain A.J. Kenealy (1908)

The Naval History of Great Britain: 1793-1827 by William James (1837)

The Dictionary of the Vulgar Tongue by Captain Francis Grose (1785)

Journal of a Residence among the Negroes in the West Indies by Matthew Gregory Lewis, 1775-1818 (published 1845)

Dictionary of Phrase and Fable by E. Cobham Brewer (1898)

Pallas Armata, the Gentleman's Armorie by John Williams (1639)

Under the Black Flag: the Romance and Reality of Life Among the Pirates by David Cordingly (1997)

Historic Costume in Pictures by Braun and Schneider (1880)

GLOSSARY of TERMS and PHRASES
Which May Be Unfamiliar to the Gentle Reader

While some words or phrases may be familiar, a few definitions have been changed to suit the narrative of this story. No disrespect is intended by this poetic license. I feel obligated to point out that the characters of the *Water Witch* often use vulgar language; the modern reader may find some terms offensive.

Abaft: Behind, as in "abaft the **stern**" – behind the rear of the ship.

A bientôt: (French) Till we meet again.

Abraham's bosom: Heaven. The Christian paradise. "And it came to pass that the beggar died, and was carried by the angels into Abraham's bosom." – Luke 16:22, King James Bible.

Acid of sulphur, dulcified: A type of sulphuric acid, sweetened. Used in medicine.

Addle pate: A stupid or thick-headed person; or one who is easily fooled, gullible.

Affando: An old fashioned fencing term for a lunge.

Aft: Towards the rear (**stern**) of the ship; the rearmost part of the ship.

Agouti: A large rodent native to South America and the West Indian islands.

Aguardiente: Portuguese or Spanish brandy, quite coarse and unrefined.

A la prochaine fois: (French) Until next time.

Ale draper: The keeper (landlord) of a tavern.

Alicant: A type of Spanish wine

All-a-gog: Enthusiastic, or anxious, or impatient, depending on the context.

All-a-mort: Confused; struck dumb.

Aloof: At a distance.

Andante: (Italian) Lit., "walking pace". A moderately slow music tempo.

Anti-pyretic: A substance that prevents or reduces fever.

Ape leader: An old maid, so called because of the popular old-fashioned belief that her fate after death would be to lead apes into hell as punishment for neglecting to follow the Biblical command to increase and multiply.

(Keep your) Ass at anchor: Stay seated; or do not move from the spot.

Athwart-ships: Located at right angles to the ship's centerline.

Athwart the forefoot: A command given by a captain to the gun crew, meaning to fire a warning shot at another vessel, i.e. just in front of the other ship's bow.

Attaco responsivo: An old-fashioned fencing term referring to a counter-attack.

Backstay: A rope running from the masthead to the ship's sides. Backstays lead **aft** or to the rear; forestays lead forward.

Ballocks: Slang term for testicles.

Baracoon: A pen where slaves are brought after being unloaded from the ship, and where they are kept imprisoned prior to sale.

Barque: A three masted vessel which is square rigged on the **foremast** and **mainmast**, and fore-and-aft rigged on the **mizzenmast**.

Bashan bull: Bashan was an ancient area of Palestine, where the bulls were particularly noted for their size and strength, as well as the loudness of their roaring.

Bastinado: A type of baton used in torture for beating the soles of the feet.

Bean sidhe: (Irish) The banshee, a supernatural creature of the Fae, noted for its piercing shriek.

Beast with two backs: A euphemism for the act of heterosexual copulation.

Beau nasty: A person who dresses in rich and fashionable clothing but has questionable hygiene practices; a slovenly fop.

Beggar's pudding: A bread pudding flavored with rosewater, currants and ginger.

Belay: To secure or make fast a rope. Also, to disregard, such as "Belay that order!"

Belaying pin: A moveable wooden pin or bar to which a line (like rigging) can be secured.

Best (and small) bowers: The bow anchors. "Best" is starboard, "small" – though identical in size to its partner – is located on the port side.

Bien mieux: (French) An expression of approval. Good show. Well done.

Bilboes: A heavy iron bar with a pair of sliding shackles used for restraining prisoners; the shackles are usually fastened to the ankles.

Binnacle: The wooden stand upon which the ship's compass is supported. It is usually protected by a hood or cover.

Bistoury: Long, narrow knife with a straight or curved edge; a surgical instrument.

Blatteroon: An overly talkative, untactful person, one afflicted with verbal diarrhea.

Blunderbuss: A smoothbore, large caliber firearm with a short stock and a flaring, bell-shaped muzzle introduced into England in the late sixteenth century. A short-range scatter-gun, designed to fire shot (such as grapeshot) over an area without the requirements of aiming. Carried primarily as personal protection against thieves, or by ship captains to fire into crowds, such as during mutinies or while boarding another vessel with hostile intentions.

Bonebox: The mouth.

Botta in tempo: An old-fashioned fencing term, referring to a type of attack which distracts an opponent by a feint, thus leaving them unprepared to parry immediately.

Botta segrete: An old-fashioned fencing term, meaning an attack in secret.

Bow: Towards the front of the ship; the foremost part of the ship. The opposite of **aft** or **stern**.

Bow-chaser: A gun set in the **bow** of a ship. Usually located both **port** and **starboard**.

Bowsprit: The large spar that runs out from the **bow** of the ship. The bowsprit supports the jib sails.

Brace: A rope attached to the end of a **yard**, used to move the sail. To brace – as in "brace the mainsail" – is to turn or move a sail's position using braces. To "brace up" is to haul on the **lee** braces in order to bring the **yard**s nearer fore-and-aft. To "brace in" is to bring the **yard** more square.

Brail(s): Small ropes attached to the edges of a sail, utilized to truss it up before furling. To "brail up" is to haul up the lower corners of a sail by pulling on the brails.

Breech: The back part of a cannon, the rear, as opposed to the **muzzle**.

Brigantine: Or brig. A square-rigged, twin-masted vessel.

Brisote: (Spanish) A strong north-east wind; a trade-wind found in the Caribbean.

Bruja: (Spanish) Lit., *witch*. Can be used as its literal meaning, or as the equivalent of bitch if used in its most insulting connotation.

Bum-fiddle: A vulgar euphemism for breaking wind.

Bunkbox: A type of sleeping arrangement found in private cabins aboard ship, such as the captain's quarters, consisting of a lidless wooden box with rope netting stretched across the bottom to support feather or flock mattresses. The sides are relatively high, thus helping to prevent the sleeper from being pitched onto the floor by the ship's movements. This is considered a luxury, as the rest of the crew sleeps in hammocks.

Burgoo: A thin oatmeal gruel, usually eaten for breakfast and much despised by sailors.

Butterbox: A derogatory term for a Dutch ship.

Cable tier: Part of the **orlop deck** where spare cables are stored.

Cacothymia: (Greek) A malevolent or evil spirit.

Caimito: A star-shaped fruit (also known as star-apple).

Callaloo: Leafy-green vegetable similar to spinach.

Calm of Cancer: An area of the northern hemisphere where a ship is likely to become becalmed. See **Horse Latitudes**.

Canister shot: See **case-shot**.

Capstan: A spool-shaped winch with a single drum used for winding in cables (particularly the anchor cable), hawsers or chains. Sockets around the upper edge are fitted with wooden bars. To use the capstan, crewmen push the bars while walking in a circle.

Careening: The act of a ship being hauled ashore, to allow for the hull to be scraped clean, repaired, caulked and pitched. A necessary task, since ships with clean bottoms sail faster and are more maneuverable.

Caruncula lachrymalia: A medical term, referring to the tear-ducts of the eye.

Case-shot: A number of small iron or lead balls (shot) packed into a round tin case and used as ammunition for cannons. An effective medium-to-long range anti-personnel shell with explosive impact that scatters shrapnel. Also known as **canister shot**.

Cast up (one's) accounts: To vomit.

Cat-head(s): Short timber beams that project horizontally on either side of the **bowsprit**. The cat-heads suspend the ship's anchors clear of the **bow**.

Chain-pump: Used to pump bilge water on ships. Composed of a chain on a series of discs.

Chain-shot: Two cannonballs connected together by a chain, used primarily to clear another ship's deck of masts and rigging, as well as combatants.

Charm-needler: A tattoo artist who utilizes magic in his/her work, creating inked charms for specific purposes which remain marked permanently on the client's body.

Cheese-parer: A derogatory term for a citizen of the Netherlands (the Low Countries).

Chemise: A woman's undergarment, usually resembling a loose, knee-length dress. May have sleeves or not.

Cherimoya: Tropical fruit with a custard-like texture; the flavor is said to resemble mango, banana, coconut and strawberry mixed together.

Cheroot: A type of small cigar.

Chirurgeon: An obsolete term for a surgeon.

Chupe mantequilla de mi culo, hijaputa cabrona: (Spanish) Suck the butter out of my ass, you whore's daughter bitch. An insult of the highest proportion.

Clew: On a square-rigged vessel, the lower corner of a sail. On a fore-and-aft rigged vessel, the aft-most corner of a sail. Clews are also used on the lower and inner corner of studding sails. **Sheets** are attached to the clews.

Clew down: To unfurl a sail.

Clew line: Ropes which come down from the **yard**s to the **clew**s (lower corners of the sails); they are used to haul up the sails.

Clew up: To draw a sail up in preparation for furling.

Cock o' the company: A pretender. A weak character who associates with low types for the purposes of appearing more courageous than he is in reality. Considered an insult.

Cockpit: Located on a lower deck, where wounded men are taken for treatment by the surgeon and his mates during a sea-battle.

Cods: Slang term for testicles.

Colors: The flag flown to indicate a ship's nationality.

Coña: (Spanish) An insulting term for the female genitalia. Cunt.

Condiddler: Slang term for a thief.

Cook off: When a fresh gunpowder charge is put into an overheated gun barrel, the danger is that it may "cook off" – ignite prematurely due to the heat.

Corpus sanctos: (Latin) Lit., *holy body*. Refers to St. Elmo's Fire, an eerie blue or white glow which sometimes appears on the masts of vessels before or after a thunderstorm. Unlike **witch-fire**, St. Elmo's Fire is caused by a naturally occurring electrical discharge.

Counterfeit crank: A thief or swindler who employs disguises to fool their victims.

Cromster: A three masted merchant vessel which is, in appearance, something like a smaller version of a Spanish galleon.

Crow's nest: A look-out station atop the **main mast**.

Cunny: A rude euphemism for female genitalia.

Dandy: A fine dresser; one who enjoys wearing flashy and fashionable clothing. Depending on the context, may also be an insult directed at a vain and shallow person.

Dasheen: A starchy edible tuber; the leaves, stalks and shoots are also edible.

Devil's dung: The spice, asafœtida.

Diet of Worms: For the purposes of this story, a euphemism for the after-life. Bess O'Bedlam may have picked up the name (though obviously not the meaning) from the historical Diet of Worms which took place in 1521, an assembly of the estates of the Holy Roman Empire that is most famous for issuing an edict against Martin Luther and the Protestant Reformation. It is unlikely that the uneducated Bess comprehends the source of her threat.

Doe je ogen open, liefje: (Dutch) Open your eyes, dear.

Doubloon: A unit of Spanish money; a gold coin.

Doxy: A prostitute. A woman of ill-repute.

Electuary: A medical remedy made as a syrup.

Ensign: A flag flown by a ship to indicate its nationality. See **colors**.

En tremblant: (French) Jewelry mounted so that it quivers (or trembles) at movement.

Excusez-moi: (French) Please excuse me.

False colors: To fly false colors is to bear aloft a flag of a nation other than your own. This is an acceptable ruse of war, though one's true colors are usually shown just prior to the attack.

Fanfaronade: Bragging, boasting.

Fart catcher: A servant (such as a footman or lady's maid) who follows closely behind his/her mistress or master.

Fata morgana: A type of optical phenomena; a mirage.

Fiddle-faddle: Nonsense.

Fiddler's Green: The mythical sea farer's paradise that is filled with an inexhaustible supply of wine, women and song. The heaven to which a sailor aspires when he dies.

Fife rail: A rail that runs around the lower part of each mast (such as fore, main and/or mizzen) to which **belaying pins** are secured.

Fils de bas: (French) Bastard. A very old-fashioned term.

Fistula: An abscess, usually painful.

Flat-in: The act of bringing the **clew** of a sail towards the middle of the vessel, so as to get more effect from the wind.

Flintlock (pistol): A single-shot firearm. Once loaded with gunpowder and shot, the flintlock is fired by fully cocking back the hammer (or dogshead or cock) and pulling the trigger. The piece of flint in the hammer strikes sparks from the frizzen (a piece of steel), which falls into the priming (or flash) pan. The gunpowder in the priming pan ignites, which flashes through a small hole in the side of the barrel, thus igniting the gunpowder *in* the barrel, firing the shot.

Florin: The principle unit of Dutch currency; a coin.

Flummery: Refers to the deliberate attempt to fool another by lying or misdirection.

Fo'c'sle: See **forecastle**.

Forecastle or fo'c'sle: The foremost deck of a ship; located forward of the **foremast**. The crew's sleeping quarters (barring the captain and officers) are located beneath the forecastle.

Forechains: In general, chains are the hardware used to secure the lower **shrouds** of the mast outside the ship's side. The **forechains** belong to the **foremast**; mainchains to the **mainmast**; and mizzenchains to the **mizzen mast**.

Forefoot: The foremost part of the ship's keel.

Foremast: The foremost mast on a ship.

Foresail: Or fores'l or forecourse. The principal and lowest sail on the **foremast**.

Fortnight: A measurement of time - two weeks, or fourteen days.

Foretopgallant masthead: At the head of the **fore-mast** is the fore-topmast, and at the head of that is the foretopgallant mast.

French disease: A term used by (primarily) English sailors for the pox, or venereal disease. French sailors generally termed it the "English disease".

Frigate: A three masted, fully rigged vessel.

Fussock: A shiftless, lazy person, usually female.

Galleon: A large, three masted Spanish vessel used for trade or war.

Galliot: A single or two masted Dutch cargo vessel.

Gallipot: Another name for an apothecary. Refers to small clay pots which hold medicines.

Garçon manqué: (French) Lit., *pretend boy*. A tomboy.

Gimbals: A pair of rings, moving on pivots, which keep instruments and other items level when the ship pitches and rolls.

Gleet: An obsolete term for gonorrhea.

Godskannonne: (Dutch) Lit., *God's cannons*. An exclamation denoting dismay, anger or other strong feelings and emotions.

Gropecunt Lane: A street in 18th century London, north of the River Thames, more properly named Grub Street, infamous for its proliferation of prostitution. May jokingly refer to any area where a gentleman may enjoy the services of a prostitute in semi-privacy.

Grumbleguts: An insulting term for a greedy person.

(to) Gull: The act of cheating or swindling; to cheat or swindle another, as in a criminal act, or to play a trick on them in the spirit of mischief.

Gunwale: The upper-most edge of a vessel's side; the heavy **strake** that binds the top plank of the hull. (Pronounced gunn'l)

Gunpowder tattoo: A permanent marking or "tattoo" on an area of the body caused when an explosion, such as the firing of a **flintlock**, causes grains of gunpowder to blow back at the shooter, and penetrate the skin. May also refer to a superstitious practice of sailors, who cause gunpowder to be mixed into tattoo ink in the belief that doing so will promote longevity.

Half a pistol shot: The preferred distance for naval engagements – about one hundred yards.

Handsomely: To do something gradually, not all at once.

Hardtack: A hard-baked, long-lasting biscuit (a cracker to most Americans) which is tough and relatively tasteless. It is composed of water, flour and salt. Also known as **ship's biscuit**.

Haut goust: (French) Lit., "high flavor". The expression refers either to meat that has hung too long and become tainted, or a very vile and disagreeable odor.

Herb-wife: One who utilizes herbs, plants, spices and roots in healing; a healer. Also, one who uses herbs, plants, spices and roots for magical purposes.

Horse Latitudes: Located at about 30° latitude in both the north and south hemispheres; areas of the ocean where the wind is light, and the weather hot and dry.

Hurdy-gurdy: A musical instrument.

Hurricano: An obsolete term for a hurricane.

Hussif: A small case containing pins, needles, scissors and other sewing equipment.

Iron Sickness: An affliction suffered by a ship whose nails and bolts are corroded with rust.

Jackeen: Slang term for a drunken, dissolute person.

Jaggery: An unrefined palm sugar.

Je suis désolé: (French) I am very sorry.

Jij Spaanse tyfus hoer: (Dutch) You Spanish typhoid whore.

Jolly-boat: A small boat used for shore excursions, carried aboard a ship.

Justaucorps: A fashionable gentleman's coat that fits fairly close to the body; it is knee-length, with full skirts and wide, turned-back cuffs.

Keel: The keel is the backbone of the ship. In ship construction, the keel is laid first; the sternport, stem and ribs are attached to it.

Knots: The measurement of speed aboard a ship.

Kom es hier: (Dutch) Come here.

Krijg de pest, vuil kutwijf: (Dutch) I hope you get the pest (the bubonic plague), you dirty cunt. An insult of the highest proportions.

La belle poule: (French) Lit., *beautiful hen*. A compliment said to a female.

La coña de tu madre: (Spanish) Your mother's cunt. A very nasty insult.

Larboard: On board a ship, facing towards the **bow**, larboard is in the left direction.

League: Approximately three miles.

Látigo para desollar: (Spanish) Lit., *whip without mercy.* A flaying whip with metal stars knotted into the tails; a terrible instrument of punishment.

Lee: The side sheltered from, or away from, the wind.

Liefje: (Dutch) My love. An endearment.

Lively: Do something quickly, at once.

Livre: (French) A livre is the standard French currency of the day.

Main deck: The principle deck of a ship.

Mainmast: The central-most, and usually the tallest, mast.

Mainsail: Also mains'l or maincourse. The principle and lowest sail on the **mainmast**.

Malanga: A starchy, tropical tuber with a nutty flavor.

Mal de mer: (French) Sea sickness; a form of motion sickness characterized by headache, sweating, dizziness and nausea. Severe cases usually include uncontrollable vomiting.

Maldita puta: (Spanish) Nasty whore or nasty bitch. An obvious insult.

Malmsey: A sweet, strong wine.

Mamoncillo: (*Melicoecus bijugatus*) Also called the Spanish lime.

Marrowbones: Referring primarily to the knees.

Merdaille: (French) Scum. An old-fashioned insult.

Merde: (French) Lit., *shit.* An exclamation.

Marlinspike: A tool used for splicing rope. Made of iron and sharply pointed.

Mijn lief: (Dutch) Lit., *my love.* An endearment.

Mijn liefje, mijn duifje: (Dutch) Lit., my little love, my little dove. Endearments.

Mizzenmast: The rear, or aftmost, mast of a three-masted ship.

Mobcap: A large, frilly cap with a high crown, worn primarily by married or widowed ladies.

Moidore: A unit of Portuguese money; a silver coin.

Monkey's Fist: A type of very complex knot used as a weight for a heaving line.

Montante: An old-fashioned fencing term, referring to an upwards, vertical attack.

Muckle: A great deal, a lot, a quantity.

Mumchance: Silence.

Murrain: A curse.

Muzzle: The mouth of the cannon, located at the front, as opposed to the **breech**.

Narwhale: An Arctic whale. The male of the species (*Monodon monoceros*) has a long, spiral-twisted horn. Also known as the sea unicorn. The tusk is thought to bring luck.

Oloroso: A type of fine, dark, dry sherry from Andalusia.

Orion: A constellation. The three "belt" stars appear to point to Sirius, the brightest star in the constellation Canis Major. In the northern hemisphere, Orion appears in the southern sky.

Orlop: Or orlop deck. The lowest deck of a ship, often containing supplies such as cables, cargo, the ship's sick-bay, the **powder magazine**, and some officers' quarters.

Peepers: The eyes.

Piece-of-eight: A unit of Spanish currency; a silver coin.

Pizzle: A penis, usually referring to an animal's.

Pleiades: Also known as the Seven Sisters. A star cluster appearing in the constellation Taurus. In the northern hemisphere, the Pleiades appear in the southern sky above and to the right of the constellation Orion (the Hunter).

Plum duff: A boiled suet pudding with dried currants or raisins.

Poopdeck: Or poop. The short, elevated aft-most deck of a ship that lies above the quarterdeck. The captain's cabin is usually located beneath the poopdeck on larger vessels.

Portable soup: For many years, a staple victual on shipboard. A bouillon of meat and vegetables boiled, reduced, defatted, and reduced again to a gluey, jelly-like consistency, then dried into cakes which would keep for years. Originally thought to be an anti-scorbutic.

Poteen: Irish moonshine; rough home-brewed liquor.

Powder magazine: Or magazine or powder room. A storeroom, normally located on the **orlop** deck. Gunpowder is stored here.

Presbyopia of Argus: Lit., the elder eye of Argus. A potent protective spell.

Presto: (Italian) A very fast music tempo.

Prestissimo: (Italian) A music tempo that is as fast as possible; faster than **presto**.

Preventers: Additional ropes used to prevent spars from being carried away if the usual stays fail and give way.

Punkah: (Indian) Usually a frame covered with canvas and suspended from the ceiling; a servant pulls a string that makes the fan go back and forth, circulating air in the room.

Purser's slush: Salt beef or salt pork was boiled to cook it, and make it more palatable. The grease that was skimmed from the water was called slush; this slush belonged, by custom, to the purser, who usually sold it to the crew in the form of tallow candles (called purser's dips).

Puta: (Spanish) Whore or bitch. An obvious insult.

Putain de merde: (French) Lit., *shit whore*. An exclamation of agitation or extreme emotion.

Quarterdeck: The area which lies **aft** of the **mainmast** on the **main deck**. It is an elevated deck before the **poopdeck**; the ship's wheel (helm) and **binnacle** are located on the quarterdeck. It is normally reserved for officers.

Querida: (Spanish) An endearment similar to darling or dear, used when speaking to females.

Ragabash: An idle, ragged person; a person of ill manners.

Rammer: See **ramrod**.

Ramrod: Another term for the **rammer**. Part of the gun crew's equipment, the ramrod was used to push a charge of gunpowder and shot down the **muzzle** of the cannon.

Raparee: (Irish) A bandit, a freebooter.

Rattletrap: A somewhat insulting term for the mouth; or a loud annoying chatterbox of a person.

Reef: A horizontal band of canvas sewn across the width of a sail. To reef a sail is to roll up a portion of a sail and secure it, thus reducing the exposed surface of the sail.

Regardez vous: (French) An imperative. Look here. You look here. See here. Look at this.

Sanguis draconis: (Latin) Dragon's blood. Refers to an aromatic resin, *Daemomorops draco*.

Scapegallows: Said of one who deserves and has narrowly escaped being hanged.

Scold's cure: Slang term meaning death.

Scuttlebutt: A cask of water found on deck for the use of thirsty sailors.

Sea lawyer: A term used to describe an argumentative or contentious sailor or seaman.

Sen'night: A measurement of time – one week or seven days.

Scurvy: A vitamin C deficiency commonly suffered by sailors, due to a lack of fresh vegetables and fruits aboard ship. Symptoms include tenderness of the gums, loosened teeth, foul breath and pains in the limbs. Curable with the introduction of ascorbic acid into the diet, such as lemons or limes. May also be considered an insult, as in "scurvy sea dog."

Sercial: A dry Portuguese madeira wine.

Sharper: A professional card cheat.

Sheet(s): A rope fastened to one or both lower corners of a sail in order to alter its direction, extend it, or retain the sail in a particular position.

Ship's biscuit: See **hardtack**.

Shrouds: Large ropes, lines or cables affixed on either side (**port** and **starboard**) of a mast and running down to the deck to support the mast.

Slap bang or nothing: Cash must be paid or no sale.

Sloop: Any relatively small (single or two masted) ship of war.

Snickersnee: Slang term for a fight, particularly one involving blades.

Something-to-be-praised: Physician, chemist and alchemist Paracelsus (Philippus Aureolus Theophrastus Bombastus von Hohenheim, 1490-1541) created an alcoholic tincture of opium which he called *laudanum* – lit., "something to be praised".

Spanker boom: An **aft** boom to which the spanker sail is attached.

Spermaceti: A white, waxy substance rendered from sperm oil. Found mainly in the head cavity of the sperm whale.

Spyglass: A telescope.

Squalembrato: An old fashioned fencing term referring to an oblique downwards motion made during the attack.

Stocatta: An old fashioned fencing term referring to a blow struck at an opponent's belly.

Standing rigging: Lines which are fixed and under tension to hold various spars in place.

Starboard: On board a ship, facing towards the **bow**, starboard is in the right direction.

Stern: The rear of the ship. Opposite of the **bow**.

Straights: Refers to the Florida Straights, located between Cuba, the Bahamas and the Florida Keys; the Gulfstream flows through the Straights. Much utilized by captains while voyaging from the New World on the return trip Europe.

Strake: Range of planks abutting against each other and extending the length of the ship.

Stramazone: An old fashioned fencing term referring to a cut made with the tip of the blade.

Swivel gun: A breech-loading weapon used aboard ships. Swivel guns are mounted on a swivel yoke and affixed to the ship's rail. Meant to be effective at short-range only (approximately 25 yards). A form of more maneuverable cannon.

Taffrail: The rail that runs around the ship's **stern**.

Tricorn: A three-cornered hat. The wide brim is turned upward to form three angles.

Tropic of Cancer: North of the Equator, it is one of the five major circles of latitude.

Tun: A barrel.

Tup: To engage in sexual intercourse.

Uw dienares, juffrouw: (Old Dutch) Lit., *your servant, madam.*

Uw spraakt Nederlands: (Old Dutch) Lit., *you speak Netherlands*

Variables: An area of low pressure calm and light variable winds near the equator. Also known by sailors as the doldrums.

Votre serviteur: (Old French) Lit., *your servant.* A polite expression.

Vuile tyfus hoer: (Dutch) Lit., *Dirty typhoid whore.* An insult of high proportions.

Waist: Between **quarterdeck** and **forecastle**, the central part of the upper deck.

Weather: As in the "weather side of a ship". See **windward**.

Weather gage: In terms of a ship's position during a battle, it is a favorable position upwind of the opponent, thus allowing for greater maneuverability and the ability to adjust one's course at will to allow the **starboard** and **port** guns to reach the proper elevations.

Weatherglass: The ship's barometer. Made of blown glass, pear-shaped with a curved spout and filled with liquid, it is used as a rough gauge for weather. When the liquid rises in the spout, it indicates foul weather is on the way.

Weevil's wedding cake: Ship's biscuit; hardtack.

Wheel-lock: An obsolete firearm; the precursor to the **flintlock**.

Wind-sail: A canvas funnel used to ventilate a ship's lower decks by drawing air down from an upper deck.

Windward: In the direction from which the wind blows. The **weather** side of a ship.

Witch-fire: A magical, colorful non-combustible flame conjured up by a charm or spell.

Wort-cunning: The knowledge of the magical properties of herbs, spices, roots and plants.

Yard: A long, narrow wooden spar affixed to the mast, which supports the sails.

Yardarm: The outermost end of a **yard**.

Yellow fever: A tropical virus transmitted by mosquitoes. Symptoms include jaundice, black vomit, red facial rash and severe diarrhea. Not necessarily fatal but contagious.

Yellow jack: A yellow-colored flag flown to indicate that a ship is under quarantine due to an infectious disease.

CPSIA information can be obtained at www.ICGtesting.com
Printed in the USA
LVOW101951300413

331652LV00002B/535/A